HER
SILENT
CRY

D0910579

BOOKS BY LISA REGAN

HER
SILENT
CRY

LISA REGAN

bookouture

Published by Bookouture in 2019

An imprint of StoryFire Ltd.

Carmelite House
50 Victoria Embankment
London EC4Y 0DZ

www.bookouture.com

Copyright © Lisa Regan, 2019

Lisa Regan has asserted her right to be identified
as the author of this work.

All rights reserved.
No part of this publication may be reproduced,
stored in any retrieval system, or transmitted, in any form or by
any means, electronic, mechanical, photocopying, recording or
otherwise, without the prior written permission of the publishers.

ISBN: 978-1-83888-004-0
eBook ISBN: 978-1-83888-003-3

This book is a work of fiction. Names, characters, businesses,
organizations, places and events other than those clearly in the
public domain, are either the product of the author's imagination
or are used fictitiously. Any resemblance to actual persons, living or
dead, events or locales is entirely coincidental.

For Dot Dorton, for changing my life.

CHAPTER ONE

Their argument crashed in angry waves against the door between us, slamming against the wood, pooling on the floor and slipping underneath where I could hear every word. Most of the time, I didn't understand what they were saying or even why they were fighting. I only understood that she was about to get hurt; the silent way, or the screaming way. I was never sure which was worse.

No matter how badly he hurt her, she always found her way back to our room eventually. She'd lower herself into our creaking bed, hissing her breaths through gritted teeth, and reach for me. I learned to be very careful when I moved under the covers. Sometimes even the slightest pressure would make her gasp with pain. As gently as I could, I would curl my back into her stomach and wait for the trembling fingers skittering over my scalp to eventually fall into a slow, soothing rhythm.

I had so many questions, but I didn't ask them. I didn't want the man to hear me, to remember I was there too. When the ragged edges of her breath smoothed out, she'd let out a soft sigh that meant that she had reached a point where her pain was bearable.

"It's okay," she'd say. "It will be okay."

She was always a bad liar.

CHAPTER TWO

Little Harris Quinn's shrieks carried across Denton City Park's playground, piercing Josie's ears. As she chased him from the swings to the slide, she looked around to see if any of the other adults were bothered by his high-pitched sounds of delight, but no one even noticed. All the other adults were similarly focused on their own children as they sprinted back and forth, calling out excitedly.

"Mom! Watch me!"

"You can't catch me."

"I want to go on the see-saw!"

Josie followed Harris over to the jungle gym in the center of the playground. It was shaped like a castle with a long, curved bridge that led from a set of low-slung steps to a large slide on the opposite side. Harris climbed up the steps and raced across the bridge.

"Careful," Josie called after him, but he was already at the top of the slide. She narrowly missed bowling over two toddlers as she raced to the bottom of the slide before he flew off the shiny end into the dirt. She scooped him from mid-air at the base of the slide and he squealed. "JoJo!"

She planted a kiss on the top of his head before he began squirming. "JoJo, down! Again!"

Reluctantly, she set him back down and watched him run back to the steps. It was best to stay at the bottom of the slide, she thought, to catch him. For just a few seconds, while he was on the bridge, he was out of her eyeline. Her heart pounded in her chest until she saw the flash of his blond hair and bright blue dinosaur shirt at the top of the slide. As he sat down and pushed himself forward, a little girl pushed in front of Josie and started climbing up the slide. In her mind's eye, Josie saw the disastrous collision about to take place. The little girl had to be six or seven years old based on her size—almost twice as large as Harris. She had on white sneakers, stretchy blue pants and a sparkly pink top decorated with a unicorn. On her back, she wore a small backpack in the shape of a butterfly. Her sandy hair, like corn silk, was tied back in a loose, messy ponytail. Josie opened her mouth to speak, to tell the little girl to stop going up the slide, or to tell Harris not to start down the slide, but the words lodged in her throat.

Moving closer to the slide, her hands reached out to grab Harris before he slid straight into the butterfly girl. A woman suddenly appeared on the other side of the slide. "Lucy," she barked firmly. "You know you're not supposed to go up the slide that way. Get down before someone gets hurt."

Little Lucy kept climbing, but the woman's hand shot out and gripped her arm, stopping her. "Look at me, Lucy," she said. "What did I say?"

Lucy froze in place and looked up at the woman. Instantly, Josie saw the strong resemblance; the same heart-shaped face, periwinkle blue eyes and narrow nose neatly flared at the nostrils. The woman's hair was perhaps two shades darker than the little girl's, but they had to be mother and daughter.

Lucy bit her bottom lip, relaxed her grip on the slide and, in a jumble of thin, gangly limbs, began to slide slowly downward on her stomach. "Sorry, Mom," she mumbled. Once she reached the bottom, her mother took one of her hands and dragged her out of the path of Harris, who slid down seconds later. Quickly, Josie scooped him up again, holding onto his wriggly body tightly.

Lucy's mother caught Josie's eye and smiled. "I'm sorry," she said.

"Oh, it's fine," Josie said. "I'm just glad no one got hurt."

The woman laughed. "Who knew playgrounds could be so dangerous, right?"

"Seriously," Josie replied. The truth was that taking Harris to the playground took years off her life. There were far too many opportunities for him to stumble and hit his head on something; to fall off something and break a bone; to be inadvertently hurt by another child running too fast or climbing up the slide the wrong way.

"How old is he?" the woman asked as Lucy tugged at her mother's hand, trying to pull her away to another part of the playground.

"Two," Josie answered. "Almost three."

With a wistful smile, the woman said, "Oh I remember when mine was two. What a great age."

"Oh, he's not—" Josie was about to explain that she wasn't Harris's mother, that she was only watching him for a friend, but Lucy whined, "Mom! I want to go on the carousel!"

Harris stopped wiggling in Josie's arms. "Me too!" he said. "JoJo, horses again!"

Josie shifted him in her arms. "Again?" she said. "We already went on three times."

Just the thought of it made the acid in her stomach churn. She'd been feeling peaky on and off for a week now, and three rides on the spinning carousel had certainly not helped.

"Mo-om," Lucy said, now tugging her mother away from the slide and toward the opposite end of the playground where the shiny new carousel had been installed weeks earlier, thanks to the machinations of the mayor.

An amusement park a few counties away had gone out of business, and Mayor Tara Charleston had seen an opportunity to "enhance Denton's lovely public park" as she phrased it when she convinced the city council to spend an exorbitant amount of money to have the carousel deconstructed, transported to Denton, and rebuilt inside the city park. At least the city had saved money by having art students from Denton University restore it. Now its bright carnival colors flashed in the afternoon sunlight as it spun, its horses rising and falling in concert with the jubilant music that played while it went round and round. Just looking at it from the playground area made Josie's stomach turn.

"JoJo, please," Harris tried again, squirming in her arms.

Before she could try to talk him out of it, a man's voice said, "You're Josie Quinn."

Lucy and her mother stopped and turned back, watching as the man walked up from behind Josie and extended a hand. Josie had seen him in the park when they arrived, walking around the perimeter of the playground, talking on his cell phone. He was lean and tan with salt-and-pepper colored hair. In a blue polo shirt, khaki shorts and a pair of loafers, he looked as though he should be on a golf course rather than a playground, but the late April weather was warm enough for his light-weight clothing.

"I'm Colin Ross," he told her, his hand still extended.

Josie shifted Harris in her arms so she could shake the man's hand. Lucy and her mother walked up closer. Lucy's mother looked from Colin to Josie and back. "Colin," she said. "You know this woman?"

He turned to her and smiled. "Amy," he said. "You don't recognize her from the news?"

Tension knotted Josie's shoulder blades. As a detective for the Denton Police Department, Josie had solved some of the most shocking cases in the state, many of which had made national news, but she still wasn't used to her celebrity. Or notoriety.

Amy stared at Josie with uncertainty until, finally breaking the tension, Josie extended a hand. "He's right. I'm Josie Quinn. I'm a detective with the police department."

Amy's hand flew to her mouth. "Oh my God, you just solved the Drew Pratt case!"

Josie nodded, noticing that Colin was beaming at her. "My team solved the case, yes."

Colin said, "She's fantastic. Do you know who her father is?"

Josie opened her mouth to say that her father was dead but before she could, Colin said, "Christian Payne."

A year ago, Josie had found out that she'd been kidnapped as an infant. Her real family believed she died in a fire. She had only been recently reunited with them. It was still hard to get used to having an entirely new family. "You know him?" Josie asked.

Colin smiled. "We both work for Quarmark."

"Right," Josie said. "Big pharma. Do you work in marketing as well?"

"No, I'm on the team that develops the pricing structures for new drugs Quarmark rolls out onto the market."

"Fun stuff," Amy remarked.

"Daddy," Lucy whined. "I want to go on the carousel."

"JoJo," Harris said, pointing over Josie's shoulder. "Swings!"

Josie was relieved he had changed his mind. "Just a minute, buddy."

Amy placed a hand on her husband's back. "Honey, Lucy wants to go on the carousel. Do you want to go on with her or should I?"

Colin smiled down at his daughter. "Maybe all three of us could go on."

"Which horse will you go on, Daddy?" Lucy asked.

"I don't know," he said. "I have to have a good look at them before I choose." He shot Josie another smile. "It was great to meet you."

"You too," Josie said. As the Ross family drifted off toward the carousel, Josie set Harris down on the grass and he raced off to the swings. As she helped him into one of the empty swings and began pushing him lightly, she saw that Amy and Lucy Ross had gotten on the carousel. Colin stood just outside the fence, talking on his cell phone again. So much for a family carousel ride.

"Higher!" Harris cried. "Please, JoJo?"

Josie smiled down at his crown of golden blond hair and pushed a little more forcefully, even though sending him a fraction higher caused a small uptick in her anxiety. She didn't know how his mother, Misty, brought him here all the time. It seemed so fraught with danger. To Josie, Harris still seemed so small and fragile. She couldn't help but fear that he'd break a bone or crack his skull with one bad fall. In her mind she heard Misty, her own mother Shannon, and her grandmother, Lisette all laughing at her—which they frequently did when she fussed too much over Harris's safety. They all said the same thing: "Kids are more resilient than they look."

As another wave of nausea rocked Josie's stomach, she wondered how mothers handled the whole parenting thing. The more independent Harris became, the scarier everything seemed. She was watching his grip on the chains on either side of the swing when she first became aware of Amy Ross's voice in the distance. She was calling out for her daughter.

"Lucy? Lucy!"

Josie looked over at the carousel and saw Amy still on the ride as people were slowly making their way off the platform and out of the metal fence that surrounded it.

Her tone became louder and higher-pitched. "Lucy! Lucy!"

Colin stopped pacing and pulled his cell phone slightly away from his ear, as though tuning in to the panic in his wife's voice.

"Lucy!"

Amy raced round and round the platform, weaving in and out of the horses, more frantic with each passing second.

Without realizing it, Josie had stopped Harris's swing. "JoJo?" he asked, looking up at her.

"It's okay, buddy," she mumbled, scooping him out of the seat and walking toward the carousel.

People continued to spill out of the perimeter as Colin tried to walk in through the exit. The teenager who had been monitoring the ride stood by the entrance gate, gawking at Amy. The line of people behind him waiting to get on stared as well. As if sensing so many eyes on her, Amy stopped moving and looked at them.

"Did anyone see my daughter? She was just here. She was on the blue horse. I was on the purple one. She got down before the ride stopped. Did anyone see her get off? Lucy?"

No one answered. Colin, phone still in hand, was now on the platform, working his way through the horses and stopping to look inside two chariots with red velvet seats facing one another. "Where the hell did she go?" he asked.

Amy said, "Did you see her come out?"

"No, I didn't see anything," Colin said. "I was on the phone."

Amy again appealed to the people waiting in line. "Did anyone see a little girl get off the carousel alone? She's seven. She has blonde hair. She was wearing a bright pink unicorn shirt and a butterfly backpack."

A few people shook their heads, but no one volunteered any information. Josie was at the fence now, studying the carousel. There really was nowhere to hide. She thought back to when Amy's voice first caught her attention. A crowd of people had flooded through the exit gate. Josie didn't remember seeing Lucy among them, but she could have raced out before Josie looked over.

"Amy," Colin said, approaching his wife. "Where the hell is she?"

"I don't know!" his wife shouted. "She was right here. She was with me. I only looked away for a second. Oh my God." She reached both hands to her temples, and her next words were a screech. "Somebody *do* something!"

Josie shifted Harris on her hip and moved inside the gate. She caught the eye of the dumbfounded worker. "Shut the ride down," she told him.

"What?"

"Shut the ride down. No one gets on or off until this child is located." She turned to the Ross parents. "If she's not here, she's elsewhere in the playground."

Amy's eyes searched the playground behind Josie. "I don't see her. She's not out there."

Josie said, "Look at me, Mrs. Ross."

Amy met her eyes.

"Let's fan out, we'll check the rest of the playground. She could be inside one of the jungle gym areas."

Colin and Amy raced out of the carousel enclosure, calling for their daughter. A few people who were in line to get onto the ride joined them, calling out Lucy's name. Josie followed, shifting a squirming Harris from hip to hip. "Down, JoJo," he said.

"Just a minute, love," Josie told him. "We're trying to find a little girl, okay?"

"I help?" he asked.

She smiled at him. "You stay with me. That's how you'll help me."

Amy flashed a photo she had taken of Lucy only minutes earlier when she climbed onto her carousel horse. Josie's arms ached with Harris's weight, but her anxiety wouldn't let her put him down. A feeling of dread seeped into her skin, making her feel clammy and uncomfortable.

"She probably just wandered off," Josie told Amy when she started to become hysterical again, but with each moment that ticked by with no sign of Lucy, Josie began to suspect something far worse.

Josie walked the perimeter of the playground. Behind the carousel was a tall chain-link fence that separated the play area from the softball field on the other side. A few people played toss in the outfield. Josie walked the length of the fence to make sure there were no breaks in it. Where the fence ended, waist-high shrubs separated the park from a strip of pavement and the street beyond. Bungalows sat peacefully across the street. Although many cars were parked along the sidewalk, no traffic went by in either direction. She followed the shrubs to the play area's entrance, a wide walkway beneath an arch that read 'Denton City Park Playground'. Beyond that more shrubbery separated the play area from the sidewalk for several yards until it terminated at a wooded area. Josie knew that on the other side of the trees was one of the jogging paths that ran through the dense forest of the park. A child could easily slip into the woods. The treeline ran the rest of the length of the play area until it met with the beginning of the fence on the other side. Still, Lucy would have had to exit the carousel and cross a significant area before running into the woods. Surely someone would have seen her.

The tightness in Josie's chest only increased as she studied the trees. The area at the back of the play area was larger and hilly and led deeper into the park which extended a few miles in each direction.

Too much ground for her to cover, even with the Ross parents helping.

She used her free hand to pull her cell phone out of her pocket and called dispatch.

"Detective Quinn," she said when the officer answered. "I need two to three units over at the city park playground. I think we've got a missing child."

CHAPTER THREE

Fat tears rolled down Amy's face as she stood next to the jungle gym, phone in hand. Colin paced nearby, his face pale and lined with fear. A dozen parents gathered around as Josie gave them instructions. "Please don't leave until you've given your name and phone number to one of the officers," she told them. "I'd also ask that you check your cell phones for any photos or video you may have taken in the last hour to see if you've captured Lucy Ross in the background."

Josie catalogued their faces in her mind. She wanted to make sure her team didn't miss anyone. A man from the back of the crowd said, "Can we help you look?"

"I'd prefer it if you stayed in this area and talked with the officers," she answered.

There was no evidence that Lucy had been abducted, but the thought had certainly crossed Josie's mind. She knew it was extremely unlikely that any of the frightened parents before her or their exhausted children had had anything to do with Lucy's disappearance, but she couldn't take a risk and allow any of them to be part of the search. What if one of them had done something to Lucy? She might be sending them out into the park to cover up what they'd done. The thought sent a chill through her. Against her shoulder, Harris snored, having fallen asleep in spite of all of the commotion.

"You're not going to let them help?" Colin asked. "We need to get out there. The sooner we start looking—"

His words were swallowed up by the wail of police sirens as two marked Denton cruisers pulled up outside the play area entrance, followed by Detective Gretchen Palmer's unmarked car. Relief washed through Josie as her colleagues got out and jogged over. As Josie briefed them, Amy pulled up the photo of Lucy she had been showing the other parents so the officers could have a look at it. Josie assigned two of the officers to work the crowd, taking down names, addresses, phone numbers and getting any cell phone photographs or video footage that existed. Gretchen said, "We'll need more bodies to search the park."

Josie sent Hummel and one of the other officers off in separate directions to search the wooded areas that abutted the play area while Gretchen called for more units. Amy tapped her on the shoulder. "I want to look," she said. "I'm going to look."

Josie turned to her. "Of course. We just need to ask you some questions first. It won't take long."

Colin stepped up behind his wife. One hand still held his cell phone while the other pushed through his graying hair. "I don't understand what happened," he muttered.

Gretchen hung up her phone, introduced herself to the Ross parents, and took out her notepad. Josie began, "How old is Lucy?"

"Seven," the two parents answered in unison.

"Is she in the first grade, then?" Gretchen asked.

"Yes," Amy said. "She goes to Denton West Elementary. It's right—it's only a few blocks from here."

"How about your home address?" Josie asked.

Amy recited it and Gretchen wrote it down. It was only two blocks away, Josie noted. To the Ross parents, she said, "I think we should have someone take a quick look at your home in case Lucy went there for some reason. Do you think she would know how to get home from here?"

Colin answered, "Yes."

Simultaneously, Amy answered, "No."

Colin looked at his wife. "She would know how to get home from the park, Amy."

Amy wiped away a tear as it streaked down her face. "No, she wouldn't. She got lost on her way back to her classroom from the nurse's office at school two weeks ago."

He looked stricken. "What?"

Amy folded her arms across her chest. "You would know that if you were home more often."

"I call every day when I'm on the road," Colin shot back. "One of you could have mentioned it."

Gretchen cleared her throat to bring their focus back to her. "Mr. and Mrs. Ross," she said. "Regardless of her age or sense of direction, it just makes sense to check your home, especially since it's so close."

As Detective Finn Mettner walked past, Josie flagged him down with her free hand and instructed him to escort Colin to his residence to check for Lucy.

"Does Lucy know her address and phone number by heart? If she got lost and a stranger asked her to tell them, would she be able to?"

"Yes," Amy answered as Colin followed Mettner out of the park.

"That's good," Josie assured her.

Gretchen asked, "Has Lucy ever wandered off before? Here or maybe in a store or anything like that?"

Amy shook her head, more tears spilling down her face. "No, she's not prone to wandering off. She always stays near me. It's a rule. She knows how I am about—"

She broke off as a sob rocked her body. "Oh God, my baby. You have to find her. We have to find her!"

Josie's voice was firm and clear. "Mrs. Ross, look at me."

Amy's eyes wandered all around the playground area before landing on Josie's face.

Josie said, "We're doing everything we can to find her right now. Tell me, does Lucy have any medical conditions we should be aware of?"

Amy's eyes drifted once more to the cluster of parents and children in the center of the play area standing before two Denton officers who were busy taking down information. Then her gaze traveled outward to the wooded areas on the periphery of the playground where several other officers threaded through the trees, searching for Lucy and calling out her name.

"Mrs. Ross?" Gretchen prompted.

"No, no medical conditions. She's very healthy." She looked at them again. "This is not like her. You don't understand. She wouldn't run off."

"Did you see her leave the carousel?" Josie asked.

Amy shook her head. "No. I was trying to get down off that stupid horse. I got tangled in the strap. She got down before me and she ran off. I lost sight of her in the crowd."

"So you didn't see her go to the exit?"

"No, no. I didn't see her after she got down off her horse and ran off. I looked and looked—oh my God."

"How often do you come to the park?" Gretchen asked.

"A few times a week. I mean, usually she comes with the nanny."

"What is the nanny's name?" Gretchen went on. "Where is she now?"

"Jaclyn. Jaclyn Underwood," Amy said. "She's away. Her family is from Colorado. She went home to visit for the weekend."

"Where in Denton does she live?" Gretchen asked.

She rattled off an address in Denton, close to the college campus. "She's a student at Denton University. She picks Lucy up from school and spends a few hours with her before dinner. Listen, is this really important? I want to go look for Lucy."

"Of course," Gretchen said. "I'll be here coordinating the investigation." A business card appeared in Gretchen's hand, and she gave it to Amy. "My cell phone number is on there."

Clutching it in her fist, Amy ran off. Josie watched as she followed the perimeter of the play area before disappearing into one of the wooded areas, following behind several of their officers.

Harris stirred, his blue eyes opening, then sighed and turned his head. Josie felt a patch of sweat where his face had rested. She patted his back and looked to Gretchen.

Gretchen tapped her pen against her notepad. "What do you think?"

"I don't know," Josie said.

"You don't think she wandered off?"

Josie shook her head. She had nothing to base this feeling on, no evidence that anything nefarious had happened to Lucy Ross, so she didn't bother trying to explain herself.

Gretchen sighed and pointed at the carousel. "Let's start at the beginning."

CHAPTER FOUR

The teenager in charge of the carousel sat in his tiny ticket booth at the entrance to the ride, his face peeking out the small window, watching the commotion with wide, frightened eyes. He stepped out as Josie and Gretchen approached.

"What's your name?" Gretchen asked him.

He held a bright red ballcap in his hands. His fingers worked the bill into a U shape. Dark hair hung over his eyes. He gave a quick flick of his head to his left, shaking the locks out of his face. "Logan," he said.

Gretchen introduced herself and Josie. "How old are you, Logan?"

He shifted from foot to foot. "Eighteen."

So they could speak to him without having to contact a parent or guardian. Before either of them could pose another question, he asked, "Did you—did you find her yet?"

"No, not yet," Josie said.

"You want me to keep the ride closed?"

"Yes," Gretchen said. "Until we know what we're dealing with here."

"Logan," Josie said as she pulled her phone out, holding Harris against her with one arm while awkwardly using her other hand to enter her password and pull up the photo of Lucy Ross she'd had Amy text her. She turned the screen toward him. "Do you remember seeing this girl on the carousel?"

He studied the photo. "I guess. I mean, a ton of kids get on this ride during the day. It's hard to remember them all."

Josie asked, "What time did you get here today?"

"Like, noon."

Josie checked the time on her phone. It was almost four-thirty in the afternoon. Gretchen asked, "And how long are you supposed to keep the carousel open?"

"Till six."

"How long have you been working here?" Josie asked.

"Like, three weeks."

Josie showed him Lucy's photo again. "Do you remember seeing this girl or not?"

His fingers curled the bill of the hat again. "Yeah, she had on a colorful backpack, like, a bug or something."

Josie looked at Gretchen. "That's right. She had one on. It was small and looked like a stuffed butterfly, but it was a backpack."

Gretchen said, "You saw her get on the carousel. Did you see her get off?"

He shook his head. "Nah, I was taking the tickets from the people in line waiting to get on. I didn't know anything was wrong until her mom started yelling her name."

"At that point, you turned back toward the carousel," Josie said. "Did you see her at all?"

"No. I'm really sorry."

"It's okay," Gretchen said. She nodded toward the carousel. "Do you mind?"

"Oh, yeah, sure."

He led them through the small fenced area where prospective riders waited. He reached over the gate and unlocked it, holding it open to let them pass through. He stood just inside the gate while Josie and Gretchen stepped onto the carousel platform.

"Are there any cameras at all?" Josie asked.

"No. We don't have any cameras."

With a sigh, Gretchen added, "And there aren't any in the city park."

"Right," Josie said. "Not enough crime to warrant cameras."

Shifting Harris again, Josie weaved through the colorful horses. "I talked with them before they got on," she told Gretchen. "Here, this is the one she was on. It's the same as the one in the photo."

"And Amy was on one of the horses as well?" Gretchen said.

"Right. This one, I think."

The horse Josie had seen Amy lingering near when she was confronting the crowd of onlookers was next to Lucy's horse but slightly in front of it. "The ride was full," Josie added.

Gretchen turned in a complete circle. "Okay, so let's say she's slightly behind her mom. The ride starts to slow down to a stop. She hops down from the horse and takes off." She pointed to the exit gate. "She could easily have made it out."

"No one saw her," Josie said. "No one saw her exit, and no one saw her in the playground after."

"No one was looking," Gretchen pointed out. She gestured toward Harris. "You were here with him. How many boys with dark hair did you see in the playground today?"

"I have no idea."

"Any of them wearing… let's say… a blue shirt?"

"I don't know," Josie said. "I see your point."

"Everyone on this ride and everyone in the playground was focused on their own kids. Even if she had run out, it's quite possible no one noticed."

"Which is why the other parents' photos will be helpful."

They both looked over to the cluster of parents and their restive children. All of them had their phones out, as did the two officers assigned to the group. Josie knew they would ask the parents to text them any photos or videos they had, and they'd give all of it a cursory review.

"We should talk to the kids, too," Josie said. "They might have been more likely to notice Lucy."

"Yes," Gretchen agreed. "We should."

As they angled around the horses to the outer edge of the carousel, something on the column in the center caught Josie's eye. "Wait," she said.

She went back toward the center of the ride. The column was wide, made of thick wood panels adorned with ornate molding and covered in oil paintings of landscapes; fields with farmhouses in the distance, old mills next to waterfalls, and gardens rife with colorful flowers. Josie ran her fingers alongside the edge of one of the panels. "Gretchen," she said. "This is a door."

Gretchen came closer, beckoning Logan to follow. Toward the lower end of the panel was a latch and a small knob painted the same bright red as the wood around it. Josie wouldn't have noticed it had she not been so close to it. She tugged on the knob and the panel opened like a door.

Logan said, "Uh, you can't go in there."

Josie and Gretchen shot him stern looks. He smiled, his face flushed red. "Oh, right. You're the police."

Josie handed Harris over to Gretchen. He was awake now, but in that post-nap state where he was content not to do much but observe things quietly. She stepped into the column. Small wooden squares were spaced out along the floor—close enough together for her to walk on but far enough apart that she could see beneath them where metal poles ran from the center of the inner wheel out to the vertical poles that controlled the horses. Above her head were more poles reaching out toward the ride's edges. Across from her was one small shelf built into the back of one of the panels with what looked like a small, black tool bag on top of it.

Logan poked his head in behind her. "That belongs to my boss," he said. "It's in case he needs to tighten things up or whatever."

On closer inspection, Josie saw that the bag was old and well-used. Its zipper hung open, and inside she could see a few wrenches and screwdrivers. She turned to Logan. "Is the door always open? Does it lock?"

"It's always open," he said. "I mean, as far as I know. No one really comes in here. No one even notices the door, I don't think."

Josie took one last look around, but she didn't see any sign of Lucy, or any sign that any person had recently been inside the column. Stepping back out, she took Harris from Gretchen's arms.

"JoJo, I'm thirsty," he said.

"I know, buddy," she said. "I'm going to call your mom to come get you. She should be on her way to my house right now."

They thanked Logan, instructed him not to let anyone else inside the perimeter and walked over to the small crowd of parents. The uniformed officers hadn't yet found any signs of Lucy on the photos and videos the parents had provided. While Josie contacted Misty and asked her to come to the park instead of Josie's home to pick up Harris, Gretchen got consent from the parents to address the school-age children. She had them sit on the grass in a circle and she told them that a little girl named Lucy had gotten lost in the park after riding the carousel. She passed around Josie's phone with the photo of Lucy on the screen. Josie watched them hand the phone around the circle. She estimated the youngest of them to be four years old and the oldest somewhere around ten. Three of them remembered seeing Lucy at the playground. One even remembered seeing her on the carousel ride with her mother, but none of them had seen her once the ride stopped.

As the gathering of parents and children dispersed, Misty DeRossi appeared at the playground's main entrance. Josie's boyfriend, Lieutenant Noah Fraley, trailed behind her, moving rapidly on a pair of crutches. It had been about a month since he broke his leg jumping from the upper window of a burning building.

"Mommeee!" Harris cried, reaching for Misty as she got closer. She took him from Josie and hugged him tightly.

"Noah wanted me to bring him," Misty explained. "I was already at your house when you called me. You sounded like something was wrong."

Noah reached them a second later. "A kid went missing?" he asked.

Josie explained the situation to both of them.

Misty said, "Are you sure she just ran off?"

All three of them had been deeply scarred by the missing girls' case that had rocked the city of Denton three years earlier. Any reminder of it was difficult to process. "I don't know," Josie answered honestly. "But I want to stay and help with the search."

"Of course," Misty agreed.

They said their goodbyes and she headed off with Harris. Noah stood in place, leaning on his crutches. Josie said, "You didn't have to come."

He smiled. "I can find a way to make myself useful."

Josie spotted a bench near the entrance to the play area. "Come on," she told him. "You can monitor who goes in and out while we search."

CHAPTER FIVE

Josie had just left Noah on the bench when Mettner returned with Colin in tow. Lucy's father's face had paled by two shades since Josie last saw him. She knew immediately that his daughter had not somehow made her way home.

"She's not there," Mettner confirmed.

"Where's my wife?" Colin asked.

Josie gestured toward the forested areas behind her. "She joined the search. We've got a dozen officers out there looking for Lucy right now. If she's wandered off, we'll find her."

"What if she didn't wander off?" Colin asked, voicing the question that had been running on a loop in Josie's head since she heard those first few strained, desperate notes in Amy's voice as she called out for Lucy.

Josie opened her mouth to give some stock police response, but Colin just walked away, off to join the search himself. The three of them watched him go.

Mettner said, "Apparently he travels a lot for his job."

"Well," Josie said. "That explains their little spat over Lucy's sense of direction—and the need for a nanny. Did he mention what the wife does for a living?"

"She's a stay-at-home mom," Mettner answered. "She doesn't work."

Noah interjected. "Did you say she has a nanny? She must do something. I mean why would you have to hire a nanny if you were a stay-at-home mom?"

Josie raised a brow in his direction. "Kids can be a lot to handle alone. Misty struggles."

"Misty works sixty hours a week," Noah pointed out. "And she has you and Harris's grandmother to help her."

"Maybe Amy Ross doesn't have family nearby," Mettner suggested.

Josie raised her hands in the air. "We don't have time for this. We need to get out and look for this little girl." She glanced at Noah. "I've got my phone if you need me. Gretchen will be stationed right over there. She's coordinating. Mett, let's go."

With Mettner only a few yards away from her, they set out into one of the patches of forest surrounding the playground. They could hear the sounds of others searching all around them—the rustle and snap of tree branches and several different voices calling out Lucy's name. Occasionally, Josie paused to text Gretchen to see if anyone had found anything. There was nothing. Gretchen had sent additional units to the houses that sat across from the park to conduct door-to-door enquiries and to search their backyards in case Lucy had exited the park instead of going deeper into it. An hour passed, then another, then another. They emerged from one forested section, crossed a different area of the park, and entered an entirely different section of trees. They walked until they reached the edge of park where the Denton University campus began. From somewhere behind her, Josie heard Amy calling out her daughter's name again and again in a strained, near-hysterical tone. The light overhead faded, casting darkness over the forest.

As she circled back to the playground, the park's overhead lights blinked on. Gathered around the entrance to the park were a number of officers, including Gretchen and Noah. As Josie got closer, she saw that both Amy and Colin were there as well as Denton's Chief of Police, Bob Chitwood. All had donned jackets. Colin held his wife against his chest with one arm while his other hand clutched his cell phone.

"Anything?" Josie asked Gretchen as she joined the group.

A grim set to her mouth, Gretchen shook her head.

Mettner jogged up behind Josie. He quickly looked around the group, assessing the situation. He said, "Not even a sign of her?"

Gretchen said, "No. Nothing."

"Can we ask for an Amber Alert?" he asked.

Josie and Chitwood answered at the same time. "No," they said.

Josie continued, "We have no evidence that she was abducted. As far as we know, she ran off. Amber Alerts are specifically for abducted and endangered children. We can call the state police, though, and the sheriff's office to ask for assistance."

Chitwood held up a cell phone. "I already did. I asked for bodies to search through the night, and the sheriff is bringing their K-9 unit."

Gretchen addressed Amy and Colin. "Can you go home and get something that smells like Lucy for when the dogs get here?"

Amy's head lifted from her husband's chest and swiveled in Gretchen's direction. "Yes," she said.

Josie nodded toward one of the uniformed officers who escorted the parents out of the park. She turned to Gretchen and Chitwood and said, "We should call the FBI."

Chitwood scoffed. "No one is calling the FBI, Quinn."

Josie put a hand on her hip. "They have a rapid deployment team for missing children."

"Isn't that just for abducted children?" Mettner asked.

"Yeah," Chitwood added. "It's called the Child Abduction Rapid Deployment team—CARD."

"No, not just abducted children," Josie said. "Any disappearance of a child of tender age. That means under twelve years old. Their CARD team was deployed in North Carolina last month when a four-year-old boy disappeared from his backyard."

"That's right," Noah said. "They found him alive in the woods."

"And we'll find Lucy Ross alive in this park tonight," Chitwood said. "There's no need to call the damn FBI. We're equipped for this, and we'll have the Staties and the sheriff helping us."

"Sir," Josie protested. "The CARD team could be here in less than two hours."

"For the love of God, Quinn," Chitwood said. Everyone stared at him, mostly because he hadn't yelled at her. He always yelled—at everyone. But now his tone was low and frustrated, almost like he didn't have the energy to argue with her. "Not every disappearance is an abduction."

"Children don't just disappear into thin air," Josie pointed out.

"You have no proof that this was an abduction. Believe it or not, Quinn, kids do wander off."

"If Lucy Ross wandered off, someone would have found her by now."

Chitwood turned to Noah. "Fraley, how long did it take the CARD team to find that boy in North Carolina?"

Sheepishly, Noah said, "Four days."

Josie suppressed her eye-roll. "That was an extremely rural area. In any direction you go through this park, you come out in a residential area. The college campus is at the north end. Someone in this city would have seen her by now. There is not enough 'wilderness' for her to get lost in."

Chitwood stepped toward her, his arms crossed over his thin chest. Even in the dull yellow light, Josie could see wisps of his thinning white hair floating over the top of his balding head. "We're going to find this kid, Quinn. We don't need the damn FBI."

"Sir, with all due respect—"

"Quinn," he cut her off. "When you start a sentence like that, I know you're going to say something to piss me off. Why not save us both the trouble of me threatening to remove you from your job?"

Josie felt heat sting her face, but she couldn't stop herself. "If you're refusing to call the FBI because you don't want it to look like you can't handle your own city, I urge you to consider that the life of a seven-year-old girl is more important than your pride."

In the low light of the park's overhead lamps, she could see his acne-scarred cheeks flush beneath his stubble. Again, she waited for his loud, angry tirade, but it didn't come. Instead, he swallowed several times, his Adam's apple bobbing. Then in a tight voice, he said, "Quinn, this has nothing to do with my pride. I've been at this a long time. Since you were in diapers. We have the manpower and the resources to handle this. You don't need to take every situation to a ten, Quinn. We can handle this. We don't need the FBI."

Gretchen stepped forward. "Then we need the press."

Josie felt a wave of relief. Surely, Chitwood could not refuse them press coverage to help search for Lucy. She also knew—as did Gretchen—that the FBI's CARD team didn't need to wait for the local police department's invitation if they were made aware of the disappearance of a child under twelve. There was a good chance that if they somehow saw the news coverage, they would descend on Denton whether Chitwood liked it or not.

Chitwood said, "Call WYEP, get them to send a crew out here. Set up a mobile station in this area. We'll search through the night and take volunteers in the morning if she isn't found tonight."

CHAPTER SIX

Within an hour, a large tent had been erected at the entrance to the playground with folding tables and chairs inside to be used by Denton PD as a mobile command post. Someone had brought coffee and pastries, although no one touched them. Noah sat at one of the tables with a department-issue laptop, uploading the footage and photos that the officers had taken from the other parents at the playground that day. Gretchen and Chitwood sat facing Lucy's parents. Josie peeked outside to where a news crew waited to interview someone from Denton PD. Members of the sheriff's office and state police troopers milled around, ready to embark on more searches. Josie knew they would work through the night, in teams, until Lucy was found. She heard Colin's voice in her head once more: *what if she's not found?*

Shaking it off, she turned back to her team. "WYEP is here. Gretchen, you want to give them a statement?"

Gretchen stood but Chitwood placed a hand on her forearm. "I want Quinn to do it," he said.

Josie said, "I'm not the lead on this one, Chief. I just happened to be here on my day off when Lucy disappeared."

Chitwood raised a brow. "I know that, Quinn. I want you out there as the face of the department."

"Sir," Gretchen protested.

"Listen, Palmer," he replied. "You don't have the—" he broke off when he noticed the Ross parents were staring at him. Clearing his throat, he went on. "Quinn is a local celebrity, and she's great on camera. That's all. I think if we put her in the press and keep you here working the case, we'll get better results."

Josie knew the real reason he didn't want Gretchen in front of cameras on a high-profile case was because seven months earlier, Gretchen had been embroiled in a scandal that had nearly cost her her career. She'd only been let back on the force because of Josie's machinations and when she returned, she'd been forced to spend time on the desk. For once, Josie understood Chitwood's reasoning. He was putting the case first. Still, Josie felt uncomfortable. She looked pointedly at Gretchen, but she just smiled and said, "I always hated doing press."

Relieved, Josie turned to Colin and Amy. "It would be great if you could join me out there. I know you're upset but if you could say a few words, it might help."

Colin squeezed his wife's shoulder. "I think it's best if Amy talks."

"No," Amy said. "I—I can't."

Colin frowned at her. "Amy, you're her mother. People connect to mothers. All you have to do is go out there and ask people to come help in the search. That's it."

Her eyes were wide with something beyond nervousness. More like terror, Josie thought. Amy clasped her hands together and held them to her chest. "I can't be on TV," she muttered. "I can't be on TV." Her gaze traveled back to Josie. "Please, just find my little girl. Please."

Chitwood, Gretchen and Colin all started speaking at once, but Josie held up a hand to silence them. Some people were not equipped to speak in front of cameras at their best, let alone at their very worst and most frightened. "It's okay," Josie said.

"Quinn," Chitwood began.

"No," Josie said. "Mrs. Ross is right. The only face people should see on television tonight is Lucy's."

"We'll give them the photo we were using earlier," Gretchen said.

"Mettner," Josie called out and from somewhere in the rear of the tent, he appeared. "Yeah, boss."

"Just Josie is fine," she said. "Mett, call Lamay and have him bring over a podium, then can you take that photo of Lucy and run it over to Staples, see if they can blow it up for us? That's what we want people to see."

"You got it," Mettner said, jogging out of the tent.

Josie felt a clammy hand squeeze her own. She looked down to see Amy's pale face staring up at her, more tears streaming silently down her cheeks. "Thank you," she whispered.

One of the sheriff's deputies poked his head into the tent. "K-9 unit is two hours out."

"Two hours?" Gretchen said. "They can't get here any faster?"

He shook his head. "Sorry, ma'am. They were already out on a case when you called up."

Josie looked to one of the tables where a large brown bag sat, containing one of Lucy's dirty shirts that Amy had taken from her hamper to give the dogs her scent. She looked back at the parents. "It's okay," she told them. "We'll have teams out there searching continuously before the K-9 unit gets here."

The press conference went off without a hitch, the blown-up photo of Lucy smiling while sitting on the carousel horse striking in its size, color, and because of the vibrant smile of the young girl. The WYEP producer promised it would be their top story. Afterward, Gretchen urged Amy and Colin to go home and get some sleep.

"I can't," Amy said. "Lucy's still out there somewhere. I can't sleep. I can't sleep until she's home with me."

Colin rubbed his wife's back. "Ame, we need to rest."

She glared at him. "Fine. You go rest. I'm waiting here for my baby."

"Amy," he said, his tone edging into annoyance.

She pulled away from him. "This is your fault, you know."

He stumbled back a little, as if the accusation had delivered a physical blow. "What?"

She reached forward and snatched his cell phone from his hand. Before he could react, she threw it against one of the tent walls where it made a *pop* sound before crashing to the ground. "You and your stupid phone," she spat. "If you had been able to put it down for five minutes to go on the ride with Lucy or even to watch her, maybe she would still be here."

"You can't—" Colin began but his words failed.

Amy's face twisted in disgust. She raised both arms, hands in fists, and beat against his chest. "If you were watching her, you would have seen where she went. Instead, you were on your phone. Do you know that every time we went past you on that stupid ride, she called out to you?"

She hit him again and he took it. A single tear rolled down his face.

Amy kept going, her voice getting higher pitched. "She said, 'look at me, Daddy! Look at me! I'm on the blue horse.'"

"I didn't hear her," Colin said softly. He caught his wife's forearms. "Amy, it was one phone call."

"It's always just one phone call, isn't it? You bastard. This is your fault."

"How is this my fault? You were on the ride with her. You were supposed to be watching her."

"Screw you," Amy shrieked. She wrenched her arms free and went after him with a force that seemed otherworldly, jumping at him, her fists flailing. As Colin fell onto his back, Josie and Mettner jumped forward, each of them hooking an arm under Amy's armpits and dragging her back. Her shrill screams continued unabated. Her limbs continued to flail. Josie caught an elbow to her nose, and she felt blood stream down her face. Gretchen joined the fray, the three of them trying to get Amy under control. Finally, Mettner wrapped his arms around her, trapping her arms against her body. Amy continued to curse her husband. She fought against Mettner's arms, but he held fast to her. It took a moment for Josie to process the words that Mettner said over and over again into her ear. "Mrs. Ross, please calm down. Lucy needs you. She needs you to be calm. Please."

Josie wiped at her face with the sleeve of her jacket until Gretchen's hand appeared in front of her, holding a paper towel. Without taking her eyes off Amy, Josie tried to wipe away the blood on her upper lip and chin. Noah lurched over on crutches. "Hey," he said. "You okay?"

Josie nodded. In front of her, Amy's cries slowly subsided to a low, sad keening. In Mettner's embrace, she sagged. "My baby," she wailed. "Please find my baby."

Noah's fingers gently tipped Josie's chin up toward him. "You think it's broken?"

Josie shook her head. "I'm fine."

Gretchen pulled a chair over and Mettner let Amy sink into it, releasing her at last. Josie stepped around Noah. She walked over to Amy and knelt before the woman. "Mrs. Ross," she said. "Look at me."

"Josie," Noah said, his voice steeped in concern.

Josie ignored him. She reached into Amy's lap and took her hands. "Look at me, Amy," she said more firmly.

Amy's wide, sad eyes blinked and focused on Josie's face.

"We're going to do everything we can—absolutely everything—to find your daughter."

Amy nodded. Josie felt the woman's hand squeeze hers. She stood and turned away. Gretchen, Noah and now Chitwood all stood staring at her. Behind them stood Colin, looking stunned and disheveled. Josie gave him a nod as she pushed past everyone and walked out of the tent. She didn't slow down until she was out of the park and in the street near some parked cars. Then she bent at the waist and threw up.

CHAPTER SEVEN

At last Amy went home to get some sleep and Gretchen sent a female officer with her. Colin stayed at the tent, silent and shell-shocked, sitting in a chair in the corner as other officers came in and out to report to Gretchen and get coffee. With Mettner mediating, the parents had agreed that they would take shifts sleeping so that one of them was always at the park in case Lucy was found. The sheriff's K-9 unit arrived, and Gretchen went out into the playground with the deputy and his German Shepherd. The dog's handler took him onto the carousel, next to the blue horse where Lucy was last seen and let him smell Lucy's shirt before setting him loose. The dog sniffed all around the platform. He sniffed the column in the center of the carousel, then sniffed around the outer part of the ride between the fence and the platform. Nose pressed to the ground, he exited the gate surrounding the ride and veered right, going to the fence that separated the park from the sidewalk. There, he sat, issuing a short bark. The handler marked the section of fence and walked the dog to the other side of the fence where Lucy's scent picked up again. Nose to the pavement, the dog traveled another twenty feet or so and sat again, silent this time.

Josie walked up to where Gretchen stood with the handler.

"The scent stops here," the handler said. "It's on both sides of the fence."

"Which means what?" Gretchen asked.

The handler shrugged. "Not sure. But because it wasn't continuous from inside the park, along the fence to the pavement and outside the park, it could mean someone picked her up and hoisted her over the fence—or she hopped the fence herself. Then it stops here completely on the sidewalk. Usually when the scent stops abruptly, it's because the person got into a vehicle."

Gretchen said, "You think she was abducted?"

The handler replied, "I can't make that determination. I can only tell you that her scent was in the park, on the carousel and it ends here. Like I said, when the scent stops, it's usually because the person got into a vehicle and left the area."

Gretchen jotted something down in her notebook and thanked the handler. Together, they trudged back to the tent. Josie said, "Someone took her."

Gretchen said, "It appears that way, but how did she get from the carousel to the sidewalk without anyone seeing anything at all?"

"We have to be missing something," Josie said.

Inside the tent, Colin was still there, arms folded over his body, his chin resting on his chest. He snored lightly.

"Hey," Noah said, waving her over to where he sat in front of the laptop.

She sat beside him, feeling the exhaustion in her body and the ache in her nose for the first time. "You don't have to stay," she told him. "I can take you home—or to my house. You should put your leg up."

His fingers worked along the laptop keyboard. "I'm fine," he said. "I'd rather be here. Keeps my mind off… well, you know."

It had been less than two months since Noah's beloved mother was murdered and his family torn apart. He'd been spending all of his time at Josie's house. She knew he was struggling to come to terms with all that had happened and that he would struggle for a long time. She also knew it was especially hard for him to manage with a broken leg. She reached over and squeezed his thigh. "It's good to be of use."

"Yes," he said, bringing up a series of photos on the laptop. "Look, I've organized all the photos from the other parents. Unfortunately, no one took pictures once the carousel stopped."

"What about photos of elsewhere in the playground after Lucy went missing? Any chance she was caught in the background?" She told him what the search and rescue dog handler had said.

Noah frowned. He started clicking through the photos. "No, not that I can see."

Each photo featured a different child—smiling, laughing, running, playing. As Noah moved through them, she studied the people behind each child, looking for telltale signs of Lucy's pink shirt or her butterfly backpack. She found herself and Harris in the background of a couple of photos but no Lucy.

"Videos?" she asked.

"Two of the carousel while the ride was still in motion. Neither captures Lucy or Amy Ross once the ride stops. Once it was over, the parents stopped taping. There is another one that is more promising."

Noah closed out the photos and clicked on a small video icon. As it started to play, Josie could see that it had been taken pretty far from the carousel, but the spinning horses were clearly visible in the background. The little girl in the video was doing cartwheels across the grass. Her mother's voice could be heard encouraging her and complimenting her on her form. Behind the girl, the carousel rolled slowly to a stop. On the right-hand side of the frame, Josie could make out the rear end of the blue horse. Lucy's sparkly butterfly backpack caught the light as she scurried down off the horse and took off toward the other side of the platform. Josie followed her progress to the left side of the screen. The ride was crowded and twice Lucy was completely out of sight behind other riders and the horses. Josie caught a glimpse of her golden hair and her colorful butterfly backpack one last time before she disappeared around the other side of the column.

"It's her," Josie said. "It's definitely her. Play it again."

Noah played the video several more times and each time they watched it, Josie picked up more details. Amy, on the horse beside Lucy's but slightly in front, had got tangled in her safety belt, giving

Lucy precious seconds to race away from her mother. Colin could be seen on the right side of the frame briefly as he paced back and forth, phone pressed to his ear. The other riders were preoccupied with getting out of their own safety harnesses and exiting the ride. The exit was on the left side of the screen, and people filed out of it in a steady stream, but the woman taking the video was following her daughter's cartwheel and jerked the camera away from the exit before all of the riders had left. It was impossible to say whether Lucy had exited the ride through the gate or if she had gone around to the other side and somehow hopped the fence. But why would she? Josie wondered. She thought of Lucy nimbly climbing the slide. She probably could make it over with no problems, but she'd been on the carousel already that day—Amy and Colin had said that—so why would she have left the ride any way but through the actual exit?

"Damn," Noah groused as they watched the last few seconds of the video for the fourth time. "We really don't know where she went once she ran around that column."

"Play it one more time," Josie instructed. "The whole thing."

This time, as she watched, Gretchen and Mettner appeared behind them, watching the footage as well. Something had been bothering Josie from the very first time she had watched Lucy hop down from her horse and take off. She hadn't been able to pinpoint it until now.

"She's running toward someone or something," Josie said.

"What do you mean?" Mettner asked.

Josie touched Noah's arm and he reset the footage and played it again. "Look," Josie told them. "It's like she can't wait to get off her horse. She throws off the harness, jumps down and races off like a shot."

"Away from her mother," Gretchen noted.

"And her father," Noah said. He pointed to the right side of the screen where one of Colin's legs could be seen in the corner.

"Look how slowly all the other kids are moving," Josie said.

"Cause they don't want the ride to be over," Gretchen said.

"Right," said Josie. "But Lucy is moving with purpose."

"So she saw someone she knew?" Mettner asked.

"I don't know," Josie said. "Maybe."

"Could someone have walked out of the park with her—or lifted her over the fence to the sidewalk—before you shut the ride down and gathered the parents?" Noah asked.

"Yes," Josie said with a sinking heart. "It's very possible."

"We still have no actual evidence that anyone took her," Mettner said. "Only suspicion."

"True," Josie conceded, but in her heart, the word rang hollow.

"Boss," Mettner said.

Josie looked at him. He wore a grimace. "Whatever it is, Mett, just say it."

"You think maybe you're leaning toward abduction because of everything that went down during the missing girls' case a few years back? Like maybe you see everything through the filter of that case?"

Noah said, "You're out of line, Mett."

"It's okay," Josie said. She met Noah's eyes. A silent flood of communication roared between them. Noah wanted to make sure she really was okay with Mettner's accusation—gently delivered though it was—and Josie wanted him to know she was just fine. She flashed him a brief, wan smile. Her heart warmed at the thought that even in his grief, Noah was sticking up for her.

Mettner's hands were in the air. "I didn't mean any offense. Really. I just know, you know, that case was hard on you guys."

Noah said, "Some of us have scars from that case, it's true, but Josie has great instincts and those are not filtered in any way. If she thinks that something more is going on here than a little girl wandering off and getting lost, I believe her. Plus, the dog-handler thinks Lucy may have gotten into a vehicle."

Mettner's hands were still in the air. "Fair enough."

"It's fine, Mett," Josie told him. "No offense taken." She turned back to Noah and the laptop. "Can we watch it one more time? Can you slow it down? Maybe go frame by frame from the time she jumps down from the horse to when she disappears from the screen?"

"Sure," Noah said, resetting the video.

Josie, Mettner and Gretchen all leaned in to watch as Noah clicked from frame to frame. As Lucy reached the left side of the screen again, Josie saw something dark edge out toward her from the column in the center of the ride. "Stop," she said. She gestured to it. It looked like the point of something extending toward Lucy from behind the column.

"What is that?" Noah asked as he tried to zoom in.

They all leaned in closer, squinting as though that would make it clearer. The closer Noah zoomed, the grainier the picture became.

"It can't be a hand or a leg," Mettner said. "It looks like the corner of a square."

Gretchen and Josie spoke at the same time. "It's the door."

CHAPTER EIGHT

They raced back out to the carousel, flashlight beams sweeping the area. Noah trailed behind, going as fast as he could on his crutches. Josie and Gretchen showed them the door. Mettner climbed inside as Josie had done earlier. There was nothing there. Josie said, "Someone call Hummel and have the Evidence Response Team come out and process the inside."

Mettner closed the door and pulled his phone out. The four of them ambled back to the tent. Gretchen said, "You think she went in there?"

"I don't know," Josie said. "If she was hiding in there, she would have still been in there when we started looking for her."

Noah said, "Wouldn't someone on the ride have noticed the door opening?"

"You would think," Gretchen said. "I'll call everyone on the list of parents whose kids were on the ride tomorrow morning and see if anyone remembers seeing the door open."

Mettner hung up his phone. "Hummel will be here in fifteen. What if someone else was inside the door?"

Noah said, "I thought you weren't down with the kidnapper theory."

Mettner shrugged. "I never said I wasn't. I just said we didn't have any evidence that she was kidnapped."

Gretchen said, "It seems unlikely that a kidnapper could successfully take a seven-year-old from inside the carousel. I mean, the only way out is through that door."

When they got back to the tent, Colin had gone and Amy sat in his place on a chair, bundled in a thick fleece jacket. Her sandy hair hung limp and unbrushed. Her eyelids were swollen. She looked up hopefully when they came in. "Anything?"

They all shook their heads. Josie said, "Not yet."

Amy frowned. "What—what happened to your face?"

Everyone froze and stared at her. Mettner said, "You don't remember?"

Amy said, "Remember what?"

She had been so hysterical, Josie wasn't at all surprised that she didn't remember struggling against her and Mettner. She probably didn't even realize she had hit Josie. Besides, it was an accident. Josie cut in, "I ran into a tree branch. Mrs. Ross, do you think you could look at some video footage and photos for us from today?"

Amy jumped to her feet. "Yes, please. Anything that you think will help."

Noah patted the chair next to him and Amy took it. They went through the footage of Lucy getting off her carousel horse and running off. None of them mentioned the door opening but Josie did explain that they believed that Lucy was running toward something or someone. They asked Amy to review all the photos they had from the day to see if she recognized anyone in the background that Lucy may have been excited to see. Two hours slipped past, but Amy didn't recognize anyone in the photos.

Two of the rotating search teams returned, having found nothing, and two fresh teams went back out. The ERT had finished processing the inside of the carousel, but the results of their findings would take time to get back. Gretchen decided that two of the detectives from their investigative team should go home and sleep for a few hours. Josie and Mettner volunteered. Noah and Gretchen would stay on-scene until they returned and then they would go and do the same. They were all hoping for many volunteers to help with the search in the morning.

CHAPTER NINE

I saw the silver woman from the window again. She was standing outside in her large garden with her back to me, a watering can in one hand. I called her the silver woman because her hair was the color of a coin I once found under our bed. After my sweaty palm clamped around it to recover it, I unfurled my fingers and let the sunlight glint off its surface. The man on the coin had long hair just like the silver woman, and today her hair was tied back in a ponytail just like his. Turning side to side, she sprinkled the water on the flowers at her feet. I willed her to turn around, to look up and see me staring at her. But she didn't. I even tapped a fingernail against the glass to try to get her attention, but it didn't work. I thought of rapping on the window with my knuckles, but that would make too much noise. I knew I was supposed to be quiet and still.

I pressed the coin against the window with my thumb, wishing it could break through the glass. Then I could go outside. I could get close to the flowers in the silver woman's garden. Maybe she would even let me use her watering can.

The coin slipped from beneath my thumb, slid down the window, bounced off the sill and clattered to the floor. The noise bounced off the walls of the small room. I felt a squeeze in my chest. I had been warned about making too much noise. She had told me not to watch the silver woman. "Don't draw attention to yourself," she always said.

When I heard her at the door, I scrambled down from my perch at the windowsill, scooped up my coin, and jumped back onto the bed. I pushed the coin under the pillow.

"What are you doing?" she asked.

"Nothing."

"I heard something in here."

"I didn't do anything," I said.

"I heard you moving around. What did I tell you?"

I pulled my knees to my chest but didn't answer.

"I know you remember. You have to be as quiet as you can or he'll hurt us," she said.

"I want to come out there with you," I told her. "Pleeease."

She gave me a pained smile. "I know you do. When he leaves, I'll take you out there."

He didn't leave for a long time. Then she took me into the other rooms. I loved to explore them even though I had seen them many times before. They were at least different from my own room. I tried to discover a new detail each time: the one yellowing, chipped tile in the kitchen; the scrape of the brown fabric on the lumpy recliner chair against my skin; the large grease spot where his head rested when he sat in the chair and smoked. Beside the chair was a small table with a remote control that I was never to touch. Next to that was a round ashtray overflowing with cigarette butts. My fingers lingered over the mound of discarded, smoked cigarettes. I wanted to touch them, but she shooed me away. I jumped on the couch instead and skipped around on the carpet until she snapped at me. "You have to be still. If you break something, he'll—"

She stopped.

I stared up at her. "He'll hurt us?"

"Or worse," she said, whispering as though he was still there somewhere, listening in secret. She gripped my arm, squeezing hard. "Promise me," she said. "Promise me you will do exactly as I say."

I stared into her wide eyes. "I promise."

CHAPTER TEN

At home, Josie showered and tried to clean up her face as best she could, but she already had two black eyes forming. So much for Chitwood's idea for her to be the face of Denton PD. She fell into her bed, so exhausted that her entire body felt achy. She wished Noah had come home with her. Thoughts of Lucy Ross swirled in her head. God, she hoped she was wrong about the girl being kidnapped, but she just couldn't shake the bad feeling sitting on her shoulders like a weighted cloak.

As she put her phone on to charge, she noticed several missed text messages. She swiped to bring them up, hoping they were filled with good news about Lucy. A sigh escaped her lips when she saw they were from her sister, Trinity. She sank onto her bed and read them.

Just heard you have a missing girl in Denton? What's going on?

You there? Everything okay? What's the scoop?

Please tell me what's going on. I hope you find her soon.

Call me as soon as you get this message. Hope you find the girl soon. Let me know if there's anything I can do.

Josie had no doubt her twin sister was genuinely concerned about Lucy, but she also knew that Trinity's compulsion to chase a good story overcame almost everything else in her life. Trinity had started out in Denton as a roving reporter for the local station, WYEP, before rising to stardom on the national stage. Then a source fed her bad information, her career fell apart and, disgraced, she was banished back to Central Pennsylvania. She had clawed her way back to the national network stage, and was now a news anchor for a famous morning show. It helped that her hometown of Denton was a seemingly never-ending source of scandalous stories that captured the imagination of the entire country. Trinity wanted to talk to her about the Lucy Ross case because there might be a story worth mining. Three years ago, Josie would have wanted to strangle the woman. Now she knew that despite Trinity's burning ambition to be at the top of her field, she did have people's best interests at heart. More than once, Trinity's reporting, research and ingenuity had actually helped people.

Josie's finger hovered over the call button, as she stared at Trinity's name. But she didn't feel like talking to her sister after the day she had had. Instead, she scrolled through her contacts until she found Christian Payne's name. She had already hit 'call' before she realized just how late it was. Still, Christian answered on the fifth ring, his voice thick with sleep. "Josie?" he said.

"Oh, I'm sorry," Josie said. "I didn't realize it was this late."

"Is everything okay, honey?"

At once, Josie felt simultaneously warmed and put-off by his familiarity. She was still getting used to the fact that Christian was her real father. The man Josie had believed to be her father died when she was six, but in her heart, she wasn't sure she would ever think of Eli Matson as anything but her dad. Still, she knew it wasn't Christian's fault that they'd been torn apart and had had to spend thirty years unknown to one another.

"Yeah," Josie said. "Everything's fine. I'm sorry. We can talk in the morning."

"Josie," he said, sounding more awake now. "For the last thirty-some years I would have given my own life to get a phone call from you at all—to know you were alive—so you get to call me in the middle of the night just as much as you want. What's on your mind?"

In the background, she heard a door creak. She imagined him walking out of the bedroom he shared with her mother and padding down the hall to the stairs, heading for the kitchen of the house they lived in, two hours from Josie. "It's a case," Josie explained. "A little girl went missing today. Her father is Colin Ross. He said he knew you."

"Yeah, he works in our pricing division," Christian said easily. "I'm really sorry to hear about his daughter. My God. Is he okay? What happened?"

Josie gave him a brief rundown of the situation. Christian said, "What can I do?"

"Well, I just hoped to get your impression of Colin Ross."

"My impression?" Christian asked haltingly. "You think he had something to do with his own daughter's disappearance?"

"I think," Josie said, "that we can't rule anything out."

"Jesus."

"Do you know him well?" she asked, forging onward even though the conversation had become awkward.

He sighed. "Not that well. We're not what I would consider close, but we've had a few drinks and been on a number of business trips together. When he worked in New York City, I'd see him several times a year. I had to travel there frequently for the company. Marketing works closely with his department once a drug is rolled out. He lived there for many years. His parents still live there, I believe. That's where he met his wife."

"What do you think of him?"

"Colin is a good guy. He's really settled down since he got married."

"What do you mean?" Josie asked.

"Just that he used to… how should I put this? Enjoy the ladies. He saw a lot of different women but never committed to any one of them."

"What happened?"

"I don't know. He met Amy. She wanted nothing to do with him. I don't know if that was the reason he became obsessed with her, but he pursued her relentlessly. Some of his colleagues in the New York office used to joke that he wore her down. I used to think that once he convinced her to marry him, he'd get tired of her. No one at Quarmark thought it would last."

"Well, it has," Josie said.

"Oh, I know," Christian said. "All he talks about is his family. It used to be when we'd get together for drinks he'd talk about the latest woman he'd been with, but I really think that becoming a father changed him. Settled him down. Either that or he's just getting old." He chuckled but the sound quickly died. "I can't believe it. That poor little girl."

"We'll find her," Josie said with more authority than she actually felt.

"I believe you will," Christian said. "You know, your sister will be blowing up your phone the minute she hears about this."

Josie laughed. "She already has."

They said their goodbyes and Josie put her phone back on to charge and laid back in her bed. Silence roared through the house, the loneliness cloying and creeping. She thought of the bottle of Wild Turkey she'd bought a month ago, just after Noah's mother was murdered. It was still in her kitchen, at the very back of one of her cabinets. Just one shot and she would fall easily to sleep. But her stomach had been on edge for over a week now, and she didn't want to make it worse. Besides that, she had learned the hard way that nothing good came of her consuming Wild Turkey in *any* quantity.

She heard a car pull into her driveway and sat bolt upright. A moment later she heard two car doors slam and then a knock on her door. It was dark outside, but the motion sensor light above her front door snapped on. Through the peephole, Josie saw Misty with a sleeping Harris in one arm and her tiny Chihuahua Weiner mix breed dog in the other. Josie threw the door open and herded them all inside, taking Harris from Misty's arms. "Misty, it's the middle of the night. Are you okay?"

"I am so sorry," Misty said. "We're fine. I just—I couldn't—"

In the dim foyer, Josie saw tears glistening in Misty's eyes. She locked the front door and waved Misty into the living room. Harris slept peacefully on Josie's shoulder. Misty's tiny dog searched its new surroundings warily. "What's going on?" Josie said. "Did something happen?"

"Oh no," Misty said. "My God, what happened to your face?"

"Oh, nothing," Josie said. "I'm fine. What about you guys? What's going on?"

"I'm so sorry. I know this is ridiculous. It's just that I… I just—I can't stop thinking about that little girl who went missing. I saw you on the news. I know that you said that 'it is believed she wandered off' but still, the thought of that little girl missing took me right back to when Harris was born. You know, when they took him from me."

"Oh, Misty," Josie said softly. With one hand, she reached out and squeezed Misty's shoulder. Misty had given birth to Harris at home with the help of a woman who had turned out to be on the run from some very dangerous people. Misty had been beaten badly, and Harris had been kidnapped.

Misty said, "I know I don't remember much of what actually happened, but…"

"You were still very traumatized," Josie said. "I understand."

"I just couldn't stay in that house tonight. Every noise freaked me out. I hope you don't mind. Harris and I feel safe here."

Josie smiled. "I'm glad you came over. Come on upstairs. I have a king-size bed. We can all fit."

"Thank you, Josie."

She would never admit it to Misty, but Josie was grateful for the company. They settled Harris in between them, and Misty's dog slept at the foot of the bed. The steady sounds of Misty, Harris and the dog breathing began to lull Josie to sleep almost instantly. As she was about to drift off, Misty whispered, "I keep thinking about that girl's mom. What she must be feeling. I can't even imagine if Harris—"

"Don't," Josie said. "Don't imagine it. We'll keep him safe. Always."

"But how can we?" Misty asked. "How can we in this world where terrible, terrible things happen?"

"I don't know how," Josie answered honestly. "But I would die trying. That's what I know."

Her speech had slowed. She was so fatigued, and sleep grabbed at her, pulling her under. Misty was still speaking. The last words Josie heard before her consciousness fell away were, "How can we keep our kids safe when you can't even tell the difference between someone who's bad and wants to take your child away and someone who isn't? Bad people are all around us, Josie. But they're disguised as good people. Regular people."

Something in the back of Josie's mind shouted out. The voice told her to hold onto it for when she woke, and then she was out cold.

CHAPTER ELEVEN

Josie woke to the sound of Harris's voice coming from somewhere downstairs, then Misty's little dog, Pepper, yapping. She opened her eyes and looked to her left, but the bed was empty. Turning in the other direction she looked at her clock to see she had slept for three hours. The scent of coffee wafted up the stairs. Normally, it would be a salve to her exhausted and frayed nerves but today, as soon as the smell hit her, nausea took hold and her stomach bile rushed up into her throat. Throwing the blanket aside, she jumped up and raced to the bathroom. She dry-heaved into the toilet a few times but nothing came up. Cold sweat broke out across her forehead. As she sank to the floor and pressed her back against the cool bathroom tiles, she willed it to pass. She had to get back out to the park today and help look for Lucy.

She heard her front door open, the clunk of Noah's crutches across the foyer floor and then his voice. "Hey, little buddy!"

Then Harris: "Noah, Noah! Hey, who's that?"

"This is my friend, Mettner," Noah said. "He gave me a ride home."

Home. Noah referred to Josie's house as home. She felt a warm little squeeze in her heart. Standing, she splashed her face with water, brushed her teeth without looking in the mirror and went downstairs. She could tell by the look on both Mettner and Noah's faces that she looked bad.

Mettner said, "Geez, she hit you hard, huh?"

Josie touched her nose and cheekbones. Both were tender. "It's okay. Any news?"

Both of their faces fell. "No," Noah said. "Nothing. We had people searching all night, and the volunteer search starts in an hour. People are already gathering at the park. Looks like it's going to be a great turnout."

Harris ran in and hugged Josie's leg. "JoJo, I watch TV?"

"Sure," Josie said, stroking his hair. "Make sure it's okay with Mommy, okay?"

He ran off. Josie said, "I have to get over there and relieve Gretchen." She remembered the thought that had sparked in her sleepy mind just a few hours ago. "I need to look at the photos and video again, too."

"I'll meet you over there," Mettner said.

*

On her way to the park, Josie called Trinity, who had called three times while Josie slept. "It's about time," Trinity answered, not even bothering with pleasantries.

"I'm sorry," Josie said. "I've been working. Do you even sleep?"

"Don't worry about my sleeping habits. Tell me about this missing girl. You know I don't like getting my information from the local correspondent at WYEP."

Josie gave her a rundown, concluding, "I don't know that there's a story here, Trin, but if you want to help, the parents used to live in New York City. That's where they lived before their daughter was born. Maybe you could track down some of their old friends. Colin Ross's parents still live there. You could talk to them maybe. See what kind of people we're dealing with."

"You think one of the parents had something to do with this?" Trinity asked.

"I don't know," Josie answered. "But if either one of them has anything nefarious in their past, I know you'll find it and that you'll find it faster than the FBI."

Trinity laughed. "You're damn right I will. I'll be in touch."

Josie hung up as the city park came into view. The playground area was packed with people, the line of citizens ready to help search for Lucy extending all the way outside the entrance and down the sidewalk. Josie felt encouraged by how many people were willing to get up early and donate their time to help a little girl. They stared at her as she walked past the line and into the playground toward the tent. It took her a moment to realize it was because of her black eyes. She picked up the pace and slipped into the tent. Mettner had beat her there. He sat in front of the laptop and beckoned her over. "Here's the footage and photos. Take a look. I'm going to tell Gretchen she can go home and help get this search organized out there."

Josie started scrolling through the photos. She wasn't entirely sure what she was looking for. The idea that Misty's words had sparked was still a shadow in her mind. It hadn't entirely solidified. Gretchen appeared beside her. "Hey, oh wow. You look—" She broke off.

Josie smiled, the movement hurting her face. "I know. It's fine. What's going on? Anything? I haven't seen either Amy or Colin."

"They're out with the search party. Mettner and the uniforms are organizing them now. I've got no news. Hummel got a bunch of random prints from the inside of the carousel column. None of them came up in AFIS. I talked to all the parents who were here yesterday and on the carousel when Lucy disappeared. None of them remember the door in the column opening. None of their children remember the door opening."

"They didn't remember seeing Lucy either," Josie pointed out. "But we know she was there."

"True," Gretchen conceded.

Josie stood. "Well, we'll just keep looking. Why don't you go home and get some sleep."

Gretchen didn't argue. Josie took over command. She itched to get out and search the woods even though a part of her was convinced that Lucy was not there. Those woods had been searched several times already—all through the night—and no sign of the girl had been found. But she had to stay at the command post to coordinate all the various teams of law enforcement and civilians there to help. She stood at the front of the tent as the morning's massive search got underway. They'd start at the park and then work their way outward, searching the yards of residences in a one-mile radius as well as the college campus. If that didn't turn anything up, they'd expand the radius.

She saw Amy and Colin walking together deeper into the city park. Both looked exhausted and pale. Amy wore jeans and had pulled a black sweater tight around her torso. Her sandy locks were thrown back in a messy ponytail. Colin wore a bright blue windbreaker and his thick salt-and-pepper hair looked like he hadn't combed it at all this morning. He pushed both hands through it, in what was obviously a nervous habit. The two walked side by side but didn't touch.

Josie studied the long line of searchers who stared at the couple as they walked into the trees. The age range was diverse. A number of students from Denton East High School as well as Denton West had shown up. They wore sweatshirts with their high schools' names and mascots emblazoned on them. There were housewives, young professionals, retirees and what looked like a few college professors. One older man with gray hair and a neatly trimmed gray beard wore a tweed suit complete with a tie. He sipped coffee from a paper cup as his eyes followed the Ross parents' movements. It was an odd choice of clothing for a search and contrasted with the garb of several volunteers who had shown up in bright orange vests and Mossy Oak ballcaps. Josie suspected they wore their bright colors hoping to draw Lucy's attention should they find her in the woods.

Several amateur search and rescue dogs had also arrived. From where she stood, Josie spotted a lumbering bloodhound that looked very familiar. Even before she spotted his owner, her heart started tapping double-time in her chest. Then she saw him. Luke

Creighton; tall, broad-shouldered, and bearded with shaggy hair. They'd been engaged once. Then he had gotten tangled up in a complicated case, had made a series of bad decisions, and ended up doing six months in prison. During her last big murder investigation, she had seen him again after two years. That case had taken her to Sullivan County, three hours north, where he lived on a remote farm with his sister. Josie had been forced to enlist his help locating a witness who turned out to be a victim. It had been a difficult time with the investigation into Noah's mother's murder and Noah had decided that he and Josie needed to take a break. Josie had ended up spending the night at Luke's. Which in itself wasn't so bad, except that she'd gotten drunk and blacked out. She had no idea what had happened that night. She was quite certain that nothing romantic or sexual had happened between them, but the truth was, she couldn't really say. She'd left the next morning before he woke up. She had hoped she'd never have to see him again.

He spotted her from where he stood. Her cheeks flamed as he lifted a hand and waved to her, a warm smile on his face. She waved back stiffly, praying he wouldn't come over to talk to her. He didn't. Instead, he walked off with a group of searchers and disappeared deeper into the park.

Relieved, Josie returned to the tent, picking up the walkie-talkie that Gretchen had left and assuming command. The searches went on through the entire day. By her estimate, over a thousand people had shown up to help look for Lucy. Local businesses donated food and drinks to the effort—keeping searchers and law enforcement well fed and caffeinated. A few students from the college's robotics engineering department arrived with drones equipped with cameras which they used to fly over the city in a grid pattern, searching for any sign of Lucy. WYEP sent three news crews to cover every aspect of the search. Thankfully, Chitwood showed up to do the on-screen interview. Amy and Colin somehow stayed off the press radar, alternating between searching and resting in the command tent. Gretchen and Noah returned sometime in the afternoon after having rested and showered. Chitwood left after talking to the press. He stopped in several times during the day but spent most of the day at the police station, coordinating the officers he had left to handle the routine issues that arose in the city. By the time the last rays of sunlight disappeared from the horizon, no sign of Lucy had been found anywhere in the city.

Most people had gone home. Only a handful of dedicated volunteers, state police officers and sheriff's deputies remained to assist Denton PD. Josie's team was left despairing, standing around the command tent facing Amy and Colin with no more answers than they had had the day before.

"How does this happen?" Colin asked. "She was right out there. She was on the goddamn carousel. Detective Quinn, you said yourself that children don't disappear into thin air."

"What are you saying?" Amy asked, her voice shaking. She had been strangely silent all day. Josie wondered if she was taking something for her nerves. Josie thought about what it would be like to have a child of her own and for that child to be missing. She would need drugs just to keep breathing, let alone to stay calm.

Colin raked his hands down his face. "I'm saying she couldn't have wandered off. We would have found her by now. The K-9 officer said she could have gotten into a car."

"But why would she get into a car with someone else? Why would she run away? You saw her," Amy said. "She jumped down off the horse and ran away. She ran away. Why?"

Josie again thought of Lucy's excited movements, how she'd moved with purpose, the same way little Harris ran when he saw his mother after a long day with Josie or with his grandmother. Josie said, "Please don't take offense to this, but I have to ask: is Lucy your biological child? Both of you?"

The two parents stared at her. Gretchen picked up the line of inquiry. "We didn't get into this yesterday because the assumption is that Lucy wandered off and simply got lost. But since we haven't found her or any sign of her, we need to ask questions now. We have to know if there are other parents involved. Is Lucy a result of your marriage or did one of you bring her from a prior relationship?"

"Oh," Amy said. "She's ours. Neither of us had children before we were married."

"How about grandparents? Is she close to either of your parents?" Josie asked.

Colin said, "Amy's dad was never in the picture and her mom passed away before we met. My parents live in New York City. We take Lucy there to visit them three or four times a year."

"They don't come here?" Gretchen asked.

"They don't like it here," Amy blurted. "It's not 'urban' enough for them."

Colin shot her a cautionary look, and Josie had the feeling the two of them had had this argument before—clearly his parents and his wife didn't always get along.

Josie asked, "How about aunts and uncles? Do either of you have siblings who are close to Lucy?"

Amy shook her head. "I had two sisters. One died in a car accident along with my mom. I haven't spoken to my other sister since the accident. That was over twenty years ago. We… never got along. I don't even know where she lives now."

"What's her name?" Josie asked.

"Renita Walsh," Amy said. "Although if she got married, it may have changed."

"Younger or older than you?"

"Two years older."

"Have you ever tried to contact her?" Josie continued.

Amy shook her head. "No. Like I said, once Mom was gone, there was no reason for us to keep in touch. I went to New York City. I don't know what happened to her after that. Colin has a brother, but he's a bigwig at some company in Hong Kong. We see him once a year, if that."

"What about Lucy's friends? Does she have many friends at school?" Josie asked.

"She has a couple of girls that she really likes," Amy answered. "I can give you their names." She took out her phone. "I can give you their mothers' names and numbers as well."

Josie nodded toward Mettner who walked over to Amy with his own phone, pulling up his note-taking app so he could take down the information.

"Why are you asking this?" Colin said. "You think someone we know took Lucy?"

"Not necessarily," Josie said. "I think she saw someone as the ride ended and that she was in a hurry to get to that person. I'm wondering who it was and if they saw anything suspicious or strange—if they realized that Lucy was running toward them at all."

"We'll make a list," Colin answered. "Everyone we know. Everyone Lucy knows. You can investigate all of them."

Gretchen said, "That's not a bad idea."

Both parents brightened at having something useful to do. They sat at a table with Mettner and Noah, and Noah began making a list on a legal pad while Mettner tapped notes into his phone.

Again, Josie returned to the photos and footage from the day before. She replayed the video of Lucy running around the center column of the carousel and that dark square jutting out as she ran around the left side. The door. The door had opened, but no one remembered seeing it open. Gretchen had told her that every parent she talked to said the same thing: they didn't even know the door was there. Gretchen had asked the parents to speak to their children to see if any of them remembered seeing the door open. No one did. How was it that the carousel had been at capacity and no one noticed the column door open? It happened the same way that no one noticed Lucy exiting the carousel, Josie realized.

All those parents were only concerned with getting their children off the ride, and the children were likely focused on whatever was next—the swings, the slide, perhaps ice cream. But surely if Lucy had gone inside the column, someone would have noticed that.

It still bothered Josie that no one they questioned remembered seeing Lucy after the carousel shut down. She'd been wearing that bright pink shirt and colorful butterfly backpack. It was impossible to miss. Lucy hadn't discarded it because no one had found it. She had to have left the park wearing it. But then why wasn't she in any of the photos taken in the play area by parents during or after the carousel ride?

Misty's words from the night before floated back to her in pieces. What was it she had said while Josie was drifting off to sleep? Something about bad guys not looking like bad guys. Something about...

"Disguises," Josie muttered to herself.

"What's that?" Gretchen asked.

"We showed everyone a photo of Lucy wearing that pink shirt and the butterfly backpack," Josie said. "Nobody saw her."

"Right," Gretchen said. "But we know she didn't leave her backpack behind because no one has found it."

"But maybe people are all looking for that backpack and not really Lucy," Josie said.

"What are you talking about?" Amy asked.

Josie looked up from the laptop, realizing she now had the attention of the entire room. Her gaze zeroed in on Amy. She beckoned the woman over and motioned for her to sit in the folding chair beside her.

Once seated, Josie said, "You'd know your child anywhere, wouldn't you? I mean if you were trying to find Lucy in a group of children, what would you look for? Not what she was wearing—that changes every day—but maybe you'd look for her blonde hair or for the size of her frame."

"It's the way she walks," Amy answered, understanding what Josie meant. "She breaks out into skipping all the time. She'll go a few steps and then start skipping, and I have to tell her to stop and slow down. Now she does it without me even telling her. It's like she hears me in her own head telling her to stop skipping." Amy let out a little laugh which quickly turned into a sob. Her hand flew to her mouth, and Josie could see her fighting to hold it down. Josie reached over and squeezed her shoulder. "Okay," she said. "I'm going to play this video again. Tell me what you see."

She replayed the video. They watched the footage that was now forever burned into both their consciousness; Lucy hurrying down off her horse, running from the right side of the carousel platform to the left and around the column. They watched the sharp edge of the door open. Then Lucy was gone, the door closed. "Keep watching," Josie said. "Tell me what you see."

Just seconds later, Amy let out a gasp. She shot up from her chair and it toppled behind her. "Oh my God. Oh my God. It's her. That's her!"

Colin ran up behind his wife and looked over her shoulder. Josie rewound the footage again to when Lucy disappeared. As the other parents gathered their children and slowly made their way off the platform to the exit gate, a small child came skipping out from behind the column from the same direction that Lucy had disappeared while on the opposite side, Amy had just untangled herself from the safety strap and was now looking around for her daughter.

A large, black sweatshirt covered the small child's torso, trailing down to the middle of her thighs. The hoodie was pulled up, but a flash of golden hair showed as she half-ran half-skipped her way off the platform and then weaved around the bodies between the platform and the fencing, until she came to the exit gate which was also opposite to where Amy was now more actively searching for Lucy, though she hadn't started calling for her yet. At the exit gate, a little boy dropped what looked like a stuffed elephant and his mother stopped to pick it up, backing up the entire line. A dad went around them, dragging his toddler by the hand. Then came the small figure in the sweatshirt, skip-walking out of the exit gate followed closely by a mother holding one small child on her hip while pulling an older child by the upper arm behind her. The mother's head was turned over her shoulder, and it looked like she was saying something to the older child. It had been chaos.

Josie rewound it, and they all watched it several times. Lucy ran through the exit gate and off to the right, out of frame. Immediately, Josie went to the photos, scrolling through each one. They found the girl in the sweatshirt in the background of two other photos, one in profile and one of her from the back. In each one she was headed in the direction of the fence that separated the playground from the street on the other side.

"Oh my God," Amy cried.

"Where did she get that sweatshirt?" Colin asked, voice trembling.

"Can you be absolutely sure it's her?" Mettner asked.

"Well, no," Josie conceded.

"It's her," Amy insisted. "I know it's her. I would know her."

"With all due respect, Mrs. Ross," Metter said. "You did see this video several times yesterday and failed to identify her."

"Mett," Gretchen cautioned.

Amy shot him daggers. "I was looking at where she went. I was looking for her pink shirt or her backpack. I didn't—why would I notice a girl in a sweatshirt? Lucy wasn't wearing an adult's sweatshirt."

"We all missed this," Josie pointed out.

"You can't say for certain it's her though," Mettner argued. "Where did she get the sweatshirt?"

"I think—" Josie broke off because the idea sounded borderline absurd when she decided to say it out loud. "I think it was inside the column."

"And she just knew it was in there? Decided to take it and throw it on? Then race out of the park?" Noah said.

"If this was planned," Josie said. "If someone took her and planned this out…"

"Someone would have had to prep her," Gretchen said.

"Prep her? What do you mean?" Colin asked.

Gretchen looked at Amy. "Would you say that you and your daughter are close?"

Amy put a hand to her chest. "Of course we are. She's my little girl."

"Does she tell you things?" Josie asked.

Amy's expression became pinched. "What do you mean? She's seven. What 'things' are there to tell?"

"Things about her day," Gretchen said. "About school. About people who talk to her."

Amy looked mystified. "I—I guess. I mean, she mostly talks about bugs."

"Bugs?" Josie said.

"Well, not really all bugs. She's obsessed with ladybugs, moths, and butterflies. She made her own luna moth. I didn't even know a luna moth was a thing."

"Where did she learn about it?" Josie asked.

Amy shrugged. "Where else? School."

"Who else besides you, your husband, and your nanny is she exposed to on a regular basis?"

"I—I don't know. She's seven. She goes to school. She comes home. Sometimes she comes here to the park. Sometimes we go to the mall. She goes to her school friends' birthday parties some weekends."

Gretchen asked, "Have you ever seen her talking to any adult at any place you've been with her? An adult you didn't know?"

"Of course not," Amy answered. "I wouldn't just let her talk to a stranger."

"What about your nanny?" Josie asked.

"Jaclyn is very attentive. I doubt that she would allow that."

Josie looked around. "Who talked to Jaclyn?"

Mettner piped up, "I did. I called her and interviewed her. She's due back in town tomorrow."

Gretchen said, "Great. When she gets back, I'd like to talk to her at the station."

"The station?" Colin said. "You think our nanny had something to do with Lucy disappearing?"

"No, not necessarily," Gretchen answered. "But we have to consider all the possibilities here. If Lucy didn't wander off, then she was taken. If someone had enough contact with her to come up with a plan where she was supposed to get a sweatshirt from inside the carousel, put it on and leave her parents behind to exit the park, then we need to find out who that person is—and we have to assume that person took her."

Amy's knees wobbled and she fell. Before she hit the ground, Colin caught her. He lifted her limp body, trying to keep her upright. Fresh tears streaked her face. "Oh God," she sobbed.

Josie stood up and spoke to Colin. "Look, why don't you take your wife home and get some rest. It's been a long day, and we need to look strongly at the possibility that this is an abduction, which changes the direction of this investigation significantly. There's a lot of work we need to do right now. We'll let you know as soon as we know more."

He looked like he wanted to refuse, but Amy was becoming more hysterical by the second. Finally, he nodded and dragged his wife out of the tent. Once they were safely out of earshot, Josie said, "We need to talk to the parents of her school friends. We should talk with her teacher as well. Also, we need to shake down every sex offender within a five-mile radius of her home and school. Someone had access to her. Someone convinced her to leave her parents behind."

"Jesus," Noah said, his voice heavy and sad.

"And I think we need to issue an Amber Alert and call the FBI," Josie added.

Gretchen said, "Chitwood will never go for it."

Josie took out her phone. "I don't give two shits what Chitwood will or won't go for."

CHAPTER TWELVE

The Amber Alert went out moments after Josie hung up with her contact at the State Police. All of their phones started blaring alarms. Ten minutes later, Josie's phone rang. Bob Chitwood's name flashed on the screen. She hit the answer icon and barked, "Quinn."

Without preamble, Chitwood said, "This your doing, Quinn?"

Josie girded herself, waiting for his tirade, for him to possibly fire her for insubordination. "Yes."

"You call the FBI, too?"

"Yes, sir. We have reason to believe now that this may have been a kidnapping." She started to launch into an explanation, but Chitwood interrupted her.

"Shut up, Quinn," he snapped. "I don't want to hear it."

"Sir?" Josie said, perplexed.

"I never said not to follow the evidence. But Quinn, by God, you'd better be right about this, or—"

"I know," Josie cut in. "Or you'll have my ass in a sling by the end of the week. Duly noted, sir."

There was a long beat of silence. Just long enough to make Josie a little nervous. Then Chitwood said, "I'm glad we have an understanding, Quinn. Now get to work."

He hung up, leaving Josie staring at her phone as though it was some alien object she had just discovered.

"What was that about?" Gretchen asked.

"I don't know. Maybe he's taking anger management classes or something?" Josie mused.

Gretchen, Mettner and Noah all erupted into laughter. Noah said, "Maybe we can get him into etiquette classes after that."

"We can try," Josie joked. "Come on, Mett, we'll go interview some of these other moms. You know where they are?"

Mettner followed her to her car, scrolling on his phone as he walked. "Amy only gave me the names of two moms. Is that normal? For a seven-year-old to only have two friends?"

Josie glanced back at him. "I don't know, Mett. But let's start with them. We can always ask them if there are any other moms we should approach."

They got into the car and pulled away as Mettner rattled off a nearby address. "Ingrid Saylor. Her daughter is in Lucy's class."

When they arrived at Ingrid's home a few moments later, all the downstairs windows were lit up. Josie and Mettner stepped onto the large wraparound porch. Voices could be heard from inside as Josie reached for the doorbell. A woman in her thirties with short, stylish brown hair answered, smiling at them. As she took in their Denton PD polo shirts, the corners of her mouth drooped. Her bottom lip quivered. "Oh no," she said. "Is this about Lucy?"

Mettner said, "It is about Lucy, but we don't have any news."

Josie extended a hand. "Ingrid Saylor? I'm Detective Quinn, this is Detective Mettner. Amy Ross gave us your name. She said your daughter is friends with Lucy. We were just hoping to ask you some questions."

Ingrid pulled the lapels of her gray knit cardigan tight across her chest and stepped aside so they could enter. "I'd be happy to speak with you. Actually, quite a few of the mothers are here right now."

"Mothers?" Mettner said.

Ingrid waved them deeper inside the large home, through a foyer to a spacious kitchen where several women gathered around an island countertop, nibbling on an array of finger food and sipping from fluted glasses. Ingrid said, "These are some of the mothers of children in Lucy's class." Josie counted six mothers altogether, and every one of them stared as she and Mettner entered the room.

Ingrid introduced them and offered them something to eat or drink, which both Josie and Mettner declined. Mettner tapped furiously on his phone, taking down each woman's name, address, phone number and child's name for the reports he and Josie would need to prepare later.

"We were all at the search today," said Ingrid. "We've been out all day helping look for Lucy. I invited everyone back for a drink."

"It was a long day," one of the other mothers noted.

Josie managed a tight smile. "It's been very difficult for everyone involved. We're grateful for your help. In a search like this, every person is a big help. We were wondering what you could tell us about Lucy and Amy Ross. Do you see them often?"

A short, curvy woman with curly blonde hair lifted a hand to draw attention to herself. She had introduced herself as Zoey when Mettner was taking names. She was the other name on the list of mothers that Amy had given them. "My daughter and Lucy are best friends. I try to get them together at least once a week. Usually, I go through the nanny."

"For playdates?" Josie asked. "Amy doesn't bring Lucy?"

Zoey shrugged. "Well, sometimes but not usually. I take my daughter to the park and they meet up there."

Mettner raised a brow. "You said once a week? What does the nanny do while the kids are playing?"

"She's usually on her phone. Most parents are. I mean, the playground is pretty safe—" she broke off and her face flushed. Stammering, she added, "I-I-mean, it—it was."

"It's okay," Josie said. "I imagine at seven years old, the girls don't need that much supervision on the playground."

"They're pretty self-sufficient," Zoey said. "And they know we're right there if they need anything or if they fall or anything like that. I mean, it's not like we ignore them completely. We just don't follow them around every inch of ground they walk."

"Of course," Josie said. "Tell me, have you ever noticed Lucy talking to any other adults at the park?"

Zoey thought for a moment. "I don't really remember. I guess she could have."

"I saw her talking to an adult," Ingrid volunteered.

All eyes turned to her. Mettner asked, "When was this?"

"A few months ago—January fifth. We had a birthday party for my daughter at the funplex near the mall. Amy brought Lucy. The kids were running all around. Lucy and a few other kids had gone into the arcade. Amy was getting tokens from one of the change machines for the games and Lucy was on the other side of the arcade, playing skee-ball. I walked by and saw a man talking to her."

One of the other mothers said, "You never told us about that."

Ingrid took a sip of her wine. "I didn't think it was important. As I got closer, I saw he was getting a ball out of the ball return for her. It was stuck. But then he seemed to linger so I called out for Lucy. She turned toward me, and he walked away."

"What did he look like?" Josie asked.

"He was young. Maybe mid-twenties. Caucasian. Tall. I couldn't see his hair because he had a baseball cap on."

"How was he dressed?" Mettner asked.

"Casual. Jeans and a sweatshirt. I really didn't think anything of it."

"You thought enough of it to intervene," Josie pointed out.

She didn't miss the eye-rolls of at least two of the other women. Ingrid said, "I only 'intervened' because Amy is insane about Lucy talking to people she doesn't know."

One of the other mothers laughed. "She never lets Lucy do anything. That poor girl. It's no wonder she had no friends."

"Jaime, stop, you're drunk," Zoey chastised.

Jaime waved her glass in the air, the liquid sloshing around. "You know it's true. Amy is a helicopter parent. She hovers *constantly*. It's a wonder she even has a nanny, the way she is with Lucy." She looked around the room. "Colin's not so bad but he's hardly ever home. Tell me, has Amy ever just dropped Lucy off to any of your houses so she could play with your kids? Has she ever let Lucy come to anything unless it's parent-attended? Have she or the nanny ever *not* gone on a school trip?"

A ripple of discomfort ran through the room, each woman shifting their weight and looking everywhere but at each other.

"She's overprotective?" Mettner asked.

Ingrid said, "It's more than that. We're all overprotective. Amy is… it's like she doesn't want anyone else to get close to Lucy, even other children."

"You have to let them bond," Zoey added. "That means giving them time together without micromanaging. She hardly ever does play dates. She really only brings Lucy to birthday parties."

"Does Lucy get invited to many birthday parties?" Josie asked.

One of the other moms laughed. "At this age, everybody gets invited. Even the ones we don't want to invite."

Mettner looked up from his phone. "Is Lucy one of the kids you don't want to invite?"

"Oh no," Ingrid said. "Lucy is very sweet. Very quiet. It's just that Amy keeps her on such a tight leash, it's like she can never have fun. Well, unless the nanny brings her."

"I think she's very lonely," Zoey added.

"You mean Lucy?" Josie asked.

All the women nodded.

Mettner asked, "Does Lucy have trouble making friends?"

"Oh no," Jaime said. "Like Ingrid said, she is the sweetest little thing. Always the best-behaved child at any party. I'll say that for Amy—she raised a well-mannered, pleasant little girl. She must rule with an 'iron fist'."

The other women chuckled. Josie raised a brow and Zoey quickly said, "We're laughing because Amy is way too nice to do anything with an 'iron fist'."

"Lucy just takes after her," Ingrid explained.

Josie asked, "Do you ladies spend much time with Amy?"

Jaime gave an immediate eye-roll, drawing an elbow in her side from Zoey, who said, "Amy is a closed book. She keeps to herself. Her husband? Very sociable but never around."

"Amy's nice," Ingrid said. "Very nice. Just hard to get close to. Our kids have all been in school together since Pre-K. We've become close. We always include Amy—"

"But she never takes us up on our invitations," Jaime said.

"I think she's lonely, too," Zoey said.

"I feel like she isolates them," Ingrid said thoughtfully, garnering more nods. "Even more than they already are with Colin out of town ninety percent of the time."

"We don't even know what she does with her time," Jaime complained. "I mean she's home all day, and she has a nanny. We don't even know if she has hobbies—or maybe she's having an affair."

Ingrid laughed. "Please, not Amy. She and Colin are still in love with each other."

"If I only had to see my husband a few days a month, I'd still be in love, too." Zoey quipped.

Laughter erupted around the countertop. Josie had the feeling that the discussion was about to turn to gossip, so she said, "Would you ladies be willing to talk to your children? Ask them if Lucy ever said anything to them about talking to or being around adults besides her parents and nanny?"

"Of course," the women murmured.

Josie passed out several business cards. "My cell phone is on there. Don't hesitate to contact me. Any time—day or night."

Back in the car, Mettner was still tapping furiously into the note-taking app on his phone. As they pulled away, he said, "None of that sent up any red flags."

Josie sighed. "No, not in terms of the parents. I still can't see either Colin or Amy being involved in Lucy's abduction, but it seems there were enough opportunities when Lucy was with the nanny for a kidnapper to get close to her and prepare her to leave her parents behind."

"You think the guy who helped her with the skee-ball machine at the funplex was prepping her?" Mettner asked. "Planning this whole thing out?"

"It's impossible to know. You can call the funplex and see how long their security footage goes back. If it goes back that far, we might be able to get video of the encounter."

Mettner tapped into his phone. "Here's the number," he said, before dialing. Josie listened to Mettner's end of the conversation with the manager of the funplex. After several minutes, Mettner said, "So you only keep your CCTV footage going back one month? Okay. Yeah. Well, thanks anyway." He hung up.

"Another dead end," Josie muttered.

Back at the command tent, Noah continued rechecking the photos and video while Gretchen paced behind him, flipping through her notebook. Josie and Mettner filled them in on what little they'd learned.

"You think someone was approaching her while she was with the nanny or while Amy wasn't paying attention?" Noah asked. "Getting her ready for this? Talking her into leaving her parents behind?"

Josie nodded. "I think it's looking more and more that way."

"She retrieved a sweatshirt from inside the column," Gretchen said. "Put it on and ran away from both her parents. Getting a seven-year-old to do something like that would require a lot of preparation."

Mettner said, "This guy could have been talking to her every day while she was at the park with the nanny for all we know."

"Doing the prep here would make the most sense," Josie said. "It's possible he even got onto the carousel with her at some point to show her the door."

"They would have had to have some sort of signal," Noah said. "So she would know when to do it."

Gretchen said, "She had to have seen him when she was on the ride. He had to be here. She saw him. He gave her a signal and she jumped down off her horse, opened the column, put on the sweatshirt and raced out of the park."

"I've been over this footage and these photos at least one hundred times," Noah said. "I can't find a damn thing."

"Maybe we should look again," Mettner suggested. "None of us—not even the parents—saw Lucy skipping around in the sweatshirt the first dozen times we looked at that one video."

They gathered around the laptop and Noah took them through every photo and video they had gathered. They combed over them, watching the videos multiple times, but found nothing amiss.

"Maybe we should have another look at the carousel," Josie said. "From Lucy's point of view."

They walked slowly, allowing Noah to keep up with them, although he'd gotten quite fast on his crutches. He stood outside the fence, leaning on his sticks, watching from the approximate position the video they'd been relying on had been shot. Gretchen stood between the two horses that Amy and Lucy had occupied. "This guy could have been anywhere," Gretchen said. "The ride was spinning. There are portions of the park we can't see in any of the photos or footage we've got."

Josie went over and climbed onto the blue horse, panning around. With a sigh she climbed down. "You're right."

Noah said, "By the time the ride stopped, he would have been outside of the park anyway. That's where she headed—out of the park—if the K-9 unit is to be believed."

"The video footage backs that up," Gretchen remarked.

Josie retraced Lucy's steps. Gretchen and Mettner followed her. She left the blue horse behind and followed Lucy's path until she reached the door. She opened the door until Noah shouted for her to stop. "Right there. That's how it was in the video," he said.

The door was only open six inches. Plenty of room to reach in and snatch up a sweatshirt from the floor. Gretchen said, "That might be why no one noticed the door opening. She didn't open it very far."

"Only far enough to reach her hand in," Mettner agreed.

"She was quick about it, since only seconds later she appeared on the other side wearing the sweatshirt," Josie added. As she went to close the door again, something colorful caught her eye. She froze.

"Boss?" Mettner said from behind her.

"Oh Jesus," Josie mumbled.

Mettner and Gretchen crowded in beside her. Slowly, Josie opened the door all the way. "What the actual—" Gretchen didn't finish.

"What's wrong? Mettner asked, craning his neck.

Josie and Gretchen parted so that he could get a good look inside the column.

"Oh damn," Mettner blurted.

There in the center of the column floor lay Lucy Ross's bright, sequined butterfly backpack.

CHAPTER THIRTEEN

"Don't touch anything," Josie said. "Call Hummel. Wake him up if you have to. Have him come back out to process this again."

Gretchen made the call while the three of them retreated outside the carousel fencing to where Noah stood. When Josie told him what they'd found, he said, "Whoever put that there did it today."

"I know," Josie agreed.

"That's pretty bold," Mettner said.

"It was probably easy," Josie said. "No one's focus was on the carousel today. The search teams were working their way outward. We didn't have anyone guarding the carousel. Why would we?"

Noah said, "He took a chance leaving that in there if he was leaving that here for us to find. What if we hadn't come back out here? The carousel would probably be closed a few more days and even then, does the operator actually need to go into the column to start the ride up?"

"No," Josie answered. "He does everything from his little booth."

"Maybe he disabled something inside the column so that when the operator tried to fire the ride up, it wouldn't work and he'd have to go inside," Mettner suggested. "Like Fraley said, assuming he wanted us to find this."

"He wanted us to find it," Josie said. "I'm sure of it. Why else take the chance of coming back here to this crowded scene to put it here?"

"The boss is right," Gretchen said. "I'm going to call the park director, get him out here to have a look inside the column once Hummel's done processing to see if anything has been disabled."

She stepped away to make the call. Noah limped back to the tent so he could sit down. Fifteen minutes later, Hummel arrived with Officer Jenny Chan, another member of their Evidence Response Team, and all the equipment they'd need. Josie and Mettner hung back, waiting and watching as they processed the inside of the column and Lucy's bag. An hour later, all of them gathered in the tent, standing around a table as Hummel set a brown paper bag in the center of it. With gloved hands, he pulled out the butterfly backpack and put it down on the table. "We didn't get anything from this. No prints, obviously, cause it's impossible to get prints from this cloth. No DNA, nothing. But, you'll definitely want to see this."

He pulled out several items in plastic bags and laid them out: two tiny toy caterpillars, a watermelon-flavored lip gloss, a hair tie, a tiny stuffed ladybug on a keychain and finally, a sheet of white copy paper with some writing on it, scrawled in blue ink. "These are the contents of the purse," Hummel said. "You can confirm this with her parents and we'll know for sure it's hers, although given the circumstances, and this note, I'm one hundred percent sure this is Lucy Ross's backpack."

Josie leaned over the table and read the handwritten note, her skin growing colder with each word.

Little Lucy went away.
Little Lucy cannot play.
You can see her if you wait.
You must go home without debate.
Answer each call or
See Lucy not at all.

Mettner gave a low whistle. "Boss was right," he said.

"I'll get the paper in and process that for prints," Hummel said.

Josie took her phone out and snapped a picture of the note. She could barely hear over the thundering of her heartbeat. She tried to slow her breathing. Beside her, Gretchen said, "This isn't typical. People who abduct children do it for selfish reasons—usually to gratify their sick, sexual needs."

"So what are you saying?" Noah asked.

"I'm saying I think this is a kidnap for ransom."

"Call WYEP and get any footage they took today for their newscast," Josie said. "There's a remote possibility they might have picked up the kidnapper heading toward or leaving the carousel."

"On it," Mettner said.

"We need to have a much longer conversation with Amy and Colin," Josie added.

From outside the tent came the rumble of several large vehicles. Josie and Gretchen looked at one another and hurried out. The FBI arrived in force, driving in a caravan of large vehicles including what looked like a tricked-out camper and a van marked Evidence Processing. As they pulled up outside the park and began to emerge from their vehicles, Josie counted well over two dozen agents. A tall, burly black man strode across the playground, his face grim and determined. When he reached them, he extended a hand in Josie's direction. "Detective Quinn?"

She shook his hand. "Yes, that's me. This is detective Gretchen Palmer."

He shook Gretchen's hand and introduced himself as Special Agent Ruben Oaks of the FBI's Child Abduction Rapid Deployment team. "We understand you've got a missing seven-year-old girl," Oaks said.

Relief flooded through Josie at the prospect of having more bodies and more resources to help find Lucy. "Yes," she told him. "And we now know that she's been kidnapped. Please, come inside and we'll brief you."

CHAPTER FOURTEEN

"Please," she told the man. "We need heat. It's too cold in here for a child."

"Shut up," the man said. "All you do is complain."

"An extra blanket then. Please."

From under the door, I heard the sound of a slap and then the yelp that issued from her throat. I braced myself to hear him hit her again, but the next sound was her footsteps shuffling toward the door. I scurried back, hopping onto the bed as she flew into the room. In the moonlight streaming through the window, I saw a small trickle of blood at the corner of her mouth. She wiped it off with the back of her hand. "Under the covers," she instructed.

I crawled beneath the threadbare blanket we had to share, and she got in beside me. She held me close to her body and soon, her warmth radiated against my skin. "I'm sorry," she said.

I didn't say anything. She looped an arm around my chest, pulling me closer to her. She whispered into my ear. "Someday we're going to leave here. I promise you."

"Where will we go?" I asked as quietly as I could.

"I don't know," she said. "Home."

I turned my head until her breath was on my cheek. "Home?"

"Yes," she said. "Where it's always warm and there's plenty to eat. All the toys you could possibly play with, and friends. Lots of friends."

"Do we have to bring him?"

"No. We won't ever see him again."

"You'll stay with me forever?"

She planted a kiss on top of my head. "Forever. We'll never be cold or hurt again."

"I want to go now," I said.

"Not yet," she whispered.

CHAPTER FIFTEEN

The FBI's CARD team immediately sprang into action. Oaks sent several agents to visit all registered sex offenders within the city limits. They took possession of the note for processing. Josie knew if there were prints to be found on the paper, their lab would get the results back much faster than Denton and the State Police. Josie gave Oaks the names of all the parents who had been in the playground when Lucy disappeared, and he sent a team of agents to run background checks on each one of them and to visit each of them at their homes in case they had anything additional to offer.

Oaks was efficient and no-nonsense, delegating and dispensing orders with speed and assurance. Josie liked him instantly. When he had set up the FBI's mobile command and dispatched his agents, Josie was able to send most of her people as well as the state police officers and sheriff's deputies home to rest finally. Once things were well in hand, Oaks turned to Josie and said, "Well, shall we go talk to the parents?"

Mettner and Noah stayed behind to offer any support they could to the FBI team at the mobile command station. Josie and Gretchen joined Oaks and a small team of agents, driving the two blocks to the Ross home in a large Chevy Suburban. One of the other agents drove, while Oaks sat in the back seat with Josie and Gretchen. "What do we know about these parents?" He asked.

Gretchen took out her notebook, squinting at it as the vehicle sped along. Josie gave directions to the driver. "He's in big pharma. Works for Quarmark. Travels a lot. She's a stay-at-home mom."

Josie took out her phone and texted Trinity: *Did you get anything on the Ross parents in NYC?*

To Gretchen, she said, "You had a chance to interview them more extensively last night, didn't you?"

Gretchen nodded. "He's forty-eight, she's forty-four. He's from New York City. She's from a small town in upstate New York. Fulton. She and her two sisters were raised by a single mother. Her mother and one of her sisters died in a car accident when Amy was twenty-two. She never got along with her other sister, so she moved to New York City and never looked back. She was twenty-nine and working as a waitress when she met Colin. They dated for a while, got married, and Colin got the job at Quarmark. They moved out of New York City into a town close to the headquarters for a few years, then moved here. They've lived in the same house for the last five years."

Josie's phone chirped as a text from Trinity came through. *Nothing juicy. Still working. Will call you later.*

"Right here," Josie told the driver who pulled over.

"Lucy is their first and only child. First marriage for both, first child for both," Gretchen added.

Josie said, "They have a nanny. She's out of town. One of our guys did a preliminary interview with her, but we think she should be interviewed more extensively. Lucy's a first-grader. I think we should also talk to her teacher."

Oaks nodded. "Will do," he said. "Looks like they're still awake."

It was the middle of the night, but every light in the Ross family's large two-story colonial-style house was ablaze. The porch light was on and Colin answered quickly. He stared at them, his eyes drifting from Josie and Gretchen to the imposing FBI agents behind them. "Oh my God," he said. "Is there news? Did you—did something happen?"

Amy ran up behind him, clutching his shoulder to stay upright. "Did you find her?"

Josie said, "I'm very sorry, Mr. and Mrs. Ross. We haven't located Lucy yet, but there have been some developments. This is Special Agent Ruben Oaks from the FBI and some members of his team. They're here to help."

"Please," Colin said. "Come in."

The house was warmly decorated in creamy hues with pastel blue accents. Plush carpeting pulled at their feet as they moved from the doorway into the living room. A long cream-colored couch dominated the room. In one corner of the couch, a blanket with Disney princesses on it was bunched up next to two Barbie dolls. On the long, sturdy walnut coffee table sat a juice box, some coloring books and crayons. Next to the couch was a recliner, the same color as the couch. End tables held matching lamps with bases made from light blue ceramic jugs. In one corner of the room, Josie saw a wooden trunk with its lid open, toys and games spilling out of it. On the walls were framed photographs of the Ross family but most of them were of Lucy. In this one room Josie could watch her grow from a small infant to the vibrant seven-year-old Josie had met at the park yesterday. The entire space was like a comforting hug. Josie felt warm and safe here. Surely, Lucy had felt the same. Why had she left? Who had taken her? Would they get her back?

Josie pushed all the questions and the anxiety they provoked aside and focused on the task at hand. Oaks gestured to the agents he'd brought with him. Josie noticed for the first time that they carried cases. Electronic equipment, she guessed. They'd need to tap into both parents' cell phones in case the kidnapper called. Oaks said, "My team needs a place to set up. I saw what looked like a dining room table in there. Do you mind?"

"Set up?" Amy said, her voice growing higher pitched. "Set up what?"

Josie held up a hand. "We'll explain, but please, the sooner we get started, the better. This is all in Lucy's best interest, I promise."

"Okay," Colin agreed. "Go ahead."

"We'll need your cell phones as well," Oaks said. "And the passcodes."

"You're scaring me," Amy said.

Gretchen took out her notebook and pen and handed it to Amy. "We know this is scary, but I promise we will explain everything in a minute. Please just write down the passcodes to your phones here."

Amy scribbled hers on the pad and handed it to Colin. His hand shook as he jotted his own down. They handed over their cell phones to Gretchen who passed them to one of Oaks's colleagues. "The screen is shattered," Colin muttered. "But you're welcome to it."

With a nod, Oaks let Josie and Gretchen take the lead since they had already established a rapport with Colin and Amy. Gretchen delivered the news about finding the backpack and then Josie showed them photos of the items found inside it—everything except the note. "Do you recognize these things?" Josie asked.

Both parents stared at the photo of the caterpillars, lip gloss, hair tie and small, stuffed ladybug. Finally, Amy pointed. "That's her lip gloss. Watermelon flavored. I bought it for her last week. And that's her hair tie. It was actually mine, but she liked the color and asked me if she could have it, so I gave it to her."

"What about the toys?" Josie asked.

Amy shook her head. "No, no. Those don't belong to Lucy."

Colin said, "Are you sure, Ame?"

Her gaze snapped toward him. "Of course I'm sure."

"Then where did they come from?" Colin asked. "Where did she get them?"

Before Amy could answer, Gretchen interjected. "We believe she might have been given these items by someone. An adult."

Colin looked perplexed. "An adult? Like who?"

Josie took her phone back and swiped until a picture of the note appeared. "There's something else," she told them. "We found a note in the backpack. We'd like you to have a look at it."

"A note? What kind of note?" Colin asked as Amy reached out for Josie's phone. Josie hesitated. "This may be difficult for you both," she warned them.

"We need to know if you recognize the handwriting," Gretchen said.

Amy's hands shook as she and Colin studied the words. Colin's face paled. "What is this?" he said. "I don't understand. Someone took her?"

"We believe so," Josie said.

Gretchen asked, "Do you recognize the handwriting?"

Amy shook her head. Colin said, "No. I don't recognize it. Who would do this? Who would take our little girl?" Amy began to sob. Colin slid an arm around her shoulders, but she sank lower and lower into the couch. "Oh my God, someone has my baby," she cried. "Someone has my baby."

Her face, pale only seconds earlier, turned bright red. With each exclamation, her voice pitched higher and higher. When she pushed her husband's hand away and jumped up, Josie feared they were going to have a repeat of the hysteria of the night before. Not that she could blame her. Josie thought of little Harris—how much she loved him—and she knew that if anyone ever took him it would break her in ways she couldn't even imagine.

Josie stood and stepped toward Amy, quickly catching her hands. "Mrs. Ross," she said. "Please. Look at me." Amy tried to wrestle her hands away, but Josie held tight. "Please. I need you to stay calm. It's very important. We need to ask questions that only you can answer, do you understand? These are important questions that might help us find Lucy. Can you help me?"

Amy stared into Josie's eyes. Her teeth clamped together and a quiet keening sound came from her throat. Josie could feel the tension in her body through her clenched hands. "Please," Josie said. "I know that this is hard. I know that this feels impossible, but I need your help. Just the way you helped me earlier in the tent. Remember?"

Slowly, Amy nodded.

"Good," Josie said. "You know Lucy best, right?"

"Y-yes," Amy whispered.

"Okay, let's sit and you and Mr. Ross can help us right now by answering some questions. Some of them are going to seem strange but it's important that you answer all of them. Can you do that for me? For Lucy?"

Amy nodded and sank back onto the couch, but she didn't let go of Josie's hands. The bones in Josie's fingers ached. Josie had no choice but to sit down next to her.

Oaks stepped forward and motioned for Colin to take a seat as well. He said, "Mr. and Mrs. Ross, have you noticed anyone unusual hanging around lately? Outside the house, at Lucy's school, when you're out?"

Colin said, "I travel a lot so Amy would have a better idea of that."

"No, I haven't seen anyone who seemed suspicious or out of place, but our nanny, Jaclyn has Lucy after school most afternoons. You should talk to her."

"We will," Oaks said. "How long has Jaclyn worked for you?"

"For three years," Amy answered. "She's a college student. Very sweet. She's graduating soon so we're going to lose her, I'm sure. Lucy adores her. She's very responsible."

Oaks looked at Colin. "Mr. Ross?"

"Oh," Colin said. "Yeah, Jaclyn's great. A godsend."

"Do either of you have any reason to believe that Jaclyn could want to take Lucy for any reason?"

"What?" Amy said. "No. That's absurd. Jaclyn would never—"

Oaks waved a hand around the room. "This is a lovely home you have here and I assume you are financially comfortable. Jaclyn could have had help from someone else. Perhaps she saw an opportunity to line her pockets?"

"No," Amy said firmly. "Jaclyn would never do something like that. Never. We pay her well. Two years ago she ran into some trouble with her housing and we were happy to help her out with a security deposit on a new place. She knows she can come to us if she's in a jam. She's family to us."

"Amy's right," Colin agreed. "I know you need to explore every avenue, but I don't think Jaclyn had anything to do with this."

"Does Jaclyn have a boyfriend?" Oaks asked. "That you know of?"

Amy said, "No, she's single. She had one her freshman year but not since then."

"Okay," Oaks said. "Now, can you think of anyone who would have any reason to take Lucy?"

"No," Colin said. "No one at all."

"Is there anyone either of you have been having trouble with lately? Feuding or fighting with?"

Colin shook his head. "No. No one."

Amy cleared her throat. Josie could feel her squeezing her hands harder. She said, "Your job, Colin."

He looked at his wife. "What?"

Louder, Amy repeated, "Your job. Those death threats."

Josie said, "What death threats?"

Colin turned toward Amy and Josie. "Oh, those are nothing."

Amy's voice was venomous. "Nothing? Our daughter is missing, Colin. Who would want to take our baby? Who? You got death threats not even two months ago."

Again, Josie said, "What death threats?"

With a heavy sigh, Colin put his face in his hands.

Amy said, "He is in charge of pricing the drugs that Quarmark puts out in the U.S. market. He decides how much people have to pay for them."

Colin's head lifted. "I don't decide. There's a team of people and an unimaginable amount of research that goes into these things. It's not like I slap a price tag on these drugs without due diligence."

"But you are in charge of that team," Amy said. "Ultimately, you give the go-ahead. Those threats came to Quarmark addressed to you."

Oaks said, "This is something we need to look into, Mr. Ross."

"People were upset about how expensive one of Quarmark's new drugs was?" Gretchen asked.

Colin nodded.

Gretchen said, "Which drug?"

Colin sighed again, clearly uncomfortable.

"Just tell them," Amy demanded.

"You have to understand what goes into these things," Colin began.

Amy made a noise deep in her throat. "Don't even try to justify it, Colin. It was never justifiable, and you know it."

"My company is a for-profit company. If I don't help them make a profit, I don't get to keep my job."

Amy thrust her chin forward. She squeezed Josie's fingers again, as if drawing strength. "It was a cancer drug. Revolutionary. It stops most cancers from metastasizing. Stops the spread. It could save millions, or at least extend their lives."

"How much is Quarmark charging for it?" Oaks asked.

There was a long silence. Finally, Amy said, "Colin's team priced it at fifteen thousand dollars a month. Insurance companies cover a lot of it, but people are still paying thousands of dollars a month in copays for it. Thousands. What cancer patient do you know who has thousands of dollars laying around to pay for one drug?"

"Ame," Colin cautioned.

Trying to keep them on track, Josie interjected, "You got death threats after the drug went onto the market?"

"Not right away," Colin said. "But after several months, we started to get them."

"*You* started to get them," Amy clarified.

"I got most of them. It's public record that I'm the head of pricing."

"How did these threats arrive?" Gretchen asked.

"Some by mail, some by email," Colin said. "All to my office which is almost two hours from here. I mean I travel most of the time, and even when I'm home I don't need to be in the office all the time. But these people didn't target me at home—only at work."

Josie said, "It's not that hard to find out where someone lives, Mr. Ross."

"Do you have copies of these threats?" Oaks asked.

"In my desk at work. I have copies of everything. I turned over the originals and any emails to our legal department, but I kept copies."

"Why did you keep copies?" Gretchen asked.

He shrugged. "Just in case… something happened, I guess."

Oaks said, "We're going to need those. I'll send an agent with you when we're done here to retrieve them. We'll wait till first light. We'll track down every person who threatened you or your team and pay them a visit."

Amy's grip on Josie's fingers finally loosened. "Thank you," she mumbled.

Colin said, "Fine, but I think this is a long shot. Why would someone angry over the price of a cancer drug take my child?"

"What's more precious than your own life?" Josie said. "For a parent? What matters more than your own life?"

Colin didn't answer. He didn't have to. They all knew the answer. You didn't have to be a parent to recognize that the bond between a parent and their child could be one of the most powerful things in the world.

"There's something else I'd like you both to do for us. It's pretty standard. Of course you can refuse, but we hope you won't."

Colin said, "What is it?"

"I'd like you both to take polygraph tests."

"What?" Amy gasped. Josie nearly cried out when the pressure on her fingers became unbearable. "Why? You think we did this?"

"No," Oaks said. "But it doesn't matter what I think. It matters what the evidence in the case shows. In almost every abduction case, we have to look at the parents first. Eliminate them so that we can direct our resources to other, more fruitful avenues of investigation."

"We were both there," Amy said. She looked at Josie. "You were there. You saw us."

"I did," Josie answered. "But Amy, this really is standard procedure. You both take them, you both pass, and your involvement in Lucy's kidnapping can be ruled out."

"How could we have kidnapped her?" Amy went on. "Why? Why would either of us stage our own child's kidnapping?"

Oaks said, "Exactly. So it shouldn't be an issue to do the polygraphs."

Colin said, "Ame, it's fine. Let's just do it, okay? We need to keep the focus on finding Lucy."

Amy didn't say anything, but she didn't protest further.

Oaks said, "I'll have the polygrapher here as soon as possible. Now, based on the content of the note found in Lucy's backpack, we believe this kidnapper is going to try to contact you. Do you have a landline?"

"No," Colin said. "Just our cell phones."

"Not a surprise these days." Oaks said. "What my team is doing in there right now is setting up their computers so that we can intercept and trace any incoming calls to either of your cell phones. Now, we have to do this through the legal department of your cell phone carrier. You'll have to sign some consent forms."

"Done," Colin said.

"Great. We'd like you to answer your cell phones as normal. Keep them charged up. We'll get it set up so that we can hear whatever you're hearing. Keep in mind, this isn't like television or like the old days—we don't need you to keep the kidnapper on the phone for any amount of time. With Wi-Fi and IP addresses and the software we've got, everything can be traced and tracked quickly. We get a call, we pinpoint a location, we send a team out. That's how we're going to do this."

Colin and Amy nodded. Finally, Amy relinquished her grip on Josie's hands.

"Now," Oaks said. "If you'll come into the other room where my team has set up, we'll get started."

CHAPTER SIXTEEN

Back at the command center, the first few rays of daylight were creeping up the horizon. They had been up all night. Josie felt a bone-deep exhaustion that seemed to be shared by everyone on her team, given the haggard look of Gretchen, Noah, and Mettner. Oaks gathered them in the tent. To Josie, he said, "You have a real rapport with Amy Ross. A connection. Do you have children?"

"No," Josie said.

"You were at the playground when this happened."

"Yes. I was babysitting my friend's son."

"Okay, well we're going to need you to be present with Amy Ross as much as possible."

"Not a problem," Josie said.

"Also, your team knows this city far better than any one of my people. If we get a call from the kidnapper, we're going to need you guys to get us to his location as quickly as possible."

"You think he's still in the area?" Gretchen asked.

Oaks said, "We can't be certain, obviously, but we'd like to be prepared if he turns up locally." He paused and looked at each of them. "Why don't you and your team go home and get some rest. Come back in later today and we'll catch you up. I'll have my team going full tilt at this until then."

No one argued. They were all too tired, and it was clear that Oaks had no intention of shutting them out of the investigation if they went and got some rest for a couple of hours.

Once Oaks had all their phone numbers saved, Josie walked with Noah to her car and drove them both to her house. Misty's car was gone but inside were still signs that she and Harris were staying. Her little dog, Pepper, slept in the corner of Josie's couch. Harris's toys were scattered across the living room floor. "Watch where you walk," Josie said.

"I'm going straight to bed," Noah told her as he hopped along with his crutches in one hand, using the banister for balance as he climbed the steps.

"I'll be right up," Josie said, heading into the kitchen where she dialed Trinity.

"Are you just getting up?" Trinity asked.

"Going to bed," Josie replied.

"Some things never change. What've you got?"

"You know I can't talk to you about an active investigation," Josie said.

"Oh," Trinity said. "So there's a lot more to this than anyone initially thought."

"I didn't say that."

"You didn't have to. If it was just a case of this girl wandering off, you'd just tell me there was no news. So what are we talking here? Sex offender?"

Josie said nothing.

"It's not a sex offender?"

Josie remained silent.

"Then it's something else. But still a kidnapping."

Frustrated, Josie said, "How are you doing this?"

Trinity laughed. "Never mind that. I know you can't tell me things, so let me tell you what I've found out. Colin Ross lived in New York City for decades before he met his wife. Apparently he was quite the ladies' man. I talked to a few of his old girlfriends—if you can call them that. He wasn't big into commitment. At least, not until Amy."

It was the second time Josie had heard this. A voice in the back of her mind wondered if perhaps the weight of having and providing for a family had become too much for Colin. Had he arranged to have Lucy eliminated somehow? But no, that made no sense. If that were the case, they would have found her body by now, not a note suggesting the parents wait for a call from the kidnapper.

"What about financially?" Josie asked.

"His parents are both professors. Upper-middle class but certainly not rich. Colin worked several jobs to put himself through the MBA program at NYU. Got the job at Quarmark right out of school and worked his way up the ranks. He's been the head of the pricing department for several years, bringing in six figures a year."

So a kidnapping for ransom made sense, Josie thought.

"I talked with his mother. She said he's been in touch with her but that he asked her not to come to Denton. She says that they don't get along with Amy. She thinks that Amy has consistently tried to isolate Colin from everyone and everything he knows."

"Has Amy ever denied them access to Lucy?" Josie asked.

"No. They don't particularly like her, but she's always been good about making sure they have a relationship with Lucy. At least, that's what Colin's mother told me."

"What about Amy? Anything interesting in her past?" Josie asked.

Trinity sighed. "No. Her life is as boring as the day is long. Lived in New York City for over seven years before she met Colin. Took odd jobs, mostly waitressing work to keep a small, shitty apartment in Brooklyn that she occasionally shared with roommates. I could only find one of the roommates. She had nothing to offer. Amy was nice, quiet, kept to herself."

Between the death threats from his job and his money, Colin was looking like the most probable reason behind Lucy's kidnapping. Someone was out to either punish him or just get a big payoff.

Trinity said, "I'll keep digging since I just heard from a reliable source that the FBI is now involved. I shouldn't let you know what I find since you won't tell me anything, but I will because you're my sister."

"And because you care," Josie pointed out. "You care that a seven-year-old girl's life is on the line."

"Caring is overrated, dear sister," Trinity said.

"Liar."

Trinity laughed. "We'll talk soon."

Josie ended the call and trudged up the steps where Noah could already be heard snoring. She collapsed into the bed next to him, and a few minutes later, she felt Noah's hand slide into hers. Their fingers interlaced, and she fell asleep instantly.

CHAPTER SEVENTEEN

Josie woke to the sounds of Misty, Harris and Pepper downstairs. She checked her phone but there was no news. Lucy Ross had not been found. The kidnapper hadn't called yet. Beside her, Noah stirred, his hand reaching for her. She turned toward him and pressed herself against his body, resting her cheek on his bare chest. He pulled her into him, his fingers brushing through her hair. "You have guests," he said.

"I know," Josie mumbled. "She's kind of freaked out right now."

"You think she made coffee?"

Josie laughed. "I'm sure she did. She's got a two-year-old and a full-time job. She's chronically sleep-deprived."

"You haven't had coffee in a few days," Noah said.

"What?"

He pressed a kiss into her scalp. "You think I haven't noticed?"

"That I haven't had coffee?"

"That you haven't been feeling well."

"It's stress," Josie said dismissively. "With your mother passing, the case, and now this little girl."

"It hits hard, doesn't it?" Noah said. "Lucy Ross."

A lump formed in Josie's throat. "Yes."

He hugged her close. She felt his breath on her forehead. "Let's get to work, then."

*

Josie texted Mettner and Gretchen to find out where they were—both had slept as long as she and Noah, which was most of the day—and promised to meet them at the mobile command center in a half hour. Josie and Noah showered and grabbed a quick bite to eat. Misty had made them an early dinner that was so delicious, Josie was tempted to ask her to move in permanently. On the way to the command center, Josie texted Oaks who said he'd meet them there to brief them.

Gretchen showed up armed with coffee and Danishes, but Josie could only stomach one cheese Danish before the nausea overcame her once more. She drank some water instead, willing her unruly stomach to settle as Oaks went over everything his team had accomplished while Josie and her team rested up.

"We got nothing from the note. No prints. The paper was just standard copy paper that could have been obtained at any office supply store, and the ink appears to be regular blue ink found in any common ballpoint pen," Oaks began. The four of them sat at one of the card tables while Oaks stood at the head. "We talked with the park manager who looked inside the carousel column. One of the poles that controlled some of the horses had been disabled."

"So when they started the ride, it would have been a problem," Josie said.

"Right," Oaks went on. "Several of the horses wouldn't have moved up and down while the ride was in motion, so someone would have had to go into the column where they would have found Lucy's backpack."

"What about the other leads?" Josie asked.

Oaks continued, "Sex offenders checked out. They're all accounted for and have alibis for when Lucy went missing. The parents who were at the park check out. No red flags. We did, however, find seventy-four credible threats to Mr. Ross related to the cancer drug he told us about last night."

"Well," Gretchen said. "That seems a lot more significant than he initially let on."

"We think he was trying not to scare his wife," Oaks said. "Quarmark's legal department had already reported these threats to the local police. No one appeared to have any active plans to kill or harm Mr. Ross. My team has alibied half of those seventy-four people so far for Lucy's kidnapping. We should have the rest checked out within the next twenty-four hours."

Josie felt a wave of relief. It would have taken her small department weeks to do the work the FBI was able to accomplish in less than a day.

Oaks continued, "We took a closer look at the nanny and she checks out. She's been in Colorado visiting her family for the weekend just like Mrs. Ross said. Her travel plans were made several months ago. We can't link her to anyone who might have had the desire, wherewithal or capability of pulling off a kidnapping. She gave us permission to search her apartment, and her landlord let us in. Nothing unusual there. We interviewed a few of her friends and professors. Nothing suspect. She said she'd let us know as soon as she's back in town which should be sometime today."

"What about the first-grade teacher?" Josie asked.

"She checks out, too."

"Did either of them report seeing Lucy talking to anyone unusual in the last several weeks or months?" Josie said.

"No, nothing. We also looked at phone records for both parents. Couldn't find anything out of the ordinary. We polygraphed both of them this morning. Dad passed no problem, but Amy failed her polygraph."

"What?" Josie and Gretchen blurted in unison.

Oaks spread his hands, palms up. "Remember, these tests aren't entirely accurate. A person's emotional state has a lot to do with whether they pass or fail. As you know quite well, Mrs. Ross has been very volatile. It could be the emotional stress skewing her results or it could be the fact that she had been lying to her husband about taking online college courses."

"Did she tell you that?" Noah asked.

Oaks shook his head. "No. She told us she was enrolled in online courses but our search of her computer and a check with the university confirmed she hasn't ever been enrolled, despite being accepted into the program over a year ago."

"The husband didn't notice that her tuition wasn't being paid?" Gretchen asked.

"She has a discretionary fund that the husband deposits into but doesn't monitor."

"You mean an allowance?" Noah said.

"Basically, yes. The husband manages their finances, pays all the bills, gives her cash for groceries and anything she needs for Lucy. This is just for her, it seems. He said originally it was for spa days and yoga classes, but then she decided she wanted to go back to school so he put more into it. He doesn't even know how much is in there."

Gretchen raised a brow. "Must be nice."

Oaks continued, "The husband gave us access to all their finances. There have been no tuition payments to any college out of that or any of the accounts they own."

"Did you confront her about it?" Josie asked.

"No. We would like you to talk to her. Like I said, she seems to have some kind of connection to you. We'd like you to be on hand at her home as much as possible, particularly if a call from the kidnapper comes in and she becomes hysterical. Maybe you can get her to open up. Nothing in our investigation so far has turned up anything suspicious, but the failed polygraph is a red flag we can't entirely ignore. If you can get her to admit to you that she's been lying to her husband about the college courses, then perhaps she'll be willing to talk to you about any involvement she might have in Lucy's disappearance."

"You really think she did this?" Josie asked.

"I don't know," Oaks said honestly. "But I can't ignore the possibility, no matter how remote."

"Where's the motivation?" Gretchen said. "She has the perfect life. Rich husband, gorgeous house, beautiful daughter. She even has a nanny to help her with childcare. She has no stress. She can fill her days with anything she wants. What does she get out of staging her own child's kidnapping?"

No one answered for a long moment. Then Mettner said, "Maybe she's sick in the head and just really good at hiding it."

"I don't think this was her," Josie said. "But I agree we can't ignore any avenue of investigation no matter how unlikely it seems. I'll do what I can to draw her out."

"Why not just bring her in and interrogate her?" Mettner asked.

"Because you only get one shot at that," Gretchen explained. "As soon as we start treating her like a suspect, she'll get an attorney. The parents will shut us out, and any information that Amy might have that would help us find Lucy alive will be out of reach."

"There may come a time when we have to bring her in," Josie said. "But right now, with Lucy at risk, I think the gentle approach works best."

"I'm with Detective Quinn on that," Oaks said. "We also need someone else at the house in case the kidnapper calls and we trace him locally. We need someone who could navigate this city in their sleep. Obviously Detective Quinn can do that, but I'd like to have some backup on that front." He looked at Gretchen, but she pointed at Mettner.

"I'm a transplant," she said. "Noah's still not very quick with his broken leg, but Mett grew up here. He's your best bet."

Noah said, "I can't get around well but anything you can give me to do, I'll do it."

Oaks smiled. "We've got plenty of work."

CHAPTER EIGHTEEN

The Ross home was swarmed with FBI vehicles and news vans. Inside, two agents were stationed at the dining room table, their laptops open, waiting for a call to come in. Colin sat at the table with them, attempting to make small talk. Amy paced in the kitchen, her arms wrapped around her middle. The kitchen was large with an old, rustic wooden table in the center of it. Various casseroles covered its surface. When Amy saw Josie, she motioned to them and said, "The neighbors brought them and some of the parents from Lucy's school. Isn't that nice?"

"Yes," Josie said. "Very thoughtful."

A tear rolled down Amy's cheek and she swiped at it. "I can't eat. Can you?"

Thoughts of her sensitive stomach and what the constant nausea might mean flooded Josie's mind, but she pushed those aside and gave Amy a wan smile before inching further into the room. "I can never eat during big investigations."

Amy stopped moving and looked at Josie's face. Her mouth turned downward. "I did that to your face, didn't I?"

Josie nodded. "This is nothing. I've been in worse situations. I know you didn't mean it."

"Sometimes I get… lost," Amy said. "It's like I get lost in my own mind, and I can't get back. It hasn't happened to me in years—decades, really. I just… I can't handle this. Lucy. She's my baby. I can't." Her shoulders shook with the effort of holding back her sobs. Josie circled the table and stood before her.

"Mrs. Ross," she said.

Amy swallowed. "Amy, please. Call me Amy."

"Amy."

"Colin called my doctor. He prescribed me Xanax. Did you know that?"

"I didn't. I suspected you might have taken something. I think that's smart if it helps you keep your wits about you."

"It dulls it," Amy replied. "That's all. Oh, my Lucy." Her voice lowered, as though she were about to tell Josie a secret. Josie leaned in to hear her. "Do you know what men do to little girls when they take them?"

Josie felt that sick feeling take hold of her again, and she steeled herself against it. "Yes," Josie said. "I do know."

Amy nodded and turned away. She put her palms on either side of the sink and leaned into it. A small window over the sink looked out into the backyard which was filled with toys and one large play set shaped like a treehouse. "I knew you did. I can tell. Did they tell you I failed my polygraph?"

"Yes," Josie said.

"They think I did this now? That I would… that I would do something like this to my own child?"

"Polygraphs aren't always reliable," Josie said. "You're under a tremendous amount of stress. That could cause your results to be inconclusive."

Amy looked over her shoulder at the doorway as though making sure no one else was listening. "I've been lying to my husband. I told him I wanted to go back to school, get a college degree. I did everything I was supposed to do—got transcripts, did the application, wrote a stupid personal essay. I got in. But then I lost my nerve. He thinks I've been taking classes. I haven't."

"People have lied about worse things," Josie said. "So what do you do with your time? While Lucy is in school?"

Amy sighed. "I clean around here. You'd be surprised how much mess one seven-year-old girl makes. I sometimes go to yoga. Sometimes just go for a run. Then I start dinner."

That hardly filled a whole day, but Josie didn't push. Instead, she asked, "Your nanny picks Lucy up from school?"

"Yes. Jaclyn brings her home and keeps her occupied while I finish dinner. Jaclyn usually starts her on her homework. She stays and has dinner with us most nights. My God, I haven't even talked to her since… this all started. She's visiting her family. I should really call her."

"My team and the FBI talked to her already," Josie said. "She's due back in town today. She was very upset about Lucy. I'm sure she'll call you once she gets settled in. Tell me, why didn't you take a class? Why not start with just one?"

Amy looked at her, a broken smile on her face. "I'm not college material, Detective."

"But you got in," Josie argued. "What field were you going to study?"

Amy shrugged. "I wasn't sure. I didn't have to declare a major right away. I was only supposed to be starting my general education credits. Anyway, it doesn't matter now, does it? None of it ever mattered. All that's ever mattered is Lucy, and I failed her. What kind of mother loses her daughter on a carnival ride when she's seated right next to her?"

Josie reached out and touched Amy's shoulder. "This is not your fault. That I know absolutely. Don't waste time or energy blaming yourself."

Amy didn't look convinced, but she mumbled a thank you.

The sound of a cell phone ringing from the other room startled them both. Amy pushed herself away from the sink and ran into the dining room. None of the agents looked up, not even Oaks. Colin simply stared at the center of the table where Amy's phone danced as it vibrated with each ring. She reached forward and snatched it up. "It's Jaclyn," she said.

Oaks raised a hand. "Mrs. Ross, the call we're waiting for is from the kidnapper. You should keep the lines open in case he calls."

Amy looked at the phone screen, uncertainty creasing her brow. Her forefinger hovered over the answer icon.

Colin said, "Don't answer it, Ame. Jaclyn will understand."

Josie said, "The note said 'answer each call'. Each call."

Oaks said, "We know who this number belongs to—the nanny—not the kidnapper."

The phone stopped ringing. Amy looked up from the screen, looking from Josie to Oaks and back again. A long, tense moment stretched out in the room. Josie heard the wall clock ticking, the sounds of reporters talking outside.

The phone rang again, making them all jump. Amy bobbled it in her hands. "It's Jaclyn again."

Colin said, "Don't."

Josie reached over and swiped the answer icon. She nodded and Amy pressed the phone to her ear. When she said hello, her voice could be heard from a small speaker on the other end of the table. But the voice that answered her was not female—not Jaclyn. It was male—deep and cold.

"Hello, Amy."

It felt like all the air in the room had been sucked out. Colin sprang out of his chair. The two seated agents began tapping away at their laptops. Oaks leaned into the living room and waved Mettner in. Amy reached out a hand and Josie took it.

"Who is this?" Amy asked.

The man laughed. "I'm the man you've been waiting for. You have been waiting for me to call, haven't you? The police let you see my note, didn't they?"

Amy turned to Josie, eyes wide and uncertain. Josie mouthed the words: *Ask him about Lucy.*

With a small nod, Amy asked, "Where's Lucy?"

Oaks and Mettner leaned over the shoulder of one of the agents, looking at the laptop screen. Oaks read off the address in a low voice and Mettner said, "We can be there in ten."

"We were already there once today after the nanny gave us permission to search her apartment. Take the unit outside," Oaks told him as Mettner ran out the door.

On the phone, the kidnapper laughed. "Oh, Amy. You really don't understand what's happening, do you?"

"Where is my daughter?" she shrieked.

"I can't tell you," he replied. The glee in his tone made rage boil in Josie's stomach.

Colin went over to his wife. He held out his hand for the phone, but she turned away, releasing Josie's hand and moving into the corner of the room. "What do you want?" she asked.

"What do I want?" he echoed. "What I want is to know how it feels, Amy?"

"How what feels?"

"Oh come on now, Amy. We both know what I'm talking about."

Her voice was a screech. "I don't know what you're talking about. I want my daughter back. Give me my daughter back."

"Only if you tell me how it feels, Amy. How does it *feel*?"

"I don't know what you're talking about. Just tell me what you want. We'll do anything. We just want Lucy back. Just bring her back to me."

"You know I can't do that, Amy."

"You can. Just tell me what you want, and I'll give it to you."

"I want you to wait."

The line went dead.

CHAPTER NINETEEN

Oaks rushed from the room. Amy sank to the floor, sobbing. Colin dropped to his knees and gathered his wife into his arms. He held her tightly, whispering into her ear. It took a moment for Josie to realize what he was saying. "It's okay. You did great. We can still get her back."

"I lost her," Amy cried. "I lost her again."

"No," Colin told her. "You didn't lose her. You asked him what he wanted. That's what they told us to do, remember? Ask him what he wanted. You did exactly what you were supposed to do."

"He doesn't want anything," Amy said.

"It's a game," Josie said. "He's playing some kind of sick game. He'll call back."

She walked over to the agent that Oaks and Mettner had been speaking with, whose screen showed the address of a small apartment complex near the university. She pointed to the screen. "I'm going there."

The man nodded. "We've already got several teams en route. I'll radio in and let them know you'll be joining them."

Outside, Josie jogged through a throng of reporters to get to her car. She sped off in the direction of Jaclyn Underwood's apartment. Amy and Colin were so upset and so focused on getting Lucy back, that it hadn't yet occurred to either of them to wonder why the kidnapper was calling from Jaclyn's cell phone. Jaclyn—who had already been vetted by the FBI and who had only returned to Denton hours ago, if that.

Josie's heart gave a wobbly beat as she pulled down Jaclyn's street. Emergency vehicles clogged the area in front of the complex, a two-story blocky building with twelve units on each floor. Every unit had its own small patio—with the upstairs units boasting balconies. There was a main entrance in the front, center of the building. FBI agents jogged back and forth from this entrance to their vehicles. The Evidence Response van was already there. Josie's eyes tracked the lower units until she found Mettner standing outside one of the patios on the end unit.

"Mett," she called as she approached him.

He turned to look at her, and she could tell by the pallor of his skin that what she'd suspected when she left the Ross home was true.

"The nanny's dead," Mettner said. "He must have just left here. We've got local units out searching the streets while the FBI processes the scene here."

"Where's Oaks?"

"Inside. Go around the front."

Josie showed her credentials to the agent at the front door, noting the overhead camera at the entryway. Inside, she went down a short hallway and then turned left. At the end of the hall was another agent with a clipboard. Beside him was a female agent doling out protective equipment. Josie donned a Tyvek suit, skull cap, booties and gloves and stepped through the door. She counted three agents processing the scene—taking photos, vacuuming for fibers and dusting for prints. The apartment was small, it's living area only big enough for a loveseat across from a small table with a television on top of it. Behind the television, gauzy curtains swayed. Beyond them, Josie could see Mettner standing outside. She stepped closer and saw that the sliding glass doors had been left partially open. Next to that was the kitchen which was barely large enough for the table and chairs crammed into it. She turned away from the kitchen and walked down a small hallway. There was the bathroom on her left and a bedroom with a desk and several bookshelves in it across from that. At the end of the hall Oaks stood in what Josie assumed was the doorway to Jaclyn's bedroom. He turned when he heard her approaching. "How did you know?" he asked.

"Know what?"

"That it would be the kidnapper calling?"

"I didn't," Josie said. "I was just going by what the note said. Right before the call came in, Amy told me she felt badly for not having talked with Jaclyn. She told me about the college courses, by the way."

"That's good," Oaks said. "She trusts you."

He turned his body in the doorway so Josie could slip past. She stayed on the edge of the room. One of the FBI agents was photographing Jaclyn Underwood's body which lay face-up on her bed, a stab wound roughly two-inches long near her solar plexus. From what Josie could see, she had been a striking young woman with deep olive skin and long, dark hair. Her face was frozen in an expression of surprise, her brown eyes wide and glassy. Blood darkened the form-fitting, yellow cotton shirt she'd been wearing and the purple bedspread below her. Next to her body was a discarded cell phone.

"He came here and used her phone to call the parents," Oaks said. "Then he killed her."

"He called Amy," Josie said. "He wanted to torture her. Now in addition to taking Lucy, he's killed someone she was close to—Amy cared for this girl a great deal."

Oaks shook his head. "Amy Ross barely has a life outside of her home. We couldn't find any evidence that anyone would want to harm her. No evidence that she's feuding with anyone. We went through her phone records and emails. We talked with her neighbors and other parents at school. They say she's distant, but no one has anything bad to say. She would have to socialize to develop enough of a personal relationship with someone that they'd want to hurt her this badly."

"Then we're missing something," Josie said.

Oaks said, "Maybe we need to take a closer look at the husband. Maybe this person is trying to hurt her and Lucy to get to him."

"He seems a more likely target," Josie said. "He's built up some wealth working for Quarmark and there have been lots of death threats against him. This could be related to the drug pricing. Think about it—family members have to stand by and watch their loved ones suffer and die because they can't afford the treatment they need."

"And this guy is torturing Colin by making him watch his wife suffer, by making him wonder if his daughter is okay or not. He has to watch the slow death of his family."

Josie nodded. "Did you find the murder weapon?"

"No," Oaks said. "We believe he took it with him."

"He came in through the sliding glass doors?" Josie asked.

"Looks that way," Oaks said. "There are some droplets of blood on the floor inside and out the glass doors, so we know he went out that way."

"There's a camera at the main entrance. We should check the footage."

"There's a rear entrance, too," Oaks said.

"I can go talk to the building manager, get whatever footage they have," Josie offered.

"That would be great. I'm going to have a couple of agents canvass the other tenants and the neighbors."

Josie took a last look around the room. On the floor beside the bed, Jaclyn's suitcase lay thrown open. On top of the folded clothes was a hair dryer and an open cosmetics bag. Josie could see cream concealer and powder foundation, mascara and lipstick. "She must have been unpacking," she said. "He snuck in and surprised her. He didn't spend much time. He came here with the intention of killing her and using her phone and that was it."

"We're dealing with a ruthless individual," Oaks agreed.

Josie went back out into the hallway. She took another peek inside the bedroom Jaclyn used as a home office. The books on her shelves were a mix of contemporary novels and textbooks, most of which had to do with architecture. Sadness washed over Josie. Jaclyn Underwood wouldn't be designing any buildings. She would never graduate from college after working so hard to get this far. She would never get married or have her own children. All that life unlived. Young victims almost always pierced her veil of professionalism—not that she ever showed it. Jaclyn Underwood, like so many before her, would visit Josie in her nightmares for years to come. The thought that she would likely be the one to have to tell Amy about Jaclyn's murder made her heart even heavier. She was about to turn and leave the room when the edge of an object poking out from beneath Jaclyn's desk caught her eye.

Josie dropped to her hands and knees and peered beneath the desk. It was a compact, similar to the one Jaclyn had in her suitcase except it was a much more expensive brand, and the color was Ivory Nude. Josie stood and took a more careful look around the room. She opened the closet which was packed with exercise equipment—a yoga mat, a portable elliptical machine, exercise bands and small dumbbells. Dresses hung from the rod. On the shelf above the rod were some shoeboxes and a pillow. Josie stood on her tiptoes to confirm that the pillowcase had the same pattern as Jaclyn's bedclothes. She left everything as it was so it could be photographed and went across the hall into the bathroom. The toothbrush holder sat to the right of the bathroom sink, a shiny chrome cup with four holes in the top. All of them were empty which made sense since Jaclyn had been in Colorado for the weekend. She hadn't had a chance to remove her toiletries or cosmetics from her suitcase. Josie studied the empty toothbrush holes, seeing exactly what she had expected to see.

"Oaks," she called. "Can I talk to you a minute?"

Oaks crowded into the bathroom with her.

Josie pointed to the toothbrush holder. "What do you see?"

Oaks raised a brow but studied it. "I see a college kid who hasn't cleaned her toothbrush holder in months, probably."

He was right. It took time to build up the whitish-green crust that rimmed the toothbrush hole.

"But there's two," he added.

"Exactly," Josie said.

One of the toothbrush holes was deep in crud while the other had only a thin layer but enough to indicate that someone else had been storing their toothbrush there for a shorter amount of time. Josie said, "In the spare room, under the desk is a compact."

"Compact?"

"Foundation," Josie said. "Women's make-up. You know, it's a little circular thing that opens. Mirror on one side, skin-colored powder on the other?"

Oaks laughed. "Okay, yeah. I got you. So what?"

"It's not Jaclyn's."

"How do you know?"

"Because Jaclyn's is in her suitcase."

"Maybe she had two," Oaks said. "How many do you have?"

Josie smiled. "I do have two but mine come in the same color and brand. Come with me."

Oaks let her pass and followed her back into the bedroom. She knelt down over the open suitcase. "Was this photographed?" she asked.

"Yes," answered the FBI agent on the other side of the room, dusting for prints.

Gingerly, Josie lifted the compact just enough so she could read off the brand and shade from the bottom. "Revlon ColorStay. Medium Deep. This runs maybe ten dollars at your local drug store. Look at Jaclyn's skin. It's not fair. It's olive."

"I'm listening," Oaks said.

She led him back to the spare room and pointed to the floor beneath the desk. "You can look but I already read it. It's Estée

Lauder. Ivory Nude. Goes for about forty dollars and is sold at higher end department stores. Jaclyn is a college student. College students don't spend forty dollars on foundation at Macy's. They go to the local CVS."

"How do you know all this?"

"Because I've bought make-up—and when I was in college, ten dollars on make-up was a lot. And no matter where you buy your make-up or how much you spend on it, you don't get the wrong shade. Google it. Ivory Nude is nowhere near the shade Medium Deep. This is someone else's compact. I think it fell and got kicked under here accidentally or something. Whoever it belongs to probably didn't even realize she left it."

"Jaclyn has friends, you know. It could be one of theirs."

Josie nodded. "It could be. All of this could be perfectly innocent." She walked over to the closet and tugged the door open again, pointing to the pillow on the shelf. "This pillow is from her bed. There are three pillows on her bed now. All with the same matching pillowcases. Just like this one. Why is this one in here?"

Oaks said, "Someone was staying here with her."

"Yes," Josie said. "Maybe not for long, but long enough to have kept her toothbrush in the bathroom, which tells me it wasn't just a friend crashing here for a night or even a weekend."

"She told my team she had no roommates or recent visitors."

"Did you ask her how recent?"

Oaks sighed. "Let me make a phone call."

CHAPTER TWENTY

Josie tracked down the building manager and took a look at all the video footage inside and outside of the building. The exterior camera at the front entrance showed Jaclyn arriving almost two hours earlier, dragging her suitcase with her. The foyer camera captured her as well. Only one other person entered after her before the FBI arrived and the building manager identified her as a tenant on the second floor. The rear exterior camera didn't show anyone entering or exiting. Josie asked the manager for a copy of the footage even though all it showed was that the kidnapper-killer was smart enough and had done enough reconnaissance to enter and exit through the sliding glass doors, where he wouldn't be caught on camera.

She met Oaks outside, gave him the footage and briefed him on what she had found, which was nothing of substance.

"I talked to the agent who spoke with Ms. Underwood on the phone," he said. "He asked her if she had had any visitors in the past few weeks and she said no. I've already dispatched a couple of agents to question her friends and neighbors about anyone who might have been staying with her going back at least six months. We'll print the compact and see if we can get any DNA from it—the pillow, too. Just in case. You think this person had something to do with Lucy's disappearance?"

"I think that this kidnapping was planned for a long time," Josie answered. "I think Lucy was well prepared. I don't know how or by whom or when it took place. By all accounts the only adults she has been around on any regular basis are her parents, nanny and teacher and they all check out."

"Except Amy," Oaks said. "She failed her polygraph."

"You said yourself that doesn't necessarily mean anything," Josie pointed out.

Oaks nodded. "I know, I know. I'm not entirely sold on the mother being behind this. But you agree the kidnapper had help?"

Josie nodded. "Yes. I do, and what better way to subtly find out the intimate details of a family's life and routine than to get close to the nanny?"

"Well, we'll see if it leads to anything once all the evidence is processed and analyzed," Oaks said. He looked toward the street where Dr. Anya Feist, Denton's medical examiner emerged from her truck, striding toward the front of the building with a grimace on her face. Josie waved to her and she stopped walking. She raised a brow, pointed to Josie and mouthed, *what happened to your face?* Josie waved back and mouthed, *don't worry about it*, before watching Dr. Feist disappear into the building.

"I'll get back to the Ross house," Josie said even though the task ahead of her weighed heavily on her shoulders.

CHAPTER TWENTY-ONE

Amy took the news of Jaclyn's murder exactly as Josie had expected—her hysteria reducing her to a loose-limbed pile of grief on the dining room floor. She reached out, and Josie got down on the floor with her and held her close. Colin had taken the news in stunned silence but with each passing moment, the lines in his face deepened with tension. Josie could see him clenching his jaw. While Josie tried to calm Amy again, Colin left the room, returning a moment later with a glass of water and a Xanax.

He thrust both toward Amy. "Take this," he said roughly.

Amy took the pill and then Josie helped her up and sat her in one of the dining room chairs. Colin paced around the table while the FBI agents in the room tapped away on the keyboards of their laptops, headphones on. Josie had no idea whether they were listening to anything on their headphones or if they wore them simply to avoid the awkwardness of watching a grieving woman break down.

Josie gave Amy a few minutes, hoping the Xanax would dull the edges of the horrific news long enough for her to ask some questions. When her eyes grew dim and vacant, Josie said, "I know this is the worst possible time, but I need to ask some questions."

"Of course you do," Colin said. "Questions and more questions. I have a question. Where is my goddamn daughter?"

Josie said, "We're doing everything we possibly can to find Lucy."

Colin scoffed. "Well, you're doing a piss-poor job of it. Go ahead, ask your questions."

Josie addressed Amy. "Before Jaclyn went away, did she ever say anything to you about having a guest at her apartment?"

Amy shook her head. "No."

"Did Amy ever take Lucy to her apartment?"

"No. They came here after school. Sometimes Jaclyn would take Lucy to the playground but mostly they came here."

"Did Lucy ever meet any of Jaclyn's friends, that you know of?"

Amy shook her head. "No. Not that I'm aware of. Jaclyn picked her up from school and brought her home. Sometimes if Lucy finished her homework before dinner and the weather was nice, they'd walk down to the playground together."

"Was Jaclyn attentive, would you say?" Josie asked. "Was she the type to keep Lucy in her sight at all times or do you think she might sit on a bench and scroll on her phone until Lucy had finished playing?"

"She was always attentive when I saw them together," Amy said. "Obviously, I don't know what she was like when she was alone at the park with Lucy. I assume she played with Lucy and interacted with her like always."

"But you don't know for sure," Colin said, his voice low and edgy. There was a coldness to his tone that Josie hadn't heard before.

Amy's eyes tracked him as he paced on the far side of the room, the table between them. "What?" she asked.

Colin pointed at her. "You left our daughter with a stranger every single day. You let her go off with a stranger, and you have no idea how this woman treated her."

"What are you talking about? Jaclyn wasn't a stranger," Amy protested. "Jaclyn was our nanny."

"Yes," Colin spat. "You just had to have a nanny, didn't you?"

"Colin, I—"

"You and your fucking anxiety. You had to have a nanny because you couldn't possibly handle those two hours between school and dinner with your own goddamn child, could you?"

Amy put her hands to her chest, looking stricken.

Colin kept going, his movements more frenetic now. He pointed a finger at her. "Her murder is on you, you know that?"

Josie stood up, her tone a warning. "Mr. Ross."

He ignored her, his words still directed toward his wife like knives being thrown across the room right into her heart. "You had to have a nanny, and because of you, she's dead. How old was she, Ame? Twenty? Twenty-one? I bet her family wishes she never met us. She could have worked at a restaurant or been a lifeguard or something like that. But she was here, doing what you should have been doing and now she's dead."

Amy said, "I loved Jaclyn. I would never put her in harm's way."

"But you did."

"What? How was I supposed to know Lucy would be taken from us? How was I supposed to know that this sicko would hurt Jaclyn?"

He waved a dismissive hand in her direction, his face twisted and pinched as though he had eaten something sour. "What the hell do you do all day, Ame? You're here all day. Lucy goes to school at eight-thirty. Jaclyn picks her up. What's the matter with you? There are single moms out there working multiple jobs, caring for multiple children and they don't need nannies."

Tears rolled down Amy's cheeks. "Colin, please."

"I want to know, Ame. You got a girl killed today. So I want to know, what do you do all day?"

Josie waited to see if Amy would lie to him and say she was taking college courses, but she didn't answer him. Instead she said, "You're being cruel. You promised you would never be cruel."

He stopped pacing and looked directly at her. "And you promised you would take care of our daughter while I was away—that you would protect her."

Amy sprang out of her chair. "You were there, too. Or have you forgotten? Maybe you could have stopped all of this before it started if that damn phone wasn't the most important thing in your life."

"Don't make this about me," he shot back.

"Then don't make it about me," she hissed. "We're losing focus. We need to focus on Lucy. She's out there somewhere with a killer, Colin. A killer! Oh my God."

Amy turned away and ran out of the room. Josie and Colin stared at one another for a long moment. Then Colin dropped into the nearest chair, put his face in his hands, and cried.

CHAPTER TWENTY-TWO

I heard their voices again. I went under the bed, but I could still hear them. I tiptoed to the corner of the room furthest from the door. I still heard them. I climbed up onto the windowsill, but I still heard them.

"You can't keep a child like this," she told the man.

"Like what?" he scoffed.

"In these conditions. Children need to be outside. They need sun and food—we both need more food."

"For chrissake," the man complained. "All you do is complain about what you're not getting. I'm sick of it."

"I'm not asking for much. Basic necessities."

The man laughed, but I didn't like the sound at all. "You're both alive, aren't you? You're doing pretty well."

Her voice got quiet and bitter. "You did this. You wanted this. I never wanted this, but here we are. If you're tired of the way things are, let us leave."

The man's voice became a growl. "You're not going anywhere with that kid. You understand me? I'll kill you both. No one will ever find your bodies. Now get the hell out of my sight before I get really angry."

Seconds later, she stepped into the room. When she saw me, she waved a hand frantically in a beckoning motion. "Get down from there," she said in her harshest whisper.

We sat on the bed cross-legged, facing one another. The man wouldn't bring us toys or books, she said, so we played games with her socks. She made shapes with them and told me their names.

Horse. Mouse. Dog. The letter A. But today I didn't want to play. When she made the shape of a heart, I swiped the socks off the bed, onto the floor.

"Hey," she said.

"I want to go home," I said.

She looked at the closed door. "Soon," she said. "Very soon."

I didn't believe her.

CHAPTER TWENTY-THREE

Josie didn't follow Amy right away. Instead, she went into the backyard, sucking in the fresh air and wishing she had some Xanax of her own, or maybe some Wild Turkey. But the moment the thought came into her head, her stomach clenched. If this went on much longer, she'd have to see a doctor. *Or visit the local drugstore*, said a low voice in the back of her head. She pushed it back, down deep into the recesses of her consciousness. She wasn't ready to go there yet. Not while Lucy was in the hands of a madman and an army of law enforcement was powerless to recover her.

Josie took out her phone and called Noah. He'd already heard most of the news from the FBI agents at mobile command as well as other Denton team members. They talked for several minutes, Josie asking unnecessary questions just to keep him on the phone. The sound of his voice was the only thing that cut through the grief she'd been drowning in all day. "Come back to the tent," he told her.

"I can't," she said. "I'm needed here."

"Okay, well call me later. Oh wait…" Josie heard him talking to someone in the background. Then he came back on the line. "I've got the WYEP footage from yesterday."

"I'll be there in five," Josie said.

The volunteer searchers from the day before had gone, although many people still lingered around the playground, drinking coffee, chatting and hoping to help—or to hear some news, Josie thought. She spotted Luke and his bloodhound among the handful of people who had brought their own dogs to assist in search and rescue. The college students with their search drones were still there, most of them fiddling with their machines while one of them used a large handheld controller to fly one of the drones over the park for what Josie imagined must be the dozenth time. The most popular local coffee shop, Komorrah's, had set up a small table at the entrance, offering free coffee and pastries to law enforcement and civilian searchers. One of the local restaurants had set up another table nearby offering hot meals and various beverages. A crew from WYEP sat on benches nearby, all of their heads bent to their phones, except the cameraman who panned the area repeatedly with wary eyes, camera at the ready on his shoulder.

Inside the tent, Josie found Noah sitting at one of the folding tables, tapping away at a laptop in front of him. "You should ask those kids from the university for their drone footage," she said as she sat next to him.

He turned and smiled at her. "Already did but we didn't get anything. They were flying their drones over the rest of the city while the carousel was unattended."

"I just can't believe this guy snuck into the carousel while all these people were here," Josie said.

"It's kind of genius though," Noah said as he pulled up the footage he had received from WYEP. "He blends into the crowd. No one is looking at the carousel."

As the footage began to play on the laptop, Josie's heart sank. "There were easily a thousand people here yesterday, and they all had backpacks."

The camera focused on the entrance to the park, where the tent could be seen in the background. The reporter taped a spot while people milled around behind her. Then the footage cut to the line of searchers inside the park, panning the crowd. It focused on the carousel a few times for several seconds, but no one could be seen inside the perimeter of the ride. The reporter did another spot with the carousel behind her but again, no one suspicious appeared. Then the footage cut to various places around town where volunteers searched for Lucy.

Noah said, "He could easily have gotten into the carousel's column once the search was underway. WYEP wasn't taping there all day."

Josie leaned across him and reset the footage to the beginning so they could watch again. "But he has to be here," she said. "He must have been in the crowd."

"Right but how could we possibly tell what he looks like? It's not like this guy's going to be wearing a T-shirt that says 'Kidnapper' on it. I mean all these people look the same—non-threatening. Except this guy." Noah pointed to the screen. "He doesn't look threatening. Just out of place."

"Oh, tweed suit guy? I noticed him, too. I was thinking maybe he was a professor."

"Should we find out who he is?" Noah asked.

"It can't hurt," Josie said. "But I don't think the kidnapper would make himself so obvious. I've got to get back to Amy. Can you send this to my phone?"

"Will do," Noah said.

"Let me know if anything develops."

Her eyes searched the thin crowd of people as she made her way from the tent to her car, but no one stood out. Luke waved to her, and she gave an abrupt wave back, rushing to her car before he could approach. As she started her engine, nausea took hold of her stomach again.

CHAPTER TWENTY-FOUR

Josie found Amy on the second floor inside a room that was clearly Lucy's bedroom. It was decorated in pink—pastel pink paint covered the walls; pink unicorns danced along the border near the ceiling. Amy sat in a pile of stuffed animals on top of a twin bed ensconced in a white bedframe with a gauzy pink canopy draped over it. The carpet was plush and dark pink. All the furniture was white—dresser, toybox, and a small desk and chair. In one corner was a large easel with a three-drawer storage cabinet. Crayons, markers, construction paper and other craft items spilled out of the drawers. On the easel was a large picture drawn in crayon of a little girl with blonde hair standing next to a larger figure in a tan shirt and shorts with a net in his hand. Above their heads floated a dozen butterflies.

In fact, all over the room were signs of Lucy's obsession with butterflies. There was a discarded net and jar next to the door. A blanket with butterflies on it was draped over a beanbag chair. Lucy had put butterfly stickers on the front of her dresser. A large poster hung on one wall with several butterflies on it, the names of their classifications below each one. Thrown in one corner was what looked like a pair of butterfly wings Lucy could wear on her back. Next to the desk was a large circular net enclosure filled with small plants. On closer inspection, Josie thought she saw actual cocoons hanging from a small plastic circle.

Amy's voice was barely a whisper. "It's a butterfly garden. You send away for the caterpillars."

Josie peered inside counting six cocoons dangling from the white round piece of plastic. "There are actually caterpillars in there?"

"Yes. They should emerge as butterflies in a few days. This is the third time we've done it."

"I had no idea you could even do this," Josie said, amazed.

Amy gave a small laugh. "Colin thinks it's gross, but Lucy just loves it. They come in a small plastic cup. You just leave them in there and in about a week, they attach themselves to the lid and form their cocoons. Then you take the lid off, stand it up inside the net using that little log and wait for them to emerge. They're so beautiful when they come out. We set them free in the backyard."

"Wow," Josie said. "She really is obsessed with butterflies."

"Obsessed is putting it mildly. She wanted us to change her name to Chrysalis."

Now Josie laughed but it quickly died in her throat because any thought of Lucy automatically led to the questions that ran in a loop in her brain: where was she, and was she still alive?

"That was after we visited the butterfly room. We did a weekend in Philadelphia. The Academy of Natural Sciences has one. It's lovely. They keep it at eighty-five degrees. You just walk around in there. Butterflies are everywhere. Lucy was wearing a bright red shirt, and they kept landing on her. She said—" Amy broke off, her lower lip trembling. Then she took in a deep breath and continued, "She said it was the best day of her life. She likes ladybugs, too. She knows all kinds of weird facts about them. She knows that they hibernate over the winter, and that they look for the west-facing walls of light-colored houses to burrow into the siding. She used to say to me that if she ever got lost, she would fly back to me like a ladybug. Go west and look for our house. She was so glad it was light-colored. Fly home to me. I wish she would."

Josie walked over and sat next to Amy on the bed. Amy said, "I'm sorry about downstairs."

"Don't be," Josie said. "You know that Jaclyn's murder is not your fault, right?"

Amy's voice squeaked. "Isn't it? He's right, you know. I don't need a nanny. I should be able to do this myself. If it weren't for me—"

"If it weren't for you, Jaclyn would have been working a lot harder at a job she loved a lot less for practically no money at all. The only person who put her in harm's way was the person who killed her. No one else is to blame. No one."

"I'd like to believe that."

"When you and Colin were… arguing, you said he promised not to be cruel. Has he been cruel to you in the past?"

Amy waved a hand. "Oh no. Not him. I would never have given in to him. He chased me, you know. He was so persistent. I didn't want a man at all. He wore me down in the best possible way. But before I said yes to marriage, I made him promise he would never treat me cruelly. The man I was with before him, a long, long time ago, was very cruel. I didn't ever want to be in that position again."

"That man—" Josie started.

"He's dead," Amy interrupted. "He passed years ago, or so I heard. It wasn't serious anyway. Kid stuff. Like I said, a long, long time ago. It was barely a relationship at all. It's just that that was my only experience and it was bad, so I wasn't looking for a man. That's all."

"You left him?"

"Yes. He didn't try to come after me, if that's what you're getting at. Ultimately, he didn't care enough to come after me. Ancient history."

"Amy, I have to ask. Is there anyone who would do this? Take Lucy, kill Jaclyn?"

"That would be so easy, wouldn't it?" Amy said. "It would lead us right to him. But no, I can't think of anyone."

Josie measured her next words carefully. "We all have secrets, Amy. I have some whoppers. Google me. You'll see. There's no shame in having a past."

"I don't have a past," Amy insisted. "I barely have a present."

"This is personal," Josie said. "Whoever this guy is, he's targeting you and Colin for personal reasons. Colin seems like the obvious target—he's already got death threats from his work with Quarmark. Can you think of anyone who might want to target him? Maybe someone you wouldn't want to mention in front of Colin?"

Amy raised a brow. "What do you mean? You think… you think he was having an affair?"

"I don't know what to think," Josie said. "But I've been in this business long enough to know that people keep all kinds of secrets."

"Not Colin," Amy said. "He's an honorable man—in spite of what you saw downstairs. He has nothing to hide."

"What about you?" Josie asked carefully.

Amy pointed to her own chest. "Me? You think I have something to hide?"

"You understand that I have to ask. If there's anything you haven't told us, anything that you maybe didn't want to say in front of your husband, you should tell me now. If you have even the slightest suspicion at all that someone you know might have targeted Lucy to get to you, it's important that you tell me now. Before this goes any further."

"I wish I knew which direction to send you. Do you think I would keep any secret from you if it meant saving my daughter's life? I don't know anyone who would want to do this to Lucy or to me."

Josie didn't push. They sat in silence for a moment. Then Amy said, "Do you think she's still alive?"

"I don't know," Josie answered honestly.

"I just wish he would tell us what he wants. We have money. This could all be over quickly."

Kidnapping Lucy for money was the most logical scenario, but Josie didn't think this was about money. If it was as simple as that, the kidnapper wouldn't have murdered Jaclyn so he could call Lucy's parents, only to goad them. He wouldn't waste his time or resources—he would make a ransom demand right away. This was about more than money, Josie was sure of it, but she didn't say that to Amy. It would do her no good. She had already told Josie that she couldn't think of anyone who would target her. Either she was lying—and if she was still willing to lie after Jaclyn's murder, Josie couldn't imagine her ever willingly coming clean—or the kidnapper was targeting the Ross parents for some other reason—a reason that neither Colin nor Amy knew about.

Again, Josie thought of the death threats Colin had received at work because of the cancer drug. How many people had died because they couldn't afford Quarmark's miracle drug? Certainly seventy-four people blamed him for their loved ones' suffering, even deaths. Perhaps one of them believed the best way to take revenge on Colin would be to take the person he loved most away and then make the next most important person in his life suffer by taunting her. In the current scenario, Colin was almost a bystander. Forced to watch powerlessly while his daughter's life hung in the balance and his wife became increasingly hysterical and unstable. Was it, as Josie and Oaks had discussed earlier, somehow symbolic of the way family members had to stand by and watch their loved one fight cancer—all the while knowing there was a drug that could stop the disease in its tracks, or at least slow it down, but unable to afford access to it? If that was the case, there would be no ransom demand and the endgame would be Lucy's death.

A shiver ran the length of Josie's body.

Beside her, Amy had picked up a stuffed unicorn. She hugged it to her. "They all smell like her," she told Josie.

Josie looked behind them at the row of colorful stuffed animals all neatly seated along the wall. She reached out and touched a teddy bear with a red bowtie around its neck. How she would have loved to have a room like this when she was a child. She hoped they could bring Lucy home to this room so she could sleep in her beautiful princess bed again.

"Oh, careful," Amy said.

Josie pulled her hand away. "I'm sorry. I should go."

"Oh no," Amy said. "I didn't mean—that bear is one of those stuffed animals you can record messages on. Colin leaves a standing message on it for Lucy when he travels, but it's really sensitive. Once, he was on a trip and I was cleaning up and moved the bear and somehow erased his message. Lucy cried for hours."

"Oh," Josie said. "That's a good idea. He travels a lot, it seems."

Amy nodded. "He's barely here at all, to tell you the truth." Gingerly, she picked up the teddy bear. "Lucy still worships the ground he walks on even though she hardly sees him. This bear is her special connection to him." She did a mock impression of Colin, making her voice low like a man's. "I love you, little Lucy. Sweet dreams. That's usually what he says."

Josie couldn't help but think of the note the kidnapper had left inside Lucy's butterfly backpack. *Little Lucy cannot play.* Was it just a coincidence?

"Sometimes if he knows she's got a test coming up or he's promised her something when he gets back, he'll mention it. I think this last trip was his standard love you message." Amy felt the bear's paws until she found what she was looking for. "Here," she said. "It's a little button inside."

She squeezed the bear's paw, but it wasn't Colin's voice that filled the room.

The kidnapper's voice turned Josie's insides to ice. His tone was cold, his words dripping with contempt and getting louder and louder with each word until he was shouting. "Hello, Amy. How does it feel? How does it *feel*? How does it *feel*?"

CHAPTER TWENTY-FIVE

Amy let out a bloodcurdling scream. Josie jumped up from the bed. Before Josie could stop her, Amy threw the bear from her lap. "Don't touch anything," Josie said, but her words were swallowed by Amy's shrieks. Within seconds, the two FBI agents stationed downstairs in the dining room burst through the door. Josie used her body to block them where they were. "Stop," she said. "Don't touch anything. Go back into the hall. This is a crime scene."

Amy collapsed onto the floor inches from where the bear had landed, still screaming. One of the agents looked over Josie's shoulder at her and then back at Josie, his eyes wide with shock and confusion. "What the hell happened?" he asked. "Is she hurt?"

"No," Josie said. "Just get back. Please."

Both agents raised their hands in the air and backed out of the room. With adrenaline surging through her veins, Josie walked over to Amy, squatted down, picked her up in a fireman's lift and lugged her out of the room. She turned to her left and kicked open the nearest door, which luckily was Amy and Colin's bedroom. She gently deposited Amy onto the bed. The woman's screams had receded to grunts. Her eyes stared straight ahead, wide with terror but seeing nothing at all. Josie spent several minutes trying to soothe and comfort her, to bring her back from the edge of hysteria but this time, it didn't work. It wasn't until Colin appeared in the doorway, face stricken, and called Amy's name that she finally snapped back.

"He was here," Amy told him. "He was here in our house."

"What are you talking about?"

Amy looked at Josie. "Show him."

The last thing that Josie wanted to do was hear the awful sound of the kidnapper taunting Amy again, but she drew herself up and went into the hallway. The two FBI agents stood like sentries on either side of Lucy's bedroom door. Josie walked past them into the room. She took a pair of gloves from her pocket—she always carried some on the job—and snapped them on. She pressed the bear's paw just as Amy had, and again the terrible message played. Colin stood in the doorway with the two agents, looking like he might throw up. Josie felt the same.

One of the agents said, "I'll get Agent Oaks on the line. Get our team over here to process this."

Josie shook her head. "They've got their hands full at the murder scene. I'll call my team. They can be here in five minutes. We'll brief Oaks as soon as he's free."

*

It felt like an eternity had passed by the time Lucy's room was processed and Oaks returned from the Jaclyn Underwood murder scene. It had grown dark outside though none of them would ever know it thanks to the number of press vehicles outside with their cameras and lights ready to go for the eleven o'clock newscast. At some point that day, the case had gone national even though Oaks's press liaison hadn't told reporters much other than that they were now treating Lucy's disappearance as an abduction. Reluctantly, Josie called Trinity.

"You have something for me?" Trinity asked. "I'm going to come there and cover this story myself."

"I'm sorry," Josie said. "I've got nothing, and don't try to do that psychic twin thing to me again."

Trinity laughed. "I don't have to have a psychic twin connection to know you want something. What's up?"

"Amy Ross might have had an abusive boyfriend before she met Colin."

There was silence, then the rustling of papers and Josie knew Trinity was looking through her notes. "The roommate I spoke with never mentioned that—or any boyfriends."

Josie thought about how Amy had described the relationship as "kid stuff." To Trinity, she said, "Then maybe you have to go back further."

"Well," Trinity replied. "Looks like I'll be making a trip to Fulton, New York, before I see you in Denton."

Oaks had already dispatched agents to Fulton to look into Amy's background, but she also knew that much of the time, Trinity worked faster than the police. In addition, her celebrity often caused people to tell her things they would be reluctant to share with law enforcement. Trinity also wasn't bound by concerns about the admissibility of evidence or the need for warrants. If she stumbled on a rabbit hole, she could plunge in without reservation. If there was anything that anyone from Amy's past wanted to keep hidden from police, there was a good chance that Trinity could uncover it. "Keep me posted," Josie told her.

The night wore on, and Josie felt as though time itself had broken down. Only hours had passed since she had woken up with Noah in her bed, but she felt like she had been with Amy for weeks and that it had been ages since she had seen anyone from her team. So she was relieved when Mettner followed Oaks into the Rosses's dining room. She'd briefed him over the phone while Hummel and Denton's ERT worked in Lucy's room, looking for any trace the kidnapper might have left behind.

Oaks looked exhausted and haggard as he made her go over the story again. "Did you ask Mrs. Ross if the bear was missing at any time in the last few weeks?"

"Yes, I did," Josie answered. "After she calmed down. She said it's never been missing."

"Mr. Ross got home from his latest trip the day before Lucy disappeared," Oaks said.

"Yes," Josie agreed. "Amy said that Lucy listened to Colin's message the night before he came home. It was his voice, his message."

"So the kidnapper had to have changed the message between then and now."

"Amy said no one besides the family and nanny have been inside the house for months. No friends or repair people. No one who could have changed the message. Based on everything Amy told me about their routine and Colin's travel schedule, I think the kidnapper got in while the Ross family was at the park—before he took Lucy or during the initial search before the FBI stationed themselves inside the house."

"How did he get in? Nothing was disturbed. No sign of forced entry."

Josie said, "I think he might have a key."

Oaks raised a brow. "That's a stretch, Detective Quinn."

"Is it? Who even knew about the bear? Think about it. That bear was a special gift from Colin to Lucy. The only people who knew that it had a recording device in it and what it was used for were Colin, Amy, Lucy and the nanny."

"So we're back to the nanny."

"What if someone got close to the nanny? Stayed with her. Asked her all about the family she worked for—their routines, their habits. Got a copy of the house key. Amy told me Jaclyn had a key. It would be a simple thing to make a copy while Jaclyn was in one of her classes."

Oaks folded his arms over his chest. "We lifted some prints from the compact in the spare room, but they didn't match anyone in AFIS. We're trying to get DNA from hair we found on the pillow, but if the print didn't turn anyone up, I doubt a DNA profile will do the trick. We might not find this mystery woman unless one of the neighbors or one of her friends knows something about her, but we'll keep working that angle. So far, none of Jaclyn Underwood's friends remember her having had a live-in guest in the last year."

Josie told him about Colin's messages usually starting out with the words 'Little Lucy', the same as the kidnapper's note. "I don't know if it means anything," Josie concluded. "But worth mentioning."

"Good work," Oaks said. "By the way, my team finished checking out the rest of the people who have made threats against Colin at Quarmark. They all have alibis for when Lucy went missing."

Josie said, "But there could be people out there who are equally as upset about the price of Quarmark's new cancer drug who didn't make death threats."

"Yes," Oaks agreed. "That's true. That's what's scary. We really have no idea who we're dealing with."

"Yet," Josie said. "We'll find him. My team checked the rest of the house to see if there were any other messages that the kidnapper might have left for the parents, but we didn't find anything."

"Where are Mr. and Mrs. Ross?"

"Upstairs resting."

"That sounds like a good idea. Go home, Quinn. Grab a few hours. Take Mettner, too. We've all had a long day. Come back in the morning. Bring someone from your team. We'll keep working every angle until something breaks."

Josie didn't argue. She picked Noah up at the mobile command station on her way home, never so relieved to see his face and hear his voice. Misty and Harris were asleep in the spare room by the time they made it up the stairs to Josie's room.

"Did you eat anything tonight?" Noah asked her as she climbed under her covers. He always worried about her staying fed, hydrated and caffeinated.

"Yes," she lied, not bothering to tell him her stomach had been far too churned up to eat after the evening's events. "Just come to bed. I've missed you all day."

CHAPTER TWENTY-SIX

Josie dreamt of Lucy—of racing after her in the park and in the Rosses's home, which had endless twisting hallways. Every time she got close to the girl and reached her hand out to grasp her arm, Lucy would disappear into thin air. She woke breathless and covered in sweat and immediately headed for the shower. Once both Josie and Noah were ready for the day, she dropped Noah off at the mobile command center. Instead of driving to the Ross home, she doubled back and pulled into the parking lot of Denton West Elementary. It was a one-story sprawling brick building surrounded by immaculate landscaping and perfectly pruned bushes and trees. Josie found a parking spot in the visitors' area. There was still an hour before students would begin to arrive for the day. She walked to the front entrance. Beside the double doors was a small brown box with a little button on it. Next to it a laminated sign announced that all visitors must report directly to the office. Josie punched the button and then looked up at the camera above the two doors. She took out her police credentials and held them up. Seconds later, there was an audible click as the locks on the doors disengaged.

Inside the building, more laminated signs directed her down the hallway to the right, past several classrooms and the entrance to the auditorium until she reached the office. Her elementary and high schools on the east side of Denton had been like this as well, with the office far from the entrance. She had always wondered why schools didn't put their offices closer to the front doors. Inside the office, a pert secretary sat behind a desk with a headset on. Josie explained why she was there, showed her ID one more time and waited while the woman made a phone call. Finally, she was given directions to Lucy's first grade classroom.

After navigating a few more hallways, Josie found Lucy's teacher, Violet Young, standing just outside the classroom, waiting for her. Josie estimated Violet to be probably in her mid to late twenties. She was curvy with long auburn hair. A burgundy sweater clung to her torso, and stretchy black pants disappeared into knee high brown boots. A necklace made from dried macaroni hung from her neck. She smiled broadly as Josie came down the hallway.

They made introductions, and Violet invited Josie into her classroom, which was filled with tiny desks and chairs between a large teacher's desk and a brightly colored carpet with the alphabet on it. A whiteboard took up nearly one entire wall. Posters and student artwork fluttered from the other walls. Violet walked to her desk and perched on the end of it. "Has there been any news?" she asked.

"I'm afraid not," Josie said.

Violet's gaze swept downward but not before Josie saw her eyes moisten. "This is just unbelievable. We've all been devastated. Our sweet Lucy. I can't even imagine—"

Josie interrupted before she began to cry. "We're doing everything we can to find Lucy. Working around the clock to bring her home."

Violet looked back up at Josie. "FBI agents were here yesterday. They interviewed most of the staff."

"Yes," Josie said. "I know. They are doing an amazing job. I'm not here to second-guess the interviews they conducted. I've been assigned to Mrs. Ross."

Violet's hand fluttered to her macaroni necklace, her fingers running over the dried pasta noodles. "How is she?"

"As well as can be expected under the circumstances," Josie said. "Do you have kids?"

Violet smiled. "No. My students are my kids. At least for now. My husband and I are on a five-year plan to get married, buy a house, get our careers in order and then have kids. Three more years and we can start trying!"

She said it with a note of desperation, as though she had rehearsed this stock answer and given it so many times, she hoped no one would see through it. Josie knew at once the five-year plan was the husband's idea, not Violet's. "Well," Josie offered. "You'll have all your affairs in order by the time you start your family. Speaking of family, I've been spending a lot of time with Lucy's parents the last two days, and I just thought it might help me connect with them better if I knew more about Lucy. I just kind of wanted to see where she spends her days, ask you what kind of student she is, that sort of thing."

"Oh, yes, of course."

Violet weaved through the maze of little desks until she came to one in the center of the room. Her hand rested on its surface, and Josie walked over to stand next to her. "This is Lucy's desk," she said. All the desks stood on four metal legs, with an open hollow area beneath the faux wood surface so that students could slide their books and other supplies inside. Each desk had a colorful laminated strip of paper on it. On the top were numbers from zero to ten, then the student's full name carefully written in marker, and below that the alphabet in upper and lower case. Josie pointed at the little cubby beneath the surface. "Do you mind?"

"Of course not," Violet said.

Josie squatted down and peered inside the small space. There was a pencil case, some glue, a stack of notebooks and folders and some plastic, toy butterflies. Next to them was a small cylindrical object that appeared to be made of green construction paper.

"It's a cocoon," Violet told her. "Well, Lucy would say a chrysalis. I assume you know about the butterfly obsession."

Josie couldn't help but laugh with delight at the secret stash in Lucy's desk. "Yes, I'm well aware. Tell me, what kind of student is Lucy?"

Violet folded her hands together at her waist. "Oh, she's very bright, and very sweet. She gets distracted easily though. She can be very... single-minded." At this, she laughed and gestured toward the fake butterfly habitat Lucy had built inside her desk. "It's a battle to keep her on-task sometimes. Then again, she is only seven."

Josie stood and walked over to one of the walls where pages of student artwork hung. "How is she socially? Does she make friends easily?"

"Oh yes. She's very sociable. The other kids love her. Though, sometimes I think—" Violet broke off, a frown on her face.

"Sometimes you think what?" Josie coaxed.

"I really shouldn't say. It's not relevant."

"It doesn't have to go beyond this room," Josie promised her. "I'm very interested in your observations."

Violet looked away again. Her hands waved in the air as she spoke. "Sometimes I think that because Mr. Ross is away all the time and Mrs. Ross seems so... distracted... that Lucy feels—subconsciously—that she has to do things to make people happy in order to get attention and love. It's almost like on some level she feels invisible except when she does something nice for someone or does what some other kid tells her to do. Like she doesn't believe people will just like her for herself."

It was a lot to unpack but Josie started at the beginning. "You think Mrs. Ross is distracted?"

"The times I've met her, yes. She just seems like her mind is always elsewhere. I don't doubt she loves Lucy, that's not what I'm saying."

"I know," Josie said.

"It's just that sometimes—like at school events or on trips—Lucy will be talking away, and Mrs. Ross will be staring into space. At some point, Lucy realizes that her mom hasn't heard a word she's said, and she just stops talking. I mean, not always. A lot of the time, Mrs. Ross seems very engaged, but you can tell by the way

Lucy sighs and rolls her eyes when she isn't paying attention that it's not a one-time thing."

Sadness tugged at Josie's heartstrings. Lots of parents paid little attention to their children though. That didn't mean that Amy was capable of staging her own daughter's kidnapping. "I did speak with some of the other mothers who implied that Mrs. Ross is a bit... overprotective."

Violet laughed. "Yes, that's accurate. But there's a difference between being physically present and mentally present. I would say that Mrs. Ross is more physically present than any parent I've ever met—almost to the detriment of Lucy's friendships with other children—but like I said, you can tell that much of the time, her mind is elsewhere."

Josie brought up one of the other points that Violet had made. "When you say Lucy is pleasing, can you give me any examples that you have observed here at school?"

Violet took a moment to think about it. "Well, there's another little girl in class who will only give Lucy the time of day if Lucy gives her the cookies from her lunch every day. Lucy does it, even though sometimes you can tell that she really wants those cookies for herself. But then at recess the little girl will tease her or ignore her. I've talked to Lucy—and of course, to the other girl—several times about the dynamic and about how to be a good friend, but Lucy still gives in to her a lot."

"Lucy sounds like she has a good heart though," Josie said.

"Oh yes," Violet said. "Without question."

Josie motioned toward the drawings on the wall. "Which of these are hers?"

Violet walked with Josie along the wall, pointing out each series of drawings. "This assignment was to draw somewhere they had gone on vacation. Here's Lucy's—the beach. She loves the beach. These were from an assignment where they had to draw a self-portrait and then underneath their portraits, they had to draw three things that they enjoy or love." Lucy's three items, unsurprisingly, included a butterfly as well as a book and two stick figures holding hands—one with short hair and one with long hair. "Those are her parents," Violet said.

Again, Josie felt a deep ache in her chest for Lucy. All the other children had drawn their favorite toys or an object from their favorite sport, a mythical animal or a cartoon character. Clearly, Lucy's world was narrower than that of her classmates. There was something to the other mothers' assertions that Lucy was isolated.

"Here," Violet said. "These were from a class trip we took to a nearby orchard and pumpkin patch. The kids had to draw their favorite thing about it. As you can see, almost everyone chose the hayride or the small petting zoo. And this display was from a trip we took to the college campus. The drama department was putting on a production of *Charlotte's Web*. The kids had to draw their favorite character."

"What about these?" Josie asked as she came to a section filled with drawings of various bugs—what looked like beetles, ladybugs, bees, some bugs Josie couldn't identify and butterflies. She immediately recognized Lucy's picture because she had seen a version of it in Lucy's room already. It was an adult stick figure in brown clothing with a net holding the hand of a small, blonde female stick figure. Butterflies flew overhead.

"We had a bug expert here a couple of months ago," Violet said. Josie raised a brow. "A bug expert?"

Violet smiled. "Oh, the kids loved him. He's actually a bee-keeper. Lives about an hour from here, halfway between here and Philadelphia. He brought beetles, tarantulas, a Madagascar hissing cockroach, some ladybugs, butterflies and a stick bug. He travels all over the state visiting schools."

"How long was he here?" Josie asked.

"Oh, only a couple of hours. He's got a pretty polished presentation."

"Did he seem as though he took a special interest in Lucy?"

"No, not really."

"Do you have his name and contact information?"

"I gave it to the FBI," Violet said. "They wanted a list of all visitors to the school in the last six months." She walked back over to her desk and shuffled through some papers until she found what she was looking for. She handed Josie a scrap of paper with a name and number written on it. The name was John Bausch. Josie took out her phone and snapped a photo of the details. "Did you take any photos when he was here?"

Violet took out her own phone. "A few, yes, although they were mostly of the kids and the insects."

"You're allowed to take photos of the children?"

"Oh, yes," Violet said. "The school sends home a waiver at the beginning of the school year that parents have to sign giving us permission to take photos of the children during school activities. We usually have a few families who don't want their children's photos taken, but this year we had permission for the entire class. We are only allowed to share photos we take on the secure district website and app, which only faculty, staff and parents are able to access. I don't have them on my phone anymore, but I can show you through the app." She swiped and scrolled through her phone until she found the series of photos and handed it to Josie.

Josie swiped through the pictures until she came to a few photos of John Bausch. In each one of them he was either in profile or his head was bent down toward the children. He was young, perhaps mid to late twenties, with thick brown hair and a clean-shaven face. He wore a pair of khaki pants and a tan polo shirt. Josie wondered if Bausch was the adult in Lucy's drawings. "Can you send these to me?" Josie asked.

"Well, I can't," Violet said. "But I can talk to the principal. There may be some legal issues—"

"A warrant," Josie said. "I can get one of those within the hour and have it sent over to the principal."

"That would work," Violet agreed.

Josie handed Violet a business card, urging her to call if she thought of anything that might be useful.

She walked back over to the wall and tapped a finger against Lucy's butterfly drawing. "Do you mind if I take this?"

Violet hesitated for a moment and then said, "Sure, I guess."

CHAPTER TWENTY-SEVEN

Josie and Oaks stood in the Rosses's backyard, the only place on the premises where they could speak without being overheard by Amy or Colin. Oaks looked as though he still hadn't slept. A patchy gray beard had grown in along his jawline and chin. His arms were wrapped tightly over his chest as he regarded her. "You knew we interviewed the teacher, and you went to see her anyway. Are you second-guessing my team, Detective Quinn?"

"No," Josie said. "On the contrary, I think your team is doing a fine job, and you're covering way more ground than my team could ever hope to cover in such a short amount of time."

"Then why did you go to the school?"

She couldn't entirely explain it. It was her instinct driving her, and she wasn't even sure where it was going to take her. "I just needed to talk to someone close to Lucy besides her parents," Josie said. "Violet Young told me that Amy often seemed distracted."

"You were looking for something you could use to try to get Mrs. Ross to open up to you," Oaks said.

"Sort of," Josie said. "The fact that the kidnapper knew about that teddy bear—the one with the recording feature—and got into the house to use it, unseen, is really bothering me."

Oaks nodded. "It's bothering me as well."

"I can't shake the thought that whoever took Lucy got close to her. Somehow."

"Yesterday you were insistent that whoever was staying with the nanny was that person," Oaks pointed out.

"Yes," Josie said. "I still think that's the most likely scenario, but I feel like we are missing something. How did the kidnapper get enough access to Lucy to convince her that she should leave her parents? Enough access to put this plan into place; a plan where she would retrieve a sweatshirt from inside the carousel, put it on to avoid being noticed, and run off to this person? Someone who got close to the nanny could have done it. Someone who routinely approached Lucy at the park whenever the nanny took her there and was on her phone. But school was the only place where Lucy was completely out of her mother's sphere of influence."

Oaks sighed. "I'll have the staff checked out."

"Thank you. And I think we should take a closer look at John Bausch."

Oaks's brow furrowed. Then he said, "He was one of the school presenters, wasn't he?"

"Yes. Great memory," Josie remarked. She knew the FBI was literally tracking down thousands of leads. Even the most mundane and unlikely of suspects were on their list. "He's the bug expert who visited Lucy's school a couple of months ago. I had my people send a warrant to the school for the photos the teacher took of him with the children the day he was there."

"You know, I had a team go to the school. They got a list of all special visitors and presenters at the school going back six months. John Bausch was on that list. I'm quite certain he had an alibi for the day Lucy went missing. One of my agents contacted his office." Oaks pulled out his phone. After several swipes and scrolls, he tapped his index finger against the screen. "Here it is. I've got a note here. My agents talked to his assistant, who is also his wife, and she faxed us a copy of his schedule for the week Lucy went missing. He was in Philadelphia for the weekend, and he was meeting with someone from the Academy of Natural Sciences around the time that Lucy disappeared. That was confirmed by a rep for the Academy. What do you propose we do?"

"Bring him in."

"You want us to bring in a guy who lives an hour away who has a solid alibi?" Oaks asked.

"Listen, we know we're not dealing with just one person here," Josie said. "So maybe Bausch has an alibi, but I don't know if that firmly rules him out. He may have had help—maybe from the mystery woman who was staying at Jaclyn Underwood's apartment. Maybe she was his accomplice, and her job was to get close to Jaclyn so she would find out as many intimate details about the Rosses's lives as possible—and get a copy of Jaclyn's house key made."

Oaks's pinched expression told her he was struggling to find the strength in her reasoning. From her back jeans pocket, Josie pulled out the drawing from the school, unfolded it and handed it to Oaks. "Lucy drew this after Bausch came to her school. There's another one up in her room. Same drawing."

Oaks raised a brow. "You want me to bring this guy in based on a child's drawing?"

"Do we have more pressing leads than this?" Josie pointed out.

"It's a stretch to call this a lead, Detective Quinn. This man was at Lucy's school once, two months ago. He has a confirmed alibi for the day that Lucy vanished. There were a half dozen guests at Denton West in the last six months: Bausch, two different children's authors, the mayor of Denton, the fire marshal and a professional athlete from the Philadelphia Eagles. All of them were checked out. All of them had alibis for the day Lucy vanished. Would you propose we bring in all of those people?"

Josie put a hand on her hip and said, "Only if they chase butterflies."

Oaks gave her a stunned look before bursting into laughter.

Josie waited for him to finish before she said, "You'd have to be blind not to notice Lucy's obsession with butterflies."

Oaks nodded. "Indeed, you'd have to be, and I see your point—if you were an adult trying to gain Lucy's trust so you could prepare her for something, using her interest would be a great place to start, but it's a little coincidental, don't you think? A guy who handles butterflies for a living kidnaps a child who loves butterflies?"

"Not just butterflies," Josie argued. "He's primarily a beekeeper, from what Violet Young said. He brought lots of different insects with him."

"Okay so aside from that you still want to bring in a guy who already checked out?"

"Let my team do it," Josie said. "My colleague, Detective Gretchen Palmer—she can do it. I'll have her track him down and bring him into our stationhouse. We'll talk with him. If it's nothing, it's nothing. But if it's something…"

Oaks sighed. "Then you'll have my support. You know that."

"Thank you," Josie said. As Oaks walked back inside to check on Colin and Amy, Josie took out her phone and called Gretchen.

CHAPTER TWENTY-EIGHT

The day was painfully long. Several calls came in to Amy's cell phone: the principal of Lucy's school, calls from Ingrid and Zoey, the mothers of two of Lucy's friends, and one from the pharmacy to let her know that a prescription was ready. Each time the phone rang, the two FBI agents stationed inside the house, Oaks, Mettner and Josie all converged on the dining room waiting with bated breath until Amy answered, her voice always tremulous, saying a hesitant hello as though she was afraid of what the word would unleash. But the kidnapper didn't call.

The lack of progress on any leads and absence of any contact from the kidnapper made everyone jittery and agitated. It left far too much time for Amy and Colin to start asking difficult questions that had no ready answers.

"Do you think she's still alive?"

"What is he doing to her?"

"What does he want?"

"Why won't he call?"

"Why is this happening?"

Their lives were in a state of suspended animation. But that was what the kidnapper wanted, Josie realized. Neither Amy nor Colin could live their lives not knowing where Lucy was or what was happening to her. It was the cruelest kind of torture. Josie didn't have to have children of her own to understand this. He was getting pleasure from this, which was why Josie was certain that he would continue the game. He couldn't take Lucy away from them permanently. Eventually, after a great deal of time had passed, they'd start to resume some of their normal activities. They would begin to live with the uncertainty, begin to eat and shower again and Colin would force himself to go to work because the bills needed to be paid. The absence of Lucy and the not knowing would become their new normal. They would never be at peace again, but they would move out of the acute stage of horror into something more chronic. The kidnapper would want them to stay in the acute phase for as long as possible, she imagined. He was going to drag this out.

Unless they found him first.

When Gretchen showed up late in the afternoon the sight of her was so soothing that Josie wanted to jump into her arms. She brought coffees and pastries for everyone with a special bag for Josie filled with three cheese Danishes. Because the press was camped out front—and growing in number with each hour, it seemed—Josie and Gretchen snuck into the yard.

"I thought you could use a break," Gretchen told her.

Josie took the coffee from her and set it on the table in the center of the Rosses's back patio. The smell of it still made her a little queasy, but the Danishes went down without any issues. "Thanks," Josie said. "Did you guys track down the guy in the tweed jacket? From the WYEP footage?"

"Not yet. We know he's not a professor at the college though. I've got a couple of people working on that."

"Did you get in touch with Bausch?"

Gretchen nodded. "He was in Allentown doing a school presentation today, but he said he would drive up tomorrow. He was very cooperative."

"Good," Josie said.

"You want to sit in?"

"Yeah. I'll come over when he gets there."

A few moments passed in companionable silence. Gretchen sipped her own coffee while Josie polished off her third cheese Danish.

Gretchen said, "What do you think this guy's endgame is?"

"I don't know," Josie said. "He's not operating like a pedophile. They try not to draw any attention to themselves. They will usually either keep the child or they'll act out their fantasy and kill the child within the first few hours."

Gretchen nodded. "A pedophile would be pretty unlikely to be taunting the parents like this."

"Which is not to say this guy doesn't have perversions, but I don't think that's why he took Lucy."

What Josie didn't say, what she couldn't bring herself to say out loud, but what they both knew was that even if the kidnapper was after money or something personal to Lucy's parents, that didn't mean that Lucy would come home alive.

*

By dinnertime, when there had been no more calls, Oaks sent Josie home. Noah, having had someone drop him off at her house, was already at her dinner table with Misty and little Harris. "Hope you don't mind pasta," Misty said.

"It's delicious," Noah informed her around a mouthful of spaghetti noodles.

"Jojo!" Harris called as Josie took a seat at the kitchen table between Noah and Harris's high chair. She smiled and kissed the top of his head, inhaling the scent of his shampoo, the smell more soothing than a hot bath after a long day.

His pudgy hand reached into the plastic bowl before him and pulled out a sauce-covered noodle. "Sketties!" he exclaimed.

Misty set a plate of steaming spaghetti in front of Josie and sat on the other side of Harris. "Spaghetti," she enunciated.

He ignored her, thrusting the noodle at Josie's face. "You eat," he said.

Josie let him feed her the noodle, slurping it out of his hand at the last second, unleashing a torrent of giggles. "Again, again!" he said, digging into his bowl for more noodles.

Josie repeated the noodle slurp three more times until everyone at the table was laughing. Harris's giggles had always been contagious.

Finally, Misty said, "Harris. You eat your own food. Let Jojo eat her dinner."

Josie took a noodle off her own plate and held it out to Harris who tried to imitate her without success, finally just snatching the noodle from her and jamming it into his mouth with his fingers.

They kept the conversation light, with no talk of Josie or Noah's work, of Lucy Ross or missing children. Immediately after dinner, Josie and Noah collapsed into her bed again, too tired to even talk. Nausea woke her at five-thirty in the morning, while the rest of the house was still quiet. As she emptied the contents of her stomach into the toilet, she prayed Noah wouldn't wake up and find her ill. Luckily, no one came to the door. She propped herself up against the edge of the bathtub and covered her stomach with both hands. The voice in the back of her head goaded her again. Why was she still sick? Was it really just stress? Or was it something more? Just as the question: *what if I'm pregnant?* floated to the surface of her mind, she heard footsteps outside the door. Then, from beneath the crack in the door, she heard Harris's voice, a loud whisper: "JoJo?"

Smiling, Josie hefted herself up and opened the door. Harris squinted up at her, blinking against the light. She lifted him into her arms. "Does your mom know you're awake?"

He wrapped his arms around her neck. "Jojo, drink," he said.

Josie smiled. "You're thirsty? We'll let Mommy sleep then. Let's go down to the kitchen."

*

Josie was at the Ross household bright and early once more. Oaks was there with a new shift of agents to man the phones and laptops.

"Have you even slept?" Josie asked.

Oaks smiled. "A few hours here and there."

She didn't bother to tell him to get some rest. The only reason she was able to sleep at night was because she knew his team was able to work around the clock and that the Ross family was in good hands.

"We got the DNA processed from the Jaclyn Underwood scene," Oaks told her. "We found one hair with the root attached on the pillow in the closet which we believe may belong to whomever was staying with Jaclyn, and we found trace amounts of skin beneath two of Jaclyn's fingernails, which we believe may have come from the killer. No hits though."

"I didn't think there would be," Josie sighed.

"But we did match the prints on the compact at the nanny's house to an unknown print in Lucy's room."

Josie felt a small thrill of excitement. While it wouldn't help them find the kidnapper or his accomplice, it linked the two crime scenes. "So the female staying at Jaclyn Underwood's apartment was also in Lucy's room. Amy said that Lucy had never met any of Jaclyn's friends though—that she knew of."

"Well, I asked her again if Jaclyn ever brought any friends over, and she said never. Why do I feel like these assholes are right under our noses?" Oaks asked, raking a hand down over his face and then rubbing at his eyes.

"Because I think they might be," Josie said. "Are we missing something big?"

Oaks shook his head. "I don't see how we can be. I've got dozens of agents working leads around the clock plus the work your department is doing."

Before Josie could say anything more, Amy's cell phone rang. Oaks and Josie turned and stared at the screen. The name read 'Wendy'.

Amy raced in from the kitchen and Colin appeared in the other doorway just behind her, having come from the living room. Josie had noticed the couple hadn't been speaking to one another much since the evening before.

"Who's Wendy?" Oaks asked.

Amy looked from the phone to him. "Wendy Kaplan. She's a friend from yoga." Her hand hovered over the phone. "I'll tell her I need to keep the line open."

She picked up the phone and said, "Hello?"

There was a moment of perfect silence before the kidnapper's voice sent a wave of revulsion through the room. "Hello, Amy."

She took a sharp intake of breath and pressed her hand to her chest. "How is Lucy?" she asked, and Josie could tell she'd thought long and hard about what she was going to ask him when he called next.

"How do you think she is, Amy?"

"I want to talk to her. Can I talk to her, please?"

Laughter filtered through the line. "Oh, Amy," he said. "Sad, silly, brainless Amy."

Undeterred, Amy said, "Have you hurt her?"

"Well, that depends on what you mean by hurt."

Amy gasped. Tears gathered in her eyes. Colin squeezed past the agents and went to Amy's side. He held out a hand for her to give him the phone, but she turned away, her voice cracking as she begged the kidnapper to let her talk to Lucy.

One of the agents waved Oaks over and pointed to the screen. Oaks beckoned for Josie, and she went over to take a look at the address. "I'm not sure of the exact address," the agent whispered. "But I did a property search for Wendy Kaplan and this one here" —he pointed to a house on the screen as shown from Google's satellite map—"belongs to her."

Unfortunately for them, Wendy Kaplan lived on the outskirts of Denton. "Fifteen," Josie whispered, indicating how long it would take to get to Kaplan's house. "At least." She started to move toward the doorway, but Oaks whispered back, "Stay with Mrs. Ross. I'll take Mettner. He's right outside."

As Oaks departed, Josie turned back toward Amy. Tears streaked her face. "What do you want?" she sobbed into the phone. "Just tell me what you want."

Josie expected more taunts but instead, the kidnapper said, "A million dollars."

Everyone in the room went perfectly still. The two agents looked at Josie and then at one another before turning their attention back to the computer. As if on a switch, the kidnapper had gone from taunting Amy to making his demand.

When she didn't answer, the kidnapper laughed. "Oh, you didn't really want to know what I wanted? Were you only asking because you think that's what a distraught mother is supposed to ask?"

Amy opened her mouth to respond but nothing came out. Colin grabbed the phone from her hand and barked into it. "We want proof of life."

Amy tugged at Colin's arm, trying to wrestle the phone away from him. "No," she wailed. "Just give it to him so we can get Lucy back."

Colin pulled away from her. "Prove to us that Lucy is alive and you can have the money."

Josie heard anger in the kidnapper's voice when he spoke next. "You don't get to make the rules. Any rules. You give me a million dollars, and I give you Lucy back. That's it. That's all."

Amy was practically hanging from Colin's arm, shouting to be heard. "You can have whatever you want. Just give me my daughter back. Please."

Colin said, "Alive. I want her back alive."

There was a long moment of silence. Josie thought for a second that the kidnapper had hung up, but then she heard him exhale. "A million dollars," he said. "Not a penny less. No conditions."

Then the line went dead.

Colin tossed the phone onto the table and pressed his palm to the top of his head. Amy started hitting him with her open hand, slapping him and screaming, "You bastard. Why would you do that? Why?"

Colin didn't fight her. He kept his hands up, blocking her blows as well as he could. "What if she's already dead?" he said.

"Don't," Amy shrieked. "Don't you even say it. Why would you ask for proof of life? Just give him whatever he asks for so we can get Lucy back."

"Ame, we're talking to a guy who kidnapped a seven-year-old girl. You think I should trust him?"

"Oh, so what? You're not going to give him the money if she's dead?"

"What?"

"You know damn well 'what'. You're not willing to do anything to get her back, are you?"

"Of course I am," Colin said. His hands came down and hung slack at his waist. "I just wanted to know she was okay. That's all. I wanted to…" he stopped. When he spoke again, his voice cracked. "I wanted to hear her voice, Ame. Oh God, I just want to hear her voice."

He dropped to his knees and Amy dropped to hers in front of him. She took him in her arms. "Me too. Me too."

CHAPTER TWENTY-NINE

Wendy Kaplan lived on the top of a mountain in a development called Briar Lane. The small collection of modular homes could only be reached by one of the long, narrow rural roads that snaked from Denton proper out into the thick forests surrounding it. Even if Josie hadn't been familiar with it, she would only have had to follow the long line of news vehicles to find Kaplan's house, which was now surrounded by police and emergency vehicles. Josie parked outside the police perimeter and walked a half block to Kaplan's address.

Like most of the newer developments in Denton, all the houses in Briar Lane looked the same. They came in three colors: tan, gray and white. Some of the residents had added a little character with landscaping and lawn ornaments. She passed a gray house on her right that she knew quite well. It gave her a shiver to think that this missing girl case had now come back almost to the very place that the famous missing girls' case had started for Josie three years earlier. She knew they weren't related in any way, obviously, but she couldn't stop the sense of foreboding that overcame her.

Kaplan's house was a few doors down, tan-colored with a beautifully landscaped garden in the front yard. An FBI agent stood in the driveway in front of a small red sports car. He nodded at Josie and said, "They're around back."

Josie walked between the houses, noticing that Wendy Kaplan had had a tall white privacy fence installed around her backyard. Another agent stood there with Mettner, guarding the entrance.

Josie felt an uptick in her heartbeat. "Mett," she said. "Why does this look like you're standing outside of a murder scene?"

He grimaced. "Sorry to tell you, boss, but Wendy Kaplan is dead."

Josie found the FBI Evidence Response van and suited up appropriately. When she returned to the backyard gate, she found that Mettner had gone off to walk the outer perimeter to see if there were any clues to be found. Josie signed in with the FBI agent and stepped into Wendy Kaplan's backyard. Like the front, it was beautifully landscaped, leaving little actual yard, its centerpiece a beautiful stone fountain. The water at its base was filled with koi. Between the fountain in the middle of the yard and the sliding glass doors at the back of the house, Josie spotted a woman's prone body. She was face down. Judging from her stretchy black yoga pants and pink tank top, she had been either returning from or getting ready to go to a yoga class. Her greying hair was long and fanned out over her shoulders, the tips of it turned red from the ever-widening pool of blood in the grass around her torso. One arm was trapped under her body. The other was flung outward to her side, fingertips covered in blood. She hadn't been dead very long. Oaks stood over her, two other agents at his side, all of them dressed in white Tyvek suits. Josie hung back while he gave out directions.

When he had finished, Oaks walked over to where Josie stood just inside the gate while his agents photographed the body and began processing the scene. "We haven't turned her over yet," he said. "But I'm guessing another stab wound."

"Jesus," Josie said. She turned and looked up and around but couldn't see any of the neighbors' upstairs windows. No one would have been able to see anything happening in Wendy's backyard.

"Looks like she put up quite the fight," Oaks said. "The house is a mess. Phone is in the kitchen on the counter. There's blood on it, so we think he killed her first and then returned to the house and used it to call Amy." He motioned toward the sliding glass doors. "I'd like you to have a look, if you don't mind."

"Of course," Josie said.

They stepped gingerly through the glass doors. Debris crunched beneath their feet the moment they hit the tile of the kitchen floor. Not glass from the doors, but from the shattered remains of dinner and glassware that had been broken in Wendy Kaplan's struggle against the killer. The draining board was on the floor. Pieces of thick ceramic plates and mugs lay all over the place. The wooden kitchen table was on its side, one of its legs snapped off. Every appliance that Wendy owned was in a broken heap on the kitchen floor. Her refrigerator door had a large dent in it.

Josie felt a swell of respect for the woman. It seemed wrong that she should die after putting up such a fight. "I hope she hurt him," she said, eyes searching the detritus.

"Me too," Oaks answered. He stood in one corner, arms crossed.

Josie stopped her search momentarily and looked over at him. "Is this a test?"

He laughed. "No, not a test. I'm just interested in what you see. Your impressions."

Josie edged around the debris to the door that led to the front of the house. She walked carefully through the dining and living rooms to the front door. Nothing looked disturbed—not even the locking mechanism on the entry door. She walked back to the kitchen.

"She let him in," Josie said.

"There was no forced entry," Oaks agreed. "My agents and your guy had a look around. No broken windows, no interruption in the privacy fence, no disturbance of the sliding glass doors."

"But then they got to the kitchen and at some point, she realized he was a threat. What do we know about Wendy Kaplan?"

Oaks pulled out his phone and scrolled through some notes. "As you know, my team checked out everyone considered close to Amy and Colin Ross. Kaplan was near the top of the list with the nanny. Here we go—she was older than Amy, in her late fifties. Divorced, no children. No boyfriends. Worked in the publishing industry in New York City for many years. Now she does some freelance work from home. Bought this house about three years ago. No record. No red flags. Alibi for the exact time Lucy disappeared—she was on a Skype conference call with several colleagues who confirmed her presence on the call, as did her actual phone and computer records."

"So she lived alone?"

"Yes."

"A woman from a large city living alone would not let a stranger into her house just like that," Josie said.

"Maybe he threatened her," Oaks said. "Pulled the knife or even a gun and demanded she let him in."

"You get anything from the neighbors?" Josie asked. "Directly across the street?"

"My agents are still canvassing but first thing we did was go to the house across the street. No one home. It is a weekday, remember? Most people are at work."

"But he would have needed a vehicle to get up here," Josie said.

"Yes," Oaks agreed. "That's why I've got agents out canvassing the rest of the development to see if anyone who was home saw an unusual vehicle."

Josie looked around the kitchen once more. "If he had threatened her at the door, she would have fought then. She never would have let him in in the first place."

"How can you be sure?"

Josie motioned to the destruction all around them. "I know this kind of fight," she said. "I've fought this kind of fight. The kind of person who fights this hard—the single woman living alone who fights this hard— doesn't let a strange man into her home."

"How scientific," Oaks said. At first, Josie thought he was being sarcastic but when she saw his smile, she knew he was joking. Mostly. It was true. It wasn't a good argument. Not based on facts or science, just on Josie's gut. But her gut rarely failed her.

Oaks continued, "How does he get her to let him in then?"

Josie shrugged. "Manipulation. I'd check to see if Wendy had any home repairs or anything like that scheduled for today. Maybe he was impersonating someone else. Either that or he told her a story, lied to her and told her something that was intriguing enough to her to get her to let him in. Then they get to the kitchen and at some point, she realizes he's going to hurt her or kill her, and she tries to fight him off."

Josie went back into the other rooms and took a more careful look around. The living room was sparsely furnished with a single couch, coffee table and a large screen television on the wall. It was a room for one, but it gave off a relaxing, joyful vibe with bright contemporary artwork hanging from the walls and a small sculpture of a happy Buddha in the center of the coffee table. The dining room was more of a home office with a desk and several bookshelves. An open laptop sat in the center of the desk. To the left of it was a pile of typed pages. It was a manuscript, Josie realized. Its title was *The Mistaken* but the name of the author had been torn off. Perhaps she had used it for scrap paper? Behind it was a coffee mug with a pile of books on it beneath the words: *Drink Coffee. Read Books. Be happy.* Kaplan had been using the mug as a pen-holder. Perhaps she had been on the phone, needed to write something down quickly, snatched a pen from her cup, and scribbled on the first thing available, the title page of the manuscript.

To the right of the laptop was a wireless mouse. With her gloved hand, Josie nudged it and the screen lit up. She leaned in to see that Wendy had been reading her email the last time she sat here. All of it appeared to have to do with a trip she was planning to New York City in the next few weeks. The desk chair was several feet away from the desk. Had she been sitting there, planning a trip when the killer knocked on the door?

Josie tried to recreate it in her mind. Wendy, sitting at her desk, making plans to visit old friends in New York City. Answers the door to a man she doesn't know. Something he tells her or says to her compels her to invite him inside.

"Has anyone checked upstairs?" Josie asked.

Oaks poked his head out of the kitchen. "We cleared it, obviously but we haven't processed it yet as it looks like the struggle took place right in here."

Josie went upstairs and had a careful look around but Oaks was right, nothing looked disturbed. She doubted the killer would have had any reason to go upstairs. Back downstairs she waited near the front door while the evidence processing team descended on the kitchen. Her eyes went once more to the living room and then to the dining room/home office, eyes locking on the desk chair. It didn't have wheels, which made sense. The room was carpeted. Wheels wouldn't have traveled easily on the carpet unless Kaplan had had one of those plastic desk mats.

Oaks walked up beside her. "What's on your mind?"

Josie pointed to the chair. "That's bothering me."

"The office?"

"The chair. If she stood up and pushed her chair back, it wouldn't be that far across the room." Josie stepped back into the room, positioning herself between the chair and the desk. Oaks followed.

"You would only need this much room if you were trying to get under the desk."

"Maybe she dropped something," Oaks suggested.

Josie dropped to her hands and knees and peered beneath the desk. There, all the way in the back, against the wall, was a small mass of white paper. Josie wrestled her phone from inside her Tyvek suit and turned on her flashlight app, shining it onto the crumpled paper.

Oaks squatted and looked in over her shoulder. "See," he said. "She dropped a piece of paper."

Josie studied it a moment more, realizing quickly where she'd seen something like this before. "It's not a piece of paper," she said. "It's a chrysalis."

"What?" Oaks asked.

"A cocoon," Josie said. "It looks exactly like the one I saw inside Lucy Ross's desk at school. Oaks, she was here. Lucy was here. The killer brought her with him. That's why Wendy Kaplan let him in. She put Lucy in here while she and this guy talked in the kitchen."

"That means Lucy could have seen the struggle, the murder," Oaks said.

"Or maybe she just heard it and so she hid under here. When he was done, he came in here looking for her."

"He tossed the chair back," Oaks said. "Dragged her out from under there."

"But she left this," Josie said.

"You think a seven-year-old is smart enough to leave us a clue that she's alive?" Oaks asked.

"I think that this gave her something to focus on besides what was happening in the other room. She's doing whatever she can to mentally distance herself from whatever she's seeing and experiencing," Josie answered. "But if she's still alive, we've got a chance of bringing her home."

CHAPTER THIRTY

I woke up and she was gone. My nose felt cold. Without her in the bed, the blanket did little to keep me warm. I crept out of the bed, to the door which was cracked. The outer rooms were dark. Even the glow of the television had been extinguished. Then I saw her, just a shadow, moving through the rooms. I watched her for several minutes. She had some sort of sack and she was throwing things into it. Finally, she came to the door. "Oh good," she said. "You're awake."

I stared at her. She knelt down and touched my face. "Remember I told you we'd leave this place?"

"To go home?"

"Yes."

I nodded.

"We're leaving now. You have to be absolutely silent and still, do you understand?"

Again, I nodded. She scooped me up and carried me through the darkness. With infinite slowness, she turned the two locks on the big door that led outside and pulled it open a fraction at a time. The fresh air felt good against my skin. Anticipation tickled the back of my neck. I couldn't wait to leave.

Once she stepped out into the night, she ran, jostling me against her, her bare feet slapping against the ground. Lights shone from overhead, casting circles on the sidewalk in front of us as we fled. Her breath was a series of gasps. She held me so tightly against her that my ribs ached.

After several minutes, her pace slowed and her grip on me loosened. She looked behind us and when she turned to me once more, a smile split her face. It was the biggest smile I'd ever seen. "Do you hear that?" she whispered.

Confused, I glanced all around us, listening as hard as I could. There was nothing. "Hear what?" I asked.

"The silence," she said. "We made it." She set me down, holding onto my hands. "Come on. We have a long way to go still."

There was a lightness about her then, a sort of joy that seemed to radiate from her. I felt it envelop me. I started to skip along beside her to keep up and she didn't even tell me to stop.

It was only when a bright light appeared behind us that I felt tension in her hand. Then came a roaring noise, shattering the stillness of the night. She looked back and with a cry, turned and ran between two houses, dragging me along with her. I glanced back and saw two bright lights. They followed us, then stopped. A door slammed. Our bodies crashed against a fence. Then came his voice, sending ice down my spine.

"Just what the hell do you think you're doing? Get back in the fucking truck. Now."

"No," she gasped. "No."

Hands grabbed roughly at our fused form, dragging us backwards. I held tightly to her neck, not wanting to be separated from her.

"If you think I'm letting you take that kid, you're out of your damn mind. I told you, I'll kill you."

He pushed us into the cab of the truck and the door slamming sounded like the last thing I might ever hear.

CHAPTER THIRTY-ONE

Mettner was given the unenviable task of returning to the Ross home to let them know that Wendy Kaplan had been murdered. While Josie and Oaks were at the Kaplan scene, Gretchen called to say she had John Bausch, the bug expert, at the Denton PD headquarters.

"Do the preliminary stuff," Josie instructed her. "I'm on my way."

She hung up and looked at Oaks. "My team has John Bausch. But before I leave, I think we need to take a much closer look at the list that was made of people closest to Amy and Colin. Specifically, Amy."

"You're thinking what I'm thinking then," Oaks said.

"That this guy is using people close to Amy to make contact so he can't be traced on any phone he purchases himself?"

"Right," Oaks said. "With the technology available to us today, we'd be able to pinpoint his location quickly and with pretty good accuracy if he called on his own phone. Once we had the number, we'd be able to go through the phone providers to track the location of the phone. It would have led us to Lucy before this thing ever got off the ground."

"But if he goes to the homes of people close to the Ross family and uses their phones, he can leave without being tracked."

"Right," Oaks agreed. "Clever, really."

"Yes. But this means that he has a list just like we do. We have to figure out who's next on that list before he tries to make contact with Amy again."

"Already on it," Oaks said.

On the way to police headquarters, Josie kept thinking about the chrysalis Lucy had left behind at Wendy's house. The very thought that the girl might still be alive was enough to make her heart soar. But then her hopes were immediately smashed back to earth by the fear that the kidnapper would kill her before they had a chance to beat him at his own wicked game. Because it was a game of some sort, and he was winning.

The police headquarters building came into view, surrounded by press vehicles. It was a historic three-story building which used to be the town hall but had been converted to the police station sixty-five years ago. It was huge and gray, with ornate molding over its many double-casement arched windows and an old bell tower at one corner. Josie parked in the municipal lot around the back to avoid the reporters stationed out front. She made her way to the second floor, past the great room where the detectives' desks were, and down a long hallway to the door of one of the interview rooms. She stood outside and texted Gretchen that she had arrived.

A moment later, the door opened. Gretchen waved her in, but once through the doorway, Josie froze in her tracks. At the table sat a slightly overweight man, easily in his sixties, with long gray hair tied into a ponytail at the nape of his neck and a thin gray beard. He smiled at her benignly. "This is Detective Josie Quinn," Gretchen said to the man. To Josie, she said, "This is Mr. John Bausch."

Josie stared at him a moment longer, dumbfounded, before she managed the words, "I'm sorry, sir. I need to speak with Detective Palmer in private for a moment."

Without listening to his response, Josie turned on her heel and walked out. Gretchen followed her to the viewing room a few doors down, where they were able to see the man in the interview room over CCTV.

Gretchen said. "What's wrong?"

Josie pointed to the screen. "That is not John Bausch."

Perplexed, Gretchen raised an eyebrow. "Yes, it is. According to his driver's license, it is."

Josie looked at him once more. "Then that's not the man who visited Lucy's school. Did the school send over the photos that Violet Young took the day he was at the school? We sent them a warrant."

"Wait here," Gretchen said. "I'll run it down."

While she waited, Josie watched the man in the interview room. He sat calmly, hands folded over his stomach, whistling softly. Completely relaxed.

Something was very wrong.

"You were right," Gretchen said when she returned. She handed Josie her phone, which displayed one of the photographs of the young man claiming to be John Bausch that Violet Young had taken.

Josie pointed to the CCTV screen. "That's the real John Bausch, obviously, if he showed you ID, but he didn't give a presentation at Denton West Elementary."

"But he said he did presentations here in Denton," Gretchen replied.

Josie handed Gretchen her phone back. "That's what he said? Presentations? As in more than one?"

Picking up immediately on what Josie was getting at, Gretchen said, "How many elementary schools are in Denton?"

"Five," Josie answered, "including the Catholic school."

"But he knows he's here because of Lucy Ross. He knows she's missing. He says he doesn't remember her, but he remembers doing a presentation at her school."

"Did he specifically say Denton West?"

"Well, no," Gretchen said. "He said he was presenting at a bunch of schools in Denton around that time."

They returned to the interview room. Gretchen immediately launched into her questions. "Mr. Bausch, do you remember specifically the names of all the elementary schools you visited here in Denton?"

Bausch smiled. "Detective," he said. "I visit hundreds of schools a year. I don't remember all their names. My wife keeps the schedule. She gives me an address, I type it into the GPS and I go. Like I said, I was here in Denton and visited a bunch of schools, but that was a couple of months ago. I don't remember all the specifics."

Josie said, "You told Detective Palmer you had visited many of the Denton schools. Did any of them cancel?"

He scratched his head. "Come to think of it, I think one of 'em did. But I had a morning booking here in Denton that day and an afternoon booking in Bellewood, about forty miles from here, so I just went to the one in Bellewood and didn't give it much thought. Like I said, my wife does all the scheduling. She'll be happy to talk to you about it. Give you any records you need."

Gretchen gave Josie a nod, pressed some buttons on her phone, and slipped out the door. Josie knew she was off to call Bausch's wife for whatever records she had. Josie took out her phone and found the photos Gretchen had just texted her of the man who had gone to Lucy's school posing as John Bausch. Turning the phone toward John Bausch, she asked, "Do you recognize this man?"

Bausch studied the phone for a moment. Josie scrolled through several of the shots, but Bausch shook his head. "Never saw him," he said.

"You don't have any assistants or helpers?" Josie asked. "Any employees?"

"No, just me and my wife. Never had any helpers. Never needed any. Don't make enough to hire employees."

"How about a son?" Josie asked. "Someone you plan to pass the business along to when you pass?"

"No," Bausch answered. "No sons. I have a son-in-law but he's in the military. Stationed in Texas about now. Been there for about a year, I think. That ain't him in those pictures anyway. He's got to keep his hair high and tight to be in the marines. Still, I'm guessing you'll want his name and all that, too."

Josie smiled. "Yes, please."

CHAPTER THIRTY-TWO

Oaks arrived at police headquarters a half hour later, looking more exhausted than ever. Large bags drooped under his eyes. Creases covered his suit. Josie pulled him into the first-floor conference room and briefed him on the John Bausch situation. Swiping a hand over the gray stubble on his chin, Oaks sighed. "Whoever this guy is, he's been planning this for a while."

"I think we should run with this," Josie said. "Release his photo to the press as a person of interest. We've only got him in profile, but it might be worth it. Violet Young saw him up close. We could have her work with a composite artist."

"I'll get one over to the school to talk with her. In the meantime, we'll use what we've got. We'll crop out the kids and put something together," Oaks agreed.

"That brings me to my next concern," Josie said.

"Which is what?"

"This guy has Lucy. We know she's alive—or at least she was earlier today when the kidnapper called from Wendy Kaplan's phone. Lucy's photo has been all over this city, on the television, on social media. The volunteers even had fliers made and tacked them up all over the place."

Oaks nodded as Josie spoke. He leaned a hip against the conference room table and crossed his arms over his chest. "You want to know where he's keeping her?"

"If he was keeping her at a hotel or motel, someone would have seen her by now."

"But not everyone would report it," Oaks pointed out. "Especially in some of the less savory establishments. Do you have some people who can shake down those places and see if they can turn up anything?"

"Yes," Josie said. "I also think we should have some teams look at hunting cabins in the area. The outskirts of Denton are pretty rural. Lots of cabins in remote areas that are not being used this time of year. If I were trying to stay off the radar and hide a little girl whose face was plastered everywhere, I'd think about finding someone's shuttered hunting cabin or camping out in the woods somewhere. I can ask the state police and sheriff's office to help check them out. County-wide."

"I can have some of my people help with that. We should check any campsites as well," Oaks said.

The sound of the door creaking open got their attention. Mettner poked his head in. "Boss," he said.

"Josie," she corrected, knowing it would do no good.

"We figured out who the tweed jacket guy is—he's a psychologist in private practice here in Denton."

"Did anyone interview him?" Josie asked.

"I talked to him. He said he came to offer his services to anyone who might need them, free of charge."

"Does he have an alibi for the time that Lucy went missing?"

Mettner scratched his temple. "No. Says he was home alone Sunday, reading."

Josie and Oaks looked at one another.

Mettner said, "You want me to bring him in?"

"Not yet," Josie said.

"You want eyes on him?"

Oaks said, "We're already running pretty thin. Tell you what—I'll have my team do a background check on him. See if they can turn up any red flags. You'll see if you can find any connection between him and the Ross family."

"You got it," Mettner said.

"I'll ask Amy and Colin about him. What's his name, Mett?" Josie asked.

"Bryce Graham. I'll text you guys my notes on him with his address and all that."

"Thanks, Mett," Josie said. Once he left, she turned back to Oaks. "Did your team get anywhere with any of the neighbors in Wendy Kaplan's development?" Josie asked.

Oaks shook his head. "Nothing of any substance. One woman thinks she remembers seeing a white pickup truck driving around the development earlier today but nothing more than that. But we have no way of knowing whether that's related to Wendy Kaplan's murder or not. It could have been anyone. Without a make, model or license plate, that lead is a dead end. None of those people had exterior cameras."

"I'm not surprised," Josie said.

Oaks raised a brow. "I am. Where I come from, everyone has a camera outside of their house."

"Well in Denton, the crime rate is pretty low, believe it or not. People don't see the need for them."

Oaks still looked baffled but continued on with his briefing. "We've got what we believe is the killer's DNA both under Kaplan's fingernails and on one of the broken pieces of ceramic mug. There's a chance that Kaplan wounded him during the struggle."

"You've got his blood?"

Oaks nodded. "We believe so. We'll test it along with the skin under Kaplan's nails and compare it to the skin found under Jaclyn Underwood's fingernails."

"But even if it matches and you can put him at both crime scenes, you already said there wasn't a hit on the DNA found under Jaclyn's nails. So that doesn't help us find this guy."

"True," Oaks conceded. "It will only help the district attorney if we catch this bastard and he gets prosecuted."

"Then we keep working every angle," Josie said.

"There's something I need you to do now though."

"What's that?" Josie asked.

"I need you to talk to Mrs. Ross again. The list we talked about earlier?"

"Of people who are close to her?"

"Yes, that's the one. There's no one else on it."

"What?" Josie said.

"The nanny and Kaplan were the only people she saw regularly, she claims."

"Two people?" Josie said.

Oaks said, "It's not that big a stretch given what we already know about her. Every person we've talked to has said the same things: she's quiet, keeps to herself. Isolated. Distracted."

"I know, that's true, but the kidnapper is going to target someone else to make contact with the Ross parents, and we need to figure out who that person is ahead of time so we don't have another murder on our hands."

"I think you're our best bet to get it out of her," Oaks said. "In the meantime, I'm going to put some units on the mothers you and Mettner interviewed. I know they told you that she wasn't close with them, but it's all we've got."

"Good call," Josie said.

"I'll also have my team double back on Amy's background check to see if there's anything we missed. Maybe dig deeper."

"Great," Josie said. "I'll head over to the Ross house."

Once outside, she took her phone out and texted Trinity: *Anything yet?*

The response came back within seconds. *I'm working on it. I'll let you know as soon as I have something.*

CHAPTER THIRTY-THREE

Amy sat in her backyard on a chair she'd pulled over next to Lucy's playhouse. In her arms she held a stuffed unicorn that Josie had previously seen in Lucy's bed. Amy's face was swollen, blotchy and tear-stained. As Josie approached, she said, "They told me about Wendy."

"I'm sorry," Josie said. "Truly sorry."

"We weren't even that close," Amy said, her voice raspy.

"But you had lunch a couple of times a week, didn't you?"

Amy nodded, squeezing the unicorn more tightly to her chest. "Wendy was a transplant like me. Divorced. She was well past the point of having children and had no desire to date or marry again. She was very insular. Like me, I guess."

"She didn't have many friends here?" Josie prompted.

"No. Not many."

"What did you talk about at lunch?" Josie asked.

"Things we saw on the news, projects she was working on, books. I talked about Lucy a lot. Wendy didn't seem to mind even though she didn't have her own children. She was kind to me."

Amy squeezed her eyes closed against the fresh wave of tears that came. "I can't believe this is happening."

"Where's Colin?" Josie asked.

"I don't know," Amy said. "Upstairs, probably."

"I need to talk to both of you."

From the back door, Colin's voice sounded. "I'm right here. Did you find something? What's going on?"

As he stepped into the yard, Amy stood up from her chair, squeezing the unicorn more tightly against her chest. "What is it?"

"We believe that Lucy was with the kidnapper at Wendy's house."

"What?" Colin said. "You think—you think she saw what happened to Wendy?"

"Does this mean she's alive?" Amy asked.

Josie held up a hand. "We don't believe she witnessed Wendy's murder although she likely heard it. We found a paper chrysalis under Wendy's desk."

The lines of Colin's face deepened in confusion. "What? What are you talking about?"

Amy made a *tsk* sound at her husband. "You really don't pay attention at all, do you? You really don't know what a chrysalis is?"

He glowered at his wife. "Why the hell would I know what that is? What's this got to do with our daughter?"

Amy's voice rose to a shout. Her hands squeezed the unicorn's head. "It's a cocoon, Colin. You know, the kind that caterpillars make before they turn into butterflies. You remember that your daughter is obsessed with butterflies, don't you? Or is that too much for you to hold in your head while you're traipsing all over the globe overcharging sick people for cancer medication?"

Colin stepped back as though he'd been slapped. Even Josie was momentarily stunned. Amy's comments were spiteful, and delivered with more force than Josie had ever seen from her previously.

Before Colin could snap back at his wife, Josie took out her phone and swiped to the photo one of Oaks's crime scene techs had forwarded her. "It's a cocoon. We believe that Lucy tore a piece of paper from a manuscript on Wendy's desk and used it to make this." She held the phone out and both parents moved closer to look at it.

Amy gasped. "She's alive. Oh my God, our baby is alive." She took one hand from the stuffed unicorn and clamped it over Colin's forearm.

"How do you know Lucy made this?" Colin asked. "How do you even know what it is? What if Wendy tore a piece of paper, crumpled it up and tossed it onto the floor?"

"That is Lucy's!" Amy said firmly.

Josie said, "I found the same thing in her desk at school. I believe that Lucy made this."

"To let us know she's still alive?" Amy asked hopefully.

"Maybe."

"Jesus," Colin said, beginning to pace. "This is a nightmare."

Amy turned toward him. "How can you say that? Our daughter is alive. She's alive! We have a chance to get her back safely."

Colin stopped moving and gestured toward Josie's phone. "How long ago did you find that? A few hours? He could have killed her by now."

"No!" Amy shrieked. "Don't say that."

Colin's eyes glistened with tears. "You need to prepare yourself, Ame. The person who has her—he's a killer. He killed Jaclyn and Wendy like it was nothing to him. What's to stop him from killing Lucy?"

"Us," Josie interjected.

Both parents froze and turned their heads toward her. Josie went on, "The most recent information we have indicates that Lucy is still alive. We are operating as though she is and we're going to do everything we can to find her as quickly as possible. The best thing that you two can do for Lucy is stay calm and answer any questions we have for you."

Colin rolled his eyes, drawing a glare from his wife. "Questions and more questions. What now?"

Ignoring his barbs, Josie asked, "Do either of you know a man named Bryce Graham?"

"No," Colin said. "Never heard of him."

"Who is he?" Amy asked.

"A local psychologist. He was at the search the other day at the park. He offered his services to many of the volunteers. Free of charge. We were just wondering if you knew him personally."

"No," Amy and Colin said in unison. Then Amy asked, "You think he took Lucy?"

"No, not even close," Josie said. "He just stood out to us when we were reviewing all the search footage because he was wearing a suit."

"There has to be more to it than that," Colin said. "Or you wouldn't be asking us about him."

"Evidently he has no alibi for the time Lucy was taken."

Amy gasped. "But… a psychologist? What would he want with Lucy?"

Josie held up a hand. "I didn't say he's a suspect. I just said he has no alibi. We have no reason to believe he had any involvement in Lucy's abduction. In fact, we're looking at someone else right now." She took out her phone again and pulled up the photos of the man who had impersonated John Bausch at Lucy's school. She handed her phone to Amy, who held it while Colin looked over her shoulder. "There are three more photos," Josie told them. "Swipe to the left. Tell me if you recognize the man in the photos."

Amy and Colin looked at each photo carefully. Colin's face remained blank. Horizontal lines creased Amy's forehead. "I don't know him. Who is he?" she asked.

"You've never seen him?"

Amy handed the phone back. "No. I don't think so. I mean I can't see his face, only his profile, but he doesn't look familiar." She turned to her husband. "Do you recognize him?"

Colin shook his head. "I've never seen the guy before."

"Who is he?" Amy asked. "Do you think he's the person who took Lucy?"

"The man in the photos visited Lucy's school," Josie explained. "He gave a presentation on bugs."

"Oh," Amy said. "The bug expert. I remember Lucy talking about him. He brought a butterfly, of course, and a bunch of other insects. She loved the stick bug."

Colin said, "I do remember her talking about that. Do you think he had something to do with her disappearance?"

"We're looking into it," Josie said. "The school had booked a man named John Bausch. The real John Bausch is a man in his sixties, but someone contacted his office and canceled the presentation. Then this guy showed up at Lucy's school and gave a presentation."

"What are you saying?" Colin said, tension drawing his shoulders upward.

"I'm saying that this man impersonated the real John Bausch, which in itself is a red flag. He would have met Lucy. She would have shown great interest in his presentation, I'm sure."

"She did," Amy croaked. "She said he was the best visitor they ever had."

"And neither of you remember seeing him after that? Lucy never pointed him out to you anywhere? You never ran into him?"

"No," Amy said. "She didn't. I'm sure she would have if she'd seen him."

Colin added, "I only remember her telling me about the school visit. She never mentioned him after that."

Josie put her phone away. "We're dealing with a two-month period here. Is it possible that Lucy could have seen him or been around him without either of you knowing it?"

Colin remained silent. Josie guessed it was because he wasn't home often enough or long enough to have taken Lucy places on his own.

Amy took a long moment to think about it. "Well, I guess when she was out with Jaclyn. I'm sure I would remember if she'd been talking to a strange man while we were out somewhere."

"Where did you take Lucy in the last two months?"

Colin stared at his wife expectantly.

Amy said, "I already told you this. School, the park—that's it. We had a routine. We don't live terribly exciting lives."

"Did you take her grocery shopping with you?"

"Well, sure, sometimes."

"Ever go to the mall?"

"Yes, a couple of times. They have that new arcade place—you can eat there and play in the arcade. One of her friends had a birthday party there several months ago and then I took her there again more recently—just the two of us. But Lucy is only seven. I don't let her out of my sight when we go out."

Josie thought of the man Ingrid Saylor had seen at that party, helping Lucy at the skee-ball machine while Amy got change. "Not even for a few minutes?"

"No, I mean, not really."

"Can you get me approximate dates? When you went to the mall? Since that birthday party?"

"I guess so. I can try. If I look at my bank statements—or you can. We gave the FBI access to all of our accounts. I have a debit card that draws right from the bank account Colin set up for me. I usually take out a certain amount of cash each week, but I do sometimes use it as a credit card instead of taking out cash, so the arcade would probably be on there."

"What about the grocery store? Do you use the card there or cash?"

Amy shrugged. "It depends. Why? What are you thinking?"

"It's a long shot," Josie said. "Most places don't keep their CCTV footage very long, but I might have my team ask for footage from the arcade and the grocery store for the dates you were there with Lucy to see if this guy was following you."

Colin said, "I'll go get the bank statements. I can make a list of places where Amy used the card in the last two months."

"Thank you," Josie said.

Once he was back inside, Amy plopped back into her chair. "Do you think this man was stalking us? All this time? Watching Lucy?"

Josie touched her stomach as a wave of nausea rushed over her. Heat stung her face. She hoped she wouldn't throw up in front of Amy. "I don't know," she said, willing the feeling to pass. "But I do think it's extremely likely. This kidnapping was well-planned and executed without a single mistake. If the kidnapper had made one, we would have found something by now, but we haven't."

Amy hugged the stuffed unicorn to her chest. "It's so creepy. So disturbing. I can't believe this. This—this monster was stalking my baby all this time and I didn't even know it. What kind of mother doesn't notice someone stalking her seven-year-old?"

Josie sucked in several deep breaths and the nausea began to recede. Again, questions of whether or not a baby—her very own baby—was growing inside her crowded her mind, but she pushed them aside. She had to focus on the case. She thought of what Oaks had said to her at the station.

"Amy," Josie said. "I need you to listen to me very carefully. This man who has Lucy is targeting people close to you in order to make contact with you."

"He's killing them to get to me?" Amy said.

"He's using their phones so that we can't trace him so long as he leaves the scene before we get there, and he's killing them so they can't identify him—but also, I think, because it will hurt you. This whole time we've been looking more closely at Colin, but Colin had less contact with Jaclyn than you, and I'm guessing he barely knew Wendy."

"He only met her once or twice," Amy agreed.

"What we need to know is, who will he target next?"

Amy stared up at her as though waiting for her to answer her own question.

Josie said, "Amy, do you understand what I'm asking? I need to know who is next."

"I don't—I can't—there isn't anyone."

"You saw Jaclyn almost daily. You had lunch with Wendy a couple of times a week. Who else is there in your life whom you have regular contact with?"

"No one," Amy said. "Not in a meaningful way. I see the same cashier at the grocery store most times I'm there. We have the same mailman."

"You know that's not what I mean."

"Detective Quinn—"

"Josie, please."

"Josie, I don't have many friends. None really. Not anymore. Wendy was my friend. That was it. Jaclyn helped me with Lucy. I'm a mother. That's what I do."

"Who would you call if you had a problem? Needed to vent?" Josie asked.

"My husband."

Josie sighed. "I'm pretty sure Colin will stay out of harm's way. He'll be here with us until this is over. But Amy, I really need you to think carefully about this because this guy is not going to stop. He's made a demand now—a million dollars—but he didn't tell you where to bring it to him or when which means he needs to get in touch with you again. He's going to use someone to do that. Who?"

"I don't know," Amy insisted. "I'm telling you, there's no one else."

"What about old friends? Someone from New York City or from your childhood?"

"No," Amy said. "I didn't keep in touch with anyone. I'm telling you, there is no one else. I only ever had my mother and she died years ago. I've never been good at making friends. People are—they intimidate me, make me nervous. I have my husband and my daughter. That's all I've got left."

CHAPTER THIRTY-FOUR

Noah was seated at his desk in the great room at Denton's police department when Josie arrived later that afternoon ahead of the joint news conference planned by Special Agent Oaks and Chief Chitwood. Someone had wheeled over another desk chair and his casted leg was propped on its seat. "Hey," he said as Josie walked over and squeezed his shoulder. "You here for the press conference?"

"Yeah," she said. "How'd you get here?"

"One of the Feds gave me a ride from their mobile command."

"They keeping you busy?"

"Yeah, it's not bad. They got a composite from Violet Young."

"Let me see," Josie said.

With a few clicks of his mouse, the artist's rendering of the man who had given the bug presentation in Violet Young's class flashed across the screen. "You recognize him?" Noah asked.

Josie frowned. "No."

"Well, they'll use it in the press conference. They've got a tip line ready. Hopefully someone out there will remember seeing him and know where to find him based on the drawing and the photo of him in profile. Are the parents here?"

"Downstairs," Josie said. "Mett put them in the conference room until the press conference starts. They'll be on camera but Oaks isn't having them speak."

"How are they holding up?"

"Better now that they know Lucy was alive as of earlier today."

"Oaks isn't worried about the kidnapper calling while they're here?" Noah asked.

"The agents who monitor their phones are down there, too," Josie explained. "But I doubt this guy is going to do two murders in a day and after this press conference, he's going to know we're onto him."

Gretchen bustled into the room with a stack of papers in her arms. "I got warrants for the grocery store and the arcade at the mall. Just got them signed. If they've got footage, it's going to be a lot to go through."

Noah raised a hand. "I'm happy to stay here at my desk and help with that."

"Great," Gretchen said. "By the way, the real John Bausch's son-in-law checks out."

"No surprise there," Josie said.

Mettner came in and grabbed the remote control for the television hanging on the wall in the corner of the room, flipping it on. The screen flickered to life, already tuned to WYEP, which was broadcasting the scene in Denton's municipal parking lot below. There were too many reporters to have it indoors. The four of them watched as Special Agent Oaks walked up to a podium covered in microphones, followed by Chief Chitwood and Colin and Amy. The parents clung to one another, looking frightened and lost.

"Shouldn't you be down there?" Noah asked Josie. "Oaks has you on Amy, right?"

Josie motioned to her face, which still bore dark bruising around her eyes. "Chitwood doesn't want me out there looking like this. It would be a distraction, he said."

Gretchen made a phone call and a few moments later, a couple of uniformed officers came up to get her warrants for footage from the places Amy had visited with Lucy in the last two months so they could be served as soon as possible.

The room fell silent as the press conference started. Oaks gave a brief update, sharing the photos and composite of the bug expert impersonator and asking the public for help. He took questions for a very short amount of time and then ended the press conference. Josie knew that Oaks had chosen not to have either parent speak because he didn't want to give the kidnapper what he wanted, which was to see the parents suffer. At the same time, it had been important for both of them to be present and seen on camera so the public would be more inclined to help. It had taken some convincing to get Amy on camera. Ultimately, since she didn't have to speak, she had relented.

"Well," Noah said. "Hopefully the tip line will be ringing off the hook."

"The FBI is manning the tip line," Gretchen said. "I say we all go home and get some sleep and come back at this tomorrow well-rested."

"You don't have to tell me twice," said Noah.

CHAPTER THIRTY-FIVE

At home, Josie left Noah in the kitchen with Misty, who had cooked up a large amount of eggplant parmesan—far more than necessary to feed three adults and little Harris. The smell followed Josie to the living room, making her feel sick instead of hungry. She swallowed down bile and dialed Trinity. "Tell me you have something," she said when her sister answered.

Trinity sighed. "I've got competition, is what I've got. The FBI just descended on this place like there was some damn national emergency."

"They do that sometimes."

"Well, I found the house that used to belong to a Dorothy Walsh. It was sold seventeen years ago by Renita Walsh. I couldn't get my hands on the old deeds, but it appears as though Renita got the house after the mother died and lived there for a few years before moving on. I haven't been able to find any Renita Walsh—not here, anyway. I did find information for a woman called Renita Desilva who is about the right age and now lives in Binghamton, New York. I have a call out to her but no response yet. There's one neighbor, elderly, who remembers them. The story matches up: mom and sister died in a car accident. Renita stayed in the house for a few years and then sold it to a young family."

"That's it? Did she remember Amy? Did she have anything to say about her?"

"That she was a nice girl. Very quiet."

Josie blew out a breath. "Well that just sends up all kinds of red flags, doesn't it?"

Trinity laughed. "I'm not done. Tomorrow I'm going to go over to the high school and see if I can get some old yearbooks. The elderly neighbor doesn't remember Amy having any boyfriends, but if the abusive relationship that Amy mentioned was really 'kid stuff' then maybe there will be something in the yearbooks. Then I'll go to the local library and search their database for old news stories in the *Fulton Daily News*. See if any of the Walsh ladies are mentioned there. Then if I haven't heard from Renita Desilva, I'll head down to Binghamton and make a house call."

"Great," Josie said. "Thanks. I appreciate this." Her finger hovered over the End Call icon. Then Trinity's voice came again. "Josie?"

Josie pressed the phone back to her ear. "Yes?"

"You okay? You don't sound like yourself lately."

"I'm fine," Josie lied, pressing a hand over her belly.

"Sure you are," Trinity said skeptically.

"Really," Josie said. "I am."

"I'll be the judge of that when I see you. I just need a couple more days. Two, tops."

*

The next morning, Josie and Noah reported to the mobile command tent. Gretchen's warrants had turned up some video footage from various places Amy had gone with Lucy in the weeks before Lucy's kidnapping. Josie sat beside Noah as he began reviewing the footage. "We'll start with this," Noah said. "It's from the arcade. According to the list that Colin made for us from their bank and credit card statements, Amy took Lucy there three weeks ago just to play some games."

"Let's have a look then," Josie said.

Noah pulled up the footage from the arcade, which had multiple cameras, each one displayed in a box on the screen.

"This is going to take forever," Noah groused.

"Not necessarily," Josie said. "You watch the ones on the left, and I'll watch the ones on the right."

Fifteen minutes later, Josie said, "Stop. Right there. That camera." She pointed to one of the squares on the right side of the screen. "Can you pull that one up? Just that one?"

Noah clicked a few times and the small square filled the screen. It was an angled, slightly overhead shot of several games in the corner of the arcade. One featured a large screen and in front of it, on the floor, several panels which lit up in different colors. Josie leaned in and saw that the name of the game was *Dance Off*. Computerized figures moved on the screen and in front of it, using the panels beneath her feet, a small blonde girl tried to match the figures move for move.

"That's Lucy Ross, isn't it?" Noah said.

"I think so," Josie said.

"Where's Amy?"

Josie searched the rest of the frame. In the lower, left corner stood a woman with a cell phone pressed to her ear, her back turned toward Lucy. "There," Josie said. "I think that's her."

They had to wait several seconds for the woman to turn around so they could see her face. "That's definitely her," Noah said, pausing the footage and zooming in.

"Yes," Josie agreed.

He zoomed back out and restarted the footage. Amy took a glance at Lucy, who was jumping and dancing on the platform of the *Dance Off* game. Then she turned away once more. "Who do you think she's talking to?" Noah asked.

"My money's on her husband. She doesn't have anyone else in her life—that we know of."

A few seconds later, another figure entered the frame, walking up behind Lucy.

"Look at this guy," Noah murmured.

It was a man dressed in jeans, boots and a sweatshirt with a ballcap pulled low over his face. From under the back of the cap, Josie could see brown hair. "It's hard to say, but I think he looks just like the guy from Lucy's school. The bug expert impersonator."

"Let me see if I can pull some stills," Noah said.

"Let's watch this first. We should also check the other cameras to see if we can get a clearer shot of his face when he was coming in and leaving."

Noah let the footage play. The man watched Lucy for a few seconds. Then suddenly, she turned, looked up at him and beamed. She moved off the platform, arms raised as though to hug him, but he stepped away from her and motioned with one hand toward her mother.

"My God," Josie said. "She already knew him."

"Quite well," Noah said. "She looks like she was about to run into his arms."

But on the screen, Lucy froze, then nodded and returned to her game, this time dancing with much less enthusiasm.

"He's already done a lot of work with her by now," Josie noted. "All he had to do was give her a small signal—just a little hand movement in Amy's direction—and she knew to act like she didn't know him. She knew not to alert her mother."

"This is scary," Noah said.

The man let her play for a few more seconds, every so often turning his head slightly to check on where Amy stood. Then he joined Lucy on the platform. They danced together for a few moments—only their backs visible on the camera. Lucy's movements became more enthusiastic. When fireworks exploded across the screen, the two of them high-fived. Then the man glanced in Amy's direction again, took something from his pocket and handed it to Lucy. He leaned down and whispered in her ear before rushing off.

"What's scary is knowing how much work it must have taken for him to gain her trust and have her this well-trained without any adult in her life knowing about it," Josie said. Without even realizing it, her hand went to her stomach.

On the screen, Amy walked toward the *Dance Off* game, no longer on the phone but now searching through her purse for something. She never even saw the man.

"Pause it," Josie said. "What did he give her?"

Noah took a moment to turn the footage back and try to get the best view of the object before zooming in. It was grainy but Josie was fairly certain by the size and red color that it was the ladybug keychain that Lucy had in her butterfly backpack when she went missing.

"That's the keychain," Noah said, as if reading her mind.

"Yes. Keep going."

He zoomed back out and pressed play once more. Lucy watched as her mother walked toward her, clutching the small object to her chest. As Amy came within a few steps of the *Dance Off* game, Lucy turned away from her and thrust the keychain into her pants pocket. Amy reached her and held out a hand, which Lucy took, skip-walking beside her mother as they walked out of the frame.

"Jesus," Josie said.

Noah pulled up the rest of the footage, searching for the man. They found him arriving shortly after Amy and Lucy, lingering at one of the change machines without using it, following Lucy until she started playing *Dance Off*, and then leaving immediately after the interaction.

"He doesn't appear on camera at any angle where you can see his face well—especially with that hat," Noah said.

"Of course he doesn't. He knew what he was doing. Pull as many stills as you can get," Josie said. "Then let's look at the other footage."

"This is unbelievable," Noah said. He gestured toward the screen where he had paused the video just as the man walked up to Lucy at the *Dance Off* game. "Amy is right there. Right there and she doesn't see this guy."

"She doesn't register him," Josie clarified. "Because he blends in. He's not a threat. She never actually sees him talking to Lucy, and her mind is elsewhere. Just like at the playground on the day that Lucy disappeared. She was in clear view of everyone. No one registered her presence. Every one of us goes through our days looking straight at people and things but not really taking them in."

"How many times do you think he did this?"

"A lot. Enough that she saw him as a friend. Someone she wanted to run to; someone she was excited to see."

"Most of the time had to be at the park, don't you think? While she was with the nanny?"

"Yes, and one of the other mothers said that Jaclyn was often on her phone."

"And there are no cameras at the park," Noah said. "And the carousel is there. This guy got to her without anyone ever knowing."

Josie thought about it, about all the planning that went into it. "The nanny had a mystery guest—a woman—staying with her at some point. That mystery woman's prints were found in Lucy's room."

"So we know she was involved," Noah said. "By the way, Oaks's team did manage to track down one of Jaclyn's friends who said she thought someone was staying with her for a while but never met the girl. That friend had asked Jaclyn about it, and Jaclyn said she was just helping someone out that she had met on campus. Said the girl was between apartments. That was five or six months ago."

"So the mystery woman befriended Jaclyn, manipulated her, got Jaclyn to let her stay there for a while and managed to avoid meeting any of Jaclyn friends. Whoever she is, she's good," Josie remarked.

"Yeah," Noah agreed. "Her job was to gain insight into Lucy and her family."

"Right—their routines and dynamics, their schedule. Lucy's likes and dislikes."

"The mystery woman reports back to this guy. Tells him, among other things, that Lucy is obsessed with butterflies," Noah said, picking up her line of thought.

"He sees an opportunity to make contact with her at her school by impersonating the bug expert."

"How did he know Bausch was going to Denton West in the first place?" Noah asked.

"It was on the school website," Josie said. "The school schedule, including all visitors and special events, is posted there. The public one, not the private one. All he had to do was pull up the site and he would have seen that Bausch was scheduled to come give a presentation there."

"And either he or his female accomplice could have called the real John Bausch and pretended to be from Denton West, tell him they had to cancel. Wow. This guy is ballsy as hell," Noah said.

"Yes," Josie said. "Impersonating Bausch was probably the most ballsy thing he did because he really put himself out in the open, made himself vulnerable. They must have been planning this for a very long time. He might have seen that as his best and maybe only opportunity to gain Lucy's trust."

"Cause once she meets him in a safe environment—school—she feels she can trust him."

"Right. Then when he approaches her outside of school, she already sees him as trustworthy."

"Then he starts approaching her every chance he gets."

"Building the rapport, the friendship."

"But what does he say to her to get her to go with him?" Noah asked.

Josie thought of Lucy's drawings: herself and a man in a tan suit—like the one the kidnapper had worn to her school when he impersonated John Bausch—both with butterfly nets, chasing the colorful insects. "He's going to take her to chase butterflies," Josie said.

"What? That's absurd."

"No, it's not," Josie said. "Amy told me they took Lucy to the butterfly room at the Academy of Natural Sciences in Philadelphia and that Lucy said it was the best day of her life. The kidnapper would have known about her obsession with butterflies. He would have promised her something magical. Something too magical to resist."

"What? Like some magical butterfly fairy land or something?" Noah asked. "Do you hear yourself?"

"Lucy is seven. Don't you remember being seven?"

"I barely remember yesterday," Noah complained.

"She's just a child, Noah," Josie said. "She has a big imagination, a passion for butterflies, and from everything I've gathered, she's both lonely and a people-pleaser. It would be easy for this guy to gain her trust. He paid her special attention. He was her secret friend. She was clearly enamored of him by the way she acted when she saw him. She would have wanted to make him happy. So she did what he said and kept him a secret from her mother."

"From all the adults in her life."

"Yes," Josie agreed. "He probably promised to take her somewhere. Somewhere like the butterfly room at the Academy of Natural Sciences—only he probably made it sound much bigger and more exciting. Not somewhere real because he never intended to take her there. He just wanted to promise her something that would fulfill her seven-year-old heart's desire. Something that would make her leave with him even though her parents were right there."

"You think he told her he'd bring her back?"

"Of course he did," Josie said. "He probably told her they'd go off on their adventure and she'd be back in her own bed that night. Everything this guy has done has been about manipulation."

"But why?" Noah asked. "Why didn't he just abduct her? All this preparation—for what? I mean if you're right, and this guy has a female accomplice who was getting in tight with the nanny six months ago, long before he went to Lucy's school, that's a lot of preparation for an abduction. Unnecessary preparation. Especially if all he wants is ransom. If the nanny was on her phone whenever she took Lucy to the playground, he could have taken her from there at any time. Why is he doing all this?"

"He's playing a game," Josie said, her mind swirling. "This isn't about the ransom at all. Not really."

"Then what's it about?" Noah asked.

"I don't know yet, but I need to make a phone call."

CHAPTER THIRTY-SIX

He didn't kill her. But he hurt her worse than he ever had before. For a long time, she lay on the bed, while I sat on the floor, praying for her to move. I licked my fingers and used them to try to get some of the blood off her face, but it was thick and flaky. It smeared and got into her hair and onto the pillow. We only had one pillowcase and he hardly ever let her wash it. I knew she would be mad if I got it dirty, so I stopped trying to clean her. It felt like my whole life before she talked to me again.

One of her hands reached out. I took it. "Are you going to wake up now?"

She nodded weakly.

"Can we go home?"

"Not yet."

"Did I do something wrong?"

Her eyelids fluttered. "No, of course not. This isn't your fault. I need you to remember that. None of this is your fault." Her hand squeezed mine. "I need to rest now, okay?"

I nodded, even though her eyes were already closed again. Her nose whistled as she slept. When she went limp, her grip loosened, and I took my hand back. I went back to the windowsill and stared outside. The silver woman was back in her garden again. Maybe she could take us home. I raised my hand to tap the window, but I couldn't do it.

I looked back at her bloodied face and swollen eyes. I heard her voice even though she didn't speak. *You must be as quiet as you can.*

I didn't want to be the reason she got hurt again.

CHAPTER THIRTY-SEVEN

Josie stepped outside the tent, pressing her phone to her ear as she paced. As she waited for Trinity to answer, she looked over toward the carousel where food and coffee tables were still set up. There were still some volunteer searchers lingering. Josie recognized Ingrid Saylor standing near the Komorrah's Koffee table, talking with the tweed suit guy. Josie searched her brain for his name. Bryce Graham. A few feet from them were a few volunteers who had brought their own search and rescue dogs, including Luke. He waved to her, but she turned quickly away from him and hurried out of the park toward her car.

Finally, on the eighth ring, Trinity answered with a breathless hello.

Josie said, "I am one hundred percent sure this kidnapping is about Amy."

"A kidnapping? Not an abduction?" Trinity said.

Josie made a noise of exasperation in her throat. "What's the damn difference?"

"Well when you say abduction, it sounds like some sexual predator took her, but when you say kidnapping, it makes me think of someone taking her for ransom."

"What difference does it make?" Josie grumbled. "Either way, I have to find Lucy Ross as soon as possible."

"Okay," Trinity conceded. She must have heard Josie's frustration in her tone because she didn't push for Josie to give her or inadvertently reveal any information about the case that she could use in a story. Instead, she said, "You said you think this case is about Amy."

"Yes. This is about Amy. Someone is doing this to hurt her."

"Nice, quiet Amy whose life is as boring as the day is long?" Trinity said.

"Yes," Josie said. "Tell me you got something. Anything."

"I got a yearbook photo. That's it so far. I'm on my way to the library now. Still no return call from Renita. I'll send you the yearbook photo though."

A few seconds later, Josie's phone buzzed. She held it away from her face so she could pull up the text that Trinity had just sent with a photo of a young teenage girl, the name 'Amy Walsh' printed beneath it. Josie studied it. The photo was grainy, showing a girl with dark, curly hair and a shy smile. The resemblance to Amy Ross was thin, at best. She heard Trinity's voice coming from her phone. "I haven't met her in person. That's her, right?"

Josie stared at the photo for another beat. "I suppose if she cut, dyed and straightened her hair. I'd hate to think I still looked like the girl in my yearbook photo."

"The FBI is right on my heels," Trinity said. "Have they turned anything up?"

"I don't think so," Josie said. "I'll have to talk to Agent Oaks. I'm headed over to the Ross home now. Let me know if you find out anything else at the library or if you get in touch with Renita."

"You got it," Trinity said before hanging up.

Josie took another moment to look at the yearbook photo of Amy Walsh. She tried zooming in, but it only made the photo blurrier.

"Boss." Mettner strode up behind her.

Josie didn't bother to correct him this time. "What is it, Mett?"

"The teams found a hunting cabin in South Denton that was broken into. Gun safe was breached, and the guns were stolen."

Josie took one last look at the photo and sighed. "Let's go," she said. "I'll call Oaks on the way there and update him."

*

South Denton was mostly comprised of strip malls and other squat, flat-roofed buildings including a self-storage facility and a car rental agency that broke up the otherwise thick foliage of the area. There were a few houses flung far and wide. Since it was a commercial district, many had been turned into businesses: a diner, an antiques store, a used-book store. At the very edge of town were several single-lane winding roads leading into the mountains. Josie and Mettner followed one of them two miles into the woods until they saw two Denton police cruisers at the end of a gravel driveway which was marked only by two standing red reflectors on either side of it. Josie parked behind one of them and she and Mettner walked up the driveway toward the small cabin. It was a rectangular, single-level structure, its siding made of faux logs, its roof made of red corrugated tin, peaked to allow Pennsylvania's winter snow to slide off. To the left of the small porch was a square of grass and then several feet from that a stone fire pit surrounded by outdoor lawn chairs. In one of the metal chairs sat a short, rotund man with white hair. Two uniformed officers stood in front of him, one talking while the other took notes. The owner of the cabin, Josie guessed. Officer Hummel stood on the porch, dressed in his crime scene garb, consulting with another uniformed officer holding a clipboard.

"What've you got?" Josie asked him as she and Mettner stepped onto the porch.

Hummel motioned over his shoulder toward the owner and other officers. "Cabin belongs to that gentleman. He lives in town. He hasn't been out here in over a month. We were doing the checks of all cabins in the area like you said. Found a window broken out back. Called the owner and asked him to come out. He says nothing was disturbed except his gun case. Glass front smashed, guns missing."

Mettner said, "He didn't have his weapons in a gun safe?"

Hummel shook his head. "No one comes out here. He thought a curio would be fine. It was locked but like I said, whoever took the guns just smashed the glass in to get to them. The owner says he's had this cabin for thirty years and never had a problem till now."

"What kind of guns?" Josie asked.

Hummel looked to the other officer, who flipped a page on his clipboard. Hummel read the notes scrawled there. "A Winchester Model 101, Marlin lever action 30/30, a Remington 700, and a Glock 19."

Mettner said, "He kept a handgun at his hunting cabin?"

"For him to carry on his belt when working around the property."

"For coyotes, probably," Josie said. "A handgun is easier to carry than a rifle if you're just pulling weeds or sitting out by the fire."

Mettner nodded.

Josie asked, "You think whoever broke in was staying here?"

"No," Hummel said, "Like I said, the only thing that's disturbed is the gun case. We walked the owner through, and he said everything else is exactly as he left it."

Which meant that there would be little, if any, evidence that would lead them to the person who broke in.

"You think this is our guy?" Mettner asked her.

"Hard to say," Josie said. "How many break-ins like this do we have each year?"

"One or two at most," Hummel answered. "And it's usually teenagers looking for a place to drink. They're not usually interested in the guns."

"Well," Josie agreed. "Hunting is pretty sacred around here. You don't mess with someone's weapons."

Hummel nodded. "You want to have a look around? The team's in there processing now, but you can go in. There are suits and gloves in the trunk of my car."

Josie suited up; the uniformed officer with the clipboard logged her in and she went inside the cabin. The place was not much larger than a trailer, its living room and kitchen divided by where the brown shag carpet ended and the tan tile began. Beyond that was a short hallway with two doors. Behind one was a bedroom and behind the other was the bathroom. Hummel was right—the only thing that wasn't neat and orderly was the living room where the gun curio's glass had been smashed. She nodded to the two officers inside who were taking photographs of the cabinet and the glass scattered all around it as well as dusting it for prints.

She took a moment to study the room. To her right was a wall with three taxidermy deer heads mounted to it, then the smashed-in curio. To her left was a small living room area with a loveseat sofa and two recliner chairs surrounding a television atop a small stand. If she were a frightened seven-year-old girl in this room with a scary man who was breaking the glass in the gun cabinet, where would she hide?

She got down on her hands and knees behind the nearest recliner chair.

Mettner appeared behind her, also suited up. "What are you looking for, boss?"

"A chrysalis," Josie answered. There was nothing beneath the chair. She moved over to the loveseat. Nothing. As she lowered her head to the floor and peered beneath the last chair, she spotted a small green object. "I need a flashlight," she called over her shoulder.

A moment later, Mettner handed her his cell phone with the flashlight app turned on. The beam shone on the green object—cylindrical and slightly curved. "Found it," Josie said, her heart hammering in her chest. "I'm going to take some photos of this, then I need it processed. I'll use your phone and you can text them to me. Lift up the chair, would you? Gently."

Mettner pushed the chair forward, its hind legs coming off the carpet. Josie snapped a handful of photos before telling Mettner to lower the chair. She handed his phone back to him. Scrolling through the shots she'd taken, he said, "She used leaves this time. I don't think we can get prints from this."

"That's not the point," Josie said. "The point is that we know that there's a good chance she's still alive, and now we know this guy is armed with more than a knife."

CHAPTER THIRTY-EIGHT

Josie dropped Mettner off at the command tent. As the volunteers she had seen earlier came into view, Josie said, "You should take some of these people out to the cabin after Hummel's team is finished processing it. Have them search the woods and see if they can find anything."

Mettner nodded. "Good idea. It will give them something to do. Well, except the psychologist guy, I guess."

Josie followed Mettner's gaze to see Bryce Graham seated on a bench in the playground area, now speaking with one of the mothers that they'd talked to the evening after Lucy had been taken. It was Zoey, she thought, as she felt a small pinch of irritation. She didn't know the guy, but it sure seemed as though he was using the Ross family tragedy to drum up more business for himself.

"He looks like he's got plenty to keep him busy," Josie remarked.

She drove the few blocks to the Ross home, circling the block twice to find a parking spot amongst all the press vehicles. The reporters on the front lawn attacked her with shouted questions as she made her way up the front walk. An FBI agent let her in. "They're in the dining room," he told her.

She heard Oaks speaking as she edged into the room behind him. "Remember what we talked about. The next time the kidnapper calls, I want you both to be ready."

From their places at the other end of the dining room table, Amy and Colin Ross stared at him. "I asked for proof of life already," Colin said. "It didn't end well."

Josie walked up beside Oaks. Colin and Amy glanced at her before returning their gazes to him.

"This is a negotiation," Oaks said, "You don't want to give him everything he wants right away, or he'll keep asking for more. Do you have a million dollars?"

The couple looked at one another. Colin shifted in his chair. "Not readily available. I started liquidating assets the other day. I could come up with eight hundred thousand pretty quickly but the rest… it would take longer."

"You still want to demand proof of life," Oaks said. "You did well the last time, asking for it."

"But he won't give it to us," Colin said.

"You don't know that. He wants money. Our best chance of getting Lucy back is to try to come to some kind of agreement with this monster. Show him you're willing to play his game."

"I think this is a mistake," Amy said, her voice tremulous. "Why are we taking chances with our daughter's life?"

"Do we even have a choice?" Colin asked.

Oaks looked up at Josie. "Your Officer, Hummel, sent us over a list of the stolen guns as well as their serial numbers. Did you find anything at the hunting cabin?"

Josie took out her phone and pulled up the photos of the chrysalis.

"Oh my God," Amy cried. "She's still alive."

Colin's eyes glistened as he, too, looked at the photo. He said, "We don't know that. We don't know how long ago they were at this cabin."

"That's true," Josie acknowledged.

"And now he's armed," Colin pointed out.

"He was always armed," Amy said. "He killed Jaclyn and Wendy. The police said he stabbed them."

The sound of a cell phone ringing interrupted the moment. Amy's body visibly trembled, but it wasn't her phone that rang. Oaks pulled his phone from his jacket pocket and swiped the

Answer icon. "Oaks here," he barked into it. He listened for a moment, then said, "You're sure?" He stood up, frowning. "Yes, send it over. Now, please. Thank you." He hung up and looked at Amy and Colin. "Everything's fine," he told them. "I just need a word with Detective Quinn, if you don't mind."

"Of course," Colin said, as his wife nodded.

Josie followed Oaks out to the backyard. "What's going on?" she asked.

"I just got a call from one of my agents in New York. Amy Walsh died when she was twenty-two years old."

"What are you talking about?" Josie asked, feeling her heart double tap in her chest.

Oaks pulled up a document on his phone and showed it to Josie. It was a death certificate issued by the state of New York for Amy Walsh dated 1997. As she scanned the words on the tiny screen, Oaks said, "Cause of death was multiple blunt force trauma."

Josie found the words and kept reading. "Manner of death: accident."

"That's not Amy Walsh in there," Oaks said.

"She stole someone else's identity. The yearbook photo was just close enough that someone taking a casual glance might buy it."

Oaks blew out a long breath. "No wonder she failed the polygraph."

Josie turned away from him and began pacing the yard. "I still don't think that she had anything to do with Lucy's abduction."

Oaks scratched the stubble on his chin. "I didn't peg you as naïve, Detective Quinn. I've read about you. Seen you on television. You've seen the worst this world has to offer. You don't believe that woman in there is capable of staging her own daughter's kidnapping?"

Josie stopped pacing and stared into his eyes. "I don't know."

"It would explain how distracted she's been. You said yourself: every person you and your team spoke to about her said she was often distracted."

The word called to mind the footage that Josie and Noah had watched that morning. "She's been distracted, yes, but not because she staged Lucy's kidnapping. Remember I told you about what Noah and I saw on the footage from the arcade? Amy had no idea that man was stalking them. Besides that, we have access to all of her records: banking statements, phone records, email. Access she gave to us willingly. If she was truly planning this we would have found some evidence by now."

"I think we need to take her in. Interrogate her."

"No," Josie said. "Not yet. She's cooperating with us."

"She's lying about who she is, Quinn."

"I know that," Josie said. "But we need her right now. Lucy's life may depend on her continued cooperation. If we start treating her like a criminal, she's going to clam up. As contentious as things have been between her and her husband, Colin's instinct will be to protect his wife which means he will hire a lawyer in a hot second if he thinks we are treating her as a suspect. Whoever this kidnapper is—he's from her past."

"A past we know absolutely nothing about," Oaks pointed out. "Because she's been lying to us all along."

"In any other circumstances, I'd drag her down to police headquarters and try to scare the hell out of her," Josie said. "I get what you're proposing. But I'm telling you, now is not the time. Let me try to talk with her again, see if I can get more out of her."

Oaks sighed. "Fine. But Quinn, if you can't get anything out of her and this thing drags on, we'll have no choice."

"I know that," Josie agreed. "Just give me some time."

CHAPTER THIRTY-NINE

Amy was back in Lucy's room, sitting in the beanbag chair with a stuffed ladybug in her arms. Sunlight streamed through the gauzy curtains and all of the glittery items Lucy owned sparkled, casting a kaleidoscope of colors onto the walls. Josie closed the door behind her and sat down in front of Amy, crossing her legs.

Amy said, "Why does he need guns? The kidnapper? What's he going to do with them?"

"I don't know," Josie answered honestly. "Amy, I need to talk to you, and it's very important."

Amy's glazed eyes came into focus and she looked at Josie. "Did something happen?"

Josie shook her head. "Not yet. I'm here to warn you. Soon, very soon, my colleagues are going to come for you. They're going to take you down to the police station and put you into an interrogation room, and they're going to start asking hard questions on the record."

Amy's fingers kneaded the ladybug. "What are you talking about? They think I did this? They think I had something to do with Lucy's abduction?"

"What they know is that you've been lying to us. They know that you're not Amy Walsh."

Amy started to speak but the words got choked off in her throat. She looked away and put a hand over her mouth.

Josie said, "I don't want to believe that you had anything to do with this. But Amy, from where the rest of us are standing, it sure doesn't look good."

Amy was silent for a long moment. When she looked back at Josie and spoke, her words were so low, Josie strained to hear them. "What do I do?"

"Tell me the truth. Right now. In this room. If you had nothing to do with Lucy's abduction, then whatever you're hiding won't matter." Josie pointed to the closed door. "Right now, my colleagues are starting to focus on you, which is completely understandable. I get where they're coming from. When you find out someone is lying about a bunch of things—big things—it's not a stretch to think they could be lying about the crime you're trying to solve."

"I had nothing to do with Lucy's abduction," Amy said firmly. "I swear to you. I just want her back."

"So do I," Josie said. "My focus is on Lucy. I don't give a damn about anything but getting that little girl back alive. That's it. That's all. So there is nothing you can tell me, no secret you can divulge to me, that is going to matter if you didn't do this. I don't care if you killed someone, Amy, but you need to tell me. Now. Before my colleagues come through that door and this whole thing spins out of control."

Tears rolled down Amy's cheeks. She clutched the ladybug again. Her eyes started to get that unfocused, vacant look again.

Josie said, "Why did you assume Amy Walsh's identity?"

Amy blinked, her gaze darting to Josie's face and then back to the other side of the room where the butterfly garden hung. "I had to. I needed one."

"Does Colin know?"

"Of course not," Amy responded. "He has no idea."

"How did you do it?"

Amy said, "I knew Amy Walsh. She was my friend. Her mother took me in. Let me live with them. It was only a few months. Then they died. Car accident. Renita wasn't with them, so she lived. But she wouldn't have let me stay. She never liked me. I took Amy's personal effects with me and went to New York City. I just… started using her identity. I lived in terror that someone would figure it out. But no one ever did. Until now. Did you know I'm not even forty-four? I'm only forty."

Josie tucked that fact away. "Why did you do it?"

"Not everything I told you was a lie."

"You were running from someone," Josie coaxed. "An abusive lover?"

Amy swallowed. Her face flushed. "Not a lover," she choked out.

"A boyfriend? Husband?"

"I was a prisoner, do you understand? A prisoner. I got away from him. I had no choice."

"Who was he, Amy?"

She shook her head vigorously. "I told you, he's dead. I'll never speak his name again."

"Amy, I need the truth."

Something in her eyes flared. "I'm telling you the truth."

"Then what was your name before you were Amy Walsh?"

"If you know I was never Amy Walsh, then you must know my real name."

Josie didn't want to alert her to the fact that they didn't have that information yet, so she said, "I need to hear it from you."

Amy said nothing. More tears rolled down her face. "The person I was before is a ghost. A fiction. She always was."

Josie was growing frustrated with Amy's cryptic answers. She wanted to shake the woman but at the same time, it was the most honest she had been thus far. "You were someone else before you assumed Amy Walsh's identity. I need to know who," Josie prompted.

Amy looked back at the butterfly garden, lines appearing on her forehead. "No," she said softly. "I don't think I was. I wasn't anyone."

"Amy," Josie said, trying to keep the irritation out of her voice. "I need you to be straight with me right now. Stop talking around this."

Another small, bitter laugh. "Around it? It's been over twenty years, and I still haven't made sense of any of it."

Josie wondered if the stress of Lucy's abduction and the murders of the people closest to her was sending her over the edge. She reached out and touched Amy's hand. "Tell me something about your life before you became Amy Walsh. Something true."

Amy pondered for a moment. Then she said, "I lived in Buffalo."

Josie didn't get a chance to ask any follow-up questions. A commotion erupted from downstairs, followed by pounding on the stairs. Oaks threw the door open. "Mrs. Ross's phone is ringing," he said. "Get down here now."

CHAPTER FORTY

The three of them raced downstairs and into the dining room. In the center of the table, Amy's phone rang. Josie leaned over and looked at the screen. It wasn't one of Amy's contacts. She read off the number. "Do you know whose number this is?"

Amy shook her head. "I don't—I don't know."

"On it," one of the agents said, tapping away at his laptop.

"You think it's him?" Amy asked.

"Only one way to find out," Oaks said.

Colin reached across the table, picked up the phone and answered.

The kidnapper's voice filled the room, sending a shudder through both parents. "Hello, Colin. I'd like to talk to your loving wife, please."

Colin closed his eyes and took a deep breath, phone pressed to his ear. "She can't talk right now. But I can discuss the money with you. Look, I can't—"

He opened his eyes and looked at Oaks, who shook his head and mouthed the word: *how*. Earlier, Oaks had told them to answer each of the kidnapper's demands with a how question. Colin said, "How am I supposed to come up with a million dollars?"

"Put Amy on the phone."

The agent whispered, "It came in as private. Give me a second to get a name and address."

Colin said, "How is Amy going to help you? I handle the finances. I can get you eight hundred thousand, but I need proof of life."

The kidnapper's voice became even colder. "Put Amy on the phone."

Colin looked at Oaks who nodded for him to continue. "You want to talk to her, I understand, but we need to talk money first. Like I said, I can come up with most of it, but I need a proof of life."

"It's a landline," the agent whispered. "Registered to Bryce Graham."

Josie's head snapped in his direction. "What did you say?" she whispered.

Oaks went over and stood between Amy and Colin. "Detective Quinn told me that you said you didn't know Bryce Graham. Why is this call coming from his phone?" he asked her quietly, but she wasn't listening. Her eyes were fixed on Colin, her fingers twisting around themselves against her chest.

On the phone there was a rustling sound. The kidnapper said, "You want a proof of life? I'll give you a proof of life."

Josie's heart halted abruptly then thundered back into motion, beating so hard against her breastbone she was sure everyone else in the room could see her shirt moving. She motioned to Oaks who strode over to her. "Bryce Graham was still at the city park when I left. But the kidnapper is obviously at his home."

Oaks gazed down at the screen, located Graham's address and rattled it off to an agent standing by the door. "Get a couple of teams over there now," he commanded.

The agent nodded and left. Josie said, "I'll call my team and have them check for Graham in the park."

"Put him into protective custody," Oaks told her.

Josie stepped out of the room long enough to call Gretchen and give her some terse instructions. She walked back in and over to Amy, gripping her forearm. "You said you didn't know Bryce Graham. Why is the kidnapper calling from his home?" she asked but her words were swallowed up by the sound of screaming coming over the line. The sound pierced right through Josie like a spike. Her knees weakened. It was a girl. Young. Her voice high-pitched.

No words. Just the soul-crushing sound of a small child's terror punctuated by the kidnapper hollering, "Here's your proof of life, you smug bastard. Is this what you want? Is this it?"

Amy flew at her husband and used both hands to tear the phone from Colin's grip. "Stop," she shrieked. "Stop! Stop! I'm here. I'm listening. Just stop. Leave her alone! Leave Lucy alone. Please."

The sound stopped abruptly but Josie could hear the sounds of faint whimpering between the kidnapper's words. "You tell him to stay off the line, Amy."

Colin fell to his knees, his face ashen. For a moment, Josie thought he might vomit.

"He's off the line," Amy said. "I promise. You can talk to me. Just stop what you're doing to Lucy. Tell me what to do."

"A million dollars."

"Yes."

Oaks's chin dropped to his chest.

Amy turned away from him, clutching the phone with both hands against the side of her face. Her chest heaved as she waited for more instructions.

"You'll split it up. In half."

"In half," Amy repeated.

In the background, Lucy's whimpers faded.

"You'll go to Walmart and buy two waterproof duffel bags. They have to be waterproof, do you understand?"

"Waterproof, yes," Amy breathed.

"You'll put half the money in each bag."

"Five hundred thousand in each bag, okay," Amy said.

"Be ready by six-thirty tomorrow evening."

"We'll be ready. What do I have to do?"

The line went dead.

Amy pulled the phone away from her face and stared at it in disbelief. She put it back to her ear. "Hello? Hello? Are you there?

Where do we take the money? Hello? What do we do? What do we do with the money?"

"He hung up," said one of the agents stationed at his laptop.

"No!" Amy screamed. "No, no, no!"

CHAPTER FORTY-ONE

Amy dissolved into a heap on the floor, tears streaking her face, her entire body shaking. She dropped the phone. Colin crawled to her and gathered her in his arms. Josie and Oaks looked at one another. Josie said, "Go to Graham's. I'll head over to the police station in a minute."

He raced out of the room. Josie went into the kitchen where she knew Amy's prescription for Xanax sat on the counter next to the toaster. She snatched it up, hearing the pills rattling inside. She took a bottle of water from the refrigerator and returned to the dining room. She shook a pill into her hand and held it out to Amy. Colin nudged her and she took it, washing it down with the water Josie offered.

"They're on scene," one of the agents said, tapping against a headset he had donned when Oaks's team left.

Josie gave Amy another minute and then she and Colin hoisted her up and set her gently down in a chair. Josie said, "Amy, do you know Bryce Graham?"

Amy didn't answer.

The agent said, "The house is clear. No one there."

"Amy?" Josie said, her voice taking on an edge.

Amy's chin lifted so she could meet Josie's eyes. "Yes, I know him. I was… I was getting therapy."

Colin gasped. "What? You were seeing a therapist and you never told me?"

"It was a long time ago," she muttered.

"You didn't think to mention this to the police?" Colin said, his voice rising with anger.

"How long ago?" Josie asked.

"I stopped seeing him about four months ago."

"How long were you seeing him before that?" Colin asked.

Her gaze swept toward the floor. "Since Lucy was born."

Colin threw his hands in the air. "Jesus, Amy. Why didn't you tell me?" When she didn't answer, he said, "How often did you see him?"

"A few times a week at first. Then once a week. We had a standing appointment. We only contacted one another if one of us had to cancel."

"Were you screwing him?" Colin asked.

Both Josie and Amy's heads whipped in Colin's direction.

"Wh-what?" Amy stammered.

"You saw this man for years, several times a week without ever telling me. Why would you do that unless you were having an affair with him?"

"Colin," Amy said. "You know I've always struggled with depression and anxiety. I needed help."

"No one needs that much help. No one like you. You're a goddamn stay-at-home mother, for chrissake. What is wrong with you?"

Amy said nothing.

"How did you pay for it?"

"I took the cash out of the account you made for me. He didn't charge much."

Colin put his hands on either side of his head and grabbed handfuls of his hair. He pulled violently. A frustrated growl tore from his throat. "What else are you hiding, Amy? Do you understand our daughter's life is on the line? Are you involved in this somehow?"

Josie thought Amy could not look more hurt or stricken than she already did, but she was wrong. "How can you even ask that?"

"How do you know this psychologist didn't take Lucy? What if he took her? You said you didn't know him. He doesn't have an alibi for the day Lucy disappeared."

"He wouldn't take her!" Amy shouted. "I know he wouldn't. I didn't think it was important. I thought if I told everyone about having seen him, it would cause a fight between us and take the focus away from finding Lucy. I stopped seeing him months ago. He had nothing to do with Lucy. He never even met her, and he would never do something like this anyway."

"Why should I believe you?" Colin spat back. "How can I believe anything you say? How do I know you weren't having an affair with this guy? Maybe you two cooked up this scheme to get Lucy and my money."

"That's crazy," Amy responded. "You're acting insane. Why would I do something like that?"

The sound of Josie's phone ringing cut through the tension. It was Gretchen. "We've got Graham. He's safe. We'll keep him at the station for now."

"I'll be right there," Josie told Gretchen. She hung up and looked from one parent to the other. "I've got to go," she said. "If I were you two, I'd focus on gathering the ransom. Lucy is still alive. Stop fighting and let's bring her home."

CHAPTER FORTY-TWO

As Josie drove toward the police headquarters, her phone chirped several times. After weaving through the press vehicles, she pulled into the municipal lot and snatched her phone from the passenger's seat. Several text messages from Trinity had come in, including a photo. Josie turned her vehicle off, took a deep breath and read through them.

Amy's not who she says she is.

It took hours but I found something in the Fulton Daily News Archives.

Check this out. Dorothy Walsh had three daughters: Renita, Amy and Pamela. Dorothy, Amy and Pamela all died in a car accident.

Then came a screenshot of the news article that Trinity had uncovered. It was dated October 27, 1997. The headline read: *Three Women Killed in Car Crash in South Fulton*. Her eyes skimmed the contents of the article. "Good God," she murmured. The article named all three of the Walsh women and gave their funeral arrangements, but there was nothing beyond that. No mention of any other passengers although Josie assumed Amy Ross wasn't with the Walsh women when the accident happened.

She texted Trinity: *I need a name. Amy knows we know she's using a false identity, but I can't get a name out of her. We believe that Amy Ross was friends with the real Amy Walsh. Time is critical. The FBI is on it, but you've already got a lead with Renita. Did she call back?*

Several seconds passed. Josie didn't even realize she was holding her breath until Trinity's reply came back. *Headed to speak to Renita now.*

Josie breathed out, pocketed her phone and went inside to speak to Bryce Graham. Gretchen and Mettner stood outside the first-floor conference room door. Mettner handed her a cup of coffee. The smell caused an instant wave of nausea to crash over her. For a fleeting second, her brain told her this couldn't possibly be from stress. It had to be the other thing. A baby. Whose baby? Noah's… or maybe Luke's? No, she couldn't go there. Not yet. Not now. Josie white-knuckled the mug and managed a smile. "Thanks, Mett."

He nodded. "I just talked to one of the FBI agents at Graham's house. Back door was kicked in, lock broken. Nothing appears disturbed in the house. There's an overturned chair in the kitchen where the phone is located. They didn't find any, uh, cocoons. That's it."

The sound of Lucy's screams filled her mind, making Josie feel even more ill. She hated to think about how the chair had been overturned.

"The FBI team is processing the scene," Gretchen added. "We talked to Dr. Graham briefly. We had to convince him that he'd be safer here."

"Thanks," Josie said. "Let me talk to him."

Bryce Graham sat placidly in one of the conference room chairs, an untouched cup of coffee in front of him. He stood to shake her hand when Josie introduced herself. She sat down beside him and put her coffee mug on the table, pushing it far enough away that the smell wouldn't reach her.

"What can I do for you, detective?" Graham asked. He smiled at her, the skin at the corners of his blue eyes crinkling. His expression and the tone of his voice was kind and soothing. No wonder so many of the volunteers had spoken with him.

"Amy Ross was your patient," Josie said. "You've been hanging around the park since her daughter went missing, and yet you never approached her, and you never mentioned to anyone in law enforcement that she had been your patient."

"Is there a question in there, Detective?" Graham asked. His smile and gentle tone told her he wasn't being confrontational.

"Why didn't you approach Amy Ross when you came to the park?"

"I don't know Amy Ross," he said matter-of-factly.

Josie felt a small flare of anger. She'd had just about all she could take of cryptic answers. "A seven-year-old girl is missing, Dr. Graham. Her life is in danger. I'd really appreciate it if you could cut the crap and speak frankly with me."

He folded his hands over his stomach. "I'm well aware of what's going on in this town."

Josie's phone chirped. She held up a hand, indicating for him to give her a moment. A quick glance showed a text from Trinity. She opened it.

Her name was Tessa. Renita doesn't remember her last name. Amy met her at the laundromat. She was homeless. Dorothy let her move in. I'll see what else I can get from Renita but she doesn't remember much after all this time.

Josie tapped back a response. *Amy said she used to live in Buffalo?* Trinity's reply came back instantly. *On it.*

Josie set her phone on the table and turned her attention back to Dr. Graham. "Amy Ross told me that you treated her for several years."

"I did not treat Amy Ross," he said.

"How about if I have a look at your patient files and then we'll talk again after that?"

His smile faltered. "You can't do that. There are privacy laws. You can't just—I won't give you permission to look at them."

"I can get a warrant," Josie argued.

"No, I don't think you can. I have no involvement in the case you're working on. I never even met Lucy Ross."

"You have no alibi for the day Lucy went missing. Someone broke into your house to call her mother and make a ransom demand. I think that's enough of a connection."

"I thought I was here because it wasn't safe for me to return to my home. Are you telling me I'm a suspect now?"

"I don't know, are you?"

"I most certainly am not," he shot back, shifting in his chair. He leaned forward, hands on his knees.

"Tell me about Amy Ross."

"I don't know Amy Ross."

Josie leaned back in her chair, staring at him. Her fingers trailed across the table until they found her phone. She picked it up and placed it into her jacket pocket. His eyes followed her movements. He opened his mouth as though to speak but then decided against it, clamping his mouth shut and looking away from her.

Josie said, "But you do know Tessa, don't you?"

CHAPTER FORTY-THREE

Bryce Graham's mouth hung open. Josie waited for him to speak and when he didn't, she said, "Tell me about your patient, Tessa."

"I can't. The privacy laws… I—"

"You can confirm for me that she's a patient. That doesn't violate privacy laws," Josie argued.

He sighed and looked away from her, lips pursed. Then he gave her a nod.

Josie leaned forward. "You're confirming that you have a patient named Tessa?"

"Yes," he said softly.

"Tessa what? I'm going to need a last name."

"The trust that I have with my patients is critical to my practice, Detective Quinn."

Josie stood up and leaned over him. "Let me say this again because apparently you didn't hear me the first time: there is a seven-year-old girl out there in the hands of a cold-blooded killer. Every second of my time that you waste in this room is a second I could be out there trying to bring her home. Are you really going to put the privacy of one patient—of this girl's mother—above the life of Lucy Ross?"

"My patient's privacy has nothing to do with Lucy's abduction," Graham said.

Josie turned away from him. "We're done here. I'll get a warrant, and I *will* get one. I've got a missing girl being targeted by someone who is out to destroy her mother. Said mother has lied about her identity and failed a polygraph. Said mother has also admitted to being a patient of yours. Our investigation has revealed that her real name was Tessa, and you've admitted to having a patient by that first name. Given that we don't know what else Tessa—or Amy—is hiding, a judge will rule that whatever's in your files could be important to the investigation. You'll be in protective custody until we've apprehended Lucy's kidnapper."

"Detective," he called after her. "Please. If my patients think the police have gone through my files, it would greatly undermine my practice."

Josie turned back. "Then tell me about Tessa. You tell me what you know about her and then I don't need to search your office."

"I didn't know her name was Amy Ross," he said. "She never used that name. She showed up at my office one day. Paid cash. Told me her name was Tessa. Since she wasn't using insurance, I didn't need her driver's license or anything."

"Tessa what?"

"Lendhardt," Graham sighed. "Tessa Lendhardt."

Josie took out her phone and fired off the last name via text to Trinity. "When did you find out that she had lied about her identity?"

He gave her a wry smile. "When I saw her at the park the morning after Lucy went missing. I really did go there to offer my services. Then I realized that the mother—that Lucy's mother—was Tessa. I was shocked."

Josie sat back down beside him. "Did you try to talk to her?"

"No. She seemed too stressed. I knew that she had lied to me. I thought she must have her reasons. I didn't want to make things worse for her."

Josie thought of Colin's accusation. "Dr. Graham, I have to ask, were you having an affair with Tessa Lendhardt?"

He waved a hand in the air dismissively as he shook his head. "Oh no. She was only my patient. I am a professional. I would never become romantically involved with a patient. Even if she wasn't my patient, she's much younger than I am, you know."

Josie narrowed her eyes at him. "That doesn't always stop people."

"I can assure you, ours was a doctor-patient relationship only."

"Why didn't you go to the police when you realized she had lied to you about her identity?"

"The very same reason I didn't want to discuss any of this in the first place," he grumbled.

"Patient privacy." Josie didn't want to get back into the same argument now that he was speaking more freely. "Why did Tessa come to see you?"

"Post-partum," he said. "She thought she had post-partum depression. She had given birth about seven weeks before that. She felt she was having difficulty bonding with the baby."

"Was she?"

Graham nodded. "I believe she was. I'm not sure this was due to post-partum, however."

"Then what?" Josie asked.

"Tessa refused to discuss her childhood other than to say that her father was absent, and her mother was neglectful. But I believe that she experienced significant trauma at some point in her life, which hindered her ability to bond with her child. At least at first. We worked very hard on it, and she did bond with Lucy eventually. It was quite the triumph for her."

"Could that trauma have been an abusive relationship in early adulthood?" Josie asked.

Graham shrugged. "I suppose, yes. I could never get to the bottom of it all. She never spoke of anything before her daughter was born, or if she did, it was only in the broadest strokes."

"Did she ever talk to you about being in an abusive relationship?"

"No," Graham said. "She said her husband was very loving. That was part of her issue. She had everything, but didn't feel happy."

"I'm talking about before her husband. Did she ever discuss relationships before she got married?"

"No. She refused. I tried hard to get her to discuss her past. I truly believe that processing events that have happened in a person's past goes a long way to assisting them in living better, fuller lives in the present."

"She didn't talk to you about her childhood or any of her other relationships?"

"No."

"What did she talk about?"

"Tessa had a great deal of anxiety. Crippling anxiety. She told me she was a stay-at-home mom. At first, when her daughter was an infant and then a toddler, she struggled greatly. She was alone with her child most of the time. She didn't believe she was capable of taking care of an infant or a toddler on her own. She was... afraid all the time."

"Of what?"

He shrugged again. "I don't know. She was just... terrified. I tried to work with her on deep breathing exercises, meditation, things she could do to manage those feelings. For a long time, she was taking medication. It was prescribed by her family doctor. As I'm sure you know, I can't prescribe medication. I urged her to see a psychiatrist to manage her dosages, but she simply went to her family physician."

"Did she tell you which meds?" Josie asked. "Xanax?"

"For her acute episodes, yes. I believe she was taking some other anti-depressants as well. Medications for her long-term, underlying depression. She was eventually able to wean herself off them. Her anxiety did improve over time."

"When did she go off the anti-depressants?" Josie asked.

"Oh, maybe two years ago? When her daughter was five, I believe."

"When Lucy started school?" Josie asked.

"I really don't remember," Graham said. "I just know that she's made great strides in the last couple of years."

"Was it her idea to stop seeing you?"

"Yes. She felt she had reached a stable point. I told her that she was welcome to come back at any time, and I wished her good luck."

"When was that?"

"About four or five months ago. The next time I saw her was at the park. That's when I realized that she was using a different name."

"Do you believe she was telling the truth about being Tessa Lendhardt?"

He smiled sadly. "Oh Detective, I don't think that poor woman has ever known who she really is."

CHAPTER FORTY-FOUR

While Mettner arranged for Bryce Graham to stay at a hotel under guard, Josie went upstairs to the great room which held the detectives' desks crammed together in the center of it. Along one wall Chitwood's office door stood closed. She wondered if he was inside or if he was off handling the day-to-day business of the city now that all of his detectives were tied up with the Lucy Ross case. Josie sat down at her desk and pulled up the TLO XP database used by law enforcement to search various records. Gretchen appeared behind her as she typed in 'Tessa Lendhardt' along with 'Buffalo, New York'.

Gretchen said, "The volunteer searchers have finished looking in the area of the hunting cabin that was broken into. They didn't find anything. Oaks is done at Bryce Graham's house. He'll be here any minute."

"Great," Josie said. "Let's wait for him and we'll do a briefing. I need Mett and Noah as well, and if Chitwood wants an update, now would be the time."

"You got it, boss," Gretchen said, disappearing once more.

The search results appeared. Zero results for Tessa Lendhardt in Buffalo, New York. Josie widened the search to Tessa Lendhardt in New York. Nothing. Again, she expanded her search parameters to include the whole country. Nothing.

"What the hell?" she muttered.

"Quinn!" Bob Chitwood's voice boomed across the room as he emerged from the stairwell. Behind him, Agent Oaks, Gretchen and Mettner filed in, followed by Noah, lurching along on his crutches.

"Chief," Josie said.

"I'd like a briefing. Now."

Noah pulled his chair out from under his desk and sat down, hefting his casted leg onto the surface of the desk. Gretchen and Mettner sat at their desks while Oaks and Chitwood remained standing. Everyone looked exhausted and haggard and a bit unkempt. Mettner took his phone out and brought up his note-taking app while Gretchen's pen poised over her trusty notebook.

"There's a lot to discuss," Josie said. She briefed them on everything that she had learned that day: that Amy had admitted to being a patient of Bryce Graham; that the name she had seen him under was Tessa Lendhardt; and that Amy had admitted to assuming the identity of Amy Walsh after her death. She went over everything Bryce Graham had told her about Tessa/Amy, which wasn't much.

"I checked the TLO XP database but there's no Tessa Lendhardt in the country, let alone New York."

"That can't be," Chitwood said.

Josie motioned to her computer. "Any of you are welcome to double-check my work, perhaps use a different database. I only used one spelling of the last name, so we should probably check using different spellings."

"We could also search for other people named Lendhardt in Buffalo, New York," Noah suggested. "Track them down and see if any of them knew a Tessa."

"I can have a couple of field agents in the Buffalo office work on that," Oaks said.

Gretchen said, "Maybe Lendhardt was her married name. She could have been married. We really don't know anything about this woman."

"Good point," Josie said. "We also have her elimination prints from when Hummel and his team processed Lucy's bedroom—after we found the message from the kidnapper on the talking bear. I can have Hummel pull them, and we can run them through AFIS."

Chitwood shook his head. "You won't get anywhere with that unless she committed a crime. You said she told you she's only forty, right? If she took Amy Walsh's identity twenty-two years ago, she would have just turned eighteen which means any crime that would have put her into the system would have happened when she was a juvenile. She won't be in there."

Gretchen said, "She might be in there. If she was arrested at eighteen but fled."

Oaks said, "From everything she's told us, it's more likely she was running from an abusive partner. Quinn, you've spent the most one-on-one time with this woman. You've talked to her therapist. Do you think she was on some kind of crime spree at eighteen?"

"No, I don't." Josie said. "Maybe running her prints is futile, but I still think it's an avenue we should exhaust."

Mettner cleared his throat. "Or we could confront her. Arrest her, even."

"On what charges?" Noah asked.

Mettner shrugged. "Obstruction of justice. Interfering with an investigation. Identity theft. Fraud."

Gretchen said, "Then she gets a lawyer. An expensive lawyer. She stops cooperating and maybe her husband does as well."

"We're less than twenty-four hours away from the ransom drop," Josie said. "Which may be our one and only chance to catch this guy. We need the parents' cooperation. Arresting Amy now would be a serious problem."

"She broke the law," Mettner argued.

"Yes," Josie agreed. "And when this is over, we can address her identity theft, but right now, Lucy might still be alive and the only person the kidnapper will speak with is Amy. We need her."

Oaks said, "Colin and Amy are at the bank now liquidating assets and trying to gather the cash they need. After that, my agents will take them to Walmart for their waterproof duffel bags."

"Waterproof," Noah said. "What's this guy planning?"

"We don't know," Josie said. "Which means he's going to call back."

"Which is a problem for someone in this town," Gretchen said. "Bryce Graham got lucky. The next person whose phone this guy tries to use may not be so lucky."

Oaks said, "Which means we need Quinn to talk to Amy again and try to get more out of her. No more secrets. Her secret could have gotten Bryce Graham killed today."

Josie rubbed a hand over her eyes, feeling days' worth of fatigue in every cell of her body. "I can try again, but I'm not sure I'll get anything useful in time."

"And we can't threaten to arrest her if we want to keep her in play," Noah said. "So you've got no leverage."

"Besides guilt," Gretchen said.

"I already tried that," Josie said. "She didn't give Bryce Graham up then. I doubt she'll be forthcoming this time."

"Do we tell her husband?" Noah asked.

Josie and Oaks looked at one another. Oaks nodded at Josie to make the call. She straightened her spine and looked around at the group. "No."

Mettner opened his mouth to speak but Josie held a hand up. "They're already at each other's throats. We don't have time for Colin to process the fact that his wife isn't who she says she is, and that she's been lying to him their entire relationship. I don't think she will be more inclined to come clean with him. He's going to be angry. I think she will shut down in the face of his anger and only clam up more. Besides, the focus needs to stay on Lucy—especially this close to the drop. We need them to be a united front with their sole purpose to get their daughter back."

Chitwood said, "Seems to me we need to be focusing more on the drop right now. You don't even know where it is, and what if this guy calls at six and wants the parents out to make the drop by six-thirty. Then what?"

"We'll need to mobilize quickly," Oaks agreed. "Like a rapid deployment team. The parents will need to be ready to move with us at a moment's notice. We'll need to prepare the money by recording the serial numbers and fitting the bags with trackers. I can get my team to work on that."

"What if the kidnapper calls and says no police, no FBI, and no trackers?" Mettner asked.

"I'm not giving this guy a chance to get away," Oaks said. "Not with Lucy Ross's life in the balance. We can hide our presence, but the trackers stay with the money."

"I agree," Josie said. "Let's get everything in place for when the kidnapper calls again. I'll go back to the Ross home and try to talk with Amy tonight."

Chitwood clapped his hands. "Looks like no one is sleeping tonight."

CHAPTER FORTY-FIVE

At the Ross home, the FBI commandeered Colin's home office to prepare the money. In the dining room, Amy sat on a chair, her legs pulled up beneath her and her arms wrapped around her chest. She stared at the cell phones on the table. Colin paced behind her. Josie was about to ask Amy for a moment when her own phone rang. She pulled it out of her pocket and saw Trinity's number flash across the screen. She quickly slipped out of the room, heading out the back door. "What's up?" she answered.

Trinity gave a dramatic sigh. "Tessa Lendhardt does not exist. Not in Buffalo. Not anywhere."

"Yeah, I know," Josie said. "But thanks for trying."

Trinity's laughter filtered through the line, skittering across the silence of the backyard. "You think I stopped there?"

Josie felt a small thrill of excitement, hoping her sister had found something useful. "What did you find?"

"I checked on all Lendhardts in Buffalo," Trinity said. "I found six, all men. Two of them are dead. One of those dead Lendhardts is survived by his eighty-seven-year-old widow, Betty."

"How old was the other man who passed away?"

She heard the rustle of papers and then Trinity said, "He was sixty-six when he died which was two years ago."

"Too old," Josie said. "I'm assuming that the Lendhardt that Amy Ross was married to—assuming she was married and not just dating—would be around her age. She told me today that her actual age is forty. Anyone on that list close to forty?"

Trinity went silent for a minute before she read off the ages of the other four Lendhardts. "Twenty-six, seventy-three, fifty-seven, and eighty."

"Not even close," Josie said, trying to hide the disappointment in her voice. "I've got to talk to her again."

"Well, first thing tomorrow I'm going to talk to the Lendhardts that I can locate and the neighbors of the ones who have passed away."

"You think they'll talk to you?"

"I'm famous, dear sister. Everyone talks to me. Listen, I had this idea. Can you get me a photograph of Amy Ross? A current photo?"

Josie thought about it. Holding the phone to her ear, she made her way back into the house, through the kitchen and into the living room where several framed photos of the Ross family hung. "Yes," she said. "I can."

"Great, send it right away, would you?"

"Okay."

Josie hung up and studied the various photos until she found a good, crisp image. She used her phone to snap a picture of Amy's smiling face and texted it to Trinity. Pocketing her phone, she went in search of Amy.

She was still curled into herself on a dining room chair. Josie caught her eye from the doorway and nodded toward the living room. With great effort, Amy stood and trudged after Josie.

"Where's Colin?" Josie asked her.

"He went up to bed. I doubt he'll sleep, but he said he needed to be alone."

"Sit," Josie told her, motioning toward the couch. "We need to talk."

Amy plopped onto the couch. "Are you going to arrest me?"

"No. Should I?"

Amy stared sightlessly ahead, shaking her head. "No."

"Why didn't you tell me your name was Tessa Lendhardt?"

Amy's gaze snapped toward Josie. "How did you find out?"

"How do you think?"

Amy looked away again. Her fingers moved to the collar of her sweater, tugging at it and then rolling it in her fingers. "Bryce," she said. "The FBI agents said he was okay. Unharmed."

"Yes," Josie said. "He's in protective custody."

"I didn't tell you because it doesn't matter," Amy explained.

"You say that, but Bryce could have been killed today. We could have caught the kidnapper today if you'd told us about Bryce. We could have had units at his house, waiting for the kidnapper."

Amy's nervous fingers moved from her collar to her forehead. She leaned forward, sobs rocking her frame. "I'm sorry. I didn't think—I didn't know. I would never put Bryce—or anyone—in danger." She looked back up at Josie. "I swear to you that I haven't been Tessa Lendhardt in twenty-two years. She doesn't matter. She never did. She was no one, and she had no one. God, I was just a kid."

"Who was Tessa Lendhardt?"

"I told you before. A fiction. A ghost."

"Amy, we don't have time for these cryptic answers. The drop is tomorrow. The kidnapper is going to call you again. That means he's going to find someone you know, probably someone you care about, and he's going to kill them. Both so he can use their phone without being traced and so he can hurt you. If you tell me who he's going to target, I can stop that from happening. We may even be able to recover Lucy before the drop happens. Head this whole thing off at the pass."

Amy sat forward and extended her hands toward Josie, capturing one of Josie's hands. Tears streaked her face. "I am telling you, I don't know. There is no one else. I swear."

"You said that last time and then we got a phone call from your therapist's house."

"That was a mistake. I should have told you about Bryce. But I honestly didn't think it would matter. I hadn't seen him in months, and I had no intention of going back."

"Then you need to tell me what else you think won't matter. It's the things you're not telling me that might get people killed. Maybe even Lucy."

Amy tugged hard on Josie's arm. "Please," she begged. "I'm telling the truth. There is no one else."

"Why won't you talk about Tessa Lendhardt?" Josie asked. "What are you hiding? Amy, I told you before, I don't care what you did. I only care about getting Lucy back. What's the worst thing you could have done? Killed someone? I don't care."

"That's not the worst thing," Amy mumbled.

"Isn't it? Tell me, Amy. What's the worst thing? What did Tessa Lendhardt do that you feel the need to hide all these years later, even with your daughter's life hanging in the balance?"

"Nothing. I told you. I was a kid. I was in a bad situation."

"With an abusive partner—husband, boyfriend, lover?"

Amy hesitated. "None of those things."

Josie pulled her hand away, a sigh of exasperation escaping her throat.

"Wait, I'm telling the truth."

Josie shook her head. "I'm sorry, Amy. I don't think you know how to tell the truth anymore."

CHAPTER FORTY-SIX

Oaks was in the dining room, seated in front of a laptop, typing up a report. A cup of coffee steamed beside him. He looked up at her when she walked in, his brow raised in a question. Josie shook her head. She wasn't getting anything more out of Amy. Nothing that made sense. Their only choice at this juncture was to wait for the ransom drop and hope that they could catch the kidnapper and recover Lucy—alive.

Oaks gestured to his mug. "Get yourself some coffee—or some sleep. Mr. Ross said they've got a spare bedroom upstairs that we can use."

Josie tried to sleep in the guest room—she and Mettner took shifts—but rest would not come. The hours stretched on in a tomb-like silence that enveloped the house. Amy sat alone in Lucy's room while Colin paced the dining room. Morning came and went. Then afternoon. Someone ordered takeout but no one ate. Every passing minute seemed like some kind of death knell. No one said it, but Josie imagined they were all wondering: was he going to call?

When Amy's cell phone eventually rang, the sound screamed through the house like an alarm. Amy came rushing down the stairs, stumbling and falling down the last few steps. Colin was there, and he lifted her up and half-dragged, half-carried her into the dining room. Amy's hands trembled as she picked up the phone from the dining room table and swiped the Answer icon. The room was packed, with Oaks, Mettner, Colin and several other agents crammed into it, listening as Amy gave a shaky "Hello?"

The kidnapper's voice filled the room again. This time he didn't sound as gleeful as he normally did. "Hello, Amy."

She closed her eyes and squeezed the phone until her knuckles turned white. "Do you have Lucy? Is she still alive?"

"No questions. You'll bring the money tonight. Six o'clock."

Amy looked around the room, eyes wide. "You said six-thirty."

"And now it's six. Remember, you don't make the rules. Six o'clock sharp. No police. No FBI. Just you and your husband."

Amy's eyes found Oaks. He shook his head and tapped his wrist, as though tapping a watch. It wasn't enough time.

"That's too soon," Amy blurted. "We're not—we don't have all the money yet."

"Oh, Amy," he said with a sigh. "Do you want to see Lucy again or not?"

"Of course I do," she said. "Please, I—"

"I'm sure you'll manage. Remember, no police. No FBI. If I see even one of them near either of the drop sites, Lucy is dead. Do you hear me? Dead."

Josie and Oaks looked at one another. She mouthed: *either of the drop sites?* He shook his head. This was not a good sign.

"Please," Amy cried. "Don't hurt her. I'll do whatever you say. We just need more time. The money—"

"Tonight. Six o'clock. Both of you. Alone. No tracers, no trackers, no marked bills. Nothing that allows the FBI to follow the money. Do you understand?"

"Yes, I understand," Amy said.

"You take one half of the money to the center of the football field of Denton East high school. You. Just you. Do you understand?"

"Yes. Just me. The football field."

"Your husband takes the other half and delivers it to Lover's Cave."

Amy's brow furrowed. "Wait. Lover's Cave? What's that?"

"You've got a whole army of police and FBI agents. Figure it out."

"Okay, okay," Amy said. "We'll find it. Just please don't hurt Lucy. Please."

"I will hurt her if you lie to me, Amy."

"I won't lie."

"Leave the police and FBI at home, both of you. You got that?"

"Yes, I promise. What about Lucy? Will you bring her? How do we get her back?"

There was a moment of silence. Then he said, "If you do what I say, she'll be released to you twenty-four hours after the drop, in the same place that you lost her."

"You mean the carousel?" Amy said, but he had already hung up.

Amy set the phone down and looked around at the faces in the room. One of the agents on the laptops said, "The number is registered to a Violet Young."

"Oh Jesus," Josie said.

Amy covered her mouth but not before everyone heard her shriek the word *No!*

Colin said, "What is it?"

"That's Lucy's teacher," Amy said. "My God."

CHAPTER FORTY-SEVEN

Josie squeezed in between Oaks and Mettner behind where the agent sat so she could look at the map. The agent pointed to a small red circle on the screen and said, "This is Violet Young's address, but that's not where the GPS puts the phone."

"She must be out somewhere then or he stole her phone," Josie said. "Where is the phone?"

The agent tapped on some keys and then dragged his fingers across the mousepad. Finally, another map appeared, and another small red circle hovered over a map of East Denton where a branch of the Susquehanna River flowed through that side of the city. "That's a bridge," Josie said. It was the bridge in Denton under which many of the homeless and drug-addicted took refuge. Had Violet Young been near there? Had the killer merely taken her phone and gone there to make the call? Or had he kidnapped Violet, dumped her body elsewhere and then taken her phone?

Oaks said, "Let's go."

Josie and Mettner rode together behind a caravan of FBI vehicles, speeding through Denton until they reached the bridge. Josie called Noah as Mettner drove, explaining what was going on. "Call the school," Josie said. "And try to locate her husband, would you?"

"You got it," he said. "Be careful out there."

Mettner pulled over behind the rest of the caravan, all the vehicles crammed onto the side of the road, a strip of gravel and weeds just before the bridge. FBI agents flooded the area, all wearing bulletproof vests with the letters FBI emblazoned on them. Josie and Mettner pulled their own vests out of the trunk and threw them on. Everyone gathered around Oaks, who had to yell to be heard over the traffic crossing the bridge and the rush of the river below. "The phone's signal is still strong at this location. Let's split up into six teams of two. Three on that side and three on this side, meet in the middle below the bridge."

"Wait," Josie said. "Be advised that there is a large homeless camp under the bridge. There's a lot of drug activity that goes on down there. Stay on your toes."

They split up into their teams and descended on the area beneath the bridge, searching for Violet Young, the kidnapper, or both. Several makeshift tents had been erected on the riverbank. Josie and Mettner stayed together, checking each one and finding nothing. No one was willing to talk to cops.

The six teams met up in the middle. There was no sign of Violet Young or the kidnapper. Josie said, "The phone has to be here. We should spread out, widen our search area along the riverbank."

Oaks nodded and gave a signal with his hand for his agents to move. With two FBI teams searching parallel to them, Josie and Mettner searched nearest the water, picking over rocks and trudging through mud. She was a half mile from the bridge when she spotted a small flash of color in the mud. She squatted down for a closer look. It was a cell phone with a bright purple glittery cover. "Mett," Josie called, waving him over.

He took one look at the phone and called the other teams. They backed off once the FBI's Evidence Response Team arrived. A few minutes later, Oaks confirmed that the phone belonged to Violet Young.

Josie's own phone rang. She took it out and saw it was Noah. Swiping answer, she said, "What's up?"

"Violet left for work at seven-thirty this morning just like always. She went out into the schoolyard with the kids during the afternoon recess period which was around one-thirty p.m. She did not come back in."

"Did anyone see where she went?"

"When the principal and other teachers questioned the kids, a couple of them said she looked like she was watching something out in the street. She told one little girl she'd be right back and left the schoolyard. No one saw where she went after that."

"Did you pull footage from the cameras near the schoolyard?" Josie asked.

"Gretchen did, but all it shows is Violet staring out toward the street and then exiting the schoolyard."

"Jesus. Did you talk to Violet's husband?"

"He's in Orlando on business. At the airport, actually. The principal called him when Violet didn't come back from recess. He told her to call the police, which she did. Dispatch took the call and sent a unit to the school."

"No one called the mobile command?" Josie asked.

Noah sighed. "Why would they? Dispatch had no way of knowing this lady was Lucy Ross's teacher."

Josie knew this was true, but she couldn't help but wonder whether Violet would have been saved had the teams on the Ross case been the ones to respond. "When did the husband last speak with her?"

"Last night. He's on his way back now."

Josie asked, "Violet's car?"

"Still in the school lot."

Josie sighed. "Thank you. I'll let Oaks know."

"I asked Hummel if we could run the elimination prints he got from Amy Ross through AFIS to see if her prints match any already in the database. I know Chitwood didn't think it was worth it, but I put Hummel on it anyway. I don't know how soon he'll get to it though. I had to send him over to the school to help Gretchen interview the faculty and then try to track down the kids who saw Violet leave the schoolyard."

"The drop is at six," Josie groaned. "Amy and Colin still need to be prepped. The drop sites have to be monitored, and now Violet

Young is missing, probably bleeding out while we're all standing around on a riverbank. He's spreading us thin."

"Seems that way."

Josie saw Oaks striding toward her. "I have to go, Noah. Thanks for your help."

CHAPTER FORTY-EIGHT

Josie tried to focus on Oaks's words, but her mind was calculating. It was nearly four already. They were losing valuable time. There was so much to be done. There was no way they were going to send either one of the Ross parents to the drop sites alone, which meant they'd need to hide law enforcement personnel very carefully at each location. There was no time to strategize—no time for anything. The kidnapper had done this on purpose, leaving them almost no time to prepare and making sure that Violet Young's fate was unknown so that their resources would be spread far and wide.

"Detective Quinn," Oaks said, breaking through her thoughts. "Are you listening to me?"

Josie managed a tight smile. "I'm sorry," she said. "Please, go on."

"I was saying that the phone is Violet Young's," Oaks told her. "One of my guys got a woman to talk to him. She said she saw a guy matching our suspect's description—brown hair, ballcap, mid-twenties, Caucasian—standing near the water, talking on the phone before tossing it into the mud. She remembered because the phone was purple, and she said she doesn't see many men with purple phone cases."

Josie told Oaks what Noah and Gretchen had found out about Violet's disappearance.

"You think Violet Young saw him from the schoolyard and recognized him?" Oaks asked.

Josie shrugged. "Either that or he lured her out of the schoolyard with Lucy. He had to have been in a vehicle. Maybe he drove up, let her see that Lucy was in the car, and then she ran out. If she'd simply seen him, I think she would have called the police. But if Lucy was there, right in front of her, she probably would have gone over."

"So, he abducts her from right in front of the school with Lucy in the car, kills her, dumps her body, then drives out here to call Amy." Oaks turned and scanned the group of agents milling around the area. "He changed his MO. Normally he kills them in their home. What's he doing?"

"He knows we have to locate Violet. He's taking up our time and resources, keeping us off balance in the hopes we won't be fully ready by the time the drop comes."

"Screw that," Oaks muttered. "I'm leaving two guys here to search up and down the riverbank two miles in each direction for Violet Young's body. The rest of us will regroup at mobile command in twenty minutes. I'm going to need your people."

"You've got them," Josie said.

"We're going to need four teams—one at this Lover's Cave—do you know where that is?"

"Yes," Josie said. "It's in the city park, in the woods."

"Okay. You'll show me on a map when we get back to command. Anyway, we'll need a team there, one at the football field, one to transport Colin Ross and one to transport Amy Ross."

"Five teams," Josie said. "You need a team to locate Violet Young."

"Violet Young is dead," Oaks said. "We need to prioritize and get Lucy Ross home."

Josie put a hand on her hip. "You don't know that Violet Young is dead."

"Based on this suspect's prior behavior, I know she's dead. If Violet Young was still alive, wouldn't she have made herself known by now?"

"Not if she's tied up or incapacitated," Josie answered. "What if she's seriously injured? We can't take the chance of waiting to locate her."

Oaks said, "Detective Quinn, I've been in this business a long time. You can't save everyone. Based on the information available to me, there is a high probability that Violet Young is dead. As far as we know, Lucy Ross is still alive. I need to devote my resources to rescuing her."

"I never suggested you shouldn't," Josie said.

"We don't have the manpower for a full-out search for Violet Young right now."

"All I need from you is one thing," Josie said. "Do you have someone who can download the GPS history from Violet's phone?"

"Of course," Oaks said. "I've already instructed them to do that, and they are working on it, but the GPS history on her phone only updates each hour which means that if this guy took her and dumped her during the time period between the updates, we're not going to find her that way."

"But what if her GPS updated… let's say, a half hour before she was abducted. In that case, it would update a half hour after she was abducted. The killer had her for longer than a half hour. We know that because he abducted her around one-thirty and he didn't call Amy Ross until almost three o'clock. There is a slim chance the GPS history could lead us to Violet Young."

"Okay," Oaks conceded. "But again, I don't have the manpower for this right now. Not with the drop only a few hours away."

"I've got people who can look for Violet," Josie said.

"I need your people in the field on this, too," Oaks complained.

"I won't have to take anyone off the Ross case," she told him.

He threw his hands in the air. "Fine. Let's just go. We're running out of time."

CHAPTER FORTY-NINE

The man was gone again. She didn't tell me where he went, but I loved it when he was away. I could skip through all the rooms. I could jump and run and make as much noise as I wanted. Mostly. She still reminded me that when he got back, I'd have to be quiet again. Then she must have felt guilty because she said, "I have a special treat for you today."

I ran into the kitchen and climbed into one of the chairs that surrounded the table. "Is that for me?" I asked, pointing to the small plate with a cookie in the center of it.

She smiled and the sight made the words stick in my throat. She never smiled. "Yes," she said. "It's for you."

I wanted it to last forever, but the cookie—and the smile—was gone in an instant. "More?" I asked.

"I'm sorry. You haven't had much to eat lately. I don't want you to get sick. Too much sugar isn't good."

My shoulders slumped. She touched my hand. "When I take you home, you'll be able to eat as many cookies as you want."

I smiled back at her.

"Go play," she said. "Before he gets back."

I was jumping from the couch to the armchair when a knock sounded at the big door to outside. She came out of the kitchen, a finger pressed to her lips. I had to be quiet again. She pointed toward the room, but I didn't want to go back there, so I jumped down and hid behind the chair. I listened to her steps. Then the door opening. A voice I never heard. "Hello, dear."

I poked my head out from behind the chair for just a second. Long enough to see that the silver woman was at the door. I strained to hear all her words but only caught some of them. "… next door… thought I would say hello… need any help…"

Without a word, she slammed the door on the silver woman, turning and pushing her back against the door as if the silver woman might try to get in. But we both heard her steps fade.

Her fingers trembled as she turned the locks. Over her shoulder, she said, "She didn't see you. She didn't see anything."

I ran out from behind the chair. "Cause you didn't let her in. You have to let her in. She can help us, maybe."

"No," she insisted, shaking her head. "No. No one can help us."

CHAPTER FIFTY

Bodies packed the mobile command tent: two dozen FBI agents, Oaks, Chitwood, Josie, Noah, Mettner, Gretchen and several uniformed Denton officers. Closer to the entrance of the tent were officers from the state police and the county sheriff's office. The energy in the room was electric. There was a hum of anticipation. Bodies rustled; feet tapped against the ground. In one corner of the tent, Amy and Colin stood with the agents they'd each been assigned to fit them with bulletproof vests beneath their clothes. Next to them were two large duffel bags filled with money. Oaks gave a briefing and handed out assignments, and the crowd dispersed. Josie waited until Amy had been left alone before sidling over to her.

"Amy," she said quietly. "Before you do this, we need to talk. Even if we get Lucy back tomorrow, you have to understand that without straight answers from you, everyone here is going to look at you hard for involvement in this. This guy murdered two people in cold blood—and he may have killed Violet as well."

"I—why are they letting me do this if they think I was involved?" Amy asked.

"Because Lucy's life is in jeopardy," Josie said. "And right now there is no proof that you're involved, only suspicion. I can put that suspicion to rest if you tell me the truth about your past. You said Tessa Lendhardt was a fiction, and we can't find any record of her ever having existed. You were someone else before you were Tessa, weren't you? That's what's going on here. What is your real name? Not Tessa Lendhardt. Who were you before that?"

Amy looked around the room and when her gaze landed back on Josie's face, her eyes were wide and afraid. "You won't believe me," she whispered.

"Why wouldn't I?" Josie asked.

"Because I don't remember."

"You don't remember? What are you talking about?"

Before Amy could answer, Oaks's voice boomed across the tent. "Mr. and Mrs. Ross, over here, please."

Amy raced past Josie, following Colin over to where Oaks waited to brief them, leaving Josie alone and more frustrated with the woman than ever. She took in some deep breaths and counted to ten. Mettner walked over and started talking to her, but she didn't hear anything he said. When he waved his hand in her face, she snapped to attention. "Sorry, Mett," she said. "What was that?"

"I'm going with the team headed to Lover's Cave since I'm familiar with it and the park."

"That's a good idea," Josie said. "I'll go with Amy and that team to the football field—I went to Denton East High School. Is Gretchen coming with me?"

He nodded. "Oh, and Lamay is outside for you."

"Perfect," Josie said.

She walked outside the tent, eyes tracking the crowd until she spotted Dan Lamay, their desk sergeant. He had been with the department over forty years and had seen the coming and going of five chiefs of police—Josie included. He was now past retirement age, with a bum knee and an ever-increasing paunch. Josie had kept him on as a desk sergeant during her tenure as chief because his wife was recovering from cancer and his daughter was in college. He was fiercely loyal to her, helping her when she needed it most. She had worried that Chief Chitwood would let him go, but so far, he had stayed off Chitwood's radar.

"Thanks for coming, Dan," she said. "Did you get the kids from the college?"

"Yeah," he said. "The ones with the drones? They're in."

Josie felt a thrill of excitement run through her. "Fantastic."

Lamay shifted from one foot to the other. "Boss, I, uh, I'm not sure I understand exactly what you want me to do."

Josie said, "I want you to find Violet Young."

Lamay looked around them as if to make sure that no one else was listening. "Boss, I don't get around so well these days. I'm not sure I'm the best man for the job."

Josie laughed. "You won't need to go trekking through the woods, Dan. You're going to coordinate. The FBI gave me two locations where the GPS on Young's phone put her between when she left the school and when the kidnapper called Amy Ross. You'll need to start in the center, I think, and work your way outward."

She punched the passcode into her phone and brought up the map that one of Oaks's agents had forwarded to her. Lamay took reading glasses out of his breast pocket and studied it. "Okay," he said. "I know where this is. But boss, who am I supposed to coordinate?"

"The first thing I want you to do is find Luke Creighton. I'll text you his number. You'll call him. He should still be in town. He's got a bloodhound. Ask him if he'll help you search for Violet Young. He'll say yes. You'll call those college students back and tell them where to meet you with their drones. Then call Young's husband and ask permission to enter his home to find something that Violet wore recently. You'll check her laundry bin. Maybe the pajamas she wore to bed last night. Tell him you have a search and rescue dog you'd like to use in the search for Violet. He's not going to say no. Then you'll call WYEP and tell them you need volunteers for a search of this area for missing schoolteacher Violet Young and that time is critical. Have them post all over social media to meet you at a particular place in the next half hour. Luke and the kids with the drones will get a head start."

"You think people will show up on short notice?" Lamay asked.

"This is Denton," Josie said. "Of course they will."

Lamay didn't look particularly confident, but he nodded anyway. "I'll do my best, boss."

Josie grinned at him. He had never let her down before. "I know you will, Dan."

CHAPTER FIFTY-ONE

The grounds of Denton East High School were eerily quiet. Oaks and his team had done a good job of hiding themselves. All sports activities had been canceled and although Josie couldn't see them, she knew the FBI had set a perimeter around the building as well as the football field. Josie and Gretchen passed a state police officer sitting in his cruiser about a mile away from the school entrance, and nodded at him, before driving Josie's unmarked vehicle into what was normally the faculty parking lot.

"You went here?" Gretchen asked.

"Yes," Josie said. "The field is just on the other side of the building there." She pointed out the windshield where they could just see a set of goalposts peeking out from behind the school building.

Josie turned the car off and they sat there for a minute. A man in a windbreaker, sweatpants and a ballcap walked a small dog along the grassy area surrounding the lot. "That's one of Oaks's guys," Gretchen said. "I recognize him."

"This guy has to know we're going to be here," Josie said.

"I'm not sure we should be here," Gretchen said. "If he sees you, he might recognize you from the news."

"It's just him and the woman," Josie responded. "He can't have eyes everywhere. Come on. I'll show you a secret entrance that goes under the bleachers."

They checked their weapons and from the backseat, Josie pulled out a couple of bulletproof vests which they quickly strapped on beneath their jackets. They were bulky, but Josie hoped if the kidnapper was watching all the activity around the school from far away, he wouldn't notice. Over top of those, they each pulled on a Denton East High School polo shirt. From the trunk, Josie pulled a mesh bag filled with football pads. Someone had secured them from the school earlier. Josie and Gretchen would lug them into the rooms beneath the bleachers. If, by chance, the kidnapper or his accomplice saw them, they would appear to be a couple of staff members bringing football equipment into the sports complex.

Bleachers couched in brick ran the length of the field on either side. Along the backside of one row of bleachers, Josie found the old metal door that led under the bleachers to a locker room and a couple of restrooms. It had been boarded up and painted over since she had attended Denton East. Oaks's team had gone ahead and sent some men to reopen the door so that both teams could use it without being easily seen. The wood panel where the door handle was had been pried away. Josie curled her fingers around the edge of the door and pulled. It creaked open and she and Gretchen slipped inside a dimly lit concrete hallway, dropping the bag of equipment inside the door.

They followed the hallway to another door which was unlocked and led them out into some type of boiler room. From there, they found Oaks and his team in a small anteroom that held metal benches and vending machines. It had small windows that allowed them to see out onto the field.

Josie rose up on her tiptoes and peered outside. It was a decent view of the field. Directly across from them was the other set of bleachers. On one end of the field beyond the goalpost, the school building could be seen, and the other goalpost sat in front of a wooded area.

Oaks said, "I've got snipers on the roof of the school and on the tops of the bleachers."

Josie looked to the top of the other set of bleachers, but she didn't see anyone. "They're well-hidden," she said. "Where's Mrs. Ross?"

Oaks said, "She's at mobile command. She's going to arrive in her own vehicle and walk onto the field alone. We've equipped her with a vest."

Beside Josie, Gretchen stared outside. "I don't see how this is going to work," she said. "Why does this guy want her to leave the ransom in the middle of the field? If he comes out to get it, he'll be completely exposed."

"I don't think he cares about the ransom," Josie said.

"He's just going to leave the money out there? He must know the police will be watching. Surely he doesn't believe we'd all just back off." Gretchen remarked. "Then he wants the parents to wait twenty-four hours to get Lucy back?"

"That tells me he's hidden her somewhere. Let's say he shows himself to us today. We can't kill him because then Lucy's location would go to the grave with him."

"And if we capture him, he uses her location as leverage. But why this? This big open area where everyone is exposed?" Gretchen said.

"Because he could walk right out into the middle of that field, leave with the money, and we wouldn't be able to do a damn thing. Not without potentially losing Lucy." Josie looked up and down the field once more, taking a slow pan. "Oaks," she said.

He stepped up beside her. "Yes."

"Did you have any of your people clear that end of the field? Where the woods are?"

He nodded. "Of course. Nothing back there but some rocky outcroppings."

"The Stacks," Josie said, referring to the slabs of rocks that had fallen from the side of the mountain behind the high school, forming large stacks of flat rocks.

"I'm sorry, what?"

"The local kids call them the Stacks. It's where the students go to hang out, drink, and smoke."

"Yes, our guys saw those," Oaks said.

"The top of the Stacks is an elevated position. Behind that, a half mile back is the old, abandoned textile mill."

Oaks said, "You think he'll come from that direction."

Josie nodded. "That's what I would do if I were him."

"I'll get someone out in the woods, along that ridge, and call the sheriff—they've got units to check out the mill."

"The units in the woods have to be invisible," Josie said. "If he's coming from there and he sees them, it's game over."

He nodded. "I'm on it."

With that, he took out his phone and made two calls. As she listened to him give instructions, a feeling of relief swept over her, but it wasn't enough to quell the unease building inside her. She knew the Denton woods intimately. She'd spent most of her childhood in them. Having agents patrol the ridge above the Stacks would make the area more secure, but Josie knew there were several crevices and other rock formations in that area that would make a good hiding place for someone who didn't want to be seen. The kidnapper could be already hiding somewhere and would have the advantage—however hard they tried to be invisible, he would see them coming. If they'd had more time, Josie could have had her own team—who was much more familiar with the area between the Stacks and the mill—clear those woods.

Gretchen handed her an earpiece connected to a small communication device. "Put this on. These are the comms the agents are using. We'll be able to hear everything that's going on."

"Thanks," Josie said absently.

Gretchen said, "You're staring awfully hard. You heard Oaks, right? He had a team clear that area when he got here."

"I know," Josie murmured. "I just can't shake the feeling that something about this entire set up is very, very wrong."

Behind them, Oaks said, "It's almost time."

CHAPTER FIFTY-TWO

It felt like the world had fallen into some strange, silent trance. Nothing and no one moved. They had managed to get one of the windows to slide open so that they could hear any noise outside the bleachers, but there was no sound. Not even the wind or the birds. Josie checked her phone. It was two minutes to six. The only sounds she heard were the hum of the vending machines across the room, Gretchen and Oaks breathing, and the low chatter over the comms. A voice in her ear said, "Team is in place in location two. We are about to send in the package." Josie knew that was the drop at Lover's Cave.

Oaks responded, "Copy that. Team is in position at location one. Is the package ready?"

Another voice came back. "Mother just pulled up in her vehicle. She's got the package. Heading toward the field."

The three of them waited, staring out the small windows. A minute later, Amy stepped through the entrance to the football field nearest the building, a duffel bag in her hands.

"How much does that bag weigh?" Gretchen asked.

"As it turns out, half a million dollars weighs about twenty-two pounds," Oaks said.

Amy let go of the straps with one hand to push a lock of her hair behind her ear. Josie could see her fingers trembling.

On the comms, Oaks said, "Team at location one is sending in the package. Stand by."

Another voice came back, "Copy that. Team at location two is sending in the package as well."

Amy walked slowly and unsteadily onto the field, struggling under the weight of her vest while carrying the duffel bag. Oaks had instructed Amy to leave the bag on the fifty-yard line in the middle of the rendering of Denton East's mascot, a blue jay.

"Team at location two has delivered the package. Mr. Ross is returning to custody. Stand by."

The comms went silent as Amy reached the very center of the field and placed the bag on the ground. The sound of her pounding heart filled Josie's ears. A voice she didn't recognize came across the comms. "Be advised. We have movement on the east side in the woods at location one."

Amy spun in a slow circle, eyes searching everywhere until they came to rest on the bleachers where Oaks, Josie and Gretchen hid.

"What is she doing?" Gretchen asked.

"Waiting," Josie said. "She's waiting for something to happen."

"Be advised, we have eyes on a suspect on the ridge in the woods at location one," came the strange voice.

From the window, Oaks waved to get Amy's attention but still, she didn't move.

Gretchen said, "But she knows that the kidnapper isn't bringing Lucy here."

Finally, after what seemed like an eternity, Amy started walking back toward them.

A shot rang out, cracking through the air. Everyone froze. On the field, Amy dropped into a crouch, her arms over her head.

"Agents report, agents report," Oaks said over the comms.

"Where did that come from?" Gretchen asked.

"The Stacks," Josie said. "Had to be the Stacks."

Amy wasn't moving. Her arms lowered and her eyes traveled her surroundings once more.

Another shot cracked the air.

"Agents report," Oaks hollered. He ran from the room.

Outside on the field, Amy's head peeked out from between her arms. She took one look around, sprung up and started to sprint toward the entrance.

Yet another voice sounded on the comms. "Location one, man down! Man down! On the ridge. Suspect is a six-foot male, armed with a—" Then it cut out.

Oaks's voice shouted, "Agent Morgan report! Report! Units to the ridge."

A third shot rang out. Amy's body bucked and fell. Suddenly the comms were full of voices shouting commands and positions. Josie took out her Glock and ran out of the room. Outside the anteroom were a set of steps on her left which led up to the field. Josie started up the stairs. Behind her, Gretchen shouted, "Boss, no! You'll be a sitting duck."

"I can't leave her out there," Josie yelled back over her shoulder. "If she's hit, she could bleed out."

"Just wait," Gretchen said, huffing after her. "Wait for help."

As Josie burst into the daylight, she saw Amy's crumpled form twenty yards away on the edge of the field. She heard Gretchen's labored breath behind her. "Go," Gretchen told her. "I've got your six."

Keeping her weapon pointed at the ground, Josie ran toward Amy. She was on her back, eyes fixed on the sky. "Please, God, oh please, please," she said over and over again. A pool of blood spread beneath her. Josie dropped to her knees, one hand searching the woman's body for the bullet wound. "Where are you hit?"

"I don't know," Amy said. "I think, I think down—" she pressed a hand into her lower abdomen, just beneath the vest. "Down here."

Josie found the source of the blood. She'd been shot in the lower right side of her abdomen. Josie holstered her weapon and took Amy's hand, pressing it over the hole in her pelvis. "Keep your hand here. Keep pressure as best you can."

She put one arm under Amy's legs and one under her shoulders, lifting her into the air. She was lucky that the woman was small in stature and didn't weigh much.

Amy said, "I have to live. I have to get Lucy back."

"We're going now."

Gretchen ran out and took up Amy's other side. Together they ran back toward the door at the center of the bottom of the bleachers. They were halfway there when another shot rang out. Josie braced for the impact of the bullet, for it to slice through some uncovered part of her body or Gretchen's body, or for it to hit Amy again, knocking her from their grasp. But it didn't come.

They banged through the door, Amy screaming out in pain. Once inside, they carried her down the steps and into the anteroom. Gently, they laid her out on the floor. Josie used both hands to put pressure on her wound while Gretchen called for an ambulance.

"Hold on," Josie told Amy. "Just hold on."

CHAPTER FIFTY-THREE

The ambulance had been on stand-by in case anyone was injured during the operation. Within five minutes, it was behind the bleachers where Josie and Gretchen had entered. The paramedics went to work on Amy. Josie listened to the chatter on the comms. Oaks's agents were moving into the woods.

"Stay with her," Josie told Gretchen. "I'm going out there."

Josie sprinted out the back and moved in behind two FBI agents dressed in tactical gear headed toward the Stacks. They ran in a column, crouched down, guns at the ready even though a shot hadn't been fired in several minutes. Just inside the forested area, where the Stacks began, the agents in front of Josie converged on another agent sprawled on the ground. As Josie got closer, she was relieved to see he was still alive.

"He pushed me," the agent said, his face twisted in pain. "I think my leg is broken."

As his colleagues called for paramedics, Josie moved along the vertical rock face, looking for the shortcut she'd used as a teenager—it was a break in the stone, a dirt-filled crease with enough of an angle that you could grab onto the tree roots protruding from either side of it and climb quickly to the top of the ridge. Once she found it, Josie holstered her weapon, fitted her body into the crevice, grabbed onto the nearest tree root and clambered up to the top within seconds. She looked around before running in a low crouch toward the other FBI agent who had been stationed in the woods. He lay curled on his side, both hands clutching at his leg.

Josie knelt over him and checked his pulse, which was strong. "What happened?" she asked.

"He shot me, that's what happened," the agent said. "In the leg. He came out of nowhere behind us. Pushed Morgan right off the ridge, I shot at him and he shot back. Hit me. Jesus. I need to get to a hospital."

Josie saw the blood spilling out from around his fingers as he held the side of his thigh. "I need help up here," she screamed. "We have a gunshot wound."

She pressed her hands over the top of his to keep pressure on his wound. "Did you see him?" she asked, hoping to keep him talking and alert until help made it onto the ridge.

"Yeah. About six foot. Brown hair. Caucasian. Young, maybe mid to late twenties. I think there was someone with him though. I thought I saw someone behind him. He ran back into the woods."

"Probably the woman," Josie said. "Hey, look at me. Just hold on, okay?"

He nodded but his face was pale, and the energy seemed to leave him with each breath. "I need help up here," she screamed again over the side of the ridge.

A moment later, she heard the heavy tread of boots crashing through the forest floor and she was relieved to see two more agents and two paramedics with a spine board. She watched as they loaded the injured agent on it and started making their way back down off the ridge, the long way around. The agents stayed behind, and Josie motioned away from the ridge, deeper into the forest, where the land inclined. "That way," she said. "We should spread out. The woman is with him."

They nodded at her and fanned out, walking carefully through the forest, their weapons drawn. Josie stayed south, creeping along, keeping close to the trees. In her mind, she mapped out the area ahead. When they were teenagers, Josie and her late husband Ray had run through these woods many times after hanging out at the

Stacks. When the police raided the area, they'd flee deeper, following paths only they knew about. Sometimes they'd hide in particular places they knew and other times, they'd make it up and over the top of the hill, scrambling down the other side to the abandoned mill. From there, they'd walk home. She found one of the narrow paths she remembered and followed it up, the incline getting steeper and more difficult to walk the higher she went. She stayed on course, though, because she remembered a cave that used to sit on this side of the mountain. It wasn't deep or all that small. It was just big enough to take shelter in from the rain.

A branch snapped nearby, and she froze. Back pressed against a tree, she held her gun at the ready, listening. The intermittent chatter on the comms burst and buzzed in her ear. She reached up and tore at the earbud, pulling it out and letting it hang along her collar. Again, she listened. She thought she heard footsteps ahead. She tried to move with them, gaining on whoever was out there without them hearing her in pursuit. On her right, the cave came into view. A foot protruded from the mouth of the cave.

Josie crept closer, heart pounding, blood rushing in her ears. She pressed her back against the outer part of the cave's entrance, listening. She heard nothing. No footsteps, no rustling, no breathing or any kind of movement. She peeked around the cave entrance. The foot hadn't moved. Swiftly, Josie turned into the cave, sweeping the barrel of the gun back and forth. The foot belonged to a woman, who lay in a puddle of blood and soil. She was young and pale with dark hair pulled back in a ponytail. As Josie got closer, she saw that the woman had been shot in the head. There was an entry wound to the right temple with stippling below the bullet hole, indicating a close-range shot. Whoever had killed her had held the gun to her skin and pulled the trigger. The splatter on the cave wall to the left of her head was still wet and dripping.

Josie thought about the shots that they'd heard when Amy was leaving the money in the center of the field. There had been two shots fired before Amy was hit, which had to have been the FBI agent shooting at the kidnapper and the kidnapper firing back. Then the kidnapper had shot Amy. It had been several minutes before the last shot rang out. Had the kidnapper killed his own accomplice? Why? What was his plan? Keeping all the money for himself? That didn't make sense as there was no indication that he had even taken the money. She had only half been paying attention to the chatter in her ear, but she knew the team at Lover's Cave had seen no activity of any kind since Colin left the money inside the cave.

It would seem that the only thing the kidnapper had hoped to accomplish was to kill Amy.

Had this woman tried to stop him? Had she wanted her portion of the money? Whatever the dynamic had been, she had ended up dead. Josie took out her cell phone and called Oaks, keeping her voice low. "I found the female accomplice. She's dead." She gave the location as best she could and hung up. Moving to the other side of the cave entrance, she listened again. She thought she heard the crunch of leaves, but she couldn't be sure.

She maneuvered out of the cave, staying close to its outer wall and searched the trees and brush, but she didn't see anyone. She took the path again, moving from tree to tree, trying to make herself small. The climb became more difficult. Her lungs burned. The ground beneath her feet angled upward steeper and steeper. Finally, she came to a small clearing and she knew she was close to the top of the mountain. There were several large rocks, and a ring of small stones circling a heap of ash. Beer cans littered the area. Local kids came all the way out here for privacy.

From the corner of her eye, she saw a flash of movement on her left. She took a shooter's stance and aimed in that direction. She saw the man's shaggy brown hair, dark green shirt and mud-covered blue jeans as he emerged from behind a wide tree trunk, a rifle sling across his chest. The barrel of the gun poked up from behind his left shoulder. "Freeze," she called. "Police. Get your hands up."

He turned toward her. Her mind registered the pistol in his hand. They both shot at the same time. Josie felt the impact of his bullet in her stomach, driving her off her feet, back through the air, and then she tumbled down the hill below.

CHAPTER FIFTY-FOUR

Josie lay on her back, trying desperately to suck in air that would not come. The pressure on her abdomen was enormous. *Get this vest off, get it off, get it off!!!* She tried to say the words aloud, but the wind had been knocked out of her. Her lungs screamed, her whole body buzzed with panic. She couldn't breathe; her gun was gone; and the killer was still out there, somewhere above her. Leaves crunched near her head. She tried to turn over, to get up, to scream but she couldn't. Hands pressed down on her shoulders.

"Hold still," a male voice said.

As the faces of two FBI agents in full tactical gear came into view, relief flooded her.

"She's been hit in the vest," one of them said.

"Let's get it off her."

They peeled the vest off and sat her up, the motion sending a spike of pain straight through her center. Finally, her breath returned. Gasping, she pointed toward the top of the incline. "He's up there. I fired at him, but I think I missed."

"We've got more units coming in from the other direction," one of them said. "Let's get you back to the school. There's an ambulance waiting there."

They lifted her to her feet. "I don't need an ambulance," Josie said.

"You should get checked out."

"No," she insisted. "I don't need an ambulance. I just need to… I need to go home… or I… I need my gun. My gun."

It appeared in one of the agents' hands. "Here you go. Now let's get out of here. You shouldn't be out here injured."

She took her gun and slid it into her holster, even that small movement sending pain through her belly. "I'm not injured."

"We'll see," one of them said as they led her back down the hill.

They delivered her to the back of an open ambulance, but the moment the two agents jogged back off to the woods, Josie told the paramedics she was fine and walked back to her car, trying to keep her gait steady, while a searing fire burned her center.

She dialed Noah on her cell phone, put him on speaker and tossed the phone onto the passenger's seat. "Hey," he answered. "You okay? I heard all hell broke loose over there."

Driving hurt. Everything hurt. Josie gritted her teeth and tried to make her voice sound normal. "I'm fine. Yeah, it was crazy." She caught him up on everything except the part where she got shot. "I didn't see Oaks when I came back out."

"He's over by the mill, last I heard. They found evidence that the kidnapper and his accomplice might have been squatting over there. No evidence of Lucy, though. I mean they didn't find her in there."

"He's got her stashed away somewhere. Is Gretchen at the hospital?"

"Yeah," Noah answered. "She's waiting on Amy Ross. The husband is there, too. Mrs. Ross is in surgery."

"Oh no," Josie said. "Do they think she'll make it?"

"They're not sure yet. The bullet is lodged in her pelvis. She lost a lot of blood. I have good news, though."

It was hard to imagine any news that might be considered good in the nightmare that had gripped the city. "What's that?" she asked.

"We found Violet Young. Actually, the team Lamay put together found her. Luke Creighton's dog sniffed her out in the woods. She was stabbed—"

"In the chest?" Josie interrupted, wincing with the effort the words took. She was almost home.

"Yeah. Missed her heart but caused a lot of trauma. The doctors said she'll survive. She was left pretty deep in the woods. She tried to walk out but she was too weak from loss of blood so she took shelter under some bushes in case the killer came back and waited. That's all they got out of her before she was transported to the hospital."

Josie felt a wave of relief so profound, she felt like she could breathe again.

"Josie?" Noah said.

"That's great," she managed. "Have someone get her statement, would you? Gretchen, maybe, as she's already at the hospital."

"Will do," Noah said.

"And can you call over to Dr. Feist's office? Ask her to test the female suspect's hands for gunshot residue, would you?"

She heard the sound of a page flipping over and knew he was writing her instructions down in his notebook. "You okay?" he asked again. "You sound strange."

"I'm fine," Josie said, even as pain webbed across her abdomen and into her lower back. "I just need to get changed. I got mud all over me up on that mountain."

"All right," Noah said. "Better check in when you're done. Oaks is out in the field looking for this guy, and Chitwood and the FBI's press liaison are trying to hammer something out to tell the reporters camped outside. We could use a cool head."

Josie pulled into her driveway, relieved to see Misty's vehicle there. "You're the cool head," Josie told him. "Tell them we don't have enough information right now to make a statement. I'll get there when I can."

CHAPTER FIFTY-FIVE

Once inside, Josie slumped against her door. From the living room, she heard the television playing. Seconds later, Misty appeared in the doorway, dressed in an oversized T-shirt and a pair of sweatpants, her blonde hair thrown up in a messy bun. "Josie? Oh my God, are you okay?"

Josie grimaced, holding her stomach. "Can you help me upstairs?"

Misty's blue eyes widened as she came closer. "My God, you're covered in blood. Should I call 911? Are you hurt? What's going on?"

Josie could hear panic raising the octaves of Misty's voice with each question. She waved her free hand in the air. "I'm fine. It's okay. It's not my blood."

"Oh," Misty snapped. "Well that makes me feel better. I'm calling 911."

"No, really. I don't need an ambulance. I'm fine. I… fell. I just need help getting up to the bathroom and getting cleaned up. Please."

"Should I call Noah?" Misty asked, putting a tentative arm around Josie's waist.

"No, please," Josie said. "You can help me. Where's Harris?"

Misty guided her up the stairs slowly. "He's asleep in the spare room."

"Okay, good," Josie said.

Once inside the bathroom, Josie sat on the edge of her bathtub. She tugged at the hem of her shirt. "I got shot," she told Misty.

"Oh my God! Josie, you said this wasn't your blood! You need to get to the—"

"I had a vest on. The bullet didn't go through."

Misty put a hand on her chest. "Oh, thank God. What happened?"

"Help me get this shirt off, and I'll tell you."

As Misty helped her lift the shirt over her head, Josie gave her the abbreviated version of the day's events. As she talked, Misty helped her take off her blood-splattered jeans. "I'm just going to throw these away," Misty said. "Unless you want me to wash them."

"No," Josie said. "It's fine."

Misty wet a washcloth with hot water and handed it to Josie. She watched as Josie wiped her face and arms. "Josie," Misty said. "This is not okay. Oh wow, look at your stomach."

Josie looked down at her abdomen to see an angry red-purple bruise blooming across her skin. She placed a hand over it. Tears stung the backs of her eyes.

Misty said, "I think you should go to the hospital. Get checked out. What if you've got an internal injury?"

"There's something I need you to do for me first," Josie said. "Please."

Misty listened as Josie explained what she wanted her to do. Then she put a hand on her hip and said, "Are you sure I shouldn't call someone else? Your grandmother? Your sister? Your mom?"

"No, thank you," Josie said. "Please. Just do this for me."

Misty backed out of the bathroom. "All right. Let me get you a change of clothes first. You'll be okay if Harris wakes up while I'm gone?"

Josie nodded. "Yes. Just please, hurry back."

CHAPTER FIFTY-SIX

A half hour later, the two of them sat on the bathroom floor, staring at the white stick between them.

"Why didn't you tell me?" Misty asked. "Or anyone?"

Josie laughed. "I didn't even tell myself. I mean, I thought with the way I was feeling, I might be pregnant, but I didn't want to admit to the possibility, even to myself."

Misty smiled. "You know, it's not the worst thing. You'd be a great mom. You're wonderful with Harris. He loves you so much."

Josie smiled. "And I love him. It's not that. I mean, it sort of is—when Ray and I were married, before we separated and he met you, we decided we'd never have children because we had both seen so much evil in the world and almost all of it was in our own families. What if we brought a monster into the world by virtue of our DNA?"

"But you were completely wrong about your DNA," Misty pointed out. "The woman who raised you had no blood relation to you at all."

"I know," Josie said. "And that was a kind of relief, but I haven't thought yet about whether I want kids."

"You and Noah would be naturals," Misty said, waving a dismissive hand.

Josie gently pressed her fingers against the tender, bruised part of her stomach, now covered with a T-shirt. "Well, that's kind of the problem. Last month when I was working on that big case, I had to go up to Sullivan County to interview a witness. I saw Luke."

"Your ex-fiancé, Luke?" Misty asked.

Josie nodded. "Things between me and Noah were bad. He had asked for a break. I was hurt and angry. I—I spent the night at Luke's house."

Misty's mouth dropped open. "You slept with him?"

"No," Josie said. "Well, I don't know. I got drunk and blacked out and when I woke up, we were in bed together. I have no idea what happened."

"But you think you slept with him?"

"Well, no. I don't think I would have, but the truth is that I have no way of knowing for sure."

"You didn't talk about it?" Misty asked.

Shame burned Josie's cheeks. "No. I left before he woke up." She leaned over the stick and then checked her phone. There was still one minute left on the pregnancy test before the result would show up. "Why do these things take so long?"

Misty said, "You should just talk to Luke. I mean if nothing happened, wouldn't you rather know that and have that peace of mind?"

Josie nodded. "I guess so, but…"

"But what if he tells you something you don't want to hear?"

"Right," Josie muttered. "I don't—I don't want to hurt Noah."

"Well," Misty said, picking up the stick. "I can't speak for whether you hurt him or not, but now you won't have to tell him about Luke at all if you choose not to. It's negative."

"What?" Josie gasped. She snatched the stick from Misty's hand and stared at the minus sign in the small window in the center of the stick.

"You're not pregnant," Misty clarified.

"Oh my God," Josie breathed. At once she felt relief, but not for the reason she thought she would. She wasn't relieved not to be pregnant; she was relieved that the bullet that had hit her vest hadn't hurt the baby—because there was no baby. The thought of there being no baby made her feel sad for some reason, even as the rational part of her mind argued coolly that she couldn't cope with a baby in her line of work anyway, so it was all for the best.

Misty watched her closely. Josie was hardly aware of the tears rolling down her face until Misty reached over and smoothed one away with the pad of her thumb. "Oh Josie," she said. "Maybe you do still need to talk to Luke. And Noah, too."

She did need to talk to both of them, but now was not the time. Lucy was still missing. Josie said, "I'll go to the hospital. Get this checked out. I just didn't want to find out there for the first time if I was pregnant and then possibly be told that I had lost the baby. Not in a place like that. With strangers around."

Misty nodded. "I know you hate hospitals. I'm not a fan either. Why don't I call someone on your team and have them come get you?"

"Thank you, Misty," Josie choked, unable to control the emotion that overcame her.

Misty lurched forward and threw her arms around Josie's neck, causing a sharp pain in Josie's stomach, but she held on, grateful for Misty's friendship, grateful that she wasn't alone—the way Amy was alone even when surrounded by people.

CHAPTER FIFTY-SEVEN

Mettner drove Josie to Denton Memorial Hospital where they ran a battery of tests and cleared her for duty. She was still sore and had several other bruises and cuts on her body from her tumble down the mountain that she hadn't noticed before, but she felt clearer-headed than she had earlier. She told the doctor about her ongoing nausea and he told her it was likely stress, gave her an anti-nausea drug and told her to follow up with her regular doctor if it continued. Script in hand, Josie found the elevators and went up to the fifth floor where she found Gretchen pacing outside the surgical waiting room.

"Hey," Gretchen said. "I was worried. You okay?"

Josie hugged her middle, which still felt as though she'd done one thousand sit-ups. "I'm fine. Thanks. Any news on Amy?"

Gretchen shook her head. "Still waiting."

Through the windows, they could see Colin seated between two FBI agents in the waiting room. Gray stubble covered his face. He leaned forward in his chair, elbows on the tops of his legs, his hands steepled together in prayer under his chin. His mouth moved although neither of the agents with him seemed to be responding to anything he said.

As if reading her mind, Gretchen said, "He's praying."

"It's not a bad idea," Josie muttered. "Have you heard from Oaks?"

"He's still out at the mill. Between there and the high school it's a big scene to process."

"Have they ID'd the female?" Josie asked.

Gretchen said, "Not yet. They're working on it."

"What about the money?"

"It's still sitting where the Rosses left it. Oaks put two agents on each package to watch. If anyone approaches, they'll be detained."

"That's good," Josie said. "But that money can't sit in the middle of Denton East's football field indefinitely."

"Right," Gretchen agreed.

"We should leave it there until after the time passes for him to give Lucy back though."

"You really think he's going to return her?" Gretchen asked.

Nausea kicked up in her stomach again. "No," Josie said. "I don't think he will. I think this is all about hurting Amy and as long as she's still alive, he will want to keep torturing her. Did you talk to Violet Young?"

"Not yet," Gretchen said. "The doctors were working on her, running tests."

"I'll try to speak with her," Josie said. Her phone chirped. She looked at the text message. "That's Oaks. He's downstairs in the morgue with Dr. Feist. I'm going to head down there first. Then we'll see if we can talk with Violet. You stay here. Keep me posted."

"You got it, boss."

CHAPTER FIFTY-EIGHT

The Denton City Morgue was located in the basement of Denton Memorial Hospital, windowless and drab with a lingering odor that was half chemical and half biological decay. The walls of the long hallway had originally been white but hadn't been painted in so long that they were now a dull gray, and the floor tiles had become jaundiced long ago. It was also the quietest place in the hospital—maybe even the city. Usually the silence made Josie's skin crawl, but given the chaos of the last twenty-four hours, it was a welcome relief. She saw Oaks as soon as she stepped into the exam room, his suit streaked with mud, his face haggard. He stood several feet away from the stainless-steel table which now held the woman Josie had found shot to death in the cave. Dr. Feist leaned over the woman's face, holding what looked like a driver's license up next to the woman's head.

"You okay?" Oaks asked when he saw Josie.

"I'm fine," Josie said. "What's going on? You've got an ID?"

Oaks nodded. "We found a backpack in a third-floor room in the old mill with a wallet inside of it. We pulled the license. We're running prints now to see if they match the unknowns from the Jaclyn Underwood scene and Lucy's room, but we believe it belongs to her. Dr. Feist is making the comparison now. We'll also take DNA from her body and try to match it from the hair on the pillow found in Jaclyn's closet."

"Who is she?" Josie asked.

Dr. Feist walked over and handed Josie the license. "Natalie Oliver. Twenty-four."

The woman in the driver's license photo stared back at Josie, a challenging tilt to her chin, brown eyes penetrating. She looked as though she'd been trying to appear tough for her photo, but to Josie she just seemed vulnerable. "She's from West Seneca, New York," Josie said. "What's she doing here?"

Oak said, "We don't know yet. I'll have my people do a background check on her now that we've got a positive ID."

Josie handed the ID to Oaks and took out her phone, searching Google Maps for West Seneca, New York. "This is pretty close to Buffalo," Josie said. "There has to be a connection to Tessa Lendhardt."

"The field agents in Buffalo haven't found anything yet," Oaks said. "There are some Lendhardts but they're all men."

"I heard that," Josie said, hoping that Trinity was getting somewhere with her interviews. "Did Hummel stop by?"

"To swab her hands for gunshot residue?" Dr. Feist asked. "Yeah, they should have those results back any minute."

Josie looked at Oaks who said, "I think we should have a briefing in one hour. At mobile command. There are a lot of things developing right now."

"I agree," Josie said. "But first, I want to talk to Violet Young."

CHAPTER FIFTY-NINE

Violet Young lay in a bed in the ICU, her small figure dwarfed by all of the equipment hooked up to her. Josie had a brief moment of dizziness as she entered the room, flashing back to the missing girls' case and seeing her then-fiancé, Luke Creighton, looking very similar to this—only much, much worse. In a shadowy corner of the room, Violet's husband sat in a large vinyl chair. He jumped up when Josie and Oaks entered.

"Who are you?" he barked, his hulking frame taking up almost half the room.

Josie made the introductions and immediately, the man's demeanor relaxed. He shook both their hands. "Sorry," he said. "It's just been a rough day. I can't believe this is happening. I thought Violet was gone forever." He looked back at his wife, swiping at tears that leaked from his eyes.

"I know this is a terrible time, but we'd like to ask Violet some questions, if you don't mind," Josie said.

"Of course," said her husband. "She was just awake before you came in. Violet? Vi? The police are here. They need to talk to you."

Josie and Oaks went over to the side of her bed. Her eyelids fluttered open, and she managed a smile. "Hi," she said, voice scratchy.

"We won't keep you long," Josie promised. "We just have a few questions. You were taken from the school, correct?"

Violet nodded. Her husband had taken up guard at the other side of her bed, holding her hand. "I was outside, at afternoon recess. I saw her, saw Lucy."

"Lucy was with them," Josie said.

"Yes, in a black car. They drove past the school a couple of times. I thought I was imagining it, but the car went past and came back and there she was—in the backseat, her hands pressed against the window, like she was yelling for help."

Josie felt a small ache in her heart for poor little Lucy. "You went over to the car."

"Yes. I know I shouldn't have. I should have gone inside and called the police, but I thought I would lose her. I just wasn't thinking clearly. Then I got closer to the car and saw it was a couple. For some reason, I didn't think…"

"You didn't think the woman was a threat," Josie filled in.

Violet nodded. "I'm embarrassed to say, yes."

"Did they force you into the car?" Oaks asked.

Tears glistened in Violet's eyes. "Yes. The man pulled out a gun and he told me he'd start firing if I didn't get in. I didn't want any children to get hurt so I got in."

"How was Lucy?" Josie asked.

A tear rolled down Violet's cheek. "Scared. She clung to me. I tried to comfort her. The man drove. Once we reached a more remote area, he pulled over and he took me out—out of the car. Poor Lucy. She screamed and cried and clung to me. But he was too strong. He took my phone and put me in the trunk."

"What kind of car?" Oaks asked.

"It was a small black car. Four doors. I don't know the make or model. I was never good with those things."

"Then what happened?" Josie asked.

"We drove and drove. Stopped a few times. I could sometimes hear Lucy crying. Once I heard her screaming and then it cut off, and I didn't hear her after that." More tears poured from Violet's eyes. Above the bed, one of the monitors began to beep. Her blood pressure and respirations were climbing.

"It's okay," Josie said. "It's okay. You did everything you could to help Lucy. You're lucky to be alive. We're still looking for her and the things you're telling us are very helpful. Just a few more questions, and we'll let you rest."

Violet nodded. She looked to her husband, who squeezed her hand in both of his large hands and smiled at her encouragingly.

"What happened after that?" Josie asked.

"They drove some more. Then they stopped. He got me out of the car and started marching me into the woods. He had a gun to my head. I was too afraid to run, and the woman, she was behind him and she kept yelling. She kept saying, 'Why did you do that? You shouldn't have done that.'"

"They were fighting?"

"Yes. She was angry with him for ruining some plan. He kept telling her to shut up. Then he told her to go back to the car. She refused and he hit her. Knocked her down. He told her he was in charge and the plan had changed. Then she got up and left. He—he stabbed me. He had this knife. Like a hunting knife. It was on his belt. I didn't notice before because I was too concerned about the gun. I… I tried to fight back, but he was too strong. I was scared."

"Did they call each other by name? Did you hear either of them say any names at all?" Oaks asked.

Violet nodded. "He kept calling her Nat. She didn't call him by any name."

Natalie Oliver, Josie thought.

"So," Josie said, picking up the narrative. "He stabbed you. They were fighting. Then what happened?"

"Then the woman came back. She hit him over the head with something. They started fighting again. I wanted to get up and run but I was bleeding. I didn't want to draw their attention, so I just stayed very still. He came over after they stopped and kicked me in the ribs a few times. I tried not to react. She said, 'Let's go,' and then he said he was going to finish the job."

She paused to suck in several breaths. Her face had gone even paler than when they'd walked into the room. "Take your time," Josie told her.

After a few more breaths, Violet continued, "She said I was dead already. I felt her hands on me. She checked my pulse. In my neck. She must have felt it—my heart was hammering at that point. But she told him, 'See, I told you she was dead. Leave her and let's get out of here.'"

Josie and Oaks exchanged a puzzled look. "She saved you," Josie said.

Violet nodded again. "I don't know why. There's no way she didn't feel my pulse. But she convinced him I was gone. I heard them walk off. A little while later, I tried to get up and walk, but I didn't make it very far. I was too weak. Too much pain."

"You're safe now," Josie told her. "Just rest. Thank you, Mrs. Young."

Josie and Oaks left the Youngs and walked down the hall toward the elevators. "That doesn't sound good," Oaks said.

"No, it doesn't," Josie said. "Did your team find any evidence that Lucy had been at the mill?"

"We're still processing, but so far, no. We haven't."

They didn't say it, but she knew they were both thinking it: there was a very good chance that Lucy was dead.

CHAPTER SIXTY

She was gone again in the dark. I woke up cold. I knew that if she wasn't there in the room with me then she must be getting ready to go home again. I ran to the door and looked through the crack. I waited for her shadow to appear, but it didn't. My legs felt stiff, my mouth dry. I listened hard for her footsteps but didn't hear them. She was always good at moving without making any noise. When the daylight started to creep across the living room, a spike of fear pierced my heart.

Where was she?

It seemed like hours and hours, but I don't know how long it was before he came out of one of the other rooms. I watched him in complete silence. He wore his usual flannel shirt, blue jeans and heavy boots. His thin brown hair was combed from one side of his scalp to the other, and as always, the scent of cigarette smoke trailed behind him. He smelled of cigarettes even when he wasn't smoking. He saw me sitting on the floor in the doorway. "You looking for her?"

I didn't move.

"You talk? Say something, kid."

"I—I—"

He shook his head. "Never mind. She's gone."

"Gone?" I repeated.

"She left. Took her shit and left."

I ran toward the outside door, but his hand shot out and grabbed the collar of my shirt.

"I'm going with her," I cried.

He tossed me as if I weighed nothing. My body flew through the air, crashed into the wall, and slid down to the floor. I felt the hurt everywhere at once. Something flared inside me—burning anger—and without thinking, I jumped back up and flew at him. I grabbed his thick, hairy forearm and clamped my teeth down on it.

He tried to flick me away, like I was a bug. "Dammit, kid. Knock it off."

I wouldn't let go. A growling sound started deep in my throat. Blood flowed into my mouth. With his other meaty paw, he backhanded me. Stars appeared before my eyes and my jaw went slack. I fell to the ground. "Look what you did, you stupid kid," he muttered. Blood flowed down his arm, to his wrist, snaking between his fingers. I had made him bleed just as he had made her bleed so many times.

I tried to stand up but dizziness overcame me. "Where do you think you're going?" he said.

"I'm going to find her," I said.

"You're not going with her," he said. "You stay here with me."

"She'll come back," I choked out.

Then his face was inches from mine, his breath foul and hot. "She's never coming back," he snarled. "You understand that, kid? She's never coming back."

Tears spilled from my eyes. "I want to go home."

"You're never going home."

CHAPTER SIXTY-ONE

The mobile command tent was abuzz with activity when Josie and Oaks arrived back at the city park. The park lights shone down on the play area, illuminating the law enforcement milling around outside the tent as well as the civilian volunteers Josie had enlisted to help search for Violet Young. She spotted Luke's bloodhound, Blue, lumbering around the swings, sniffing at the dirt and walked toward him. Josie knelt and called softly to Blue, who recognized her. He walked over to her, his tail wagging, and pressed the length of his body into her waiting hands. She scratched his back, rubbed his sides, and spoke softly to him. Nearby, Luke was talking with a sheriff's deputy. He smiled when he saw her, said goodbye to the deputy, and came over.

"You're okay," Luke said. "Word around here was that you took one to the stomach. Had everyone pretty freaked out till we heard you had your vest on."

Josie nodded. "A little bruising. That's all. I wanted to thank you—and Blue—for your help with finding Violet Young."

Luke smiled and gestured toward Blue. "It was all him. I'm just his ride."

"Well," Josie said. "We're lucky that you were both here."

"It was the least I could do, especially after what happened at my place. You know, I was going to make you breakfast that day but when I woke, you were gone. I figured you had a big lead to run down."

Josie's gaze fell momentarily. She shored herself up and met his eyes again. "I did," she said. "About that, Luke, what did happen that night?"

His face fell. "You don't remember?"

"I'm sorry. I—uh—I remember dinner. Then I left and came back, and we drank. A lot. I remember watching television with you. Laughing. Then we woke up in your bed. I need to know—"

"You blacked out?"

Shame colored her face. "Yes. I told you—I hadn't had anything to drink for months before that. Not that that's any excuse. I'm so sorry. I don't remember. But I need to know. If I'm going to move forward with Noah, I have to know the truth."

Luke looked back at the tent where Josie knew Noah had been all night, working the phones and a laptop because his broken leg kept him out of the field. "Oh, you think we—you think we slept together?"

"We didn't?" Josie asked. She tried to stem the monster wave of relief that started to crash inside of her, at least until she'd heard everything.

Luke laughed. "No, Josie. We didn't. Not that I didn't think about it. I mean you and I—we had some amazing times together—but no, I knew you were hung up on Noah, so I didn't even try. I told you I wasn't making a pass."

"I remember that," Josie said, cheeks on fire.

"Well, I meant it. We watched television. We laughed our asses off at some comedy special that came on. You said it was a good escape. Then when it was over you started crying."

"What?" Josie said, a little more forcefully than she anticipated. She wasn't typically a crier.

"Yeah, you spilled everything about how Noah had pushed you away. How much you loved him."

"Oh God," Josie said.

Luke waved a hand in the air. "Don't be embarrassed. It was sweet. I knew you were being vulnerable because when we were together, you always kept so much of yourself—well, to yourself. So I made some confessions of my own."

"About what?"

He looked away from her. "I'd really rather not talk about them when I'm sober."

"Luke, please."

His eyes found hers again. "Let's just say that I still have nightmares about everything that happened: my best friend being killed in front of me, me being tortured, spending time in prison. I get... scared. I told you that's why I had gotten Blue. Because I felt better with him around. That's why I still live with Carrieann. Because I hate being alone."

"I'm sorry," Josie said.

"You went to sleep in my bed and a couple of hours later, I got in. I just... I was having a lot of anxiety. It made me feel better to be close to you. Real manly, I know."

"Oh, Luke. I understand. Believe me, I do." Josie looked down at Blue who had now taken up position at Luke's feet. "But Luke, Blue was outside the bedroom door. When I woke up, his dog bed was empty, and he was outside the door."

"Against it, right?"

"Well, yeah. I almost tripped over him. I wondered if you put him out there because we were—you know."

Again, Luke laughed. He reached down and patted Blue's head. "Blue can open doors, remember?"

That Josie did remember.

"That door to my bedroom tends to swing shut on its own if it's not propped open," Luke added.

They both turned when they heard the sound of someone calling Josie's name. Noah stood at the mouth of the tent on his crutches. He balanced on them and lifted one hand to wave her over.

Luke went on, "Sometimes, when I am having a really bad night, he sleeps outside the door, pressed against it. That way no one can get to me without getting past him first. I didn't teach him that. He just figured it out. That's what makes him so special."

Josie smiled at Blue. "Oh, there are a lot of things that make him special," she said. "Stick around, would you? We might need your help finding Lucy still."

Luke looked from her to Noah and back again. "Go," he said. "That's where you should be."

As she walked toward the tent, and Noah, she looked over her shoulder at Luke one last time. "Thank you, Luke."

CHAPTER SIXTY-TWO

Noah hobbled outside the entrance of the tent to meet her. "Why didn't you tell me?" he said. "Why didn't you tell me you got shot? Jesus, Josie."

Josie stopped in her tracks. She could tell by his tone that he was genuinely upset. "I'm sorry, Noah. I didn't think it was that big a deal. I had a vest on."

"So did Amy Ross, and now she's fighting for her life. You know damn well those vests don't make you invincible. You could have been killed."

"Noah, I'm sorry."

"I had to find out from a couple of Feds who carried you out of the woods. Why didn't you tell me?"

Josie put a hand on her hip. "They didn't carry me," she said.

He pointed a finger at her. "Don't change the subject."

What could she say? She didn't tell him because she had wanted to go home first and make sure she wasn't pregnant before she got checked out at the hospital? Because, had she been pregnant, she wouldn't have known exactly whose it was? What a mess she had made of things.

Noah said, "I just lost my mother, Josie. I can't lose you, too."

"You're not going to lose me," Josie said, softening her tone. "I promise."

"You can't make that promise," he shot back. "Not in this line of work."

"Neither can you," she pointed out. "You'll be back on full duty in no time and back in the field with me."

He didn't respond.

"I'm sorry I didn't tell you the truth," Josie said. "But wait, did you say Amy Ross is alive? Did she make it through surgery?"

Noah looked away from her, and she could tell by the muscle twitching in his jaw that he was taking a moment to compose himself. He met her eyes once more. "Yes. She made it. She's in recovery now. Heavily sedated. They had to take an ovary and one of her fallopian tubes. They were able to save her uterus though."

"My God," Josie murmured. A wave of sadness enveloped her. Almost of its own will, her hand went to her own bruised abdomen. Amy was forty and likely hadn't had any plans for more children, but still, her injuries would deeply affect any decisions she made about having children going forward. Lucy was missing, the Ross family had one million dollars on the line, and now Amy's body had been irreparably damaged. What more would this case take from the woman?

"Let's go inside," Noah said. "Oaks wants to do a briefing."

Josie followed him into the tent where once more, dozens of agents as well as state police, sheriff's deputies and many members of Denton PD—including Gretchen, Mettner, Chitwood, and Lamay—were gathered around Oaks, waiting for him to speak. He held up his hand, signaling for five more minutes and walked over to Josie. "You okay?" he asked.

She nodded. "I'm fine," she said, feeling exactly the opposite.

"I'd like you to brief everyone on what happened at the football field."

"Of course."

Oaks called everyone to attention. Josie delivered an account of what had happened at the football field and behind it, in the woods beyond the Stacks. Gretchen stood and gave a report on Amy's medical condition. Mettner briefed everyone on the drop at Lover's Cave which had been uneventful and gone without incident except for the fact that the money Colin had left there was still there, untouched. Lamay spoke about the rescue of Violet Young. Then Oaks picked up with what Josie had found out from Violet.

"Sometime between the abduction of Mrs. Young from the school and the phone call that the kidnapper made to the Ross family to give the final instructions for the drop, these perpetrators did something with Lucy Ross. We don't yet know what."

"But," Josie said. "They had Violet Young's phone with them so I think we should start by searching the same two-mile radius where they dumped Violet Young."

Mettner dragged a large foam board with a map tacked to it into the middle of the room. "Here is the radius," he said, indicating an area of West Denton outlined in red. "Here is where Violet Young was found."

Josie added, "It's possible the kidnapper stashed Lucy somewhere in this radius before the drop and then went back and moved her, but this is a good place for us to start our search. We don't know for certain that that's where he left her so we should work outward from there. Any evidence that we find that indicates she may be elsewhere, we'll need to pursue immediately."

Someone from the back of the tent said, "Isn't the kidnapper supposed to deliver Lucy to the carousel tomorrow?"

Josie said, "We have to consider the possibility that he has no intention of delivering Lucy. He hasn't taken the money, and we believe he murdered his own accomplice, Natalie Oliver. We know from Violet Young that the two of them were fighting prior to the drop. We also know that both of them were at Denton East High, leaving the Lover's Cave drop completely unattended. It's not clear exactly what their intent was, but we know that the male suspect had deviated from the plan and that Natalie Oliver was not happy about it."

She nodded to Oaks, who nodded back and addressed the crowd. "Natalie Oliver had gunshot residue on her hands. The round that doctors dug out of Amy Ross's pelvis was a .308, which as you all know, came from a rifle."

"A rifle powerful enough to have hit her when fired from the cave that Natalie Oliver was hiding in," Josie added.

"The round that the medical examiner pulled from Natalie Oliver's brain was a nine millimeter, and based on the degree of damage to her skull, we believe it came from a pistol," Oaks said.

"Both could have come from guns that were stolen from the hunting cabin," Gretchen said. She flipped a page in her notebook. "The Remington 700 takes a .308 round and the Glock 19 takes a nine millimeter round."

Josie nodded and went on, "We believe that the male kidnapper was hiding in the Stacks near the football field. We believe that Natalie Oliver was supposed to be at the Lover's Cave location, but for whatever reason, maybe because of the disagreement they'd had, she instead came to the Denton East location, where she remained hidden in the cave. We don't believe that the male suspect knew she was there until she had already shot Amy Ross. Once the confrontation between the male suspect and the agents patrolling the ridge began, she took the opportunity to shoot Amy Ross. The male suspect located her in the cave, shot her in the head, and took her rifle."

"So all bets are off," Noah said. "He's on the run now. No partner and no money."

"Right," Oaks said. "We don't know what he's going to do next: try to return to one of the drop sites and take the money, or go back to wherever he stashed Lucy to get her and try the whole thing again—assuming she is still alive."

"Why would Natalie Oliver shoot Amy Ross?" Gretchen asked.

Josie sighed. "That's anybody's guess. Some type of jealousy? Maybe she felt the kidnapper's personal need to torture Amy was interfering with the kidnapping plan. The ransom seemed secondary to him. Also, he asked for waterproof bags and then had the parents drop the money at sites where water wasn't an issue. Maybe they thought it was going to rain or maybe they had originally planned the drop site near the river and then changed their plan. It's possible that could have been part of their disagreement. It's impossible to know what they were thinking or what went on between them, but at this point the more important issue is locating Lucy."

"Or recovering her body," Chitwood said.

Oaks added, "And finding this bastard before he kills again."

Josie said, "Did your guys in New York get anything on Oliver in the last hour or so?"

Oaks nodded. He shuffled through the pages in his hands. "Natalie Oliver, twenty-four years old. A foster kid since she was a baby. Moved from home to home. Aged out of a group home at eighteen. Worked odd jobs: waitress, receptionist at a gym, made some money driving for Uber, worked at a mall. Did a few semesters at Erie Community College in Buffalo. She hit the New York lottery for a hundred thousand dollars two years ago. Quit her retail job, moved to a nicer apartment in West Seneca. Paid her rent for a year. Neither the landlord nor the neighbors have seen her in six months."

"Vehicles?"

"Yes," Oaks said. "She is the owner of a black Honda Accord registered to her address in West Seneca."

"Can you check toll booth cameras? Does she have an E-Z pass account?"

Oaks checked his notes. "No E-Z pass account but we've got a team looking at cameras now and we've released the license plate number to the press in case the kidnapper is still in possession of the vehicle and driving it around."

"How about her friends, associates?" Josie asked.

Oaks said, "We're still running down those leads. As of right now, I've got units at Denton East and at Lover's Cave watching the money. Colin is with Amy at Denton Memorial Hospital. I've got three agents there, one who is specifically monitoring both their phones. We've got units searching the two-mile radius that Detective

Quinn has outlined here where Violet Young was found. The sheriff's office has their K-9 unit on site, and they'll be searching for Lucy all night. Obviously, there will be units outside, monitoring the carousel in the very unlikely event that the kidnapper delivers Lucy."

Josie added, "I'd like units on standby in case there are any developments at either of the drop locations or in the search for Lucy. Everyone available should join the search."

As everyone dispersed, Oaks said to Josie, "You should go home. Get a couple of hours of sleep."

"I can't," Josie said, even though every cell in her body yearned for sleep or just to lie down in her comfy bed.

Gretchen said, "He's right, boss. We've all been at this all day. We can rotate like we did last time. You and Noah go get a couple of hours and then you'll relieve us."

Chitwood said, "If anything develops, you'll be the first to know, Quinn."

All four of the Denton detectives stared at him. It was the least abrasive and abusive thing he had ever said to her. "Chief?" Josie said.

Chitwood rolled his eyes. "You do your best work when you're clear-headed. If I'm not mistaken, you carried a dying woman off a football field today, climbed a mountain, got shot, fell down that mountain, and now you're still here. Did you even eat anything today?"

"N-no," Josie stammered. "I—there was no time."

"Well that seals it," Chitwood said. "Take Fraley. Eat and straight to bed. We'll see you back here in three hours to relieve Gretchen and Mettner."

Josie looked around at all of them. Lamay stood up. "Boss," he said. "I'll stay here. If anything happens—anything at all—I'll call you myself."

Noah lurched to his feet and put his crutches under his arms. "Let's go," he said. "The clock is ticking."

CHAPTER SIXTY-THREE

Josie and Noah picked up takeout on their way back to her house. Misty and Harris were already asleep in the spare bedroom. They scarfed their meal down in the kitchen while Josie texted Trinity to see if she was still awake. A moment later, Trinity called.

"You're still up?" Josie asked when she answered.

"Not for much longer," Trinity said. "I was hoping you'd call. I hear the police there aren't giving the press anything but that there has been a ton of police activity in your area. I also heard from my WYEP contact that Amy Ross is in the hospital. What gives?"

"There were some developments. Amy was injured. I can't say more than that."

There was a beat of silence. Then Trinity said, "If you weren't my sister, I would never let you off the hook with just that. I'll say this: I want an exclusive when this is all said and done. I'm doing all this work, and you're not telling me anything."

Josie laughed. "Because I can't. You know that."

"Don't worry. I always get the story."

Josie laughed. "I know you do. I assume you didn't uncover anything useful about Amy—or Tessa—today since you didn't call."

"I'm sorry, Josie. I interviewed two of the living Lendhardt men here in Buffalo and the widow of one of the Lendhardts who passed away. None of them ever knew a Tessa, and none of them recognized Amy's photo or the age-regressed photo I had made of her."

"Age-regressed photo?"

"Yeah we did a story a few years back about how this genealogy company was using age regression software to restore damaged or destroyed photos. They also do it if you bring them a photo of an ancestor and for fun, you can have the photo regressed to see what the relative looked like when they were a kid. Anyway, I still have a contact at that company so I asked her to age-regress Amy's photo to between sixteen and eighteen so I could use it in interviews. I've been showing her current photo as well, but I'm thinking if she lived here twenty-two years ago or more, people's memories might be sparked by the younger version of Amy or Tessa or whatever her name is."

"That's actually kind of amazing," Josie said.

"Tomorrow I'll track down the other two living Lendhardts and then interview the neighbors of the other one who passed away since it doesn't appear that he had any family."

"Let me know if you find anything," Josie said.

She hung up and helped Noah up the steps to her bedroom. Once inside, Noah sat on the edge of her bed and propped his crutches against the end table. "How long do you think Misty is staying?" he asked.

Josie rummaged through her dresser, looking for something comfortable to wear. "I don't know," she said. "Until she feels safe going home."

Noah laughed. "You realize that could be never, don't you?"

"No," Josie said. "Misty's strong and independent. She's just having a hard time with this abduction case. I think once it's over, she'll feel better going home."

Josie stripped down, leaving her clothes on the floor and pulled a large T-shirt over her head. She climbed into bed and stretched out on her back. "Does it bother you that much?"

"No," Noah said. "It doesn't. It's just hard to remember that we have to be quiet, so we don't wake Harris."

He hefted his cast onto the bed and shifted so he was sitting up, his back against the headboard. He reached over and stroked her hair. "Why did you really not tell me about getting shot today?"

"I thought I might be pregnant," Josie said.

"Are you?"

"No," Josie said softly.

The moment stretched out between them. Noah's fingers continued to roam softly over her scalp.

Finally, Noah said, "I thought you might be too."

Josie looked up at him. "Why didn't you say anything?"

"I figured you'd bring it up when you were ready. Plus, this case…"

Josie shifted closer to him. He shimmied down so he was flat on his back and she rested her cheek against his chest. Tears leaked from her eyes and wet his T-shirt. "There's something I need to tell you."

His hand moved to her back, fingers tracing her shoulder blades. "What's that?"

"When I was on your mom's case last month and I went to Sullivan County to follow up on that lead, I spent the night at Luke's."

"I know."

Her head popped up. She looked into his hazel eyes. "What?"

"We couldn't find you, remember? I was the one who suggested Trinity check Luke's sister's place. I figured it was the one place in Sullivan County you knew how to get to, so you'd probably go there."

"Did you know Luke would be there?"

Noah shrugged. "Well, where else would he go after he left prison? That was their family home, wasn't it?"

"Yes," Josie said. "It was. You weren't worried?"

"About what?"

"I don't know, that something would happen between me and Luke."

"Josie," Noah said. "You're a lot of things, but dishonest is not one of them. So no, I didn't give it a thought."

"Well, there's something else."

"Which is?"

"I got drunk. Blackout drunk. I woke up in bed with Luke—clothed—but in the same bed. But I didn't sleep with him."

"How do you know?"

"He told me. I talked to him. Tonight. I'm sorry."

"Well," Noah said. "I'm pretty sure I was being a major asshole around that time."

"That doesn't excuse my behavior," Josie said.

Silence fell over them. Noah's hand kept exploring her upper back and the nape of her neck. Finally, he said, "I was right, though."

"About what?"

"I didn't think you would sleep with Luke and even blackout drunk, you didn't."

"Don't let me off the hook," Josie said.

"You let me off the hook after the way I acted during my mom's case," he pointed out.

"Not the same thing," Josie pointed out.

"Well," Noah said. "I can still let you off the hook if I so choose."

Josie smiled, closed her eyes, and nestled her face deeper into his chest, inhaling his scent. "I'm not as forgiving as you."

"Well, some sins are more egregious than others. Are we going to talk about the pregnancy?"

"There was no pregnancy," Josie pointed out.

Noah squeezed her shoulder. "You know what I mean, Josie."

"No, we're not going to talk about it."

"What if you had been pregnant?"

"Please don't."

"You would be an amazing mother, Josie."

She lifted her head and looked into his eyes. "Misty said the same thing but how do you know? How can you possibly know that? I had no example. I have no frame of reference. I wouldn't know the first thing about being a mother."

Noah pushed some of her brown locks out of her eyes. "You would figure it out. You would love your child. Everything else would come naturally."

"Would it?" Josie asked. "Some mothers don't bond with their children. They just don't. Look at Amy—what Bryce Graham told me—she clearly loves and adores her daughter and yet, she had trouble bonding with Lucy."

"But she did, eventually, and besides, trouble bonding hardly makes her a bad mother."

"I'm just saying that the mothering thing doesn't just come naturally. When horrific things happen to you, it changes you. Me. What happened to me in my childhood changed me."

"I agree," Noah said. "It made you a better, stronger, more caring person."

"I love that you think that," Josie said. "But can we please not talk about this now? We need sleep. Lucy Ross is still missing. I don't want to think about anything but finding her."

Noah laughed softly and kissed the top of her head. "You're making my point for me."

"I can't hear you," she muttered. "I'm sleeping."

CHAPTER SIXTY-FOUR

They relieved Gretchen and Mettner a few hours later. The night gave way to morning, the sun coming up on Denton with a relentless vibrancy that cared nothing for the turmoil currently gripping the city. Oaks assured Josie that his colleagues in the Buffalo field office were working hard to track down any leads there. Denton PD patrol officers located Natalie Oliver's Ford F-150 abandoned in a ditch along a rural mountain road. The day stretched on. Josie left Noah at the command tent to go out with searchers, traversing the two-mile radius in which they'd found Violet Young. There was no sign of Lucy or her male abductor. The money went untouched. The time for the kidnapper to return Lucy to the carousel came and went with no sign of the girl.

Amy's condition hadn't improved but decisions had to be made, so Josie sent Mettner to retrieve Colin from the hospital. A thin gray beard covered his face. He looked pale and gaunt, as though the last few days had aged him by decades. Josie offered him coffee but he declined, sinking into a folding chair near Noah, his gaze on the floor. He looked utterly defeated.

Oaks and Josie looked at one another. She nodded for Oaks to proceed. "Mr. Ross," he said. "We can't leave your money in the drop locations indefinitely. We can leave it there for a few more days, but the high school will need their field back soon. What would you like us to do?"

Colin shook his head. "I don't know. How can I make this decision? We don't even know if Lucy is alive. My wife—" He broke off, tears gleaming in his eyes. He looked from Oaks to Josie. "What would you do?"

Josie shifted uncomfortably. "I don't have children, Mr. Ross," she said softly.

"But I saw you with your son the day Lucy disappeared. At the park," he said.

Josie grimaced. "Harris is not my son. I was babysitting for a friend."

He took that in, eyes back on the floor, a muscle ticking in his jaw. "My wife trusts you," he said.

"Yes," Josie said.

Oaks said, "Mr. Ross, we can't make these decisions for you."

"Do you think Lucy is alive?"

"We don't know," Josie said honestly. "But we're not going to stop looking for her."

"Do you think he'll come back for the money?"

Oaks said, "I don't think so, but again, we have no way of predicting what he will or won't do."

"He's stopped calling. Your agents have had Amy's phone charged and monitored this whole time." He put his face in his hands. "My God, this can't be over. My little Lucy. She can't just be gone."

Josie waited a moment and when he didn't speak, she said, "There is another option."

Colin looked up at her once more. She said, "We could put you on camera. Hold a press conference. You speak to him directly."

"And say what?" Colin asked.

"Give him instructions," Josie said.

Oaks said, "It's not the worst idea. We have no way of making contact with this guy. We have no idea where his head's at now that his entire plan has gone south."

"The press is the only way to reach him right now," Josie said. "You tell him what you want him to do. Maybe we can lure him in."

"He can have the money," Colin said. "I'll deliver it somewhere and he can have it. I just want Lucy back."

Oaks said, "We'll hash this out then, sort the location and time, and contact the press. Why don't you go home and clean up? Take a shower, change your clothes. When you get back, we'll have everything ironed out, and we'll prep you on what to say and how to say it."

Colin stood up. "Yes, yes. I can do that."

Josie said, "I'll go with you. I'd like to bring a few items from Lucy's room if you don't mind. If this guy has even a shred of humanity left in him, maybe we can appeal to that. Remind him Lucy's just a little girl and whatever beef he has with Amy, Lucy has nothing to do with that."

Colin followed her to her vehicle, and they drove the few blocks to the Ross home. "The press is all gone," he mused.

Josie said, "They're stationed at all the other locations, hoping to catch something newsworthy. If they knew you were here, they'd be here."

"Your officer, Mettner? He did a good job avoiding them when we left the hospital."

"Mett's a good man," Josie said as they got out and walked to the front door.

Colin unlocked the door and let them in. The house was eerily silent, the odor of spoiled food filling its rooms. Josie wrinkled her nose. Colin said, "Must be food left out in the kitchen. We ran out of here the other day quickly, and I haven't been back since."

Josie motioned to the steps. "You go get ready. I'll clean up in the kitchen."

Colin walked to the stairs and stopped, his hand resting on the railing. "Detective Quinn, last night Agent Oaks told me that my wife… that she… that Amy isn't her real name. That she used to go by a different name. Tessa something. Is that really true? She's not who she says she is?"

Josie said, "Yes, it's true. I'm so sorry."

"Do you know what—what happened to her? Why she took someone else's identity?"

"I don't," Josie said. "I'm sorry. She did allude to the fact that she had been in an abusive relationship. We're trying to find out more about her past."

"I didn't know," Colin said. "I never knew. She always had such bad anxiety. I tried to be empathetic, understanding, but I—ultimately, I wasn't. I shouldn't have said the things I said to her the other day. I didn't mean them. And now… I might not get to tell her that."

"You don't know that," Josie said. "She might pull through. Then you can tell her anything at all that you need to tell her. Right now, we need to keep our focus on Lucy. The sooner you're ready, the sooner we can get back to mobile command and start planning for the press conference."

With a nod, Colin trudged up the steps. Josie walked into the kitchen to start cleaning up when her phone rang. Trinity. "Hey," she answered. "Did you find something out?"

"Martin Lendhardt—the other Lendhardt who died—I talked to the neighbors where he used to live. No one remembered him."

"That's not helpful," Josie said.

"Just wait," Trinity said. Josie could hear the excitement in her voice. "One of the neighbors bought his house from an elderly lady who is still alive and residing at a nearby nursing home. I talked to her. She remembered Martin Lendhardt. She said he was mean as the day is long. Moved into the house next to hers twenty-six years ago with a young wife."

"A young wife?" Josie echoed.

"Yes. A young wife named Tessa."

"Please tell me you're serious."

"Dead serious."

Josie did calculations in her head. "Wait, twenty-six years ago, Amy would have been fourteen years old. This woman said they were married?"

"That's what she said. They were new to the neighborhood. The wife never spoke to anyone. She said they often heard her screaming. They were sure he beat her, but whenever the police were called, Martin would make up some story like he had the television on too loudly, and Tessa would speak only long enough to tell the police her husband hadn't laid a hand on her."

"Jesus. I wonder if there are any police reports."

"I doubt it. He was never even arrested. Well, not for domestic violence."

"For what then?"

"Well, that's where it gets really interesting."

Josie's heartbeat sped up. "Tell me," she said.

"Tessa and Martin Lendhardt had a baby."

"What?"

"My source says that when they first moved in, she often heard a baby crying. She says eventually she worked up the nerve to go over when Martin was at work. She knocked on the door and asked Tessa if she needed help, but that Tessa closed the door in her face."

"But there's no record of Tessa Lendhardt even existing," Josie said. "How could she have had a baby?"

"Maybe a home birth? It sounds like Martin didn't let her out of the house very often—if at all."

"Was the child a boy or a girl?" Josie asked.

"She didn't know. They never let the child leave the house."

"Then how does she know that there was really a child?"

"Well, I guess she doesn't know. Not for sure. But there's something else."

"Besides a baby that may or may not have existed?"

"We'll come back to that," Trinity said. "My source thinks that Martin killed Tessa."

"Based on what?"

"About five years after they moved in, Tessa disappeared. She says she used to see her pass by one of the windows facing her house just about every day. Then one day, Tessa wasn't there anymore, and Martin was meaner than ever. She asked him where his wife went, and he said it was none of her damn business. She thought because of the way he used to beat her, he must have killed her and was hiding her body in the house. She says she called the police but that they came, went inside his house for a while and then left. She tried to get information out of them, but they wouldn't talk to her. She asked them if they'd seen the child inside the house, but they told her to mind her own business. Nothing ever came of it."

"Probably because Tessa never existed in the first place. There's no record of her. So what happened?"

Trinity drew in a breath. Josie heard papers rustling. "She's not sure what happened after that. She got put into a nursing home by her kids. Her house was rented out multiple times after that. I left her son a message, but I don't know that he'll have the information for all the tenants or that any of them would remember Martin."

"It couldn't possibly be that easy," Josie groused.

"But I checked out Martin Lendhardt, and he was convicted of child endangerment in 2002."

Now Josie's heartbeat was a series of thunderclaps in her chest. "So there was a child."

"Evidently. I couldn't get anything else. But maybe you or the FBI could access the records of his arrest and conviction?"

"Yes," Josie said. "I'll call Special Agent Oaks. Trinity, thank you for this. That exclusive is yours."

Josie hung up and called Oaks, briefing him on everything Trinity had discovered. He promised to find out everything he could about Martin Lendhardt's child endangerment conviction. Josie dropped her phone into her pocket and tried to slow her breathing. It felt like a break in the case. She hoped that by the time she brought Colin back to the command tent, Oaks would have a lot more information.

She took a glance around the messy kitchen and started cleaning up. Several half-finished mugs of coffee sat on the kitchen table. Someone had kept the Rosses's coffeemaker full and hot while the FBI and Denton PD were stationed at the house. Josie emptied them into the sink and rinsed them out. The real stink came from the trash bin, which was full of half-finished takeout, also from the myriad law enforcement officers who had been staying there around the clock. Neither Amy nor Colin had been able to eat much since Lucy went missing. She tied up the bag and wrestled it out of the bin. Turning toward the back door, something on the shiny tile floor caught her eye.

A muddy footprint. Then another partial print. From someone walking into the kitchen from the back door. From the look of the treads, Josie guessed the person who left them had been wearing boots. Her mind worked backward to every agent and officer who had been at the Ross home in the past week. None of them had been wearing boots. Besides that, it hadn't rained, and there was no mud in the backyard. Josie set the trash bag softly onto the floor. She took out her phone, fired off a text to Noah—he would respond the quickest—and then she drew her service weapon.

CHAPTER SIXTY-FIVE

As she raced up the stairs, she heard the sound of water running in the bathroom. At the top of the steps, she made a sharp right and began checking the rooms, her Glock held out in front of her. First Colin's home office, then Lucy's room. The bathroom was next. She placed one hand on the doorknob. "Mr. Ross?" she called.

No answer. He could be in the shower. Maybe she was imagining things. Even if the kidnapper had come to the Ross home after shooting Josie on the mountain behind Denton East, he had probably already left. What would he have come here for? Maybe he thought they'd brought the money back to the house and planned to swipe it while no one was around.

"Mr. Ross?"

No answer. She turned the knob. It twisted easily in her hand. She kept her gun at the ready and pushed the door open. There stood the kidnapper, pressing Colin up against the wall. He held a forearm against Colin's throat and a large knife in the little hollow where Colin's solar plexus was located. Both heads turned toward her. Josie aimed at the kidnapper. He was taller than she expected. Everything had happened so quickly on the mountain, she'd barely had a chance to register anything about him before he shot her. Now she took a good look at him. His shaggy brown hair looked greasy and unwashed. Mud streaked his face and clothes. His brown eyes widened when he saw her.

"I shot you," he said.

"Put the knife down and step away from Mr. Ross," Josie said.

Colin's voice came out strangled and raspy. "Let him kill me. He can have the money. Just get my Lucy back. Bring her home."

Josie aimed at his ribs, but she knew she didn't have a clean shot. Not with the kidnapper pressed so close against Colin. Still, she didn't waver. "I said, drop the knife and let Mr. Ross go. Now. You're under arrest for the kidnapping of Lucy Ross and three murders."

He smiled at her. "Three murders?"

"Jaclyn Underwood, Wendy Kaplan, and Natalie Oliver."

His smile failed. His mouth moved but nothing came out.

"That's right," Josie said. "We ID'd your girlfriend, and we know you shot her. This ends now. I don't want anyone else to get hurt, including you, so just put the knife down and step away from Mr. Ross."

Colin's hands were trapped between his own body and the man's forearm, keeping just enough room between the two for him to breathe and speak. "Please," he said. "I don't care if he kills me. Do whatever he says to get Lucy back. He can have the money."

The man looked at Colin briefly. "I don't want your money, asshole."

In her mind, Josie calculated that back-up units should be there within the next five minutes. Although, she realized, that might not stop this guy from plunging his knife into Colin's chest or her from having to shoot him.

"What's it about?" Colin asked, eyes bulging from his head. "Whatever it is, I'll help you. I just want Lucy back."

"Maybe one day your wife can tell you what this is all about. Or is she dead?"

Josie said, "Tessa is still alive."

His eyes darted toward her and she saw his knife-hand slacken a little. "She told you?"

"Told me what?" Josie said.

"The truth. What she did to me."

"What did she do to you?"

His knife hand lowered, his forearm coming away from Colin's throat. Still, his arm held Colin in place. "You're bullshitting me. If she had told you what she did—the truth, the real truth—you would have arrested her. She'd be in jail right now and not in a hospital."

"Amy would never hurt anyone," Colin gasped. "You must have the wrong woman. This is all a huge mistake. Please, just bring Lucy back. Whatever you think my wife did, you're wrong. Lucy has nothing to do with this. Just bring her home and I promise you, we can forget this whole thing."

The man shoved Colin hard with his forearm. Colin's neck whipped back and forth, the back of his skull smashing against the wall. "You're the one who's wrong, asshole. You know nothing about your wife. She's an evil, lying bitch. You think she cares about Lucy? You think she ever cared about Lucy? About anyone but herself? Look at what she did to me. Look!" With his free hand, he tore at his shirt, popping buttons and exposing a pale chest with a smattering of hair. In the places the hair didn't grow were large silvery scars. Old welts or cuts, Josie couldn't be sure. There were cigarette burns and a large scar on his left lower torso that looked like the permanent imprint of a belt buckle. They were old and faded but so indelible on his skin that even now in adulthood, they were unmistakable.

Childhood scars, a faint part of Josie's brain registered, but she quieted that voice because the part of her brain that was on high alert recognized that he had finally taken the knife away from Colin's body. It hung now at his side, opposite Colin. Slowly, Colin slid down the wall to the floor.

Josie said, "If Amy did that to you then we need to have a serious conversation. Put down the knife. I'll put down my gun. I'm willing to listen to you, but we don't have to do it like this."

He laughed bitterly. "I don't think so. You know when people listen? When you have a knife in your hand."

"What do you want?" Josie asked.

"I want her to pay."

"Who? Tessa? Don't you think she's paid enough? You took everyone she cared about away from her—Jaclyn, Wendy, and most importantly, Lucy. Plus, now she's in the hospital in critical condition. What else do you want? You want her dead?"

He shook his head. "I want her to suffer. The way I suffered."

Josie's mind was still working at breakneck pace back over everything she knew about this case and what Trinity had just told her. The man before her couldn't be older than twenty-six or twenty-seven. His accomplice had only been twenty-four. Both would have been infants—or at least very small children—when Amy was living in Buffalo as Tessa.

Josie said, "Was it you or Natalie? Or both of you?"

"Was it me or Natalie what?" he asked.

"You were her children," Josie murmured.

Downstairs, the front door creaked open and next came the sounds of a half dozen pairs of boots storming the house. Shouts of "FBI" floated up the steps. The man's eyes widened. He looked down at where Colin had curled into a fetal position on the tiles. He raised the knife in one hand and reached for Colin with the other. Josie fired a shot. It grazed his upper arm, but it was enough for him to lose his grip on the knife. It clattered to the floor, and Josie rushed at him, gun pointed at his chest, screaming for him to get his hands up and get on his knees. She kicked the knife away and under the clawfoot tub. She was aware of the FBI agents thundering up the stairs, their large shadows now behind her in the bathroom doorway. With a look of defeat, Lucy's kidnapper dropped to his knees and put his hands behind his head.

CHAPTER SIXTY-SIX

I waited until I heard his truck roar to life. When I heard its wheels screech away, I went to the bedroom door and started working on the lock. He let me out into the other rooms when he was home as long as I was quiet and still. He didn't let me play the way she used to—and we never had cookies. More often than not, I stayed in my own room. The smallest infraction and he'd hit me or think up something worse. Something that left scars. Sometimes I would bite him or hit or kick him, trying to leave marks on him the way he left them on me. It felt good. When I saw his blood, something inside me came alive, like a light turning on. I dreamed of getting a knife and using it on his leathery skin. But making him hurt only made the beatings worse for me. The last few days I'd stayed calmly in the living room so I could study the lock he'd put on my door. It was a simple thing. A small hook. I figured out that I could unlock it from the inside using something slim. A knife would do it. I managed to steal one from the kitchen before he locked me back up without him even noticing. I thought of keeping it for the next time he let me out. I could hide it in my shirt and slice him with it when he was distracted by the television.

But I had to stick with my plan. I had to get out, just like she had.

It didn't take long to pop the hook out of place. Excitement made my skin tingle. I didn't bother gathering anything like she had. There was nothing I wanted from this place except to get out. Even though I knew he was gone, I tried to move as stealthily as I could. I might never break that habit. In seconds, I was out the front door. The first rays of the morning sun inched along the horizon. I hadn't run for so long that my legs grew weak after less than a block. My lungs burned.

Those telltale double lights appeared in the distance. Just like the night she tried to take me home. My body wouldn't do what I told it to do. *Run*, my mind screamed. *Get away!* Instead it sank to the ground, as if my bones were dissolving. The lights stopped close to me, blinding me. A door opened and closed. Then hands lifted me off the cold pavement. Their touch was gentle, the way she used to touch me. I didn't want to cry, but hot tears streaked my face.

A face I didn't recognize blotted out the lights. A woman. Not her and not the silver woman. Someone else. "My God," she said. "Son, are you okay? What happened to you?"

A thick lump formed in my throat. I could hardly speak over it, so I shook my head. I was not okay.

Her hands cupped my cheeks. "I'm going to call the police. Just hold on. You know what? You'll come with me in my car and we'll go to the hospital. They can call the police from there. Come on. Let's go."

I let her pour me into the back of her car. As she pulled away, she asked me, "What's your name, son? Can you tell me your name?"

I remembered what my mother used to call me. "Gideon," I said. "My name is Gideon."

CHAPTER SIXTY-SEVEN

"Who the hell is this kid?" Chitwood asked no one in particular.

Josie, Noah, Mettner, Gretchen, Oaks and Chitwood all crowded into one the Denton PD viewing rooms, watching the man they'd apprehended at the Ross home on CCTV while he sat alone in an interrogation room down the hallway. They'd left him cuffed and he sat slumped in one of the metal chairs, his bound wrists in his lap. He hadn't said a word to any of them since they'd brought him in.

"He's Amy Ross and Martin Lendhardt's son," Josie said. "I'm sure of it."

Gretchen said, "You think she gave him all those scars?"

"I never liked her all that much," Noah admitted. "But I'm not sure I could see her torturing a little boy."

"No," Josie said. "It wasn't her. Martin was the one convicted of child endangerment. It had to be him."

"Child endangerment wouldn't account for the kind of abuse this kid endured, based on those scars," Noah said. "Child endangerment is when you neglect your kid or put them in a dangerous situation. This kid was abused."

"Well," Josie said. "I'm not sure what happened, but he blames Amy for whatever happened to him."

"Well, what the hell is his name?" Chitwood asked.

Oaks's phone chirped. He answered it with a brusque hello, listened for a few minutes and said, "Thank you." He turned to Josie and said, "That was one of my agents in Buffalo. They got in touch with the district attorney's office there. They were able to view Martin Lendhardt's file. He had a son—not a daughter. His name was Gideon. Gideon Lendhardt."

"How old?" Josie asked.

"He's twenty-six. I should have a driver's license photo in a few minutes. We'll see if it matches our suspect. He was found escaping Martin Lendhardt's home at age nine, malnourished and scarred. Hadn't been to school. Martin was arrested. Gideon was terrified of him and would never talk about him or anything that happened in the house. Martin's defense was that Gideon's mother was the one who beat and starved him. But she couldn't be located."

"How convenient for him," Josie said.

Oaks continued, "They couldn't prove it wasn't her. The best they could do was charge him with child endangerment. One year in prison. Gideon was put into foster care—bounced around to a bunch of different homes—which is where he stayed until he aged out at eighteen."

Gretchen said, "Natalie Oliver was a foster kid, too."

"So now we know where they met," Noah said.

"And we know that Amy-or-Tessa abandoned him. But we still don't know where Lucy is. I'm going to talk to him."

CHAPTER SIXTY-EIGHT

Josie faced off against Gideon Lendhardt. From across the inter-rogation table, he stared at her, his eyes flashing angrily. There was no guarantee that he'd talk to her, but he hadn't asked for a lawyer yet either, so Josie had to take her chances.

"Gideon," she said. "Whose idea was it to find Tessa and make her pay? Yours or Natalie's?"

He didn't speak.

Josie went on. "I'm guessing it was your lifelong dream to make her pay, but that Natalie was the one who came up with an actual plan. You two met in foster care, right? I understand you were nine when they took you away from your father for good. So you bounce around from home to home. One day you meet Natalie and the two of you become good friends. Maybe even lovers later in life?"

She could tell by the flare in his eyes that she had hit on some-thing. "You understood each other, didn't you? Both foster kids? Both kicked out of a system that couldn't care less about you as soon as you turned eighteen. Then somehow you find Tessa. You realize she's living in Pennsylvania with her husband and daughter. You want to get back at her, but you don't know how. Natalie sees an opportunity not just to get back at her but to make a little money as well. Natalie took care of the logistics, didn't she? The planning. What was in it for her? Just to make you happy? Or she wanted the money? I know she had a taste of money before you two carried this out. She hit the lottery. She knew she could get money out of Tessa's new husband, didn't she? All you two had to do was get to know little Lucy for a few months before the kidnapping, right? Earn her trust, become her friends. Promise her something irresistible—maybe taking her to a butterfly sanctuary or something. Well, Natalie probably came up with that. You just wanted to grab her, didn't you?"

"It would have been a lot less trouble," he said.

"Yes, I imagine it would have. Your plan was pretty elaborate. Especially the carousel. No cameras in the park, that was smart. Who gave Lucy the signal? Was it you or Natalie? It was you, wasn't it? Natalie was at the Ross home leaving the teddy bear with your secret message, wasn't she?"

"That was a streak of genius if you ask me," he said, smiling. "I just wish I could have been there to see Tessa's face when she heard it."

Josie felt ill seeing the glee on his face, but she forged ahead. "Where did you take Lucy?"

"You think I'm going to tell you? You're not so smart, are you? Kind of like Tessa."

Josie let the barb go. "Well, I know you moved around a lot. Camped out in the woods. Stayed at the mill for a while. Also smart—to keep moving."

He didn't respond.

"Gideon, what did you do with Lucy?"

He still didn't speak.

Josie said, "Lucy doesn't deserve this, you know. She's innocent."

"So was I," he muttered.

"Yes, you were. It must have been very traumatic, what happened to you."

"You don't know a goddamn thing," he growled.

"I know that you were taken from your father when you were nine years old. I also know that your father told child services that Tessa had given you all those scars. But if that were the case, they wouldn't have taken you from him, would they?"

He didn't answer. A vein bulged in his forehead.

"They never reunited you with your father. All those years and they never sent you back to him. We can't view your foster care file, but I'm guessing the reason they never sent you home is because you were violent, just like your father."

"I'm nothing like that bastard," he snarled.

"Well, you're not like your mother," Josie replied. "She's gentle and kind."

He pushed back in his chair a little, the legs screeching on the tile. "That's an act."

"How do you know?" Josie asked.

"Because any bitch who leaves her kid with someone like my father can't be kind. Any bitch who abandons her child without so much as batting an eyelash is not gentle or kind. Whatever she said to you to make you believe that, it's all an act."

Josie softened her tone. "How old were you when she left? Do you even remember her?"

"I remember enough. I remember waking up hungry and looking for her, and she was gone. My father told me she left us. He said she didn't love us. That she was a liar, and she wasn't coming back for me. I waited. She never came back."

"Your father put those marks on you," Josie said. "Didn't he?"

He dropped his gaze for a moment. "She might as well have. If she'd stayed, he would have taken his anger out on her, not me. She could have taken me with her, but she didn't. She went on to live some great, fancy life and left me there in that shithole where my father beat the piss out of me for no other reason than I reminded him of her. The welts, cigarette burns, yeah, those are from him."

"The others came from foster care?" Josie guessed.

"I wouldn't have been in foster care if it weren't for her. You don't get it, do you? I was tortured. My life was an unending hell. All because she left me behind. She left me there, and she never looked back."

Josie thought of one of the conversations she had had with Amy when she had told Amy she didn't care if Amy had killed someone, she just wanted the truth. Amy had said, *that's not the worst thing.* Because she had abandoned her own child, effectively sentencing him to a fate worse than death.

"How did you find her?" Josie asked. "How did you even know she was alive?"

"My dad. A couple of years ago, I went back to see him. I stayed away from him mostly after I aged out, but I found out from someone who used to live around us that he was sick, real sick. So I went to see him. The fight had gone out of him by then. He was harmless."

"He had cancer," Josie said.

"Bone cancer. Yeah. Real painful. He was at the end. I knew he was going to die, so I asked him about her. I wanted a picture. Something. We never had any photos of her or anything. It was almost like she had never existed, but I knew. I knew she had been there."

"Did he have any answers for you?" Josie prompted.

"The same ones he always had. She was a lying bitch who abandoned us. I asked him if she was still alive. He said for years he thought she was dead, that's why he never went looking for her. But then he was at chemo one day, flipping through magazines and stuff, and there was this newsletter thing one of those pharmacy reps had left, all about Quarmark and their groundbreaking new cancer drugs. He was interested in it because they had just released a drug that was supposed to stop bone cancer from spreading or stop bone mets or something. Stop cancer from metastasizing to bones—I don't know. It didn't matter. He couldn't afford the stupid drug anyway. But in that newsletter was a story about the team at Quarmark. They'd had some big, fancy, expensive celebration in New York City, and one of the guys on the pricing team was in the photos."

"And your father recognized your mother in the photo with him," Josie filled in.

"Yeah. There she was, looking like some kind of supermodel while my dad was dying in the same shithole she'd left him in—and he was so broke at the end that the bank took everything. There wasn't even anything left for me."

"So you decided to go after her," Josie said.

"I just wanted to mess with her, but then I found out she had a kid. Then I knew what I had to do."

"Natalie helped you."

"Yeah but then she lost it, said I wasn't going along with the plan like we said. All she cared about was the money. I never cared about that. I wanted Tessa to suffer. Nat said I was ruining everything. Said I was too obsessed with Tessa, decided to take her out."

"So you shot Natalie," Josie said.

He didn't answer.

Josie changed tactics. "Was that the only thing you disagreed about?"

"She got pissed when I changed the drop location. We had other places in mind—down by the river—but I changed it at the last minute. She didn't like that."

So the disagreement on the day they took Violet Young hadn't been to do with Lucy. Still, that didn't mean the little girl was still alive.

Josie felt the familiar roil of nausea in her stomach. "Gideon," she said. "What did you do with Lucy?"

CHAPTER SIXTY-NINE

Gideon leaned forward in his seat, his cuffed hands extended across the table toward her. The smile that spread across his face made Josie's skin crawl. "Guess," he said.

Josie said, "You know you're in a lot of trouble, right? If there is even a chance that Lucy is still alive, now is not the time for you to play games. Give us Lucy, and I'll talk to the district attorney about some sort of deal—like keeping the death penalty off the table."

The smile died on his lips.

"Oh," Josie said. "You didn't account for that, did you? New York doesn't have the death penalty anymore, does it? Well, here in Pennsylvania, we do."

He said nothing, his face hardening. Josie caught a glimpse of what he must have looked like to his victims, up close and personal. Terrifying. She said, "Your one and only chance of avoiding the death penalty is delivering Lucy. What did you do with her?"

A long moment stretched out between them. Josie made sure not to break eye contact first. Finally, she sighed as if she were bored and stood to leave. Her palm was on the door handle when Gideon said, "If you were me, what would you have done with her?"

Again, the sick feeling overcame Josie. She tried not to sway on her feet. Looking back at him, she kept her voice calm, unemotional. "Where's her body?"

A flush crept into his cheeks. He banged his hands against the table. "Fuck you," he said. "You think I'd kill a kid?"

Josie walked back to the table, placed both hands on its surface and leaned in toward him. "Yes," she said. "I do. You are your father's son."

He leaped up from his chair, lunging toward her, but Josie held her ground, despite the fact that her heart hammered so hard in her chest, she felt like it was going to crash through her breastbone. His face was inches from hers. She smelled cigarettes and something foul on his breath.

"I am not like him."

"If you didn't kill her, then where is she?"

"Don't try to trick me," he spat.

Josie shook her head. "You think I have time for tricks? Games? I have one job, Gideon. One. Finding Lucy Ross. That's it. That's all. So if you're not going to help me—and maybe save your own life in the process—then I don't have time for you."

She turned away from him. He shouted after her. "Oh, so you're going to walk away. Just like her. You bitches are all the same. You want to know where that little brat is? Figure it out. What would you do with her if you were me? If you really give a shit about Lucy Ross, you'll know. Hey, hey bitch, don't you walk away from me. Don't you—"

The door closed behind her.

She walked down the hall and let herself into the viewing room. Chitwood, Noah, Gretchen, Mettner and Oaks stared at her. Chitwood said, "Well, that went well."

"He wasn't going to tell me," Josie said. "He's a sad, pathetic little man. This is what he's got. This control. This game. He'll never give that up. He's got nothing to lose now."

Gretchen said, "Do you think he killed her?"

"I don't know."

Noah said, "So we need to figure out the riddle. If we're him, what do we do with Lucy Ross when the rest of the plan has gone to shit?"

Oaks said, "Well, he wouldn't return her. I don't think that was ever his intention."

Josie said, "He wouldn't return her because he would want Amy to wait and wonder, just like he did as a small child. He waited for her to come back. He wondered if and when she would return."

"It was torture for him, I'm sure," Gretchen put in.

"If he kills Lucy and we recover her body, that puts a stop to the uncertainty," Noah said.

Chitwood said, "If he kills her and hides her body well enough, the uncertainty lasts forever."

Josie could not disagree, but she also couldn't give up on the possibility that Lucy was alive. If she was still alive, she was somewhere out there alone and terrified. Time was running out. Josie said, "Let's assume for a minute that he means what he says, that he wouldn't kill a child."

"If she's alive, he left her somewhere," Gretchen said. "Where?"

"Somewhere she won't be found," Noah said.

"Which means she's as good as dead," Oaks said.

"She wouldn't be found in the woods," Gretchen said.

Noah let out a lengthy groan. "That's everywhere. Literally every place outside of this city."

"Why would he leave her in the woods?" Chitwood asked.

"Because of what he went through," Josie said. "When he was a child, Amy left him alone in the figurative wilderness. She left him with an abusive father. He had to fend for himself."

"But he made it out," Noah said. "So if the game is to recreate that scenario—a child left alone to fend for herself in a harsh environment—there has to be a chance that she could get out, that she could survive."

Gretchen said, "People can survive in the woods, even a child."

"Not a seven-year-old," Josie said.

"He's got no concept of age," Oaks remarked. "He didn't have a normal childhood. He had to learn a lot more survival skills at seven than Lucy Ross. He's not thinking of what it's like for her being seven years old. He's thinking of how it was for him."

"So we're back to the woods," Chitwood said.

"Let's get a map," said Josie.

A few minutes later they were all gathered around Noah who had pulled up a satellite view map of the county on Google Earth.

"My God," Oaks said. "This really is like looking for a needle in a haystack. How do you find a seven-year-old girl in miles and miles of forest?"

Josie stared at the map. "He would have thought this out. He wouldn't have just left her anywhere. He would have wanted to put her where she wouldn't wander into a residential area on her first foray. Here," she pointed to southern Denton where Alcott County ended, and Lenore County started. "State gameland, maybe? It's remote."

"Too many people," Noah said. "It's for public use. You've got hikers, fishers, hunters. The chances of someone running into her are a lot greater in state gameland."

"You think so?" Mettner said. "I mean, some of those areas aren't used for months by anyone. There are plenty of wild animals out there—if I'm this sick bastard and I'm playing his demented game of trying to see if a seven-year-old girl can get out of the woods alive or not, I might choose the state gameland."

"Well," Oaks said. "It has to be close by. From the time of the drop to the time Quinn caught him in the Ross house, it was only about twenty-four hours. He would have had to go to wherever they stashed her, gotten her, driven her to wherever he was going to leave her and driven back to the Ross household."

Josie said, "Twenty-four hours could put her anywhere in the state. It doesn't seem like a lot of time to us, but you could easily drive six hours from here, spend a couple of hours and drive back."

"Jesus," Chitwood said. "We'll never find her. Someone should go back in there and try to get him to tell us."

"Too bad we can't beat it out of him," Noah said.

There were nods all around the table. "I'm going to dream about beating that bastard for the rest of my life," Oaks muttered. "But that's not an option."

"He's not from here," Josie said. "Neither was Natalie Oliver."

"So?" Chitwood said. "I'm not from here. Neither is Palmer. What's your point?"

"How did he know about Lover's Cave? That's a local thing. Not on any map," Josie said.

Mettner said, "They did recon for months."

"Still," Josie said. "Chief, you've been here at least a year. Had you ever heard of it before this case?"

"No," he said. "But I'm not looking for abandoned places to squat."

"He found out about Lover's Cave from somewhere. Only locals would know about that."

Gretchen said, "Kommorah's Koffee, down the street, they've got photos of all the local landmarks and rock formations. I had heard of it because of that wall they have displaying local artists' and photographers' work."

Josie knew the wall. An entire section had been devoted to photographs taken by a local photographer who'd gone on to be quite successful and now traveled the world, freelancing for magazines and websites like *National Geographic* and the Smithsonian. The pictures were of places that only residents intimate with the city's geography would know, like the rock formations found in the forests surrounding the city. She knew them well: Broken Heart, the Stacks, Turtle, Lover's Cave, and the Overlook.

"Mett," she said. "Run down to Komorrah's and take a photograph of the wall, would you?"

Wordlessly, Mettner jogged from the room. Chitwood said, "Are you serious, Quinn? You're going to look for this kid based on some pictures hanging in a coffee shop? You do understand that Lucy could get killed out there while you're playing these games with this monster, don't you?"

"He's been in the area for months. Back before they'd taken Lucy, before anyone was looking for them, they could have gone to Komorrah's many times."

"It's very popular," Noah pointed out.

Chitwood shot him a dirty look.

Josie went on, "Maybe they were there one day, waiting for their order, and they happened to look at the wall. Maybe he got the bright idea to use one of those places as a drop location."

"I think you're talking out of your ass, Quinn."

Oaks said, "You have any better ideas for narrowing our search area, Chief?"

Chitwood didn't answer. He turned away from them and started pacing the room. Josie's phone chirped. She opened Mettner's text message and pulled up the photograph. "I see the Stacks. It wouldn't be there. They're right behind the high school where Oliver was killed. Broken Heart—that's also near Denton East. Near enough for her to find her way out of the woods pretty quickly. Turtle…"

Noah said, "That's behind a residential area. That area of woods isn't very big."

"You're right," Josie agreed. "It's not very big. It's right behind the trailer park where I grew up."

"What else is on there?" Noah asked.

"The Overlook," Josie said.

"Is that like a lovers' lane?" Gretchen asked.

Josie and Noah laughed. Josie said, "No, the name is a joke. It's this huge rock that sits smack in the middle of the woods. It stands almost straight up but it's angled so you can actually walk to the top of it."

"And you can slide back down," Noah said. "It's really like a giant slide."

Josie said, "It's huge, about the height of a tree. Flat on the top."

"It doesn't really overlook anything," Noah said. "It just takes you to the treetops. It just looks really cool. Plus, it's just weird. Sitting there in the middle of the forest."

Gretchen said, "Can you find it on this map?"

She reached over to the laptop and zoomed out of the game lands they had been looking at. Pointing to various locations to orient them, she said, "Here's west Denton—the city park, the elementary school, the Ross household. Here's the middle of the city where we are now. Here's Denton East High school, then the Stacks and behind that the abandoned textile mill. Where is the Overlook?"

Noah said, "It's north."

Josie pointed to a rural road snaking up and out of Denton proper toward the top of the screen. "If you take that route north, it would be on the left. There are some hiking trails. You might even be able to see it on satellite." She clicked, moving the area into the center of the screen and zooming in until a misshapen gray shape poking through the treetops came into view. "There," Josie said.

"Do we still have dogs?" Gretchen asked.

Noah said, "The sheriff's K-9 unit is on standby and Luke Creighton is still in town with his dog."

Oaks said, "Let's go. I don't want to waste one more second."

CHAPTER SEVENTY

It was pitch black on the mountain road going north out of Denton. It took Josie three passes to find the mouth of the hiking trail that would lead them to the Overlook. Once she located it, she pulled over and got out. Down the long winding road was an unbroken line of headlights as far as the eye could see. On short notice, they'd managed to round up over seventy people to help search for Lucy. Members of the Denton PD had come in on their night off. The sheriff's office had sent several deputies, the state police had sent troopers, and the FBI agents who had already been working the case were amassed there as well. They fanned out along the shoulder of the road, covering a half mile on either side of the hiking trail.

Flashlights bobbed in the darkness as Josie gave the signal for all of them to step into the woods. The temperature had dropped. Josie felt a slight palpitation at the thought of Lucy out there alone in the cold and the dark. There wasn't even any ambient light in this area of the city.

"You okay, boss?" Gretchen asked as the two of them picked through the underbrush side by side. Chitwood was a half mile south of them, and Oaks was a half mile north. Mettner was with Oaks.

"I'll be okay when we find Lucy," Josie said.

As they waded deeper into the forest, they could hear the sounds of branches snapping, leaves crunching beneath feet, dogs panting and running ahead, and a chorus of voices calling out Lucy's name. The Overlook was a mile into the wooded area. Josie knew there was nothing resembling civilization for several miles in every other direction. She tried not to panic, thinking of the vast area they had to cover. Her hope was that Gideon had left Lucy at the Overlook and that she had either stayed there or simply hadn't gotten very far in whatever direction she had taken.

Their flashlights illuminated the bottom of the Overlook as it came into view. They kept calling Lucy's name, but no response came. They searched around the bottom of the massive rock but found no signs of Lucy. Josie said, "I'm going to climb to the top."

Gretchen shone her light upward. "That's pretty far up, boss. In the dark."

"I have to," Josie said. "What if she's up there?"

But she wasn't. Josie reached the top in a few moments, breathless and trying to stay in the center of the rock's surface so she didn't fall off. On her knees, she shone the light around the top of the Overlook. After two sweeps, her light caught something unusual. She crawled over and saw two small flat rocks wedged up against one another making an upside down V, like a little arch. Beneath it was a small mass of leaves. Molded into a chrysalis.

"Lucy," Josie whispered.

She scrambled back down to the ground, excitement propelling her. "She was here," she told Gretchen. "She was here. She left a cocoon up there."

"Maybe she's nearby," Gretchen said. "Which direction do you think she would go?"

Josie panned her flashlight around them, seeing nothing but tree trunks. Somewhere nearby an owl hooted. She thought about Lucy. "Her mom said she has a terrible sense of direction."

"I remember," Gretchen said.

"But she was completely obsessed with bugs."

Gretchen laughed. "Not sure that helps us here."

"She liked butterflies and ladybugs best."

"Again, boss, not sure that is helpful in this particular scenario."

"If you're at the top of the Overlook, which way does the sun come up? Which way is east?"

Gretchen pulled out her phone. The screen lit up as she punched something in. "I've got a compass app. Not sure it will work out here—oh wait, here it is—east." She turned and pointed away from the bottom of the Overlook. "That way."

"Then she would have gone the other way," Josie said.

"West?"

"Yes, when ladybugs hunker down for winter, they find light-colored homes and they like to land and burrow into the west-facing walls because the late afternoon sun warms them. Lucy knew that. She told her mom that if she ever got lost, she would fly home like a ladybug. She would go west."

"But the Ross home isn't west of here, it's south."

"And Lucy Ross is seven," Josie said with a laugh. "The logic isn't precise. She would have spent the night here. The sun would have come up over there and she would have known that the sun comes up in the East. She would have flown home to the west-facing wall of her home."

Gretchen put her flashlight under her chin, illuminating her face. "At the risk of sounding like Chitwood, are you serious?"

Josie put her flashlight under her own chin and grinned. "We'll get one of the dogs, and see if they can capture her scent from the Overlook. Betcha the dog heads west."

Josie made a few calls. Luke was closest to them, with Blue. Ten minutes later, he and the dog had thrashed their way through the woods to the Overlook. Blue greeted Josie with a long, wet tongue on her hand. "Hey boy," she whispered.

They waited with bated breath while Blue tried to pick up Lucy's scent at the base of the Overlook. Finally, the dog found something, racing off into the darkness.

West.

They dove into the thick trees after him, calling out Lucy's name with more urgency. Josie's feet began to ache. She didn't know how long they'd been out looking, but it felt like an eternity. Then came

Blue's low bark. Josie and Gretchen froze, sweeping their flashlights around to locate him. The dog barked again. And again.

"This way," Josie said.

They raced toward the sound, Josie flying fast and sure-footed over the forest floor, just like she had in childhood, running through Denton's woods with Ray. Gretchen labored behind her. A flashlight beam came into view. It was pointed toward Blue, who sat at the base of a tree.

Luke said, "He found something. Blue, quiet."

The dog stopped barking, and all three of them listened. Josie stepped past the tree, her flashlight searching out any sign of Lucy. "I don't see anything," she said.

Gretchen said, "Shh. Listen."

From close by came the faint sound of whimpering. Josie spun in a circle. The sound came again. "It's above us," Josie said. She turned her flashlight upward into the trees. "She climbed the tree. Lucy!"

A sharp intake of breath sounded from over their heads. Then more quiet whimpering. All three of them shined their lights above until finally, amid a mass of branches, a small, sneakered foot came into view. Josie's heart stopped for two counts and then thundered back to life at double time. "Lucy," she called. "It's the police. We're here to take you home."

Nothing. Josie wished she could see the girl's face. "Lucy, please. We're here to take you to your mom and dad. We're not going to hurt you."

"Where's Natalie?" came a small voice.

"She had to go away," Josie said. "But she wanted me to take you back to your parents."

"You're lying," Lucy said. "All grown-ups lie."

"Not me," Josie said. "I just want to take you home."

"Did he hurt her? Gideon? He's a bad man. He acts like he is good, but he's not."

Josie said, "I know, Lucy. I'm sorry. I met Gideon today. I didn't like him at all."

Her voice was so small, Josie had to strain to hear it: "Did he hurt you?"

"No," Josie said. "He didn't hurt me. He's in jail now. He can't hurt anyone ever again."

"But he made Natalie go away, didn't he?"

"I'm sorry, Lucy, but yes, he did."

She didn't say anything after that, but Josie heard soft sobs and the creak of a branch. "Lucy," she called. "Please come down and let us bring you home."

Still she wouldn't come down. More of the searchers—alerted by phone by Gretchen—began to arrive. Josie tried again, "Lucy, your mom and dad miss you so much. We'd really like to take you to see them."

"My dad probably isn't even home," she said.

"Yes, he is," Josie said. "He has been home since you were taken. Looking for you. Just like your mom. They love you so much and want to have you home with them."

"You don't really know my mom and dad."

"Yes, I do," Josie said. "I was there that day you went on the carousel. Do you remember me? I had a little boy with me, Harris. He was coming down the slide and you were going up?"

Josie shined her flashlight onto her own face. A few seconds passed. Josie thought she saw a lock of blonde hair in the branches. Lucy said, "You don't look like you."

Josie touched her cheek. The black eyes. "I fell," she said. "On my face. But I'm okay. Do you remember me?"

No answer.

"Your mom wants you to come home because you have to release your butterflies soon. The ones in your butterfly garden. The butterflies are going to emerge at any moment. They may have already."

"You saw it? You were in my room?"

"Yes," Josie said. "Your mom showed me your room so I would know more things about you. To help me find you. She also showed me the bear your dad gave you—the one he leaves you messages on." She didn't mention that Gideon had tainted it. If it was up to Josie, Lucy would never hear his voice again.

"I talked to your teacher, too," Josie went on. "I saw the chrysalis in your desk, and the one you left at your mom's friend's house, the one in the hunting cabin, and the one on the Overlook. Did you leave them so we would find you?"

"I just like making them," Lucy said. "It makes me think of stuff that's not bad. That man put a lot of bad things in my head."

"I know he did," Josie said. "But like I told you, he's in jail now. He's never getting out. It's time to go home and see your mom and dad." Josie walked over to the base of the tree and reached a hand up. "Can you come over to me?"

Her arm ached with the effort of holding it aloft but finally, the branches above them fluttered and rustled and a moment later, a small, cold hand fit itself into Josie's. Gretchen was at her side and took her flashlight as Lucy fell into her arms. The girl curled herself against Josie's body, wrapping her thin legs around Josie's waist and her arms tightly around Josie's neck. She nestled her head into Josie's chest. Josie's abdomen ached with each step, but she didn't dare try to disentangle the girl from her. Luke, Gretchen and several other searchers lit the way as Josie carried her out of the woods and to a waiting ambulance.

CHAPTER SEVENTY-ONE

Josie rode in the back of the ambulance with Lucy. She stayed with the girl in the ER while the doctors and nurses examined her and asked what seemed like a thousand questions. She didn't leave Lucy's side until Colin burst into the room and scooped his daughter into his arms, sobbing into her hair. "Thank God," he cried. "Oh Lucy. Thank God."

Tears stung Josie's eyes. Quietly, she slipped out of the room and down the hall toward the exit. As the ER doors whooshed open, Dan Lamay shuffled in. "Boss," he called, waving a sheaf of papers in the air.

Josie stopped and waited for him. They stepped away from the doors and into the waiting area, which mercifully, was nearly empty. "What's going on, Dan?"

Out of breath, Lamay handed her the papers. "Hummel pulled Amy Ross's elimination prints and had them run through AFIS, like you asked."

Josie raised a brow. "I'm not sure that matters now. We've got Lucy. It's not up to me to decide if Amy should be prosecuted for what she's done. If the FBI wants to pursue the identity theft angle, they can do that. Anything she did or didn't do in New York is up to prosecutors there."

"Oh, I think you'll still want to see this."

She took the pages from him and began looking them over. "This can't be right," she said. "Are you sure this is right?"

Lamay nodded. "Hummel had the state police run the AFIS search twice. It's right."

Josie stared uncomprehending at the old photograph before her while Lamay filled her in. "Amy Ross's fingerprints are a match to a little girl who went missing when she was eleven years old from Cleveland, Ohio in 1990. The local police did a fingerprinting event at her school as part of an initiative in the late eighties to reduce the number of missing children. They came in and fingerprinted all the kids and sent the prints home for parents to keep on file. Her mother turned them back in to the police when she went missing and they were entered into the national database. Her name is Penny Knight."

"Penny Knight," Josie murmured, studying the face of the smiling girl from nearly thirty years ago. It looked like a school photo with its sky-blue background, and Penny posed artificially with her arms folded on top of a stack of books. Her hair was short and uncombed. Bright blue eyes gazed out earnestly over a toothy smile. Josie could see traces of the grown Amy in the girl's face—her eyes and the shape of her mouth. "Did you call Cleveland PD?"

Lamay said, "I did. She lived in an apartment in a run-down part of the city with her mother. Single mom. Habitual drug user. Apparently, Penny's dad was never in the picture. He's not even listed on her birth certificate. Her mother used to send her to the corner grocery store to buy food when she was too messed up to go herself. One afternoon she sends Penny down to the store for some eggs and milk. Penny never made it to the store and never came home. Mother didn't report it for almost two days."

"Two days?" Josie exclaimed.

"She thought Penny had gone to stay with friends and would just come home, but when she didn't, the mom reported her missing. Police could find no evidence of any foul play."

"They thought she was a runaway? At eleven?" Josie asked incredulously.

"They couldn't make a determination one way or another. They carried out a pretty extensive investigation and the mother stayed on them to keep looking until she overdosed in 1996."

"Penny—or Amy—would have been seventeen then. She didn't have any other relatives?"

"None that she or her mother were close to. Apparently, the mother's family didn't have much to do with her on account of her drug use," Lamay said. "So, whether Penny ran away or someone took her, once her mother died, she didn't have a home to return to."

"The year Penny turned eighteen was the year Amy Walsh died," Josie said. She remembered how cryptic Amy had been about her past, saying she didn't remember who she really was or what her name had been. That Tessa Lendhardt was a fiction. Because it was an identity that Martin Lendhardt had given her after he took her. Once she escaped him, she shed that identity. It had never really existed in the first place.

"My God," said Josie.

"Are you going to tell them?" Lamay asked.

"Yes," Josie said. "They need to know. But not tonight. Tomorrow, I'll talk to Amy and Colin."

CHAPTER SEVENTY-TWO

Four days later, Josie stopped outside the door to Amy Ross's hospital room, peeking through the tiny crack in the door and listening as Lucy told her mother a story about a real luna moth she had seen in the woods when she was away with the "bad people". She was seated cross-legged next to her mother, her tiny frame squeezed in between the guardrail and Amy's side. As she spoke, Amy stroked her blonde hair and stared at her, a look of pure wonder on her face. Josie listened as Amy asked her questions, and listened carefully to her answers. Not for the first time, Josie felt a tremendous wave of relief and gratitude wash over her. The Ross family had lost a lot. They'd been traumatized. Amy's secrets had been laid bare. Lucy would likely need years of therapy after the things she had witnessed while with Natalie and Gideon. They would forever mourn the loss of Jaclyn, who had been like family to them. Josie also knew that Amy carried around a lifetime's worth of guilt over the death of Wendy Kaplan. But they were all alive, and from the looks of it, Amy's secrets hadn't driven her husband away. Lucy's family unit was still intact.

"You can go right in, you know," Colin said, appearing behind her.

Josie jumped and then laughed, turning toward him. "I didn't want to interrupt," she said.

In his hands was a hot tea and a milkshake. He stepped past her and nudged the door open with his elbow. "You're not interrupting. Please. Lucy would love to see you. She was disappointed when she found out you'd been here earlier this week to talk to us without her—although I'm glad you did because she doesn't need to know about Amy's past. Not yet."

Josie nodded and stepped through the door.

Lucy hopped down from the bed when they entered and ran into Josie's arms. "Josie! I didn't think you would come back."

Josie touched Lucy's cheek and smiled at her. "I just wanted to check on you and see how you and your mom were doing. How are you feeling?"

Lucy's lips twisted. "I can't sleep. I have bad dreams."

Josie knelt and looked Lucy directly in the eye. "I understand. I used to have nightmares, too."

"You did?"

"Sure," Josie said. "I knew some bad people when I was a kid, too."

Lucy lowered her voice. "Are they in jail?"

"Yes," Josie said. "Yes, they are."

"I might want to grow up to be a police officer like you," Lucy told her. "So I can put bad people in jail."

Josie smiled. "Then who would take care of the bugs?"

"Oh, right. My mom said she thinks I'll be an entomologist." She turned back to her mother. "Did I say it right?"

"You did, sweetheart," Amy told her.

Colin walked over and handed Lucy the milkshake. "Here, Lucy. Why don't you and I take a walk while your mom and Josie catch up?"

Lucy took the Styrofoam cup and skip-walked out the door. Colin trotted after her, calling for her not to spill her milkshake. Amy smiled as she watched them go.

Josie walked to Amy's bedside. Amy said, "What did he say?"

"Gideon won't see you. Also, the district attorney would prefer if you had no contact with him."

The smile left Amy's face. "Did you tell him the truth? About his father? What he did to me?"

"His lawyer made him aware. He still doesn't want to see you or speak to you."

Amy looked away from her but not before Josie saw tears in her eyes. "I didn't want to leave him. I mean, I knew it was wrong. I tried to take him with me, but Martin caught me. He said he would kill Gideon if I ever tried to take him again. You have to understand, there was only one way out of that house, and it wasn't with Gideon."

"You don't have to justify your actions to me," Josie said. "I'm only relaying a message."

"But I want you to understand how things were. I—I was so young. I wasn't ready to be a mother. Poor Gideon. I didn't know the first thing about caring for a child—especially under those conditions. I used to tell him we were going home. I don't know why I said that. I was so stupid. I used to think maybe my mother missed me. Maybe I could take Gideon with me and she would be happy to see us—so happy she would change. She would stop doing drugs and take care of us. Then Martin told me she died, but I still told Gideon we would go. At that point, I wasn't even talking about a physical place—it was just an idea. Home. A place where no one would hurt you, where you'd never be hungry or hurt or bored. I shouldn't have done that."

"Given him hope?"

Amy nodded. "I lied to him."

"Did you?" Josie asked. "Would you have taken him with you if you could have?"

Amy looked away. Her words sounded small and raspy. "I don't know," she admitted. "Every time I looked at Gideon, it reminded me of all the terrible things Martin had done to me."

"How did you come to be with Martin?" Josie asked, unable to quell her own curiosity.

"He was a truck driver. Every so often he was in Cleveland making deliveries at this warehouse near my apartment. I walked past there almost every day. He started talking to me. He was so nice at first. My mother—she was hooked on drugs. It wasn't a good situation. Martin invited me many times to go on the road with him. Made it sound like an adventure. He was kind and funny, and he used to bring me gifts. Feed me when I was hungry."

The parallels to Lucy's kidnapping were chilling. "I went with him one day. I didn't feel like his prisoner. We drove and drove. At first, it was exciting. Then he started to do things to me. Things I didn't like. Things I didn't even understand at the time. Whenever I tried to get him to stop, he became very angry and violent. I told him I wanted to go home, but he said I was pregnant. I didn't even know. I was very naïve. I was young even for my age—mentally, I mean. So we settled in Buffalo. He told the few nosey neighbors there that I was his wife. No one questioned it. I never left the house. I gave birth at home. It's a miracle either of us even survived. It was very painful."

"No one questioned the baby? How did he even get a birth certificate?" Josie asked.

"I don't know. That must have happened after I left. Gideon looked just like him. No one would doubt his paternity. You know, all the times the police came to our house, they never asked for identification or anything like that. I told them nothing was wrong, and they left. I never once had to prove who I was. Like I said, I just stayed inside the house. Then Martin told me it was my job to take care of the baby all while he kept... assaulting me. I knew by then that's what it was—all I did in that house was watch television. That's how I learned about rape. Prime time drama. Soap operas."

"How was Martin with the baby?"

"Awful," Amy replied. "He became so much worse. Gideon wasn't a happy baby. He cried constantly. Martin refused to get me anything I asked for, anything that might help. Things I saw in commercials or on morning shows. Martin never touched him, only me. I knew if I didn't get away, he would kill me. When I left Gideon with him, I didn't think he would ever hurt him. He took more of an interest in him when he got older and cried less. I know it sounds absurd, but I was just a kid. A really stupid kid."

"You got out. Why not just go to the police?"

"And tell them what? I couldn't even remember my old name. Well, I knew my first name was Penny. But that was it. He told me my mother was dead at some point. I had no reason not to believe him. She'd already nearly died several times before that. It wasn't a stretch to believe she had overdosed for good. Besides, I didn't want to be that girl: the abducted girl, raped for years on end, who had a baby in captivity. My face plastered over every magazine and newspaper in the country. Returned to a family who had wanted nothing to do with me my entire life, who didn't care that my mom was a drug addict or that I had gone missing. I went with him. Do you understand? I went with him. He used to tell me that I couldn't go to the police because I went willingly, that I let him do all those things to me. I thought the police would blame me. I was so stupid, it never occurred to me that he would be in trouble. He must have been pretty sure of himself—you know, that I wouldn't tell—because I don't think he ever tried to come after me or find me."

"He manipulated you," Josie said. "Just like Gideon and Natalie Oliver manipulated Lucy. That's what people like Martin do."

"But it worked. I knew it was wrong to leave my mother, but I went anyway. I was so stupid. I just wanted to go on an adventure. I wanted to be with Martin because I was never hungry when I was with him."

"You were a child."

"Yes," Amy sighed, eyes turned toward the window. There was a resignation in her voice. "I was a child. But what happened to me—it happened to me. Then I was an adult, and I wanted to start over."

"How did you know what to do?" Josie asked.

Amy laughed. "I didn't. I hitchhiked out of Buffalo—only taking rides from women. Someone dropped me off in Fulton. There was a laundromat there that was open twenty-four hours. It was warm and no one bothered me. I walked around during the day and at night, I slept there. That's where I met Amy. She used to bring her washing there. I think she felt sorry for me. She gave me some clothes. Eventually, she took me home with her. Dorothy took one look at me and said I'd always have a home with her. She was so kind to me. So were Amy and her younger sister. Only Renita didn't like me. But it was wonderful. Then the car accident happened. I was devastated. I loved Dorothy like a mother. Everything I know about being a mother, I learned from her."

Josie felt sadness sweep over her. Amy had had a few months with the woman. That was the extent of her knowledge of parenting. At least Josie had had her grandmother as a stable loving force her entire life to offset the horrors she had endured.

Amy continued, "I knew Renita wouldn't let me stay. I was packing my things—I stayed in Amy's room with her. Renita was at the funeral home. A police officer stopped by with some personal effects they'd taken from the car. Amy's driver's license was in there. It was a spur of the moment decision. I took it and left before Renita came home. I took the cash from Dorothy's wallet—that was also with the personal effects— and I took a bus to New York City. By then, I had learned enough to survive. I found a shelter and stayed there until I made enough working odd jobs to get an apartment with a couple of other girls. I was Amy Walsh. I even used her high school transcripts to get into Denton University. No one ever asked any questions. Until Lucy disappeared."

"Why didn't you tell me about Gideon?" Josie asked.

"I never thought even for a moment that he was behind this."

"Did you ever look him up?"

Amy shook her head. She reached over to the side table, grimacing in pain, and snagged a tissue. She dabbed tears beneath her eyes. "I only ever looked Martin up to see if he was still alive. It wasn't until he passed away a couple of years ago—I found his obituary—that I finally felt free. The obituary didn't say anything about Gideon. I thought… I thought he was dead, too, but I couldn't find anything online. But I didn't look that hard, to be honest. I wanted that part of my life to be over. I never thought it would come at such a high price. I'm so sorry."

Josie thought about the lives lost, sadness weighing her down. As if reading her thoughts, Amy said, "I will live with the guilt of what I did and what Gideon did for the rest of my life."

Josie nodded, unable to speak. She couldn't help but wonder if any lives could have been preserved had Amy been completely honest with them from the very beginning. Josie knew it wasn't her job to judge Amy. Her job had been to bring Lucy home, and she had done it. She hadn't walked in the shoes of Penny Knight or Tessa Lendhardt or even Amy Ross. It wasn't her place to second-guess Amy's life choices, and it wasn't worth wondering what might have been. They all had to live with the aftermath of what had actually happened.

Josie's gaze swept past Amy to the windowsill behind the bed. There was a small chrysalis made from gauze pads sitting on it. She would recognize Lucy's work anywhere. She swallowed over the lump that had formed in her throat and returned her gaze to Amy. "I'm only going to say one thing: break the cycle with Lucy. She's so smart, so precious. Help her to be strong, like steel, to know her own mind, and draw her own conclusions. She deserves that."

More tears slid down Amy's face. "She does, and I will. I promise."

CHAPTER SEVENTY-THREE

Josie drove home, her mind awhirl with the things Amy had told her. The gravity of the case still felt like a drag on her, the only thing lightening her mood that Lucy was safe and sound. She pulled into her driveway, noticing that Misty's car wasn't there. Neither was the rental that Trinity had driven there. She had come and stayed with Josie for a few days, and then returned to New York City after getting interviews from everyone she possibly could. Against her better judgment, Josie had even asked Colin to grant Trinity an interview, and he had agreed, mostly so he could publicly thank all the volunteers and law enforcement who had helped to recover Lucy.

Inside, Noah sat on the couch, his casted leg on top of her coffee table. "Hey," he said, using the remote to mute her television. He patted the couch cushion next to him. "Come, sit."

She plopped down next to him and looked around the room. For the first time in over a week, Harris's toys weren't strewn all over the floor.

Noah said, "Misty went home. Although she said she'll call you next week about babysitting."

Josie smiled. "I know she will. It will be weird without them. I was starting to get used to having them. Even that little dog. Man, can Misty cook."

Noah nodded. "That she can. You know, I can cook, too."

"I know that," Josie said, staring at the television where a sitcom played silently.

"And we could get a dog if you want."

She turned to him, brow raised. "'We' could get a dog? How would that work? You'd get him on Thursdays and every other weekend?"

He reached down between them and took her hand. "Or I could move in with you, and we wouldn't have to split custody."

"What?"

"You don't have to give me an answer right now," he said quickly.

"About the dog or the moving in?"

He laughed. "Either. Both. Just think about it."

"Noah, we've been through a lot these past couple of months—with your mom's case. I'm not sure either one of us is clear-headed enough to take a step like that."

"That's why I said to think about it. I love you, Josie, and in spite of the way I acted during my mom's case, I am in this for the long haul. For good. If you need more time, if I need to prove that to you, I'm in."

He leaned in and kissed her.

"I'll think about it," she promised. "But there's something I think we really need to do first. As soon as your leg is better and before we do anything else."

"What's that?"

"Take a vacation."

A LETTER FROM LISA

Thank you so much for choosing to read *Her Silent Cry*. If you enjoyed it and want to keep up-to-date with all my latest releases, just sign up at the following link. Your email address will never be shared, and you can unsubscribe at any time.

www.bookouture.com/lisa-regan

Thank you so much for reading about Josie, her team, and their latest case! It means so much to me that you keep returning to Josie's hometown of Denton again and again to follow her adventures.

I love hearing from readers. You can get in touch with me through any of the social media outlets below, including my website and Goodreads page. Also, if you are up for it, I'd really appreciate it if you'd leave a review and perhaps recommend *Her Silent Cry* to other readers. Reviews and word-of-mouth recommendations go a long way in helping readers discover my books for the first time. As always, thank you so much for your support. It means the world to me. I can't wait to hear from you, and I hope to see you next time!

Thanks,
Lisa Regan

 LisaReganCrimeAuthor

 @Lisa1Regan

www.lisaregan.com

ACKNOWLEDGEMENTS

As always, first and foremost, I must thank my wonderful readers and loyal fans! Your enthusiasm for this series is such an amazing gift that I cherish each day. I never get tired of hearing from you lovely readers, and genuinely appreciate each and every message! Thank you so much to my husband, Fred, for your unwavering support, your humor and for always pushing me. You bring out the very best in me and I couldn't do this without you! Thank you to my daughter, Morgan, for giving up your mom for so many hours while I write. Thank you to my first readers: Dana Mason, Katie Mettner, and Nancy S. Thompson. Thank you to my Entrada readers. Thank you to my parents—William Regan, Donna House, Rusty House, Joyce Regan, and Julie House—for your constant support and for never getting tired of hearing good news. Thank you to the following "usual suspects", people in my life who support and encourage me, spread the word about my books, and generally keep me going: Maureen Downey, Carrie Butler, Ava McKittrick, Melissia McKittrick, Andrew Brock, Christine and Kevin Brock, Laura Aiello, Helen Conlen, Jean & Dennis Regan, Debbie Tralies, Sean & Cassie House, Marilyn House, Tracy Dauphin, Dee Kay, Michael Infinito Jr., Jeff O'Handley, Susan Sole, the Funk family, the Tralies family, the Conlen family, the Regan family, the House family, the McDowells, and the Kays. Thank you to the lovely people at Table 25 for your wisdom, support, and good humor. I'd also like to thank all the lovely bloggers and reviewers who read the first five Josie Quinn books for continuing to read the series and to enthusiastically recommend it to your readers!

Thank you so very much to Sgt. Jason Jay for answering all my law-enforcement questions at every hour of the day and night and never getting impatient with me. I am so incredibly grateful to you!

Thank you to Oliver Rhodes, Noelle Holten, Kim Nash and the entire team at Bookouture for making this fantastic journey both possible and the most fun I've ever had in my life. Last but certainly not least, thank you to the incredible Jessie Botterill for somehow getting the very best out of me each and every time. You never cease to amaze me, and I could not and would not want to do this without you.

49175576R00212

Made in the USA
Lexington, KY
20 August 2019